# CAMPUSLAND

# CAMPUSLAND

**SCOTT JOHNSTON**

ST. MARTIN'S PRESS 🕮 NEW YORK

First published in the United States by St. Martin's Press, an imprint of St. Martin's Publishing Group

CAMPUSLAND. Copyright © 2019 by Scott Johnston. All rights reserved. Printed in the United States of America. For information, address St. Martin's Publishing Group, 120 Broadway, New York, NY 10271.

www.stmartins.com

Designed by Steven Seighman

The Library of Congress Cataloging-in-Publication Data is available upon request.

ISBN 978-1-250-22237-4 (hardcover)
ISBN 978-1-250-22238-1 (ebook)

Our books may be purchased in bulk for promotional, educational, or business use. Please contact your local bookseller or the Macmillan Corporate and Premium Sales Department at 1-800-221-7945, extension 5442, or by email at MacmillanSpecialMarkets@macmillan.com.

First Edition: August 2019

10  9  8  7  6  5  4  3  2  1

*To my college friends. You know who you are.*

*Colleges don't make fools, they only develop them.*

—GEORGE HORACE LORIMER

# CAMPUSLAND

# Prologue

## Devon University

From Wikipedia, the free encyclopedia

**Devon University** is an American private research university located in the New England town of Havenport. With an admissions rate of 83 percent, it is considered one of the most elite universities in America.

| | |
|---|---|
| **Motto** | *Una Crescimus* (Latin, "Together We Grow") |
| **Established** | Sometime between Facebook and Snapchat |
| **Undergraduates** | 5,127 |
| **Graduates** | 4,012 |
| **President** | Milton Strauss |
| **Endowment** | $47.12 |
| **Colors** | Red and black |
| **Nickname** | Ass Monkeys |

"D'Arcy!" Milton cried from his office. "They've been messing with our Wikipedia page again!"

D'Arcy appeared at his door almost before the words came out. "On it."

It was a constant struggle to stay ahead of the pranksters. She logged on to Wikipedia and made the necessary corrections, starting with the admissions rate. She typed in 5.2 percent, only slightly higher than Harvard's. Then she fixed the rest. . . . Established: 1704. Endowment: $28 billion. Nickname: The Devils.

*Ass Monkeys*. D'Arcy chuckled at that one. Last time it was the Butt Munchers.

# Blue Nation Coffee

**SCHOOL YEARS HAD** a dependable rhythm, one Eph always found comforting. This was his favorite time, September—the anticipation, the excitement of reconnecting after summer break. Official move-in day wasn't until tomorrow, but many students had come early for orientations or team practices, so the sidewalk was busy. Walking down Ellsworth, a commercial street that ran along one edge of campus, he saw eagerness painted on the passing faces. He had little doubt his own face looked just the same.

Blue Nation Coffee was a favorite hangout for both students and faculty. It had the usual coffeehouse design elements—menu boards of colorful chalk and bare Edison lightbulbs hanging from high ceilings of antique tin tile. Today the place was a white-noise cocktail of chattering students, soft modern jazz, and grinding Fair Trade coffee beans. After waiting through the line, Eph sat at a communal farm table with two lemongrass kombuchas, one for D'Arcy. He ran his hand along the distressed wood. It had a reassuring solidness. A small, tented sign said the wood had been reclaimed from a barn in the Berkshires. That was pleasing somehow.

Propping open his brushed-aluminum MacBook Air, Eph took the comforting aroma of coffee deep into his lungs. He longed for the caffeine, but D'Arcy kept pestering him about probiotics, whatever those were.

Someone pierced the coffeehouse calm, barking shrilly into a cell phone. It was a spandex-clad woman at the head of the line. Eph recognized her from around campus, but didn't know her. The cashier stood there sheepishly waiting for the order, but the woman—evidently some-one of authority—was busy tearing someone a new asshole while at least ten people waited in line behind her. This went on for some time, with no one quite sure what to do. Eph knew they would do nothing. The woman was African-American, and in a university town allowances were made for cultural differences. A polite silence was observed until the woman hung up her phone and placed her order as if nothing had hap-pened.

Eph tried to focus on the lesson plan staring at him from his Retina Dis-play but knew it was impossible, not after his meeting with Cooley. He settled on looking busy, navigating to Blue Nation's website to see what causes they backed. Blue Nation donated a percentage of their revenue to progressive causes, so lattes came with a side of virtue. It looked like they funded lots of environmental causes and sustainable-food initiatives. They had stopped pro-viding straws, too. Eph liked straws, but heard they were bad for the environ-ment, so he supposed it was okay.

"Hey!" It was D'Arcy. His D'Arcy.

"You're late. I've been sitting here trying to look busy."

"Sorry, those *Lampoon* kids from Harvard were pranking our Wikipedia page again—at least, they're the primary suspects."

"Off with their heads." Eph said, finding the whole thing amusing. He handed her the other kombucha, which, when D'Arcy opened it, gave an au-dible hiss.

"*So?*" She smacked Eph playfully with her free hand.

Eph unconsciously flipped his hair, throwing back a youthful swoop of brown locks from above his dark-framed glasses. The gesture revealed a glimpse of a small scar on the edge of his forehead, an imperfection that highlighted an otherwise winsome face. "Cooley confirmed it. I'm up this year. April." He gave her that thousand-watt little-boy smile he had.

"I knew it! I wonder, will you remember the little people?"

She smiled back at him, her teeth gleaming impossibly against smooth chestnut skin. D'Arcy worked as an administrative assistant for Milton Strauss, Devon's president. She and Eph had met a year ago at a climate rally. Eph often imagined how they looked to others, the perfect modern couple, emerged from different backgrounds, each finding a home here in the highest echelons of academia. . . . *Oh, no . . .*

*Ebony and ivory*
*Live together in perfect harmony*

That damnable earworm! It played in his head on continuous loop whenever he thought about his relationship with D'Arcy, mocking him for any feelings of cultural smugness. *Damn you to hell, Paul McCartney.*

"It all seems unreal, to be honest," Eph said, willing himself to hear the light jazz coming from unseen speakers.

"C'mon, you totally deserve this. The book was wonderful. You're their little rising star."

Eph had recently published a book called *Ralph Waldo Emerson: Muse of the Private Man,* which had sold six thousand copies, a smashing bestseller in the world of works about nineteenth-century literature.

"Don't forget about Smallwood. Atkins's retirement means there's only one spot, and Cooley said it was between the two of us." Barrett Smallwood taught modern American lit, while Eph taught nineteenth-century, so there was a natural rivalry already.

Eph was making $85K, not bad money in Havenport, the smallish Northeastern city that was home to Devon University. After taxes, though, it was $50K, and that meant few luxuries. The perks helped, with the university providing most meals, full health and dental, plus university-subsidized housing—in Eph's case a tidy one-bedroom with exposed brick one block from campus. He supplemented his income by teaching in the summer program. All in all, things were comfortable, but tenure would more than double his salary, which meant some creature comforts would be within reach, plus he could start actually taking summer vacations. He could even put in for a sabbatical after five years.

It wasn't just about money, though. It never had been. Eph grew up modestly, so he lived frugally. He simply wanted to stay, here, in this place. Going back was unthinkable.

"Smallwood, isn't he the one who wears those funny neoprene shoes?" D'Arcy asked.

"Yes, with the little individual toes. It's his signature look. Doesn't matter if it's ten degrees and snowing. You have to admire the commitment. The kids—and frankly most of the faculty—call him Toes behind his back."

"Toes!" cried D'Arcy, laughing. It was more of a honk, really. Eph thought it was one of her more endearing habits.

"He putters around campus on a recumbent bike and calls his students 'dude,' even the women. You know, he doesn't even require actual writing in his class. He thinks it's part of an antiquated power structure or something, but I happen to know he dabbles in nanofiction on the side."

"Dare I ask?"

"It's just what it sounds like. Really, really short stories. Some of them are called twiction, a literary form required to stay under Twitter's character limit."

"Sounds cutting-edge." If D'Arcy was being sarcastic, it was hard to tell.

"Hey, maybe *I* need a signature look. Any ideas?"

D'Arcy took in Eph's ensemble: khakis, blue button-down shirt, blucher moccasins. At least he'd ditched the flannel he'd favored when he first arrived. "I think it's in my best interests not to comment," D'Arcy said, lifting the bottle of kombucha to her mouth to hide the smirk.

"I read Toes's thesis, you know. I found a copy in the stacks."

"Aren't you the literary stalker. What's it on? Do I want to know?"

"It's an exegesis of Pynchon's *Crying of Lot 49*. His theory is that it's an anti-novel with no beginning, no end, no structure . . . a rage against conformity. The paper was"—Eph groped for the right adjective—"thorough." It came out *thurr-ah*. Despite his efforts, Eph's childhood accent occasionally surfaced.

"Isn't Pynchon a recluse or something? I don't know why I remember that."

"He is. Very clever, that Toes, interpreting a recluse. Who's going to contradict you? Maybe I should have cut my teeth on Salinger."

"*Way* too obvious. Plus he's dead anyway."

"You have a point. Anyway, Cooley. He got all mysterious on me. He shut the door to his office and said he really shouldn't say any more, which of course is what people say when they're about to do just that, and then he said I definitely had the inside track. Toes has his backers, but if I stayed on the straight and narrow, it was mine. 'Don't make any waves,' he said. Then he winked."

"He winked?"

"He winked."

"I don't understand," D'Arcy said.

"That's too bad, because I was hoping you would." Eph sipped his kombucha, trying and failing to like it. He made a mental note to ask Peterson in Bio what probiotics were, exactly, and why everyone made it their business that he have more.

"Well, straight and narrow—not much of a stretch for you, my dear. And don't you think Cooley was probably just underscoring what he'd said . . . with the wink?"

"Yeah . . . maybe. But think about it, isn't a wink meant to suggest that there's *more* than what's being explicitly said?"

"You're the English professor. Isn't deep inner meaning your department?"

Eph took one more reluctant sip of kombucha. The drink's intense carbonation lit up his chest and suggested it would like to explore his nasal cavity at the slightest opportunity. *Bleh.* Back to coffee next time. "When was the last time someone winked at you?"

"I am going to say no one's ever winked at me. I think it's more of a white thing."

"Miss Williams, are you suggesting an ethnocultural skew in winking? Don't let on to anyone in Sociology or you'll cause a stir. Careers have been made on less."

D'Arcy smiled. She loved Eph's wry sense of humor.

"You know," Eph continued, "there was this TV show when I was a kid, I can't quite remember what it was called, where the father would wink at his son. It was a kind of intimate thing, a silent connection. I remember wishing my dad had been a winker."

"Should I get you a couch so you can continue sharing?"

"No, but I still wonder about Titus."

"Somehow, I don't think that Titus O. Cooley, venerable chair of the Devon University English Department, was trying to establish an intimate connection with you, silent or otherwise. Unless you're telling me I should start getting jealous."

Eph ignored her. "Still, it's kind of a dying gesture, don't you think?"

D'Arcy looked exasperated. "Are we really still talking about winking? You have managed to find a subject I have no more opinions on."

"*On which.*"

"On which what?"

"*On which* you have no more opinions."

"Shut up, just shut up."

"Sorry, if I'm going to be a tenured professor of English, I'm going to have to insist you don't end sentences in prepositions."

"Fuck off."

Eph winked.

# Devon Daily

## Devon Welcomes New First-Years

The university hummed with activity yesterday as the campus welcomed 1,498 new first-years. President Milton Strauss issued the following statement to the university community:

"Welcome, incoming first-years! You are the 315th matriculating class to grace Devon's halls. You were selected from a record number of applicants—over 36,000!—so you should feel enormous pride in your accomplishments. As Devon's most diverse incoming class ever, you represent all fifty states and over forty countries from around the world. Speaking for the faculty and the administration, we can't wait to get to know you better!"

Upper-class students clad in Devon red-and-black T-shirts were out in force to help first-years move belongings into their rooms. "We want to show the first-years that Devon is a community, and communities support each other," said Dylan Fernandez, a junior from Arizona.

Elsewhere, dozens of campus organizations set up tables in East Quad, hoping to catch the eyes of potential new members. "We're looking for freshmen interested in the Greek experience," said Tug Fowler, president of the Beta Psi house.

Farther down the row, a student identifying herself only as "Gaia" hoped to find new members for the Progressive Student Alliance. "Our interest is in action and social change, and in finding those who will join us in the struggle against the status quo," she told the *Daily*.

Of note, this is the first time incoming students are to be officially known as first-years. Over the summer, a university committee led by Dean Martika Malik-Adams, Dean of Diversity and

Inclusion, deemed the term *freshmen* gender biased and exclusionary. She also suggested that the prefix *fresh* raised issues of objectification.

"All should feel welcome here at Devon," said Dean Malik-Adams in a prepared statement, "not just a privileged few."

# Milton's Walk

**MILTON STRAUSS WALKED WITH PURPOSE.** His daily stroll had become something of a personal tradition, and it was good to see life back in the campus.

Things had been quiet over the summer, save for Model UN delegates and high school kids attending summer school programs. Parents assumed these programs increased their kids' chances of admission. They didn't, but the revenue was welcome, particularly during the fallow months. It was all about resource utilization. Sure, Devon had a $28 billion endowment, shy only of Harvard's, but there were always new demands on the school treasury, and Milton, like a Renaissance king, had to receive the myriad constituencies who sought to make a claim. The work agreed with him.

In any event, the bustle of the school year was back.

"Milt!" a student cried from across College Street. Milton smiled and waved.

"Hey, Milt!" another yelled. Milton smiled again, not the least bit discouraging of the implied familiarity. He was their friend, one of them, accessible. Social media, which often documented his comings and goings, said as much. There was even a Twitter account called @FakeUncleMiltie that tweeted witty observations about campus life. He didn't know who was behind the account, but this pleased him all the more. A secret admirer. He discreetly checked his Twitter feed several times a day: @FakeUncleMiltie was up to three thousand followers. It was a little edgy sometimes, but that was okay.

He passed through a beautifully ornate stone archway. The college campus, Milton thought, was man's perfect place, a walled garden where beauty and youth came together in pursuit of the truth. Devon was surely its most splendid example.

This pleasant thought foundered as he passed the imposing Pailey Art & Architecture Center, a building always demanding to be noticed. The brutalist architecture fad that had once swept the intellectual precincts had left almost no campus untouched, and Devon was no exception. The building's Stalinist slabs of rectilinear concrete, set here among Gothic and Georgian masterpieces, assaulted the eye. Naturally, that was the point. "The Pailey" caused a sensation in the early sixties when it was built, as did many other buildings that today offend all but the most slavish preservationists. The interior was more awkward still, with more levels than floors and oddly jutting mezzanines—a layout that seemed to intentionally thwart one's ability to get from A to B. The concrete was cold and would sweat in the warmer months, giving off a dank, musty smell no countermeasures could ever fix. It was an angry, perspiring fortress.

What of it, then? Campuses were nothing if not places of experimentation, places to provoke the status quo. In the sixties, eye-pleasing aesthetics took a backseat to establishing one's modernity bona fides. Milton was too young to remember much about the sixties, but he imagined them with fondness. If ever the status quo needed to be jolted from its somnolence, it was the 1960s. At least Devon had one of the first and *better* examples of brutalism. The Pailey was a tad less hideous than, say, Georgetown's library or that new(ish) wing of the Boston Public Library. Was that Philip Johnson? *Hmm*, best to keep his opinion to himself. There were some things the president of Devon University simply couldn't say. Actually, a lot of things, but Milton didn't dwell on it.

Not today.

Today was the day after Labor Day, back-to-school day, and the campus teemed with tanned students arriving with their equally excited parents. Milton made a point of walking toward the vast East Quad, where the first-years were housed. On the road outside, dozens of SUVs disgorged wide-eyed young men and women. Milton knew the parents, many of them, had spent over a million dollars getting their children to that curb, and goodbyes would not be quick. He remembered arriving at this same curb, decades ago, but his trip had been by train and then a taxi, a steamer trunk lugged the whole way. That's just how it was then. *Safe travels, Son.*

He stopped and helped one family wrestle a huge duffel out of a Volvo, getting it as far as the curb. The delighted parents, realizing who their benefactor was, asked for a selfie with Milton and their daughter. He knew that was coming, just as he knew the picture would get posted to Facebook. It would probably say something like "So fortunate Milton Strauss was able to help us carry all of Susie's stuff!"

Milton cherished these interactions, the acknowledgment that he, Milton Strauss, son of a tailor—a Jew!—was president of Devon University. Well, perhaps the Jewish part wasn't that remarkable anymore in this former WASP redoubt, but still. He imagined the figure he cut, the confident stride of a Man of Importance.

"Milt!" another student cried, prompting another wave. Walking on, Milton saw the future site of the two new residential houses. He swelled with pride thinking about what would surely be his signature achievement. No brutalist ruminations for new buildings on his watch, no. Designed by the renowned architect Soren O. Pedersen, these would be soaring, neotraditional Gothic monuments to academia, and—dare he think it?—to Milton Strauss. Teacher, leader, *master builder*: Robert Moses in academic robes.

Land had been cleared and the contractors were all but ready to break ground. The project would allow Devon to increase its enrollment by 15 percent, which would increase the projected admission rate from 5.2 percent to 6. This would allow room for additional first-gens and students of color. Foster Jennison, billionaire member of the class of '62, was pledging the first $250 million toward the projected $550 million cost. Milton Strauss, *master builder,* and Jennison, *investment titan,* didn't always agree on everything—Jennison had some distinctly dated ideas—but he was always at the ready for his beloved alma mater with seldom a string attached. In a remarkable display of donor temperance, he even spared the school from having to accept his intellectually tepid second grandson—the one with 1300 SATs. Yes, Jennison was a man Milton could work with. The other grandson—he was still here, wasn't he? Milton couldn't quite remember the boy's name. He must get D'Arcy to double-check on the boy's status.

Feeling a renewed sense of vigor, Milton crossed Bingham Plaza and approached Stockbridge Hall, where he and other top administrators kept offices. Oddly, a small knot of protesters were outside the entrance. It was early in the year for that sort of thing, but having spent the last several decades at Devon, Milton was more than used to it. He even had sympathy for most of the causes, having himself slept several nights in a shantytown that progressive students had constructed back during the dark days of apartheid. That had been right here, in the stone expanse of Bingham Plaza. What could they be protesting today? No doubt something well-intentioned.

The protesters spotted Milton and instantly became animated. *"Hey, Milton! Divest from Israel now! Stop the murder!"* cried one. *"Divest now! Divest now!"* Their homemade signs thrust up and down like pistons.

Milton smiled and walked over. "It's great to see everyone. Really great." He began shaking hands, much to the bewilderment of the protesters, who didn't know what to do other than shake back. "Keep up the good work, and welcome back to school!"

Then, Milton Strauss, seventeenth president of Devon University, turned and disappeared inside Stockbridge Hall.

# Lulu's Room Sucks

**THE DOOR TO** Lulu's room opened, letting in unwanted light. Her annoying roommate again. *Why can't she just disappear?* It was two weeks into the semester, and Lulu had yet to get up before ten, and now it was only because her roommate, whom she'd kicked out for the night, was coming back from wherever it was she'd gone—the Asian Student Center? That was, what? Three times so far? It would equate with however many boys Lulu had brought back.... The last one departed sometime during the night, although she wasn't sure exactly when. Right now, her immediate need was a Diet Coke. Her mouth felt like it was stuffed with cotton balls, and when she leaned forward, her brains longed to slide out the top of her head. Best to lie back again.

"This is not fair," said Song, the roommate. "It's my room, too!"

"Hey, this isn't my idea of the Connaught either, sweetie, but we all have to make compromises."

"But *I* am the only one who compromises. You do what you want!"

"This whole deal is a compromise, as far as I'm concerned. I mean, look at this dump. I've seen nicer prisons," Lulu said, ignoring that the only prisons she'd seen were in *Orange Is the New Black* on Netflix, at least on those rare nights in New York or the Hamptons when she had nothing better to do than watch television. "And you're no picnic either, your alarm going off at dawn every day—and just look at your half of the room." Lulu glared at Song's side, which was spotless. "It's like one of those labs you spend all day in."

"It's clean!"

"Could you please just stop talking now?" Lulu raised a pillow over her face. With that, Song scooped up some books, made an angry chuffing noise, and left.

An hour or so later, Lulu hoisted herself up and looked in the mirror. She was wearing nothing but an oversized T-shirt that said BUT FIRST, NACHOS.

Where the hell did *that* come from?

Whatever.

She considered herself. An objective third party would say she was beautiful, but in a way that was tired beyond her eighteen years. The kind of jaded, faintly angry beauty that comes from a youth spent in Manhattan's moneyed precincts: the Dalton School, Fifth Avenue, Barneys . . . Her father, Sheldon Harris, was a prominent entertainment lawyer and largely absent parent. Her mother was long out of the picture, having left Sheldon for a different life practically the moment Lulu was born. Mother and daughter had never even spoken.

Lulu asked after her mother often in her younger years, but Sheldon would just say that she wanted a different life and left; that is, if he said anything at all. Why couldn't Lulu know who she was? There were reasons, he'd say, as if that were an answer. It was the abiding mystery of Lulu's childhood, and one she never quite learned to live with. *Why did she leave?*

When Lulu turned sixteen, Sheldon revealed her mother's identity, saying it was time. It turned out Lulu knew precisely who her mother was, at least from a distance. Lulu tried reaching out a number of times but never heard back, not a word. It was a wall of maternal silence. The humiliation proved too much and Lulu came to share Sheldon's resentment. Since then, she'd done her best never to think about it, but sometimes her mother's high profile made that difficult. It might be one thing if the bitch were out of sight, out of mind, but she wasn't. Lulu was left to marinate in revenge fantasies, mostly involving achieving personal fame herself.

Sheldon, for his part, did the best he could to raise a daughter on a net worth of $75 million. Mostly, this had involved a string of nannies and a weekly meal together. Quality time.

Not that Lulu had any problems with this arrangement; she had her freedom and never wanted for financial resources. She adored Sheldon and was smart enough to know that being the only woman in a powerful man's life had benefits. He was also kind enough to keep only casual track of the liquor and amusing pharmaceuticals he left around. This made Lulu's apartment a frequent after-party destination for the private-school set.

Lulu wore her hair long. It was dirty blond, although kept a lighter shade with the help of outside agents. It framed a face possessed of a beautiful smile, although one rarely offered without an agenda. She was lithe, almost sinewy, thanks to hundreds of hours of spin classes, giving her a body that wore clothes well and got more than enough attention from the opposite sex. Her eyes were dark green, although today more bloodshot than anything else.

She looked around the room, glowering. It was a thirteen-by-eighteen in Duffy Hall with a single-size bed on either side, two utilitarian desks, and two dressers. Her closet was a horrifying thirty-six inches wide (she had looked up the dimensions online during the summer) and didn't fit a fraction of her wardrobe. Sheldon—that's what Lulu called him—insisted that she stay in on-campus housing for at least a year because that's what *he* did, and *he'd* had such a good experience. Lulu tried to explain that her roommate wasn't likely to be from their crowd, the way everyone was in his day, but Sheldon said some diversity would be good for her. "Multiculturalism—isn't that the thing now?" he'd said. But he didn't have to room with Song, the human robot.

In reality, the room was quite generous by college-freshman standards. There was even a fireplace with exposed brick and a mantel. All the rooms had one. The fireplaces hadn't been functional in several decades, university lawyers having ordered them plugged after students conducted one-too-many incendiary experiments, nearly burning down Wolcott House in 1972. Still, most students and their parents marveled at this hint at Devon's Edwardian past when the scions of America's elite arrived with servants in tow, and fresh firewood was always at the ready.

But to Lulu, the circumstances were beyond depressing. What with the cheap blond-wood furniture that looked like it came in a box from IKEA, and a closet that held only a fraction of her Barbour and Rag & Bone . . .

She flopped back in bed at the thought of spending an entire year in this place. Back home, she had views of Central Park and a walk-in closet, which out of necessity was where she'd left most of her wardrobe. It wasn't as if there were anything to dress for in this fashion wasteland, anyway. The boys frequently wore gym shorts, while the girls favored . . . she didn't even know what to call the look. Contemporary scruff? Pathetic, whatever it was.

Reaching over to her desk, Lulu grabbed her iPhone, held it up in the air, and took a photo. With a click, she posted the photo to Instagram, where she had over four thousand followers. She added the caption "My fab room at Devon. #sarcasm." It was immediately liked by several followers, which cheered her up, if only for a moment. Lulu photographed or filmed just about everything in her life. It was all part of building a personal brand.

Song was from Asia somewhere—Lulu briefly tried to remember where, Singapore?—and was majoring in some science or another. STEM, as they all said. Lulu didn't know or care to find out much more than that. What was the point? She'd probably leave soon, anyway. College was supposed to be liberating, but so far she found it anything but.

Less than a month ago she was in East Hampton, coming and going as she pleased in her Mini (the convertible, of course), hanging with actual friends, people who understood that pairing Prada sunglasses with Tory Burch was au courant. Why, her picture was in *Hamptons* magazine twice this summer, spotted once at a friend's party and another time at the Hampton Classic—with all the right people, of course. She'd seen Brooke Shields, the Hiltons, Christie Brinkley . . . one night she even went to Calvin Klein's house on the beach in Southampton! Sure, it was a fund-raiser, and Sheldon paid for the ticket, but whatever—she was an It Girl in the making, a glorious hatchling who would soon grace the society pages and be photographed by Patrick McMullan.

But four years in this social backwater was unthinkable. Sure, Devon was prestigious, and it always impressed people when she told them she was going there, but these were her years of being young and fabulous, and they were going to be wasted hanging around in a shitty little town like Havenport. There wasn't even a SoulCycle!

And these . . . *people.*

Yuck.

New York was where she needed to be. A dozen other pretty young things were probably making their moves right now, maybe even lining up their own PR agents.

At one point Lulu thought Devon might help her cause—the reality was that not too many young socialites had the wattage to get in—but the spotlight was not here, it was two hours away, in Manhattan.

Her town.

The people at *On the Avenue* magazine, widely read in her circle, had been talking to her about doing a feature on up-and-coming "philanthropists." It would be a multipage shoot, just Lulu and three others. She didn't know who the others were, but she could guess. Chrissie Fellows and Aubrey St. John, for sure.

Just now there was a rare opening in the world of young socialites, and a prominent piece would put Lulu on the map. Cricket Hayes, the unchallenged queen of twenty-something society, had moved to Palm Beach to dry out. New York was in need of a new star; at least that's how Lulu saw it. She'd even perfected her socialite pose: Head tilted at a ten-degree angle, body turned slightly. Mouth open just enough to reveal perfectly bleached teeth, facial expression left intentionally blank. Smiling led to smile lines and, worse, conveyed the wrong image: eagerness. The last thing a socialite could be was eager, even if it happened to be the case. Eager was for climbers, not those who had already ascended the social heights. A certain world-weariness was de rigueur.

In the meantime . . . what? Make the best of it? The thought was so depressing. The worst thing was that no one around this place, least of all someone like Song, could understand her plight. They might even mock her for it. It wasn't exactly typical to complain about being at Devon.

As Lulu looked around campus, she was struck by how much reality differed from Devon's traditional image. For one thing, where were all the white people? Okay, not white people, exactly. She wasn't some sort of *racist*. There had been blacks in her class at Dalton, and she was pretty sure one was even from East Harlem. And there was that Hispanic girl she talked to once or twice. . . . She was thinking more just about people she could relate to. Lulu had studied Sheldon's Devon yearbook, and plenty of students back then were from Hotchkiss, Andover, and other normal places. These days, those kids were all at Wake and UVA and Georgetown and other mostly Southern colleges that had not grown hostile to—how to put it?—people of a certain background. But Sheldon had gone to Devon "back in the day" and never shut up about it. He wanted the same experience for his only daughter. When she put together a good academic record at Dalton, Sheldon hired a consultant to help with her application essay, an avowal over the guilt she felt being from a privileged background.

Her application was pushed over the finish line with a substantial check. She had won a coveted spot. It also didn't hurt that she'd shown some talent for literature and writing, and by sheer happenstance the English Department was in need of bodies, having fallen out of favor for the more preprofessional disciplines. Like whatever Song was doing.

What Sheldon didn't understand, though, was that this was no longer his Devon. People still had this image of the "Devon Man." He was quite the sport and wore pastel Shetland crewnecks over Brooks button-downs while tailgating before the Big Game. That image was approximately six decades out-of-date. Today's Devon was way more South Bronx than Southampton.

In an abstract sort of way, Lulu supposed there was nothing wrong with that. Her politics, to the extent she gave them much thought, closely adhered to the agendas of the benefits and political fund-raisers to which she aspired. This meant that by default she was a Democrat, like Sheldon (or she would be, as soon as she figured out how to register). She supported all the causes of the moment. Lately, she'd memorized a wholly impassioned-sounding plea for transgender rights that seemed to play well. Not that she'd ever *met* a transperson, but she was sure if she did, she'd know how to use the correct pronoun. Pretty sure.

In her quieter moments, she sometimes felt the diversity movement had gotten a bit . . . strident? For one thing, did everyone have to talk about it so much? Seriously, was no other subject available for discussion? Diversity and inclusion. On and on. *For God's sake, we get it already.*

Lulu crawled out of bed. Throwing on some sweatpants, she walked down to the common room to get a Diet Coke from the vending machine. There she spotted Yolanda Perez, her RA. Yolanda was pinning a poster to the bulletin board, something she did almost constantly. At the bottom it had those little tear-offs with contact information. Lulu took a quick look, not that there was any chance she'd be interested.

*Support Group for Self-Identified Women. If you have experienced emotional, physical, or sexual abuse or stalking, or if there's an experience you wish to talk about, you are not alone. Advocates and your peers are here to listen and support you. Contact Fightback, sponsored by the Devon Womyn's Collective. 898-555-5943*

Yolanda must have tipped the scales at 220, and Lulu wondered who on earth would stalk her. Then Lulu thought it might be cruel to wonder that, but only briefly.

"Rough night, Harris?"

"Is it day now? How unfortunate." Lulu examined the vending machine. No Diet Coke. *Shit.* She debated taking the calorie hit of a real Coke and decided against it.

"You know, if you ever want to talk, Harris, I'm here for you."

"That's very reassuring, thank you." Lulu was already walking back down the hall to her room. She crawled back into bed, deciding more sleep was a bigger priority than any further search for Diet Coke.

# I Feel Like

**IT WAS THE** third week of classes, and Eph's English 240 was well attended, maybe seventy students. Technically, his class was a lecture, but it was still small enough to allow for some give-and-take, which Eph valued. The students settled in, virtually all staring down at their phones.

Eph took a moment to mentally pinch himself. Devon days were long and languorous, and he floated from classes to one of the soaringly beautiful dining halls, then perhaps to the Faculty Club or the gym. Campus was a stunning idyll, bathed in intellect. Eph couldn't imagine a place he'd rather be, even as he questioned whether he deserved to be there. For those inside the bubble, Devon was a reprieve from the ordinary, workaday lives of commuting and cubicles, or in Eph's case, tractors. Tenure was immutable, impregnable security; but more than that, for Eph it was validation, an imprimatur that declared he had risen above his roots. Getting denied would likely mean starting again somewhere else, the stain of rejection following him. It was unthinkable.

He flashed back to his unlikely journey, from Coastal Alabama Community College to Samford University—also in Alabama—on a scholarship. (When he said, "Samford" quickly enough, he knew people at Devon thought he was saying "Stanford," a misunderstanding he was content to let go unremarked.) From there he'd gained entry to the English Lit Ph.D. program at Florida State, skipping right over his master's. After graduating at the top of his class, he submitted an application to Devon for an open assistant professorship in American Lit, his specialty. It was a shot in the dark. He was shocked when he got the call for an interview, and more shocked still when he got the job. He found out later that the Devon English Department felt the need, however temporarily, to reach beyond its usual pool of Northeastern Ivy League academics. That window seldom opened and he got lucky.

It was nine-thirty on the dot. Showtime. He jumped right in.

"Good morning. The Civil War marked a significant turning point in American literature. The Romantic Movement that dominated the first half of the century, with writers like Hawthorne, Emerson, and James Fenimore Cooper, yielded to something new, the Age of Realism. The backdrop was an America first feeling its industrial might, an America where anyone, it was thought, could rise up to become a Carnegie, Rockefeller, or Vanderbilt. It was Twain himself who coined it the 'Gilded Age.'"

Eph began pacing back and forth, as was his habit on the academic stage. "There were critics, particularly from Britain, who said the Realists were nothing more than a derivative of English literature the likes of Dickens. I beg to differ. This new American literature was something different entirely: unbound, messy, and socially aware. There was no confusing Twain or others with any English writer. The precise turning point, if we're forced to pick one, would be Walt Whitman's 'O Captain! My Captain!,' an elegy for Lincoln, the man he admired above all. Whitman's poetry was like nothing that came before—highly descriptive, bowing before no conventions of rhyme or cadence, a riotous chronicling of the passing American scene. It was a consciously radical attempt to create a uniquely *American* poetry.

"Perhaps this doesn't seem like a big deal. I mean, who reads poetry today, right? In that time, though, poetry was easily the most read literary form. It ranked far above the novel in literary importance."

Some movement by the classroom door distracted Eph for a moment. Someone was there, in the door's small window, but the face vanished just as Eph looked over. *Was that Toes?*

"Uh, so while the Hawthornes and Emersons wrote of an idealized, naturalistic world—thus the term *romanticism*—these new writers, the Realists, wrote about the lives of everyday people, frequently using a regional patois, bringing to life vivid characters and exploring the human condition. The Romantics viewed nature as the primary channel through which self-reflection and self-realization could take place—think of Thoreau, out on his pond, striving to put into words the sound of one hand clapping—but later writers rejected this for tales of real people doing real things. Twain was the dominant force of this new realism. Hemingway would later say of Twain that all American literature can trace its roots to a single book, *The Adventures of Huckleberry Finn,* which we will read this week."

He had them. They were absorbing his every word and feverishly taking notes. He thought briefly back to his time as a teaching assistant at Florida State, where the boys would spend class on espn.com while the girls surfed social sites. He realized he was thinking elitist thoughts, but weren't there some things about which it was worth being elitist?

A girl in the front row raised her hand. She had round blue-tinted glasses and straight black hair that fell halfway to her waist. "I feel like this is all a very white perspective."

"Well, I suppose you could say that," answered Eph. "Most of the notable literature from the time was written by whites, although African-American literature began to flower in the very late part of the century when increased access to schooling led to higher literacy rates. I cover that period in a different class."

The girl was undeterred. "I feel like it's still kind of racist not to acknowledge the African-American community during the earlier periods."

"Well, as we'll see, they certainly *were* acknowledged, particularly by Twain, but there was little literature actually produced by African-Americans until later."

"I feel like"—Eph began to sense a linguistic *Groundhog Day*—"I feel like this is an injustice. It upsets me."

"The treatment of African-Americans certainly was an injustice," Eph replied.

*"Was?"* A murmur spread through the class.

"Uh, was, and *is,* but for the purposes of this class, we're going to confine ourselves to the nineteenth century, if that's all right with everybody?"

There was some audible seat rustling, but no apparent objections.

"Your term paper will be due before you leave for winter break," Eph continued. "I want you to compare and contrast a Romantic and a Realist. Choose one from each period. I want to see a deep dive. Twenty pages, give or take." He waited for the groaning to commence, but there was none. Back at Coastal Alabama Community College, a twenty-page paper was unheard of, but this was Devon. It was expected.


After lunch at the Faculty Club (a delightful poached salmon served with fennel and a beurre blanc sauce), Eph walked back to his office, which, like his class, was in Grafton Hall. In the long hallway that bisected the building, he caught Toes emerging from a meeting room along with a few others. Toes's prematurely gray hair was in the usual bun, which was pierced with what looked like a chopstick. Eph wondered what purpose that served.

"Eph, dude!"

"Hello, Barrett."

Glancing through the door, Eph recognized one or two English Department colleagues as well as some professors from the Language Department. He tried hard to suppress his curiosity, not being inclined to give Toes the satisfaction of asking. He failed.

"What's up in there? Plotting a literary coup of some sort?"

"Ha, no! This is our Esperanto working group. Some of us are trying to persuade the Devon Language Department to offer a course."

"Aren't there, like, five people in the world that speak Esperanto?"

"It might surprise you then to know there are over two million Esperantists worldwide."

"You call yourselves Esperantists?"

"That's right. Our goal is to make Esperanto the universal language, which we think will promote peace through better mutual understanding."

"Sounds like a plan."

"Say, are you interested in getting involved?"

"Not really."

"Okay, but just you wait, my friend. *Esperanto tranprenos la mondon!*" Toes waited for Eph to ask for a translation, but the request was not forthcoming. "That means 'Esperanto will take over the world.'"

"Okey-dokey."

"All right, then. Peace, brother!" Toes' shoes made a squishing noise on the marble floors as he walked away. Eph tried to find Toes annoying—well, he *was* annoying—but he was also relentlessly upbeat, which made him difficult to dislike. Much.

———

In his cramped office, Eph checked his email. The first one in his in-box was from a student.

> Professor Russell, I am in your 19th Century American Lit class (which I love!) and I was wondering if I could come by your office to discuss my paper.

Eph didn't recognize the name. It was still early in the semester and he'd only learned the names of the few who regularly spoke up. He proposed a time on Friday during office hours and got an almost immediate response.

> Thank u. Can't wait!

Can't wait? For a faculty consult?

As a professor, Eph always liked it when students reached out. It usually meant they cared about the subject, at least enough to improve their grades. Many professors at Devon were content to lecture, but to Eph, teaching was all about the interplay between teacher and student.

He looked forward to meeting Miss Harris.

# Ashley, Alabama

## WHERE ARE YOU FROM?

How Eph dreaded that question. His normal response was always pleas-antly misdirecting, especially when Devon people were doing the asking. "Flor-ida," he'd say. It wasn't that his roots embarrassed him, but he didn't want to be a curiosity, or, worse, an object of suspicion. And maybe when you got right down to it, he *was* a little self-conscious about it.

Florida wasn't too far off, not really, since his childhood home was only forty miles north of the Panhandle, and a couple of times his family had va-cationed down on the Gulf beaches. Life in the Panhandle wasn't all that dif-ferent from life in southern Alabama, so it was the whitest of lies. Floribama, some people called it. Also, he'd earned his Ph.D. in Tallahassee, at Florida State, so that established his Floridian bona fides.

Didn't it?

Up here, when he said, "Florida," people assumed he was from Boca or Naples or some other warm-weather outpost where Northeasterners always seemed to have in-laws. He did little to dispel these notions. Eph knew if he said he was from the postage-stamp town of Ashley, Alabama, he'd be treated as a lab specimen, some sort of wayward traveler from that *other* America, the one of tattoos and rednecks driving F-150s with gun racks. He'd be asked questions, ones oozing with fake sincerity, in an effort to "understand."

*Tell us what it's really like.*

He didn't feel like being appointed Devon's cultural "explainer," like that guy who wrote *Hillbilly Elegy*. Besides, he'd worked hard to get here. Or was it that he'd worked hard to get away from Ashley? Maybe it was both.

Not much ever happened in Ashley, anyway, so there wasn't much to tell. What passed for discourse were debates on the relative merits of John Deere and Allis-Chalmers, or maybe arguments over who would win the Auburn starting-quarterback job the next season. To this day, the town's claim to fame is the world's only monument to an agricultural pest. Eph had to admit it was the one story about Ashley he liked to tell. He'd shared it with D'Arcy, anyway.

The story went back to the time Eph's family first settled there, around the turn of the last century, those boundless years of America's adolescence. In 1898, the Alabama Midland Railway ran a spur behind Main Street, connecting the town to the world and setting off a flurry of commerce. The soil in Melcher County was rich and mineral laden, perfect for growing cotton to meet the growing nation's insatiable demand, so Ashley farmers stayed busy. The Alabama Midland Railway carted away the town's bounty, while the venerable Brink's corporation arrived with cash and bearer certificates, which were immediately deposited in the Merchant & Planters Bank. The town prospered.

In the summer of 1915, farmers first noticed an unfamiliar insect in the fields, an ugly-looking black thing with a mottled shell and extended proboscis. Some said it came from Mexico, which turned out later to have been the case. Few gave it much thought as it wasn't a known pest, but the boll weevil proved itself an ambitious consumer of cotton and soon, like some biblical plague, was destroying cotton crops all over Melcher County. In a panic, farmers put entire fields to the torch, sort of an agricultural chemotherapy. It did little good. The damn things would just burrow into the soil until it was safe to come out.

Facing ruin, the town fathers gathered and made a dramatic decision: they would diversify Ashley's crop base, growing peanuts, tobacco, even indigo. The boll weevil was voracious but picky, and that was its weakness. Word from other counties was that the pest didn't much care for anything besides cotton, so growing other crops was the solution.

While this may seem an obvious course of action to the modern observer, not so in those days. Cotton had brought wealth to Melcher County, and Ashley's farmers knew how to grow it and grow it well. Peanuts and the like required different growing and harvesting practices, and besides, who would grow which crop? Folks were just used to a certain way of doing things, and change bred uncertainty. Uncertainty bred fear. Some thought they could ride the infestation out, and they argued the point with vigor. In the end, though, the sight of charred fields was more frightening than the prospect of learning new crop techniques, and the town pushed forward.

The plan worked with surprising speed, and before long Ashley was prospering even more than before the pestilence. In 1919, to commemorate what they'd been through, the town commissioned a statue of a goddess holding aloft an oversize boll weevil. They erected the damn thing right in the middle of the town square. Passers-through took it as a tongue-in-cheek gesture, but it was hard to imagine the God-fearing folks of Ashley putting up an expensive statue as an ironic gag. Little did they know that a century later it would be all the town was known for, even if this renown would never extend much beyond the confines of Melcher County. Still, the Boll Weevil Monument stands as an eternal reminder to all how Ashley withstood adversity.

*So that's what it's like. We build statues to insects.*

Eph seldom dwelled on his own history in Ashley. He was the youngest of three, born to Millie and Big Mike Russell. By that time, Ashley was just another rural backwater, its glory years of wealth, industry, and cleverness decades behind it. Eph's family owned a farm—growing soybeans and peanuts, mostly. They got by, but only just. There was little money for anything but the basics.

Eph's early years were monotonous. When not in school, he was helping Big Mike and his siblings, Jack and Ellie, on the farm. He knew from an early age it was not his calling. Any spare time he had was spent reading. This did little to endear him to the neighborhood kids, and Big Mike thought it was a waste.

Still, at times in his younger years Eph valued the sameness of it all. Emerson—one of Eph's favorites—called consistency the "hobgoblin of little minds," but Eph suspected Emerson wasn't talking about kids. For kids, change is always unsettling. Sure, the small things, the things that nudge at the order of things, those you got over. Things such as that time when Eph was eight and his mom announced the family would be eating only healthy food from then on. What did this mean for Tater Tots? Spaghetti night? Or a year later, when his pet rabbit, Jedi, died. He was almost as old as Eph when he went to rabbit heaven, and the family buried him out back with a little ceremony. Eph even said a few words. He couldn't imagine the world without Jedi, but only for a few days.

Then there's big change, the kind that sends a life on a different track—the kind that leads to Devon University instead of a soybean farm. That's a different story, one that comes from a knock at the door.

# The Progressive Student Alliance

**THE PROGRESSIVE STUDENT** Alliance made its headquarters in the space of a defunct fraternity, the old DKU house. The beautiful two-story stone structure evoked an Anglican chapel in the Cotswolds. The university had been openly hostile to fraternities since the fifties and used the considerable tools at its disposal to rid itself of them. Most of the houses, though, were privately owned, and the university couldn't simply reclaim the properties. So Devon played the long game, waiting for opportunities. In its view, DKU had housed a particularly noxious gaggle of undergraduate brigands, a label with which the house residents themselves would not have quibbled.

In the mid-seventies, when money was tight everywhere, DKU fell behind on its property taxes. Like a hen appealing to the fox, the fraternity asked for Devon's help. DKU had been at the school since 1851, went the appeal. It was an integral part of Devon's history. And the order's traditional involvement in the community had to be considered. Some of the brothers had even helped raise money for, you know, that thing a few years ago. So went the argument presented by Jamie Riggs, DKU's president.

"Yes, indeed," replied the dean of student affairs. "It would be a shame to see DKU leave us," whereupon he nodded to university counsel, a man from the venerable Shearman & Sterling, who produced a check and a prodigious raft of papers, ready for signature. He held the check up so Jamie could see it, then pushed the papers across the table.

Relieved, Jamie signed here and signed there, imagining the reception he was going to get back at the house. Oh, what a party it would be. DKU lives!

Jamie Riggs would be the last of the Delta Kappa Upsilon's 127 presidents. The party that night would indeed become the stuff of legend, but mostly as a monument to naïveté. Jamie, having been hungover at the time and not expecting treachery from his beloved Devon, had not actually read the eighteen-page loan agreement and its various codicils and covenants, which, while providing funds to cover the tax payment, required repayment, in full, in a week's time.

Eight days later, at precisely nine a.m., an eviction notice was posted on DKU's front door, giving the boys until the end of the semester to vacate. The magnificent DKU house was Devon's for the bargain-basement price of $18,000.

For a number of years, the house was underutilized, serving in turn as auxiliary space for the Architecture School, a venue for performance art, and, most recently, a student-run café. A $150 million gift from Ellis Dixon, private equity mogul and member of the class of '77, made possible the building of a new, state-of-the-art student center, so the café had outlived its usefulness. Over the summer, the dean of student affairs decided to allocate the space to the Progressive Student Alliance, along with $100,000 for the group's general-purpose fund. For the PSA, it was a nice upgrade from meeting at Blue Nation Coffee. They now had a permanent base from which to forward the Struggle.

"Rufus, put on some tunes," Red said.

"Play some Björk," Gaia said.

"I'm not playing fucking Björk again," said Rufus, a sophomore and resident tune-meister. He favored bushy, seventies-style hair and cargo shorts. He linked his phone to a speaker with Bluetooth and played some Phish.

"I've been thinking," said Red. "Israel doesn't cut it." Red hadn't bothered with their little first-day protest. "There's no juice. No one around here understands the Middle East, and why should they? It was fucked-up when they were born, and it will be fucked-up when they die. That's all they know. We've tried more than once and there's no traction."

Red looked at the signs that said DIVEST NOW! and ZIONISM = RACISM!

sitting in the corner. They would be repurposed later. Despite the warm weather, Red wore a rainbow knit cap, bulging with the effort to contain his dreadlocks. When he pulled the cap off, his Rasta-style braids spilled out like a tangle of cinnamon snakes. They contrasted vividly with his pallid complexion. Plopping on the faded couch, he lit his first joint of the day. It was one p.m. Others joined him.

Red wasn't his given name, but it had followed him from birth when he came out of the womb with his unmistakably vibrant scalp. Later the name gelled nicely with his flavor of politics. He was a product of Buckley and Exeter, educational bona fides unsurpassed in the eyes of the Eastern establishment. That Red Wheeler was a product of that establishment, with a rich family and a trust fund of considerable heft, was something he had dedicated himself to living down, at least outwardly. He loved walking into his grandfather's Park Avenue offices, dreadlocks screaming defiance as he strolled by all the work-slaves.

But the truth was, having money freed him from having to make any himself, from being a cog in someone else's corporate machine. *No one* was going to exploit Red Wheeler. The rationalization gave him comfort.

Red was one of those people who just always seemed to be around. Every campus had a few, inhabitants who found creative ways to extend their collegiate experiences far beyond the usual boundaries. Red was in his seventh year, having found Devon much to his liking. He'd been a handful of philosophy credits shy of graduating for some time, a process he managed with care. Technically, he wasn't enrolled at the moment at all and lived off campus.

Being at Devon relieved Red of any responsibility, from having to figure out what The Plan was. His family was big on planning. Red, not so much. He liked things one day at a time. The pursuit of progressive causes conferred a needed sense of purpose and also acted as a shield of sorts. When you're saving the world, no one should be on your case about a goddamn *plan.* Better yet, progressivism came with its own prepackaged lifestyle of clothes and rallies and pleasing pharmaceuticals. It was a lifestyle Red fully embraced.

"The year just started," Rufus said, still on Israel. "Maybe we just need to turn up the vol on this, give it time."

Red inhaled deeply on his joint. "Fuck that . . . tried Israel last year . . . got . . . no traction." The words came out in a staccato whisper and puffs of smoke as he tried not to exhale prematurely. After a few more moments, he exhaled more fully, and a fragrant cloud filled the room.

"I still can't believe Milton said, 'Keep up the good work,'" Gaia added. She wore small round glasses and had multicolored beads woven into her hair. "I mean, what an asshole."

"Milton Strauss is a progressive, but he's also part of the power structure, which is a fundamental contradiction in the dialectic." Red really liked the word *dialectic*. "He's an old-style liberal, really . . . but still, the man can be useful. Everyone has a part to play."

The others, seven or eight of them, nodded in agreement, passing around the joint. They often deferred to Red, as he was older and had seen his share of the Struggle—G7 Summits, Occupy, Black Lives Matter, the Women's March, Antifa . . . Red was universally acknowledged to be "woke" and drifted seamlessly between causes. When Trump won, he rallied four hundred students into the middle of East Quad for a primal scream at three a.m. It got over two hundred thousand views on YouTube. He'd originally made his name as a sophomore when he led a student movement to force the endowment to divest from fossil fuel companies. Borrowing from the eighties playbook when Devon antiapartheid demonstrators constructed a shantytown, he rallied students to build a "zero net energy village" right in Bingham Plaza. Consisting mostly of unsightly yurts, slapdash lean-tos, and other tent-like structures, it prompted Milton Strauss to announce over a billion dollars of divestment. Red was quoted in *The New York Times*.

There were always rumors around Red after that, talk of some hacking, maybe even with Anonymous, the infamous hacker collective known for wearing Guy Fawkes masks. Red did little to dispel these rumors, keeping a Guy Fawkes mask lying casually around his apartment. The truth was he never got any further than Comp Sci 101 way back in freshman year.

If there had been such a thing as president of the PSA, it would certainly have been Red, but the group eschewed such bourgeois power structures in favor of the more progressive practice of "general consensus." This often took the form of finger snapping, which meant "I approve." Someone once told Red that snapping could be traced to the beatniks, who would gather in coffeehouses, reciting poems suffused with cultural rebellion. Listeners would snap as each verbal dagger struck its mark, not unlike African-American churchgoers chiming "Amen" during an inspired sermon. Red didn't know if the story was true, but he liked to think so.

"We have to make it about Devon somehow, otherwise people won't give a shit. You think the average GPA-sucking zombie around here cares about fucking Israel? But they *do* care about the cozy little bed they're sleeping in called Devon University. We need them to question everything they think they know by exposing the elitism and the systemic privilege."

Red also liked the word *systemic*.

"All these rich kids, man . . . so fat and comfortable in their patriarchal bubble, so intellectually constipated . . . they don't know struggle. We gotta bring the whole thing down." That Red was rich and had been living off his family's money at Devon for seven years went unsaid, had the contradiction even occurred to anyone. Being woke proffered a certain moral license.

As the group thought on this and other weighty issues of social justice, the purple cannabis cloud grew around them.

"You guys see the Republican Club invited that fascist Potter to speak?" someone asked. Robert Potter was a Republican senator from Texas known for his conservative stance on immigration.

"We'll see about that, won't we?" Red grinned.

"Hey, I got my first gig," Rufus said, studying his iPhone. "Beta house."

Rufus, whose *nom de fête* was RoofRaza, was a purveyor of electronic dance music, commonly known as EDM. His reputation as a campus DJ had taken hold toward the end of the previous year when the frats gave him a gig or two. "Four hundred cash money, baby."

"Fraternity dicks," Gaia said.

"Maybe so," said Rufus, "but it's beaucoup bucks."

# The Dix

**AT LEAST LULU KNEW *SOMEONE*** in this god-awful place. Shelley Kisner had been two years ahead of her at Dalton. They weren't great friends, but generally hung out in the same Manhattan circles. Shelley's family had an estate in Southampton. While not as much to Lulu's tastes as East Hampton—Southampton was filled with all those tedious *finance* types—it was something. They knew the same clubs and many of the same people. Shelley had texted a few days before, and they agreed to meet up in the Dixon Student Center, known to all as the Dix.

Lulu browsed her iPhone while waiting for Shelley to arrive. There were stories on Facebook about a devastating earthquake in Chile. Lulu's thumbs got busy.

*Thoughts and prayers for those suffering in #Chile. #SoSad*

Click, posted.

Lulu liked to send out frequent prayer requests on Facebook, not that she had ever literally prayed herself. She refreshed her screen every few seconds. Seventeen likes in less than a minute. A trace of dopamine stimulated her prefrontal cortex, giving off a slight high. She was about to hit refresh again when Shelley plopped her Fendi bag down on the table.

"Well, hey, Harris."

"Thank God, a familiar face." Lulu stood up and exchanged air kisses, both cheeks, then walked to the Starbucks vendor and ordered double espressos. The sounds of foosball punctuated the otherwise relative quiet, even though the many rows of tables were actually quite crowded.

The Dix, previously known as Bancroft Hall, was an enormous building intentionally designed to look like the Parthenon, with an imposing thirty-foot-high colonnade of Corinthian columns running down its length on either side. The inside had recently been renovated by Ellis Dixon's gift. It was a cavernous space with various food vendors around the periphery. Devon's masters once imagined Bancroft, built a century ago, as a temple of learning. They probably didn't anticipate the Subway and Einstein Bagels franchises. Flags from all the nations represented by the student body hung from the high rafters. This year there were ninety-three. Rows of long tables were interspersed with "pod" areas featuring comfortable oversize chairs and various table games.

"Why is it so damn quiet?" Lulu asked.

"Look around." Shelley waved at the silent rows of people. "Behold, a Friday night at Devon." Sure enough, other than the *clack-clack-clack* of foosball, the most noticeable sound was the *click-click-click* of keyboards. Row after row of fellow students, pecking, a susurrus of white noise. "If they're not studying, they're playing computer games online, particularly the Asians. A lot of them are probably playing together, but they won't speak, not directly. All their communication is through the games. This is their idea of socializing, having proximity to each other. On weeknights, they get serious and go to one of the libraries."

"Is it always like this?" Lulu affected a bored look. *Is that Song over there?*

"This utterly banal? Pretty much."

"I hate this," Lulu said.

"Can't say I disagree."

"Why are we here again?"

"The Dix or Devon?"

"Well, both I guess, but I meant here at the Dix."

"We are 'minding the gap.'"

Shelley had just a hint of an English accent, painstakingly cultivated during a summer spent as an intern at Sotheby's in London. *Minding the gap* reminded Lulu of—what else?—the London Underground, although she couldn't imagine what that had to do with their present situation. What she'd give to be in

London now . . . Annabel's, Henley, perhaps Ascot . . . maybe this coming summer. Sheldon wouldn't mind.

Someone dropped a full can of Red Bull nearby, snapping Lulu out of her brief reverie.

"What gap?" Lulu asked.

"The gap is that expanse of time between dinner, which the Philistines here eat at about six, if you can imagine, and the evening's festivities. It can be four or five hours. No one's ever come up with the right solution, although there's lots of pre-gaming—you know, the drinking before the drinking. Personally, I can't ingest alcohol for seven hours straight, at least not the way some people around here do. I'd be calling to the seals."

"What?"

"Vomiting."

"Thank you for that image."

"This *is* college, dear, and I did use a metaphor."

Changing the subject, Lulu asked, "So . . . what about the male of the species around here?"

Shelley leaned back. "Let me answer that with a question. How many . . . boys, in this vast expanse of the Dixon Student Center, would you let touch you?"

Lulu looked around, wrinkling her nose. Taking in a sample of several dozen nearby Devon males, she quickly realized the question had been rhetorical. She slumped in her chair.

*"But . . ."* Shelley let the word hang in the air. "There are certain ponds in which the fishing is better than, well, the Dix. They are small ones, and you need to know where they are, but they are there. Things at Devon may be desperate, but it's not beyond hope."

She had Lulu's attention.

"C'mon, let's go," Shelley said.

"Where?"

"Just trust me. You should meet some of the right people. Not everyone here is from . . . wherever it is these people are from." Shelley gave a dismissive wave to a nearby pod of students, still *clicking* and *clacking*.

"But I'm not dressed," Lulu said, still clad in an ensemble of Bandier yoga gear.

"We'll swing by your room. You're in Duffy, right? It's practically on the way."

# The Society of Fellingham

**THE EARLY-EVENING AIR** was cooling as they made their way up Randolph Street, about a block from campus. Lulu, wearing a Ralph Lauren knee-length coat, was feeling a hint of optimism for the first time in her brief career at Devon. Where were they off to?

They came to a modest three-story shingled home, wedged between two others. Shelley rang the bell, which gave off the Big Ben chimes. "I should tell you, they're a bit eccentric, but just go with it, okay?"

A tiny slot in the door slid open, the kind of thing Lulu associated with a Depression-era speakeasy. A pair of eyes glared out. "Who goes there?" The voice had a British accent. Or maybe it was what Sheldon called a Locust Valley lockjaw. Was that still a thing?

"You know who it is, Winny, you damn twit. And she's with me." Shelley nodded toward Lulu.

The slot window closed with a *thwack* and the door swung open, revealing a remarkably pale young man with slicked-back hair and a double-breasted blazer with some kind of crest on the breast pocket. "Shel! How are you, darling? How was the summer?"

"Same old. You know the drill."

"Well, it's about time you showed up. Who is your terribly attractive friend?"

"This is Harris. She's a fellow New Yorker. We like her." It was understood that *New York* meant "Manhattan," and only certain parts.

"Lulu."

"A great pleasure, Lulu Harris. I am Winslow Gubbins. You may call me Win. Welcome to Fellinghams." Win had wavy brown hair and a sallow complexion. Lulu noticed he dropped the *h* in *Fellingham*—*Felling-um*—and he said it in the plural, the way a Brit would do.

"Please, *entre*." They walked through the foyer into a living room. "It's not much, but it's home. Toby, two Pimm's Cups for our new arrivals." Win gestured to an elderly black man in a white jacket who was tending bar. He mixed Pimm's No. 1 with Sprite, garnishing the drink with wedges of orange and lime.

Lulu accepted her drink and took in her surroundings. Perhaps twenty people were milling around, chatting, all well dressed by Devon standards. One or two wore white dinner jackets, although for what Lulu could scarcely imagine. Several seemed to have accents of indeterminable origin. There was faded but comfortable-looking furniture, the bar, and a large fireplace. The décor was slightly fussy and worn. There was also a what . . . scepter? . . . over the mantel. It had colorful inlaid stones. Overall, the place looked like what it was: a small, unremarkable house in Havenport. Except for the scepter.

"Winny and I met in London when I was at Sotheby's," Shelley said. "He's as close as we come to an Englishman around here, so that qualifies him to be president of this dubious establishment."

"High Scepter, *s'il vous plaît*."

"Sorry, High Scepter. Anyway, Lulu's father is a very important entertainment lawyer," offered Shelley.

"Is that right? Whom does he represent? Anyone we know?" It wasn't clear if the question was directed at Lulu or Shelley.

"Oh, I'm sure," Shelley said, looking at Lulu over the rim of her traditional Collins glass.

"He's New York based, so Broadway and TV, mostly," answered Lulu.

"Fascinating," said Win, managing not to seem fascinated at all.

"I told Lulu that Devon is not the social wasteland she thinks it is," Shelley said.

"Well, it is, God knows, but there are redoubts of civility," Win said.

"I take it you mean here?" Lulu said. Win just smiled, eyebrows arched. "So, where is here, exactly?"

"Fellinghams. I thought we covered that."

"She wants to know what goes on here, you wanker," Shelley said.

"What goes on here, what goes on here . . . How shall I say it? We are a haven, a refuge, if you will, for a certain sort. We value the arts and have frequent soirées, most notably for Lord Fellingham's birthday. We are comfortable in formal wear, and most of us speak several languages."

"*Je vois,*" Lulu said. I see.

"Ah, *très fábuleux, ma chère.*" Win clinked his glass on Lulu's, pleased with their mutual fabulousness. "But we really should talk to Frazier." Turning, Win waved across the room. "Frazier, a moment."

Frazier disengaged from a conversation with a rail-thin brunette with enormous gold hoop earrings and traversed the room. "Hello, Shel." His eyes turned to Lulu. "Well, whom do we have here?"

"Meet Lulu . . . Harris?"

"Yes, Harris."

"Harris." Win let the word hang there for a moment, as if divining the name's uncertain provenance. "Well, Lulu, meet Frazier Langham, our society historian. Frazier, meet Lulu Harris, freshman."

"The pleasure is mine," Frazier said. He sported a blazer and rep tie, perfectly knotted. "And aren't we supposed to be saying fresh*person*, or something?"

"Wait, we have a historian?" Shelley asked.

"It's *first-year* now," Lulu said. "The word *fresh* targets us for sexual violence. I got a pamphlet. It's all there."

"A pamphlet! How wonderful!" Win clapped his hands. "You *must* bring us one. One has so much trouble keeping up with the nomenclature." He laughed, imagining he had made a particularly clever bon mot. "Anyway, Frazier here is, in fact, the society's historian. I thought he might give you the sordid details."

Frazier liked few things more than talking about Fellinghams. "I will go back to the beginning. Our little island of civility was founded nine years ago by—"

"Hold on, you sure you can keep track of all that history, Frazier? I mean, nine years . . ."

"Shut up, Shel, you harpy!" Win blurted. "It's important for any organization to have institutional memory."

"Okay, I'll be good. Do go on." Shelley smiled and sipped her Pimm's.

"The Society of Fellingham," Frazier continued, "was founded nine years ago by Sir Alexander Hargrove. A freshman at the time, he found the university's social options lacking, at least for one as he, born of the British aristocracy. The society was named for Hargrove's direct ancestor Lord Herbert Fellingham, the second Marquess of Fellingham, who lived in the seventeenth century and was a prominent supporter of James the Second. Sir Alex was a traditional monarchist, you see, and the society's mission statement asserts that we will strive to reinstate the primacy of monarchic rule, and that America, in particular, should be returned to the monarchic fold. Also, there should be many formal affairs with free-flowing alcohol."

"Long live the queen!" shouted Win, High Scepter.

All in the room stopped what they were doing. Raising their Pimm's, they shouted back, *"Long live the queen!"* Lulu sensed it was a thing.

Frazier continued, "The scepter was chosen as our symbol, and you can see our sacred scepter, handed down through generations of Hargroves, hanging over the mantelpiece. It's quite priceless."

Shelley snorted.

Frazier just ignored her. "Sir Alex decreed that only students who were members of the aristocracy could join, but he soon discovered this meant Fellinghams would have a membership of two, himself and Ahmed Farooq. Ahmed was the grandnephew of the deposed shah of Iran, so he was a fellow traveler, aristocratically speaking. Farooq's family had been chased from the family seat by street mobs during the revolution, but he still qualified. Ahmed aside, though, Sir Alex was distraught to learn that he had arrived in something of an aristocratic wasteland."

"He did know he was in, like, America, right?" Lulu asked.

"That's not entirely clear. By all accounts he was intoxicated for most of his six years here, and he may not have technically graduated. Pembroke College at Cambridge had been the family's scholastic seat for centuries, but they say Sir Alex couldn't settle on a subject of study, which makes admission at Cambridge problematic, as was the fact he may or may not have written 'Bugger off' as the response to one of his A Level essay questions. We believe he chose Devon because it's the closest approximation to Oxford or Cambridge, what with our Gothic spires and house system. But some details of the story are lost in the mists of time."

"He graduated three years ago," Shelley offered, being helpful, as always.

"Anyway, Sir Alex decided to grant admittance to others who could at least *act* with the appropriate social graces, and Fellinghams was founded with nineteen initial members. They had no house, of course, and held meetings at the residence of a former professor, one who professed to be an Anglophile. Regrettably, it turned out he was also a predatory homosexual, which made it necessary to seek other arrangements. A year later, Sir Alex set his eyes on this very edifice. Lacking sufficient funds for the purchase, as his family was some three generations removed from anything resembling actual wealth, he persuaded his now close friend Ahmed to foot the bill. Ahmed's family had managed to escape Iraq with Swiss bank accounts of considerable health, you see, so it was a small matter."

"To the damn Persian!" Win cried.

"*To Ahmed!*" answered everyone.

"So, how goes it with the whole monarchy thing?" Lulu asked, suppressing a giggle.

"Splendidly," Win answered. "We're having a party to celebrate Prince Harry's birthday next month. Perhaps you might attend."

"Huzzah!" Frazier cried, in apparent agreement.

Someone turned the music up, and the night became a blur of alcohol, toasts, and slightly loosened neckties. In the fullness of the evening, Win removed the scepter from the mantel and led a march around the living room, waving the scepter from side to side like a drum major. Each time the line passed the bar, a shot of whiskey was all but required. Presently, it was decided that food was an urgent requirement, and so Win led a small parade to Gino's Pizza down the block, everyone singing "That Gay Old Devon That I Love" along the way. Five pies were ordered in high-Elizabethan English from Gino, otherwise known as "my good man."

Gino didn't mind—this wasn't the first time. But he did wonder about the university now and then.

Shelley and Lulu walked back to campus in somewhat less than straight lines, clutching each other for support and giggling as they went. Lulu deliberately mangled a few lines of "Rule, Britannia!," another of the evening's standards.

"Don't take them too seriously. They're harmless. Win's from New Jersey!"

"The High Scepter of Hackensack?" Lulu laughed hysterically.

"It's all in good fun."

"You don't have to convince me. Those are the first people I've liked since I got here, and that incluudes the people I've had sex with." They both laughed hysterically, swerving under the wrought-iron gates to East Quad. They paused while Lulu took a double selfie, which she posted to Instagram with a click.

The inscription over the gate, which few ever took note of, read UNA CRESCIMUS.

Together We Grow.

# The English Department

**ONCE A MONTH,** the English Department had an all-hands meeting. Generally, about forty people attended these, including teaching assistants and a visiting writer or two. Eph and his colleagues crowded into one of the larger spare classrooms in Grafton. Sunlight bathed the room through the arched, leaded-glass windows.

Devon's many architectural details, particularly the Gothic ones, lent the campus a feeling of timelessness, even if it was all a bit of a conceit. Most of the buildings that appeared centuries old were actually built in the 1930s, but that feeling of permanence was just what the architects at the time were reaching for. Instant Oxbridge, just add stone and mortar. Conceit or not, it worked, leaving Devon's residents feeling part of something that had been here long before and would remain long after.

While no one, perhaps in the entire history of academia, would ever lay claim to liking faculty meetings, Eph came closer than most. They were a reminder, much like the architecture, of just where he was. With professors still filing in, he imagined the road not taken. (Okay, sure, Frost was a cliché, but Eph had a soft spot for the craggy Vermonter.) In Eph's case, that road would have involved riding a John Deere, back and forth, back and forth.

Titus Cooley, chair of the English Department, leaned back against the desk at the head of the classroom. On the north side of seventy, he had a genetically furrowed brow set above impossibly bushy eyebrows. His weathered face was like a tan-and-pink watercolor that someone had left out in the rain.

"Okay, let's get on with it. We have a few items to cover today. First, the department heads all met with President Strauss yesterday. We covered a variety of issues, but I wanted to bring some to your attention. I'm sure you're all familiar with the website Rate My Professor."

A groan issued forth. The site was widely loathed in academic circles. Rate My Professor let students anonymously rate their teachers, and most professors secretly hated any form of transparency. (Devon, like every other college, kept its official student course ratings under strict lock and key.) Rate My Professor rewarded easy graders and contributed, in the view of many, to grade inflation. That the site had recently added a teacher "hotness" ranking didn't help, either.

Titus raised his voice above the moaning. "As you may be aware, the site allows users to rate professors on a scale of one to five. Anyone can rate any professor. No actual proof that the rater attended the class, or even attended the school, is required. Furthermore, most professors have small sample sizes, thus not meeting the requirements for statistical significance. For these reasons, the university has decided to issue a statement condemning the site in the strongest possible terms."

"Here! Here!" The room vigorously approved. Eph tried not to look at the site much, but he knew most teachers, including himself, secretly couldn't resist the occasional peek. His own 4.4 rating was well above Devon's 3.6 average. The sample size was only eighteen, so it didn't mean much, but it gave him some satisfaction nonetheless. He liked to imagine people back in Ashley had seen it, somehow, but knew it was unlikely.

"Furthermore," continued Titus, "there have been some rather unpleasant occurrences at other schools. Teachers colluding to rate each other, or even rating themselves. That sort of thing. It goes without saying that such shenanigans here at Devon would result in severe disciplinary measures. I'm going to assume that this isn't going to be a problem."

There was a murmur of agreement.

"Moving on, we will be hiring a new assistant professor. I have emailed you the curricula vitae of the candidates should you have any feedback. Interviews begin next week. . . . Lastly—"

"Excuse me, Professor."

It was Sophie Blue Feather. Poetry. Arrived at Devon last year with full tenure, which was rare. Everyone quietly assumed she was Native American, but to Eph she looked white as Titus Cooley. Was he the only one who noticed? He knew better than to ask.

"Professor Blue Feather," Titus said.

Blue Feather rose out of her seat. "It appears that all the candidates you sent us are cisgender. I urge the department in the strongest possible terms to increase its LGBT representation, particularly trans. It is imperative that we break the heteronormative paradigm."

*Now there's a mouthful,* thought Eph. Professor Blue Feather herself was a self-described pangenderist. She cut a striking figure, fortyish, with severe black-rimmed glasses and a pixie haircut died Smurf blue. When Eph first met her, she came right out and said, "*Yes,* I'm pangender." It was a challenge; as if she could read his thoughts, thoughts that just may be squirmed uncomfortably in the presence of anyone whose sexuality didn't adhere to traditional boundaries. She was daring him to say something. All he could manage was to look exactly like a deer in the headlights.

Maybe it was because he didn't know what the heck a *pangenderist* was. Wasn't pan*sexual* a thing, too? Later, in private, he had turned to Google and discovered a robust palette of gender options, each with its own unique flag. Facebook, for instance, allowed users to choose from fifty-eight, although he frequently found the definitions confusing. For instance, he couldn't see that there was a difference between an *androgyne* and an *hermaphrodite*. For that matter, how was something called *neither* a gender, and why was it different from *other,* and why was there both *cisgender woman* and *cisgender female*? And wasn't a *two-spirit* just a gay Indian? Eph imagined some faceless social force conjuring up nuanced gender alternatives behind the scenes.

*Pangender,* he discovered, described people who embodied all genders within themselves. All fifty-eight? How did they decide what to wear in the morning? And just to make sure he had things straight, a *pansexual* was someone who liked getting busy with the other fifty-seven. Eph wasn't sure he knew any pansexuals, but they must be popular at parties.

"Uh, cisgender?" Titus asked, looking as though he immediately regretted asking.

"That would be *you,* Professor," said Sophie Blue Feather, pangenderist. The room broke out in laughter, although Blue Feather's expression didn't change.

"Ah, so you mean . . . normal?"

There were audible gasps. He'd used the N-word. The other one. "We don't say *normal*, Professor," Blue Feather said.

"Er, right, because I suppose that would imply, if one thought it through, that others were, uh . . ."

"*Ab*normal. Yes, Professor."

"I see . . . yes . . . right. We will look into your request, Professor, although if I'm not mistaken, HR takes somewhat of a dim view on raising matters of, uh, sexual identity in the hiring process."

"That's why you need to involve more LGBTIAQ members of the faculty in that process."

"Well, yes, certainly, as I said, we'll look into it."

Poor Titus was doing his best to keep up with the cultural tides, but the tides were moving faster than a man of his age could swim.

"Our last item," he continued, "is this business of 'trigger warnings,' which, as you know, is a topic of much discussion both nationally and here at Devon. The university has formed a new committee with representatives from every department to frame a policy, and I have asked Professor Smallwood to represent the English Department. Professor, would you please come say a few words?"

*Toes!* Eph sank in his chair, trying to decipher this development. Toes fashioned himself as the consummate outsider, a radical who paid no deference to the Man, yet here he was, chairing some new committee. Was Toes playing an inside game? At least Titus wasn't winking at him. *Christ, stop reading into everything.*

Eph wasn't averse to playing the "game" in the name of his career, at least to a point, but the subtle undercurrents of departmental politics often eluded him. The abstruse meaning behind two-centuries-old literary prose? No problem. The politics of a twenty-first-century English department? Farm life had not trained him for that.

Toes made his way to the front. *Squish squish squish.*

"May I suggest," Titus said, "that if you are triggered by the appearance of unusual footwear, you may wish to avert your eyes." The room once again erupted in laughter. Old Cooley occasionally wielded a dry wit to great effect.

"Thank you, Professor Cooley," said Toes, now beet red. "We are called the Committee on Safe and Open Classrooms. Picking up on what Professor Blue Feather said, our Devon community grows ever more diverse, and we must take care not to marginalize those who may not feel completely comfortable here. We need to remember this was a university built by white men for other white men with no consideration given to the 'other.' We still live with the echoes of that discrimination."

Toes sounded like he'd memorized this, Eph thought.

"If you consider the Americans with Disabilities Act, it was meant to provide accessibility to differently abled people. In a similar way, trigger warnings, which we prefer to call content warnings, are meant to provide accessibility to the classroom for all, ensuring a safe environment. Studies show—"

"Excuse me." Everyone turned. It was Fred Hallowell, sitting in the back. English playwrights.

"Uh, yes, Professor Hallowell."

"You can call me Fred."

"Fred, certainly."

"Are there many injuries in the classroom?"

"Sorry?"

"Injuries. Are there many."

"I don't understand." Toes suddenly looked like he'd ingested one too many turmeric balls at Blue Nation.

"Well, you said you're trying to make classrooms safe, and I'm trying to figure out why they're dangerous." There was an uneasy murmuring, not all of it sympathetic to where Hallowell was going.

"Not all violence is physical!" Sophie Blue Feather cried.

"Oh, well, yes," Toes said. "Professor Blue Feather is correct. We are not addressing physical dangers, per se, but rather psychological ones, which can be every bit as harmful. For instance, a victim of sexual assault, whom we term a *survivor*, can easily become distraught if exposed to passages in books like *To Kill a Mockingbird* or poems like *The Waste Land*. Books like *The Great Gatsby* can trigger those who have been victims of domestic violence. It is our duty as a school to protect our students from emotional trauma."

"By treating them like precious little dandelions?"

"Well, no, of course not. But as stewards of an institution that has been guilty of systemic oppression, it is our duty to make sure that we do everything we can to promote inclusiveness. No one who comes here should feel marginalized."

Hallowell was having none of it. "So we are censors now?"

"Looking after the safety of our students is not censorship, Professor!" Blue Feather said.

"Yes, that's right," Toes agreed. "While the committee hasn't come up with a set of guidelines yet, we hope to avoid outright censorship in favor of anticipatory warnings."

"Hooray for us!" Hallowell pumped his fist in the air. "Incidentally, who decides what gets a trigger?"

"We plan to form another committee to determine that in the coming months." (Eph had often noted it took almost nothing at Devon to necessitate the formation of a committee.) "We have tentatively created a series of seventeen guiding—"

"I think we've got the gist, Professor," interrupted Titus, looking to end the discussion before it went further downhill. Hallowell was tenured, and he sometimes used his untouchable status to roil the departmental waters. No waters were more easily disturbed. "The directive on this comes from President Strauss himself, so we can all look forward to a comprehensive policy later this year."

Eph thought he could hear the faintest trace of sarcasm in Titus's voice.

# Office Hours

**EPH HEADED BACK** down the hall to his office. He wasn't sure what to make of the meeting, other than that keeping his mouth shut had seemed the sensible thing. Treating college students like coddled babies didn't strike him as the best idea, but this was no time to tilt at windmills. He would keep his head down and teach.

The other day, Devon's newly formed Committee on Art in Public Spaces had used plywood boards to cover up part of a monument dedicated to Devon students who had lost their lives in the Civil War—but only the half with names of the Confederate students. Planks of wood literally covered up half of this beautiful bronze plaque. You could stand against racism and slavery, Eph reasoned, but still think some of this was overwrought.

Eph certainly *thought* of himself as a progressive, and by the standards of the Deep South, he certainly was. He hated guns, was supportive of abortion rights and the environment, and so on. Mostly, his politics were representative of what they weren't: the gun-toting, pickup-driving, shit-talking, revival-tent world of his youth. If progressive was the opposite of that, then that's what he was. But something about the latest winds blowing through campus had a dark edge, as if a subtle transition were going on from the American Revolution to the French. Devon had no shortage of Robespierre wannabes. Maybe when he had tenure, he would express these thoughts more. For right now, though, he didn't care much one way or the other about the political winds, be they blowing from the left or right. Politics would come and go, but literature was forever.

"Hello?"

Someone was knocking gently on his open door. It was his four o'clock, the girl who wanted to talk about her paper. He immediately recognized her, now matching the face with the name. She was the striking girl who normally sat on the left and didn't speak much. She was one of the few frequently late for class, he recalled.

"Come in, Miss . . . Harris. Have a seat."

Lulu shut the door.

"Uh, would you mind just keeping that open a bit? School policy." Eph recalled this point made rather emphatically in his HR training. Lulu opened the door about six inches and sat down in the chair next to Eph's desk. Eph didn't like to put the visitor's chair on the far side of the desk because he felt it made him too intimidating, less accessible. Not that he *felt* intimidating, but he remembered his own reluctance around teachers when he was younger. "What can I do for you today?"

"Well, first I wanted to say just how much I enjoy your class. It's my favorite. I find it . . . stimulating."

"Thank you." *That's nice. A bit suck-uppy, but nice.*

"I wanted to ask about my paper. I was thinking about contrasting the role of women as depicted by the Realists and the Romantics."

"Excellent idea."

"For my Realist, I thought I would go with Louisa May Alcott."

"Another great idea. She wrote about very spirited, independent women. Do you know she was from Massachusetts and actually grew up around Emerson, Hawthorne, and Thoreau? Right there you have an interesting angle."

"Well, that's where I'm having trouble. Women in the Realist era I get. Writers like Alcott portrayed strong women who defied the conventions of society to pursue their own dreams. But the Romantics portrayed them as either succubus bitches or silent sheep who served at the pleasure of their men. Or as victims to be chopped up, like with Poe. And Thoreau apparently didn't think women existed at all."

Eph chuckled and was impressed with Lulu's breezy knowledge of the subject, not considering the information that fifteen minutes with Google might confer. "So what's the issue?"

"Which Romantic do I pick? Their women were so much less interesting."

"I think you already answered your own question. The Romantics' views were not monolithic. Just a second ago you listed at least four approaches they had toward women. Pick one and run with it, although you're right about Thoreau—he may not give you much material."

"What about Emerson?"

"Emerson was quite progressive for the time. There may not be enough contrast there for an interesting paper, but you're welcome to try."

"You like Emerson, don't you?"

"One of my favorites, yes," Eph replied.

"Alcott was in love with him, wasn't she?"

"It's true. Thoreau as well."

"And they were both much older men, weren't they?"

"Yes, in Emerson's case, three decades."

"How interesting." Lulu leaned forward, smiling slightly, right at Eph.

The sudden shift in the mood made him uncomfortable. *Why is she looking at me like that?* "Well, I have a five o'clock, so . . ."

"It's four-fifteen," said Lulu.

"Uh, yes, I know, but I have to, you know, prepare."

"Okay, Professor. Thanks for your help."

She left, but just before she did, she winked.

*What is it with winks around here?* He was pretty sure this one was different from Titus Cooley's avuncular wink. Was he still attractive to a girl that age? The thought pleased him.

# Gummy Bears

**RED AND OTHER** members of the Progressive Student Alliance were hanging out on Goodwin Green, an open space near the center of Devon's campus. It was surrounded by ancient elms, now showing the slightest hint of cooler weather to come. The group sat down on a spot where the grass hadn't been worn by Frisbee throwers.

"I've got a hacky sack, if anyone's into it," Robbie Ochoa said.

"Dude, don't be such a cliché," Red said. "No one's played hacky sack since the Clinton administration. Besides, I have something better. He pulled out a cellophane wrapper and carefully unfolded it.

"Gummy bears?"

"*Special* gummy bears, from Colorado, where this particular kind of gummy bear is perfectly legal. Mock not, or I will not share." Red passed around two gummies to each person. "In these, we will find inspiration."

"Do we eat both at once?" someone asked.

"Live for the day, man," Red answered, popping them into his mouth. They all followed suit.

Gaia was staring into the distance, as if looking for something. "I don't feel anything."

"Lie back, it will come."

"I don't feel anything, either," Gabe Amato said.

"Hey, dumbass, we just took them about thirty seconds ago. Just shut the fuck up and let it come."

"I feel like you're being a dick, Red," Gaia said. "Remember your first year here? I think people were playing hacky sack then."

Red ignored her. They lay in silence for a bit, trying to discern any shift in their perceptions.

"Wait, I think I feel something," Robbie offered, looking at the sky with increasing curiosity.

"You guys act like you've never been high before when, really, it's been what, eighteen hours?" said Red.

"Never done magic *gummies*, man," Gabe said.

This prompted giggling.

"Let your minds go, my brothers and sisters, and imagine our future together. The PSA will rise up and be a feared presence on this campus. We will *make* them listen."

"Listen to what?" Gabe asked, still staring at a cloud, one that now looked a great deal like a friendly clown.

"To what? To the plight of the oppressed. To the will of the people. To every brother of color who's been gunned down by the blue and every sister ever held down by the old boys and their patriarchy. To every lake and every tree that's ever been poisoned by big corporations at the altar of mammon. To every gay, lesbian, queer, trans, bi, or questioning person struggling with their identity. To every Muslim brother, afraid of being attacked by fascists for their beliefs. To our giant *fucking* megaphone that will allow no sleep as long as we live in a society that oppresses the less privileged."

There was a pause as they took it in.

"Shit, man, could we just maybe pick one of those?" Robbie asked.

"Red's big-picture, Robbie. Focus is not his strong suit." Gaia's voice had a curious edge.

"We need to do it *all*, to address the entire matrix of oppression. But Robbie's right. We start small—and build. We need to sow the seeds of chaos, only then can we tear down the prevailing order. My friends, this campus is asleep, and *we* are the alarm clock."

"Testify!" Robbie cried. Gabe made a trilling noise like an alarm clock, which drew some giggles. At that, the group fell silent for a time, focusing on the changing cloud patterns. They swirled and danced against the blue sky.

"Man, you guys should have seen Gaia sticking it to this prof the other day. English 212," Gabe said, breaking the spell.

"Thanks for noticing, Gabe," Gaia said.

"What are you talking about?" Red asked, only faintly interested. He was more interested in the chimerical effects of THC, descending on him like a pleasant fog.

"I feel like it's a class about white supremacy," Gaia said. "I mean, we don't read *any* writers of color. I said something about it, and this dick totally blew me off."

"True dat," agreed Gabe. "You guys ever read *The Adventures of Huckleberry Finn?*"

"I don't know . . . in eighth fucking grade maybe? Why?" Red said, still trying to decide if he was interested in the conversation. The fog beckoned.

"We're reading it for class. Book's a piece of work."

"Why?"

"The N-word is all over it. Like, every page," Gabe said.

"Fuckin' A it is," Gaia added.

"Seriously?" Red was still trying to remember if they'd read *Huckleberry Finn* back at the Buckley School.

"Seriously, bro. Book's a trigger fest."

Red sat up, willing the fog away. "You have a copy?"

"Sure as hell." Gabe rolled over and fished the paperback out of his backpack and tossed it to Red.

Red flipped through it, pausing to read different passages. "Who's the prof?"

"Russell, something Russell." Gabe, once again supine, was trying to make out the shape of a particularly vexing cloud.

"Never heard of him. White dude?"

"Uh, yeah."

"Tenured?"

"How the hell should I know?"

"Well, how old is he?"

"I don't know. Thirties, I guess?"

Red grew excited. He needed to get in touch with Jaylen Biggs over at the Afro-American Cultural Center. "We're going to bring the Struggle home. It's Organizing 101. There has to be a target, and the target needs a face."

# Long Live the Queen!

**POSSESSING LITTLE HISTORY** of its own, the Society of Fellingham's initiation rights were still a work in progress. They weren't as barbaric as those boorish fraternities, to be sure. Win Gubbins had heard rumors that over at Beta, pledges were taken one by one, blindfolded, to a second-story balcony where each was instructed to tie a small rope around his scrotum. A brother would then raise a pledge's blindfold slightly, just enough for him to see he was on a second-story balcony and that the other end of the rope was secured to a cinder block by his feet. The blindfold was replaced and the pledge was asked, "Do you trust the brotherhood?" Allegedly, this was after an entire day of blindfolded activities, including sitting for hours on a basement floor while listening to the song "Baby," by Justin Bieber, at volume ten, over and over. After answering "Yes, sir!" the pledge, pants and underwear still bundled at his ankles, was told to hold out his arms, into which the cinder block was placed.

The next words were "Throw it."

By this point in the day, Stockholm syndrome was in full effect and a pledge could be counted on to do pretty much anything, including throwing a cinder block attached to his balls from a twenty-foot balcony. The rope, of course, measured twenty-two feet, which the brothers deemed a sufficient margin for error. It was a source of great hilarity, one heard.

Another time the initiates staged some performance art where they supposedly put whiskey, beer, and some visibly used feminine-hygiene products in a blender. The *note de grâce* was a live mouse that someone procured from a bio lab. It was dangled and dropped with little splash. Someone hit PURÉE and the pledges were made to drink the resulting cocktail. That skit was deemed disgusting even by Beta standards.

Win wasn't sure he believed such stories, but those Beta fellows weren't quite caught up on the evolutionary scale, so anything was possible. He did notice they made their pledges carry them around to classes one day in a sedan chair. He wished he'd thought of that one, what with its colonial overtones.

The Fellingham initiation was a more civilized affair, although it, too, would have its share of adult beverages. When Alexander Hargrove founded the society, he'd googled *English initiation rites* and discovered that at Cambridge initiates in one drinking society were forced to wear kippers around their necks for a whole day of classes. This struck Hargrove as amusing and appropriately British, so he set off on a tour of Havenport's markets in search of just the right kippers, preferably ones of considerable pungency. Discovering that Havenport was a kipper-free metropolis, he pronounced the city "uncivilized" and returned to Google, where he discovered that kippers were readily available online. He procured several pounds. Subsequently, each initiate was made to wear a string necklace of a dozen kippers for a day, strung together like puka shells. It became widely known in the Devon community that on the second Thursday of each October one needed to sit as far as possible from anyone who appeared to be wearing a food product around their neck.

It was seven o'clock, and Win expected the initiates at any moment. There were seven this year, including the fetching Harris girl, which would bring the society up to twenty-six members. Frazier, Shelley, and the others were dressed in black capes, while Win's was bloodred. Each cape had a hood, which they lowered to obscure their faces. The lights were off, and flickering candles were everywhere. Some were perfumed, to ward off the imminent arrival of rotting kippers.

"They're coming!" said Frazier, who'd been keeping an eye through a drawn curtain. Win went quickly to the mantel and grasped the scepter, then jogged back to the entry hall. He stood at the center of the others, and they arranged themselves into a phalanx, Win at its point. The doorbell rang.

"Tripp, music," whispered Win.

Tripp Maynard, another member, got out his phone, which was bluetoothed to some speakers. It began playing some Gregorian chants he'd downloaded earlier in the day.

*Attende Domine* . . .

"Who seeks entry?" Win cried, doing his best to lower his voice an octave.

"Uh, you told us to get here at seven?" said a male voice outside the door.

*Bloody idiots,* thought Win. "Who seeks entry?" He tried to sound angry this time.

"Oh, right. Uh, it is we, the postulants . . . O . . . High . . . Scepter."

Someone outside snorted.

"Enter!"


They came through the door, including Lulu, who eyed the robed phalanx and the candles with suspicion. Was this going to be a serious thing? She could only presume this was all done ironically. Best to play along.

Frazier, acting as Win's right-hand man, pointed at a trash bag near the door. "Remove those bloody fish!"

This was fine with Lulu, who, despite having lost her sense of smell by third period, still found the kippers revolting. Part of her, though, had enjoyed the day. Most people around campus knew about the kippers, and it signaled that *she* had been chosen for something that *they* had not, even if they weren't sure what it was, exactly.

Frazier instructed them to go to the living room and kneel in a row. "Postulants!" he cried. "You will now present us with your offerings."

The residential houses at Devon each had a grand dining hall with its own unique patterned china, and the postulants had been instructed to pilfer a full set. Win thought it a fun task to assign, and after all, stealing stuff was an honored college tradition. That the society was low on cash and needed some kitchenware factored only somewhat into the decision.

The postulants held out their plates, which one of the members collected. "You will now each bow before the High Scepter," said Frazier.

"But we're already kneeling," pointed out one of the boys.

"Oh, for God's sake. Just bow your head a little when he gets to you."

Win approached the first postulant, a girl from the Philadelphia Main Line. He was accompanied by another member, Fielding Wallace, who wielded a large silver loving cup. "Postulant, state your name!"

"India Knox."

*"Postulant, state your name!"*

"India Knox . . . O High Scepter."

Win held out the scepter and placed it on India's shoulder, as if she were being knighted. "India Knox, do you pledge to hold the values of the Society of Fellingham above all others, and do you further pledge to exercise everything in your power to restore the primacy of the queen's monarchy to all her former subjects?"

"Uh, sure."

"As a sign of your troth, you will now drink elixir from the Cup of the Marquess." Fielding leaned down and handed the loving cup to India, who grasped both handles and drank. Lulu looked over and noticed the cup said, *William O'Leary—for 40 Years of Dedicated Service—Appetuck Valley Volunteer Fire Department—1984.*

"Now, rise." India stood, and Win placed his right hand on her shoulder, holding the scepter with his left. "You are now a full member in good standing of the Society of Fellingham. Long may you live for its glory!"

*"Huzzah! Huzzah!"* cried the members.

Win then made his way down the line, repeating the ritual with each postulant. When he got to Lulu, she suppressed the urge to giggle, not to mention ask for the precise definition of *troth.*

"Absolutely!" she said responsively. She drank from the cup, noting that the elixir of the marquess tasted precisely like Pimm's No. 1.

When Win finished with the last postulant, he said, "One more order of business. Brother, if you would."

Frazier handed each postulant a small gold plaque printed with their name and graduation year.

"We will now proceed to the chapter room, our sanctum sanctorum," said Win.

They climbed the stairs to the second floor, where Frazier unlocked a door. "Enter," he commanded. The smallish room must once have been someone's bedroom, Lulu thought, although now it just had some old furniture. A picture of Queen Elizabeth was on one wall, along with a small painting of what could only have been Lord Fellingham himself. Numerous gold plaques, similar to the ones they'd been given, adorned the opposite wall.

"You will now affix your plaques to the Wall of Belonging," said Win.

Lulu noticed some double-sided tape was on the back of her plaque, so she pressed it on the next available slot. Alexander Hargrove's plaque was the first, so they appeared to be in chronological order. She supposed the new plaques would be screwed in later, like the rest.

When all the plaques were in place, Win held the Cup of the Marquess aloft and cried, "Brothers and sisters, your names will be upon this wall forever. To Lord Fellingham!"

"*To Lord Fellingham!*" came the response.

"*Long live the queen!*"

"*Long live the queen!*"

Win removed his hood, which signaled to the others to do the same, and declared, "We shall now all drink to excess."

A cheer went up as Tripp Maynard killed the Gregorian chants and flipped on his party mix. Someone produced a bottle of Veuve Clicquot, spraying it everywhere, and the evening was on in earnest.

For a few hours Lulu managed not to obsess about her upcoming appearance in *On the Avenue*. At last, she'd met some people she could tolerate, perhaps even like. Shelley, with whom she was growing close, even held Lulu's hair as she vomited into a second-floor toilet later that night.

But by then, her only thoughts were how cool the porcelain felt against her cheek.

# Trip Wires

**LULU SAT IN** her usual spot, waiting for Professor Russell to arrive. She had been watching the professor with greater interest of late. Something about him drew her in more each week. She loved the way his hair fell over his dark-framed glasses, and the way he unconsciously flipped it out of the way. His cheeks were slashes of pink as if painted with a wide brush. The overall effect was one of youthful innocence that belied his age.

The class was two-thirds female, which didn't surprise her at all. She doubted very much the professor knew his effect on women. He struck her as perfectly naïve, which somehow made him even more alluring.

There was nothing naïve about her usual crowd, those boys and girls in New York. Most had been drinking and using recreational drugs since their early teens. A jaded ennui was the standard calling card.

And the Devon boys? Most were silly little things who'd spent their high school years studying for AP exams and practicing violin. They wouldn't know what to do with her if they had the chance. The jocks were a bit better. They were beautiful, particularly the rowers and lacrosse players, and she'd been with a few, but they were ultimately boring, disposable. Sitting in the stands cheering on the Devon Devils was not on her college to-do list.

Older men were not a strange country for Lulu. There had been that brief affair with a friend of Sheldon's last summer. He was a mature, patient lover, not like all these sweaty and eager boys. No one ever found out about their dalliance, but the danger of it had been like a drug.

———

Eph strode into the classroom. He loved this moment. Teaching wasn't quite like being a rock star, but maybe it was, just a little. You were onstage, with a crowd, putting on a performance of something you loved. There was no better job in the world.

He looked around, taking in the silent attention for a moment. The classroom looked more crowded than usual, which meant he must be getting through to them. That was good. Positive student feedback helped when tenure loomed.

"Okay, today we're going to dive further into Twain and the Realists, who came into prominence after the Civil War. Did anyone know Twain was something of a technologist? You might be interested to know he spent many days in the laboratory of his friend Nikola Tesla and had a relationship with Edison as well. He also managed to lose nearly his entire fortune on a bad tech investment, a typesetting machine that didn't pan out. It all sounds very modern, doesn't it?"

A hand went up, a boy in the front row. "It's interesting how that contrasts with Thoreau, sitting by his pond, or Hawthorne, pondering the human condition."

"Excellent observation. I love it. Can we imagine any of these characters in today's world? I think Twain would be fascinated with the iPhone, while the Romanticists might recoil in horror at the idea of Twitter. You could have a paper there, by the way."

Another hand shot up. It was Ifeellike.

*Sigh.* "Yes?"

"I feel like I was disrespected last class."

Eph was taken aback by the confrontational tone, but decided to give her some latitude. "I'm very sorry to hear that. How so?"

"I told you how the lack of minority representation in this course's syllabus really upset me, and I don't feel like you acknowledged my feelings."

"Right, then. Consider your feelings acknowledged." Eph immediately regretted his flippancy.

"Okay, now I feel like you're just *mocking* me." Several others in the class appeared to grow more interested in the exchange. "You know, Professor

Smallwood says you can't prove there's an objective reality, so the only thing you can know is real is how you feel about something. Well, *I* feel disrespected."

*Goddamn Toes.* "Well, I'm sincerely sorry about that, and no disrespect was meant, but it's hard to get around the fact that most of the great writing in our period of study was by white authors."

"And who's deciding what's great? *You?*" Ifeellike was now in high dudgeon.

"I have my own views, naturally, but I'd say it's more of a general consensus that forms over time."

"Whose consensus? Other people of privilege? I think we all know the answer to that, *don't we?*"

"Yeah!" chimed in a few others.

"As I said last week, Miss . . ."

"Gaia."

"Miss Gaia."

"Just *Gaia.*"

"Gaia. Well, as I suggested last week, there weren't actually many African-Americans or any other people of color who had had much schooling at this point in American history, and I think the body of literature simply reflects——"

Another hand shot up; a male student. *Thank God.* Anyone but Ifeellike.

"I would like to read a short passage from *The Adventures of Huckleberry Finn.*" The student, a pallid boy with vibrant red hair in dreadlocks, stood and opened his book. Eph didn't recognize him. "'Jim was monstrous proud——'"

"Excuse me, but are you in this class?"

The student ignored Eph and started over, now affecting an exaggerated Old South accent. "'Jim was monstrous proud about it, and he got so he couldn't hardly notice the other niggers.'"

Several students audibly gasped. Eph suddenly realized where this was heading. Another student had his cell phone out and looked to be filming. How long had he been doing that? *Crap.*

"Now, let's hold on a second and discuss this——"

The student cut Eph off and raised his voice. "Chapter Two. '*Niggers* come miles to hear Jim tell about it and he was more looked up to than any *nigger.*'"

The class grew uneasy, some leaning and murmuring to one another. Eph didn't like the feel of it. "Okay, so let's take a mo——'"

The red-haired student, flipping to another page, cut him off again. "'Strange niggers would stand with their mouths open—'"

This proved too much for Ifeellike. "Professor, how can you allow this to happen?" she shouted. "There are people of *color* in this class!"

Another student, an African-American, stood up. He was seated on the other side of the room. Eph didn't recognize him, either. *What the hell is going on?*

"This is a racist class!" the boy shouted, to the class as much as to Eph. "Shame on Professor Russell!"

Looking over at the boy with his cell phone out, whom Eph noted was also African-American, Eph said, "Excuse me, it's against school policy to film in class."

"I'm not filming, I'm *documenting*."

"*Shame! Shame!*" shouted several others. A few stood up.

"Please!" Eph was almost shouting now himself. "Let's calm down and discuss this. We're all on the same side here, but sometimes great literature needs to be understood in the context of its time."

"*Down with racism! Down with white privilege!*" shouted the first African-American student. "C'mon, people, how can we accept this? Don't sit like sheep in the face of oppression!" He stood and began to walk out. At least six others immediately got up to join him, including the documentarian and the red-haired boy. At the exit, the first student turned, along with the others. "Will you sit silent for injustice?" The other boy panned his cell phone around the room. "We know who you are, *sheep*." At that, many of those remaining got up to leave, filing slowly out. Shouts of "*Racism!*" echoed outside in the hall.

Eph looked around. Mostly Asian kids were left, looking confused and a bit terrified. Cultural respect for authority and the desire for good grades kept them in their seats. Also, there was the Harris girl. She looked slightly amused more than anything else.

"All right," Eph said, trying to regain his composure. "Where were we?"

Outside, Red Wheeler gave Jaylen Biggs, president of the Afro-American Cultural Center, a high five. Ritchie Taylor, the documentarian, also high-fived both. Gaia was there, as were a handful of other PSA and Cultural Center members.

"Did you see that, man?" Red said. "Justice was on the menu today, my friends. Serving size, large!"

They all laughed hysterically.

"Fucker didn't know what hit him," Charlie Hamer said.

"Yeah, not bad. Not bad at all," Jaylen said, not appearing as buoyant as the others for some reason.

"What do we know about this guy, anyway?" Charlie asked.

"The fuck cares what we know," Red said.

"I know someone who took his class last spring," said Gabe. "They liked the dude."

"So what? I don't care if he's Santa Claus. In any war, there are victims."

That satisfied Charlie. "Then mission fucking accomplished," he crowed.

"Excuse me?" said Red.

"Just sayin'."

"The mission is *never* accomplished. The Struggle is a permanent state. How many times do I need to say that? Read your Trotsky, man. Today was just a taste. Ritchie, you come with me."

"Where?"

"To see a friend over at the *Daily.* Someone I trust. Bring that phone with you. But first, let's go somewhere private and have a good look at that video."

They walked on, a spring in their steps.

# Everybody Go Deep

**EPH AND D'ARCY** decided to take in a Devon Devils football game against a visiting team from the Ivies. Maybe eight thousand spectators were in a stadium that held sixty. The crowd looked mostly like some local Havenport kids and some die-hard alumni.

Once, Devon had been a national power, but that time had long passed. Now the school struggled for attendance, especially since the students were largely indifferent. Sometimes they came to tailgate, but would get drunk and never make it out of the parking lot. It was debatable whether many even knew the rules. Eph overheard someone nearby say that someone had committed a "foul."

What no one, Eph knew, living anywhere near the Acela line could ever understand was the role football played in places like Alabama. They might nod their heads like they understood, like it wasn't news to them: they like football down there. But they don't get it.

They don't get it at all.

The thing is, there isn't much to do in small-town Alabama. There are no art exhibits, no visiting lecturers. There's no High Line and the Dave Matthews Band is definitely not playing at the American Legion Hall on Saturday night. There are no women's marches, peace marches, antiglobalization marches, or any other marches (unless you count that time parents had a demonstration about that sex ed class, but that was a while ago). *The New York Times* is not available for delivery, and no one would do the crossword or read the Sunday Review even if it were.

But there's football, and in Alabama that means two things: Auburn and Bama, otherwise known as the Crimson Tide. As a good citizen of the Yellowhammer State, one is obliged to pick one of these teams as one's own.

Pick? No, that's not right. You inherit them, depending on family ties and geography. Then you bleed for them, the way you'd bleed for God or country. Ashley was Auburn country as the university lay just a piece up Route 29. The easiest way to start a fight in Ashley was to walk into a bar with a ROLL TIDE shirt.

One of Devon's linebackers laid on a tremendous hit, prompting the crowd to cheer (and D'Arcy to wince). Despite Devon's retreat from football excellence, the players were bigger than ever. Eph wondered why that was.

As an adult, Eph stayed in decent shape. He could run a mile in maybe seven minutes and put forty miles on his bike some Sundays. But as a kid, football was one on a long list of sports in which he'd been found wanting, although to be fair, his last data point was at the age of ten.

He developed late. A shade over six feet as an adult, he wouldn't reach that height until almost twenty. As a kid, he was scrawny and short. There are many reasons a boy doesn't want to be scrawny and short, but in Alabama, athletics would top the list. Not that Eph had anything against sports, even then. Many a night he'd lain in his bed longing for the golden arm of a quarterback or the graceful power of a wrestler. God, or random fate, wasn't on the same page.

Pop Warner was the only year of football he ever played. He shuddered at the memory.

Ashley's youth were automatically sized up for a position. Big and fat? Offensive line. A little less big? Defensive line. Really fast with a low center of gravity? Running back. Really fast with large hands? Wide receiver. Tall with a good arm? Quarterback. And so on until you got to kids like Eph: undersize, slow, and scared. They tended to get splinters in their asses, as the saying went, from riding the bench. At the Pop Warner level, though, the coaches were obliged to play everyone. This always enraged the dads of the better players, who thought that any second their boys weren't on the field undercut their chances at a Division I scholarship. That anger radiated off the sidelines like heat from a furnace. Eph, a sensitive kid, picked up on these things, and it only added to his sense of dread at being called into a game.

Usually, they stuck him in the defensive backfield and hoped to avoid disaster. A defensive back didn't get hit much, but Eph found every moment on the field terrifying regardless. He still remembered this one black kid named Jesse Greer. Jesse played running back for a rival team and must have outweighed Eph by forty pounds. To Eph, André the Giant had nothing on Jesse Greer, and the last place you wanted to be was standing between a guy like Jesse and the end zone. Not just because he was huge, either, but because he played with a sense of urgency, like he knew football was his only ticket out.

Even at age ten, on some inchoate level Eph could relate to Jesse that way, although football was never going to be Eph's particular ticket. One time he got hit so hard the rim of the helmet cut into the edge of his forehead and he needed stitches. It left a small scar.

Eph's mom, Millie, was always supportive and said the right things after games. But Big Mike, he never said much at all, except after Eph got the scar. He said it was something to wear with pride. Red Badge of Courage, or something like that. Generally, though, Big Mike's strategy for dealing with a wimpy, book-loving son was not to say anything at all, as if Eph could interpret silence in any way other than a crushing blow.

Whatever Eph was, he wasn't Jack. That much was clear. Jack was his older brother. He was good at football. He was good at a lot of things.

Sometimes, the rare times Eph dwelled on it, he thought that one interception—just one—might have changed the entire trajectory of his life.

He was eternally thankful it never happened.

# Lulu Ubers to Manhattan

**LULU WAS BACK** among her people, here for the big *On the Avenue* shoot. Because she had no Tuesday classes, she'd taken an Uber (Sheldon's account) the day before for the two-hour drive to Manhattan and spent the night at home. She hadn't bothered to call and wasn't surprised to find Sheldon away. Charlie, the doorman at her building since she was a child, greeted her warmly. "Hello, Miss Lulu. So good to have you home." She liked to think she had a great relationship with all the doormen.

She arrived in time to meet up with some city friends at Debajo, the club of the moment. They all had fake IDs, even if for a certain crowd, at certain places, it really didn't matter. Bottle service (Grey Goose) had been five hundred dollars a bottle, and at the moment she couldn't recall if she'd paid or someone else had paid. Or perhaps she'd just left. Details were a bit hazy, but no matter. Someone paid, she was sure. Pretty sure.

She and her group called themselves the Snap Pack, owing to their habit of documenting their fabulousness on social media. They'd been featured last summer on a blog called the *Rich Kids of Instagram*. While she knew the site was meant to be mocking, she also knew that people were secretly jealous. One of her friends, Thea von Klaussen, had already launched a clothing line. Being back in the city reminded her that people were moving on while she sat in classes. She was here to play a little catch-up.

It was understood that the *Avenue* in *On the Avenue* magazine referred to Park Avenue, specifically between Fifty-ninth and Eighty-sixth Streets, an area that remained a canyon of wealth and privilege where society dames practiced the hostess arts. The magazine's offices weren't actually on Park, though. Commercial space on Park was far too banal and corporate, and *On the Avenue*, while still the gazette of record for the Upper East Side set, was getting edgier in recent years in an effort to expand its demographics. That meant extending their cultural and physical reach beyond the confines of the Upper East Side.

In fact, millennials, even the right sort, didn't want to live there anymore, despite that (far) East Side real estate prices were now among the cheapest in Manhattan. For a typical twenty-something, living in, say, Yorkville was a social death sentence. The neighborhood had the faint odor of junior investment bankers, wielding their pickup routines in Second Avenue bars. It had reached the point where not even junior investment bankers themselves wanted to live there. The financial crisis of 2008 put a stake in whatever cachet that sort had left, so they sought credibility by flocking to previously unthinkable neighborhoods like the East Village and even Brooklyn.

Lulu lived on Fifth, though, which was a different animal. By virtue of its world-class views of Central Park, Fifth Avenue was forever protected from the vicissitudes of real estate trends.

Sheldon often talked about how much Manhattan had changed since his own youth. The map of acceptable places to live had expanded remarkably. Prior to the Ed Koch era, no self-respecting socialite or preppie would have been caught dead living outside a narrow Upper East Side rectangle bordered by Fifth Avenue on the west and Lexington on the east.

The irrepressible Koch willed the city out of the fetid, garbage-strewn days of the seventies (which Lulu knew mostly from movies like *The French Connection*—Sheldon loved film of the era). The term *yuppies* was coined to describe all the new twenty-somethings, with their yellow power ties and ready cash. This new breed branched out, first setting their sights on the West Side. The bodegas of Columbus Avenue yielded to trendy restaurants, designer-clothing stores, and specialty-food shops like Zabar's. Next, cultural control of the West Village was wrested from any lingering bohemians. The trend continued through the nineties as one neighborhood after another fell to gentrification. By the aughts, the map had been expanded to most of Manhattan, and even to the so-called outer boroughs (except Staten Island, of course). Some moneyed white people, those who fancied themselves progressive champions or urban pioneers, even colonized Harlem, driving up rents and infuriating local activists.

*OTA*, as everyone called *On the Avenue*, made its home in the Meatpacking District, which had long transitioned from its past of warehouses and abattoirs. Occupying land on the distant West Side, not far from Greenwich Village, it laid claim to a patina of carefully maintained grittiness, something cherished by its residents. They loved saying they lived in the "Meatpacking District," as if they were being self-deprecating. Never mind that there remained but a single abattoir, one situated right next to the new branch of the Whitney. Young neighborhood newcomers loved the ironic contrast.

Lulu arrived at *OTA* to find the freight elevator broken, so she had to walk the two flights up. (A broken elevator only burnished *OTA*'s edgier bona fides.) She felt confident in her Prada camel off-the-shoulder cashmere sweater and skinny-fit, carefully destroyed jeans. The office was in a large loft with the requisite high interior ceilings and brick walls, adorned with framed oversize *OTA* covers. The open layout had rows of long tables each lined with fashionable-looking young women and large-screen, razor-thin iMacs. Cricket Hayes stared imperiously down from one of the framed covers.

There didn't appear to be a receptionist, so Lulu walked up to the nearest person. "Excuse me, I'm looking for Wendy Faircloth?"

The woman looked up. "Oh, you must be Lulu. Let me get Wendy for you. My name is Judy, by the way."

Lulu was pleased to be expected, which of course she had to be, but it pleased her nonetheless.

The imprimatur of *OTA* could set a girl up for life, transforming another random party girl on the prowl into a branded socialite. That status was conferred with exposure, and that exposure was determined inside these exposed-brick walls. Perhaps her photo might hang here someday next to Cricket's.

*OTA* had articles, but they tended to be fluff about society decorators or the histories of older New York families. Mostly, people opened *OTA* for the party pictures, which some snarkily referred to as the society sports pages. Photographers like Patrick McMullan were dispatched nightly to the "right" events to snap pictures of city swells coming and going. *That* was the goal, to get in those pictures, with the largest footprint and the best page position possible. Pictures were forever, after all. They were the ultimate social currency.

"Hello, Lulu," said the elegant woman breezing into the room. "I'm Wendy Faircloth. Welcome to *OTA*."

Lulu recognized her right away from the masthead page of the magazine, something Lulu had carefully studied. Wendy wore a black leather pencil skirt with a white Anne Fontaine shirt. Her perfectly highlighted hair was swept up in a messy bun, intentionally arranged to appear random, as though no effort were made at all. Lulu knew just how expensive such noneffort efforts were.

"Yes, hi! I'm delighted to be here." They shook hands. Gold bangles rattled on Wendy's wrist.

"Can I have Judy get you some coffee? We just got a new Jura, and I don't want to tell you what it cost! We also have Bai tea if you're not a coffee drinker."

"Espresso would be perfect." Lulu thought that sounded more sophisticated than just *coffee*, and the caffeine hit would be welcome after last night.

"Of course," Judy said, scurrying off.

"So, you're our Devon girl. Very impressive. My son applied, but they just don't want many kids from our crowd anymore." Wendy didn't need to add she meant white private-school kids from Manhattan. "You must be a smart one."

"I got lucky, but thank you." *Maybe this whole Devon thing will be useful after all.*

"You look smashing, by the way. Is that Hermès?"

"Prada, actually."

"Ah, yes. I should have known. You wear it so well!"

"Thank you." Beaming on the inside, Lulu realized she had broken out in a large smile, which she immediately dialed back. *Mustn't be eager.* Judy arrived with the espresso, which Lulu gratefully accepted. She took a sip and mentally thanked the caffeine gods.

"We'll have a number of designers for the shoot—I have some ideas I can't wait to try on you! Come with me, if you would. The others are already here." Wendy led Lulu through the aisles of luminous iMacs, then through glass doors into a studio area where a number of people were milling about. "Come meet your fellow cover girls."

*Did she say cover?* Lulu tried once again to keep a lid on her excitement. A cover would *totally* put her on the map. They walked over to where the other girls were sampling clothes from various racks.

The competition.

"Lulu, this is Cassie Little and Christina Fellows," Wendy said. They exchanged hellos, in full *I don't give a shit* mode. Cassie, in particular, barely looked up from her phone. Lulu had met them both before, and more than once, but if Cassie and Christina remembered, they weren't letting on, and Lulu was not going to give them the upper hand by letting on herself. "And where's Aubrey disappeared to?" Wendy asked.

"Here!" came a voice from behind one of the racks.

Aubrey St. John. Spence, Columbia, St. Anthony Hall. Third-generation Wall Street money. Grandfather was chairman of Morgan Stanley and board chair at Sloan Kettering. Aubrey was the leading contender to be seated at the socialite throne after Cricket Hayes abdicated by moving to Palm Beach. *Seriously,* thought Lulu. *Who moves to Palm Beach at twenty-nine? It's* Night of the Living Dead *down there. The brand she built, just to blow it off like that . . .*

"We've met before, haven't we?" Aubrey asked.

"Maybe in East Hampton?" Lulu ventured.

"Of course." Aubrey was older than Lulu, so it was entirely possible Aubrey didn't remember, but Lulu remembered precisely. It was two summers ago, at the Katzes' clambake on Main Beach. Marvin Katz was a producer friend of Sheldon's who'd won several Emmys.

"All right, ladies, come come!" Wendy clapped her hands. "Let's get you to makeup and styling and then we'll go to wardrobe."

This process took well over two hours, although Lulu was perfectly content to be fussed over. They emerged as glamorous 1940s movie starlets with formal gowns and elegant waves in their hair, as if on their way to a ball. The set was throwback Victorian, done in olive greens and browns, with a couch, heavy drapes, and numerous large pillows. Wendy arranged the girls, putting Aubrey in the center of the couch with Lulu standing slightly to the side. This annoyed Lulu, but she knew that saying anything would be a misstep. They would probably rearrange the seating multiple times anyway.

A photographer, bald with a long ponytail, started shooting. Wendy surveyed the scene she had created. "There they are, the New Philanthropists!" she declared as the camera clicked away.

Lulu had never really done any philanthropy, if by *philanthropy* one meant actually giving money to something. But she *did* go to lots of expensive bene-fits (the tickets for which were always paid for by Sheldon), and she also lent her name to the various junior committees. Last year she'd cochaired a ju-nior fund-raiser for the Southampton Hospital. The invitation, with her name printed prominently at the top, had gone out to thousands of people, and she had even said a few words up on the stage about the importance of good health care. Lulu quietly hoped it would be a stepping-stone to the Me-morial Sloan Kettering Associates Committee, the ne plus ultra of New York junior committees.

"Come on, girls, look like you own this town!" implored the photogra-pher. "No, no, that's not it," he said, evidently not happy with what he saw. "I want serene confidence, with maybe just a *soupçon* of *fuck you*. Can you give me that?" Lulu, sneering ever so slightly, wondered if the other girls knew what *soupçon* meant. Despite her ambivalence about Devon, she found it convenient to throw her credentials in people's faces now and then, even if this time it was only mentally. It was always done subtly, of course. *You go to Wake? I hear that's so much fun. . . . Where do I go? Oh, I'm up in Havenport.*

That line of thought got her where she needed to be, the *soupçon*. She tilted her head, striking her much-practiced signature-pose-to-be.

"Excellent, girls! You are stars!"

Lulu allowed herself to think about all the wonderful things that accrued to a top socialite. Designers longed to dress you, and you got to keep the clothes afterward. You never paid to go anywhere, with event organizers thrilled just to have your name attached. There were promotional deals with perfumes and clothing lines; it was all about building your own personal brand. Some, like Cricket Hayes, had parlayed that brand into reality TV shows. Cricket even had a considerable following in Japan. Or *used* to have.

And then there was social media. A million followers translated into $10,000 for a single tweet or Instagram post. "Want to know how Old Navy makes your butt look scary good?" Khloé Kardashian got paid $13,000 for sending that one tweet. One tweet. Not that Lulu found anything tasteful about the Kardashians—they officially horrified her—or Old Navy, which horrified her even more, but the family's business model appealed to her im-mensely.

Finally, they called it a wrap. Wendy Faircloth swept back into the room, trailed by Judy, who held several bags. "Excellent job, girls. You shoot like pros. Judy has some small gifts for you." Lulu accepted her bag and took a quick peek inside. Chloé perfume, a Burberry scarf, some other things she didn't want to be caught ogling.

Before leaving, she took a detour through the clothing racks and stuffed a Dolce & Gabbana jacket into her bag. She'd had her eye on it earlier, and the magazine didn't have to pay for any of this stuff anyway, she reasoned. Then she snapped a discreet selfie, making sure the *OTA* logo on the wall was clearly visible over her shoulder. She posted it to Instagram with the caption "Can you say glam?" Seconds later, the responses started.

"♥♥♥SO GORGEOUS!!!!!!!"

She hit refresh. "★BEAUTIFUL!!!!!!★"

Refresh. "STUNNING!! LOVE U!!!!!"

With a sense of well-being she hadn't felt in months, Lulu summoned an Uber for the trip back up to Devon. On the road, the adrenaline of the day's activities wore off and the previous night caught up with her.

She fell into a contented sleep.

# Devon Daily

## Accusations of Racism Against Professor

Several students are leveling accusations of racism against Devon faculty member Ephraim Russell. Russell, an assistant professor in the English Department, specializes in nineteenth-century American literature. Accusations center on the lack of minority representation in the course's syllabus, as well as the allegedly profligate use of language many in the class find offensive and exclusionary.

"An entire century, and Ephraim Russell can't find even one writer of color to choose from?" remarked Jaylen Biggs, president of the Afro-American Cultural Center. A review of Professor Russell's syllabus by this paper confirms that all required reading is the work of white authors of European descent.

More troubling, according to some who were there, is the use of language that many feel creates an unsafe environment, particularly for students from marginalized groups. The *Devon Daily* was able to obtain exclusive video shot during Professor Russell's class, and it confirms the use of certain racially charged words. Following one student's reading of a passage containing multiple uses of the word "n****r," the Professor responds, "Excellent. I love it." Students can be heard gasping in response.

"I'm upset, I can't even tell you," said one African-American student, who declined to be identified. "I left class in tears yesterday. Professor Russell should be ashamed to let this sort of thing happen in a Devon classroom. I don't feel safe at all." When asked if Russell had provided content warnings to class members, she said no.

Martika Malik-Adams, Dean of the Devon Office of Diversity and Inclusion, said that the Bias Response Team is looking into the allegations. She added that new guidelines on content warnings are expected to be released sometime later this academic year. Each department has appointed a single representative to serve on the newly formed Committee on Safe and Open Classrooms, which will determine appropriate measures regarding content warnings. Dean Malik-Adams noted that Professor Barrett Smallwood will represent the English Department.

Professor Smallwood could not be reached for comment at press time, nor could Titus Cooley, English Department Chairperson.

# Titus Cooley's Office

**EPH SAT GLUMLY** outside Titus Cooley's office. Until seeing the piece in the *Daily*, he hadn't been overly concerned about the incident in his class. College kids did all sorts of strange things these days, and besides, why would he be a target? Mostly, that day in class struck him as odd, almost like a piece of performance art or agitprop.

He probably didn't disagree with the students' basic views, even if he thought the whole trigger-warning thing was silly. Most other professors felt the same about trigger warnings, he was sure, but were reluctant to say anything, as the concept was gaining traction. How or why this was the case was a mystery to Eph. Who drove these things, anyway? It couldn't be the ragtag bunch who'd sandbagged his class. . . .

He could hear Titus talking on the phone. The words were unintelligible behind the formidable oak door, but Eph was pretty sure the conversation was about him. He'd meant to go to Titus earlier, just in case the incident became a "thing," but he'd gotten sidetracked, and then a few more days went by and he figured it had blown over.

Then the article appeared in the *Daily*.

In the online version, there were 247 comments and counting. He'd read a few but quickly stopped. He was called a lot of unpleasant things. The word *fascist* came up a lot. Arjun Choudhary, the dean of students, canceled Eph's class today as a "safety precaution."

Titus's door swung open. "Ephraim. Come in, come in."

Eph walked into the magnificent office with its view of Bingham Plaza and Titus walked him over to a sitting area. "Let me say right off I know you're not some damned racist or, what was it . . ."

"'Fascist.'"

"No, that wasn't it."

"'White supremacist'?"

"That's the one. You're not one of those. I don't suppose you're a fascist, either."

"Thank you, sir. That's quite a low bar we're setting."

"Well, these are strange days, Ephraim, strange days."

Titus had a habit of repeating words and phrases. He pulled a pipe from a rack and carefully stuffed it with tobacco. Striking a wooden match, he held the flame steadily over the bowl, drawing it in with a series of puffs. "I know, I know, it's against the rules, but I contain the practice to this office, and no one seems to complain."

Being the éminence grise of the English Department clearly had its benefits. Eph couldn't recall the last time he'd seen someone smoke a pipe, and the smell was oaky and sweet. He found it calming.

"You could say the inmates are running things around here, you know," continued Titus. "Between you and me, Strauss is terrified of them. The students, I mean. Well, *everyone*, really, but you didn't hear me say that. But they're an angry lot, and they use social media to hype everything up. Not that I really understand any of it, all this Twitter nonsense. They even have some sort of online petition about you."

"Professor, if I may, what happened was clearly staged. Some of those students weren't even in my class, and that video had to be doctored. I never said 'I love it' or 'excellent' after the kid read that passage. I know I must have said those words at some point, but it must have been in another part of the class."

"I'm sure, I'm sure." Titus puffed again. His eyes, framed by those impossibly bushy white eyebrows, stared at nothing in particular. "It's just that this comes at a sensitive time, what with this 'content' committee being formed. Plus there's talk of a down year for the endowment, and the Board of Governors is watching matters closely."

"Respectfully, Professor, I've done nothing wrong. And how can I teach when my class is canceled?"

"I know, I know. But here's the rub of it. President Strauss is concerned about how this looks, particularly at a time when we're competing with Yale and Harvard for the best minority high school students. You didn't hear it from me, but really we're fighting every year over the same few hundred candidates."

Titus paused to puff some more, creating a small cloud over the couch. "Here's what's going to happen. There's going to be a hearing conducted by this 'Bias Response Team,' which I've never heard of, if you want to know the truth. Ten years ago—hell's bells, *five* years ago—this would have been a non-event. But it's out there, you understand? The university can't be seen as doing nothing. In the meantime, you can still teach. The university will be posting a security guard, just in case."

"A security guard, in a classroom?"

"It will be discreet. You should know Strauss wanted to shut the class down. I argued it's too far into the semester and it wouldn't be fair to the students."

"What about fair to me?"

"You don't have to convince me, but I'm afraid the matter is out of my hands."

*That doesn't sound good.* "Who will conduct this hearing?"

"Martika Malik-Adams, dean of diversity and inclusion. The Bias Response Team is part of her department. You'll want to step carefully around her."

"Thank you for the advice, Titus." Eph had heard of Malik-Adams but had never met her.

"Bit of an agenda, that one, I fear. She's also fond of wearing these pants—spandex, I think they are—which are a clear violation of the university's dress code for employees, but she's been heard to say it's a cultural choice. Naturally, no one will say anything."

Eph flashed back to the woman at Blue Nation Coffee earlier in the year. *Could that . . . ?*

"Don't worry too much, my lad. I'm sure this will work out," Titus said, not sounding convinced at all.

Riding his bike back to his apartment, Eph thought, *No wink today.*

# (Don't) Speak Your Truth

**IT WAS PEAK** leaf season in southern New England, the time of year many campuses looked like calendar photos. Devon's tree-lined walkways glowed with reds and yellows. It was a Saturday, and late enough in the morning so that much of the campus had risen from the previous night of drinking or late-night video game sessions. A small group played touch football on Goodwin Green.

Eph and D'Arcy made their way across campus toward the farmers' market held every Saturday on Havenport Green. With the hearing coming up in a couple of days, Eph was in an uncharacteristically sour mood and walked quietly at D'Arcy's side. Passing Forbes Hall, he asked D'Arcy to hang on while he ducked into the vestibule. He grabbed a copy of the latest *Devon Daily* from a pile. Back outside, he scanned it quickly, relieved to not see anything about his case. Flipping back to the front page, he examined the lead story.

# Costumes Spark Outrage

Thursday night's Halloween revels were marred by several incidents surrounding the alleged insensitivity of some costumes, with one incident resulting in violence. Accusations ranged from racism and sexism to cultural appropriation.

One student, dressed as prominent transsexual Caitlyn Jenner, attended Wolcott House's annual "Inferno" event and was confronted by a number of other students from the Devon LGBT Coalition who were angry that the student in question was not, himself, LGBT and was possibly making light of Jenner and transsexualism. The confrontation grew heated and drew the attention of some campus Democrats, also in attendance, who were offended over Jenner's coming out as a Republican. This precipitated an angry exchange between the two groups, described by one observer as a "fight over who was more offended." Sometime during the exchange, the student dressed as Jenner left the party without ever being identified. Adding to the disruption, another reveler was bitten by a small terrier, later identified as a "comfort animal." Although pets are not allowed on campus, the university now makes exceptions in cases where students feel undue stress.

Elsewhere, a partygoer at the Beta Psi fraternity, dressed as the Frito Bandito, drew the ire of members of the Latino House. Seeing a post of the offending costume on the fraternity's Instagram page, members of the Latino House demanded entry to the party to confront the student wearing the Mexican-themed ensemble. When told they were not on the party's list, a fight ensued, prompting an appearance by the Havenport police. No arrests were made.

"This is an outrage," said Vincent Lopez, a member of the Latino House. "The Frito Bandito plays into the worst sort of Mexican stereotypes. And even if it didn't, what right does this white person of privilege have to appropriate a Latino character?"

Beta Psi president Tug Fowler stated, "It was a private party, and besides, people should just lighten the f**k up."

Asked to comment, Martika Malik-Adams, Devon's Dean of Diversity and Inclusion, stated she was "troubled," and that her department was forming a committee to set costume guidelines going forward.

"You know, I've always thought myself a progressive, but sometimes I think there's a different definition up here," said Eph, tossing the paper in the garbage as he and D'Arcy walked.

"What do you mean?"

"Where I come from, I've seen racism. Real, make-your-skin-crawl racism. If there's racism at Devon, I sure can't find it. This is a liberal place and I don't think anyone would tolerate it. And seriously, have we really devolved into fighting over Frito Bandito costumes?"

"You're white."

*"What?"* cried Eph. He pulled up his sleeve, examining his arm. "Sonuvabitch, you're right!" He turned and looked at D'Arcy. "Is this going to be a problem for your parents?"

D'Arcy honked, but was still determined to make her point. "No, I mean you can't understand."

"Don't give me any credit, or anything."

"No, I mean you can't understand your own privilege."

"I grew up on a dirt farm in Alabama."

"Still, you get treated differently, more deferentially, because of your skin color. Even here. You just do."

"So you're saying Devon is a racist institution?"

"Not exactly, but this place was built by white people, for white people."

"You mean in 1704?"

"Come on, as recently as the 1950s, Devon was ninety-five percent white."

"That was sixty years ago! Don't you think the place has changed, maybe just a bit? The student body is only half white now, plus poor and lower-middle-class students get a complete free ride."

"Sure it's changed, but the place still *feels* white to some people."

"What does that mean?"

"Well, just look around." D'Arcy made a sweeping gesture at the manicured lawns and stately spires. "This isn't an environment many students are used to."

"Hey, it doesn't look like a peanut farm, either, but that's what I *like* about it. Would you feel more comfortable if they made the place look more ghetto?"

"I'm from Montclair, New Jersey, asshole."

"Okay, a bland suburb?"

"Stop it, you know what I mean," D'Arcy said.

"I do know what you mean, and I'm choosing to make light of it."

"I'm just telling you how people feel."

"And they *feel* that because Devon looks like an Anglican fantasy camp—which it totally does, by the way—that it's also somehow racist?"

"Yes . . . no. *I don't know*, but it's there. Can we please talk about something else?"

"And since when do feelings trump everything else?" Eph continued, ignoring her. "I had a student the other day tell me that something was wrong—something that was a historical fact—simply because he *felt* it was wrong. No supporting evidence. He had on a T-shirt that said ALWAYS SPEAK YOUR TRUTH. Isn't there only one truth? Since when are we entitled to our own? This kid thought it was history's obligation to validate his feelings. He then went on with all this Descartes drivel about how you can only know yourself, and therefore the only objective reality is what you perceive. It wasn't the first time a student has served that up."

"But with something as serious as racism, I don't think you can totally dismiss how the community feels. People come by those feelings honestly."

"Do they? Sometimes I wonder."

"I think so."

"Sweetheart, I love you, but I think the definition of racism is being defined down, and it's going to bite everyone in the ass when the real stuff happens. It will be the boy crying wolf."

They walked on in uncomfortable silence.

# The Farmers' Market

**"EVERYTHING IS LOCAL.** We are part of an urban farming collective," said the man in the small tent. He was shirtless under denim overalls.

Every Saturday, scores of vegans, organic-food buffs, and just plain old hungry people descended onto the Havenport Green to sample the goods at the farmers' market. Rows of tents held a multitude of vibrantly colored produce as well as spices and baked goods.

"Where do you farm in a city?" Eph asked the tent's proprietor.

"Abandoned lots, mostly, increasing the city's green-space footprint. We call ourselves guerrilla farmers."

"Huh." Eph wondered what Big Mike would make of this.

D'Arcy picked out a few tomatoes. "That's amazing. So good for the community." She handed the tomatoes to the man, whose gray ponytail reached the small of his back. "We'll take these."

They wandered the stalls, shimmying through the crowds of people carrying shopping totes made of recycled material. They walked past tall stalks of brussels sprouts, pots of virgin hand-pressed olive oils, and trays of vegan samosas. Eph noticed that just as many people were photographing food as buying it. Everywhere he looked, people were lining up batches of arugula or colorful rows of peppers *just so* and capturing the images on their phones.

"Why are people photographing vegetables?" Eph asked.

D'Arcy had to think about this. "Because they're pretty?"

Eph grunted. Back on the farm, the last thing that might have occurred to him would have been to take pictures of a pile of peanuts. "But when would you look at them? Are you going to be sitting around a year from now and suddenly have the urge to look at some rutabagas you saw twelve months ago?"

"No, I think it's more that people like to post photos of food on Instagram."

"I don't follow. Do *other* people want to look at your food pictures? That seems even less compelling." Eph watched as a nearby woman took out her phone and photographed a stacked pile of organic corn. "Seems vaguely snobby. Food snobbery!"

"Excuse me, but isn't that small-batch Guatemalan coffee you are drinking?"

"I'm drinking it, not digitizing it. Besides, it was all they had."

"I think you are losing your mind."

"You may have a point."

Finding a bench under a large elm tree, they sat down against the trunk and snacked on some scones. "Okay, let me give it another shot," said Eph, nodding at D'Arcy's kombucha. He took a swig and winced. "Yeah, no."

"Your loss. Probiotics are so good for you."

"And what are those again?"

"You know, these things . . . they're in your gut . . . they do healthy things. . . ."

"While I'm at it, these scones are a bit dry, aren't they?"

"That's the way scones are, my dear."

"Then why do people eat them?"

"They just do. Jesus, could you be any more of a dick today?"

"But I'm *your* dick."

"Yes, you are." D'Arcy smiled and leaned into Eph's shoulder.

They sat in silence for a minute, letting the beautiful New England fall day distract them from the events hanging over Eph's head. Eph inhaled deeply, trying his best to relax. The aroma of autumn's sweet decay was in the air.

"The whole thing is so damned silly," D'Arcy said. Eph didn't have to ask what she was talking about. *So much for relaxing.* "Most of those kids weren't even in your class."

"I know, but I'm getting the distinct impression that's beside the point."

In the two weeks since the "incident," Eph had continued to hold class. Attendance was down by a third, with Ifeellike and the other agitants noticeably absent. A small crowd of protesters picketed outside the entrance to Grafton before each class. They chanted and generally harassed those entering the building. The one with the red hair was always there, chanting into a megaphone. The assigned security guard prevented them from entering, but they were quite content outside anyway. Better exposure, Eph assumed. The chanting could be heard inside the building, which not only disrupted his class, but also no doubt annoyed the entire English Department. Except for Toes, Eph thought. He could swear Toes was enjoying the whole thing.

*"Hey, ho, racist profs have got to go!"*

One morning, WELX, the local television station, showed up with a reporter. She logged a short piece, but it thankfully never made the air.

The video from the class, which Eph knew had been carefully edited to put him in the worst possible light, emerged in social media channels. @FakeUncleMiltie even tweeted a link with the comment:

Racism is everywhere, even here at progressive Devon U!
#DevonShame

Eph noticed the #DevonShame hashtag had started trending both locally and statewide. He also noticed he now had forty-two ratings on Rate My Professor, and that his average had dropped to 2.6.

It had not been a good week.

"Listen, you need to be careful with Martika Malik-Adams," D'Arcy said.

"Yes, I've been warned not to look at her pants too closely."

"No, I mean it. You don't want to be in her crosshairs."

"Why, exactly? I'm sure she does valuable work. I know what I said before, but I agree this school needs diversity." Eph firmly believed diversity was a noble pursuit, even if he was concerned it had become a game of "check the box" on skin pigmentation.

D'Arcy smiled. "Eph, I love you, sweetheart, but sometimes you can be so damned naïve. Do you know how much Martika makes? Five hundred and seventy thousand dollars a year. I'll kill you if you share that with anyone, but I see the papers that cross Milton's desk. Martika is the third-highest-paid employee at Devon after Milton and the AD. She has to show something for that. Think of her as a hammer looking for nails, and right now, white boy, you are a nail."

"Yeah, Titus said something along those lines, although without the nail part . . . and without the white part. Say, you're suddenly sounding a different tune."

"I don't take back anything, but I've seen her operate. She spends a lot of time in Strauss's office, and I think even he's afraid of her. I just need you to take this very seriously. I know I don't have to remind you what an important time this is for you."

Eph had been trying not to think about tenure. "Can we go back to organic food and guerrilla farming? This is depressing, while that was merely annoying."

Just then, they spotted Toes emerging from a nearby aisle. Eph groaned quietly and lowered his head, hoping not to be spotted. Too late.

"Now, now, I'm sure he means well," D'Arcy whispered.

"Eph!" Toes cried. "Fancy seeing you here."

They stood. D'Arcy smiled while Eph looked dyspeptic, as if the effort to keep pretending this was just another pleasant day was just too much.

"Hello, Barrett." They shook hands. Toes had these really small hands, smooth and hairless, and his fingers wouldn't wrap all the way around Eph's. It was like shaking hands with a little boy. Eph waited to see if Toes would continue on his way, but he just stood there. Reluctantly: "Barrett, you know D'Arcy, don't you?"

"Sure, I think we've met. You work in Stockbridge, don't you?"

"She's President Strauss's assistant," Eph said.

"I'm impressed. That must keep you busy!"

"It does," D'Arcy replied.

"Hey, have you guys tried these small-batch plum muffins? They're unbelievable."

"No, we missed those somehow," Eph said.

"Well, here, try one!" Toes pulled one out of his bag and offered it to Eph.

"That's very nice of you, but I'm still working on this tasty scone here." Eph gestured to the puffy yellow pastry, which was missing only a single bite.

"How are those? I've been meaning to try them."

"They are excellent, if you also like shredding the Sunday *New York Times* and eating that."

"Oh, ha, funny. Okay, no scones."

They stood there for a few moments in awkward silence. Eph wondered how much work it took to maintain a man bun. *When the hell is Toes going to move along? C'mon, just put one bootee after the other. . . .*

"Ah, Eph, I've been meaning to tell you . . ."

*Here we go.*

"I feel just awful about what happened. . . . I'm sure this will all get sorted out." Toes was practically oozing sincerity. Or not. He was definitely oozing something.

"I'm sure it will. Thank you."

"It's a shame we couldn't have had our committee's guidelines in place sooner . . . it might have helped."

"I think we should establish a committee to study the recommendations from your committee."

"We could certainly entertain . . . oh, that was a joke, wasn't it?"

"Probably depends on whom you ask."

There was another long pause. Eph was committed to not further abetting the conversation, while Toes looked as if he was struggling with what to say next.

"You know, Foucault said that 'justice must always define itself.'"

"Okay, I'll keep that in mind." *Whatever that fucking means.*

"Well, you guys have a great day!"

"Nice to meet you!" said D'Arcy, calling after Toes as he retreated. *Squish squish squish.*

"I don't want the rest of this thing." Eph threw the scone at a nearby trash bin. It bounced off the rim, onto the grass.

"Missed!" said a small boy standing nearby, licking an ice cream cone.

"Toes can take his Pynchon, his Foucault, and his stupid little shoes and shove them all up his bony ass." Eph walked over to pick up the errant scone. This time he tossed it underhand from just a couple of feet. It bounced off the rim again, back onto the grass. "Shit!"

"Honey, let's find you a doughnut. I won't tell anyone."

# Devon Daily

## New Houses Break Ground

Ground was broken on Devon's two new houses yesterday. Principal benefactor Foster Jennison, Class of '62, and a host of other luminaries including Havenport mayor Sal DeSanto and Governor Sullivan Lodge III, Class of '75, joined President Strauss for the ceremony.

The new houses will allow Devon to expand its enrollment by 15 percent and will eventually accommodate just under eight hundred undergraduates. Designed by Soren O. Pedersen Associates, the houses are described as a "contemporary interpretation of the traditional Gothic style." All told, the houses have over half a million square feet of floor space. Unnamed as yet, the project is expected to take two years.

# The Hearing

**EPH, SHOULDERS SLUMPED,** walked with D'Arcy at his side for support. "Stockbridge. Could they have chosen a more intimidating place?" Eph asked. Like most members of the Devon community, Eph had never set foot in Stockbridge.

"That's probably the idea." D'Arcy's voice softened a little. "Hey, you know I have to keep some distance. Officially, I mean."

"I want you to. You don't need this." As Milton Strauss's assistant, she couldn't get involved. "Does he know about you and me?"

"I don't think so. I've never mentioned it and he doesn't really ask about my personal life."

"Probably for the best. I don't want you getting dragged down by this."

"I'm sure it will turn out okay."

"Me, too." Eph sounded less than convinced. The political winds on campus were not at his back. Even he knew that. And just in case he forgot, today's *Daily* was there to remind him.

# Devon Daily

## Russell Hearing Today

A hearing will be conducted today by the University Bias Response Team into the conduct of Assistant Professor Ephraim Russell. Professor Russell has been accused of allowing racist rhetoric into the classroom, as well as ignoring authors from non-empowered communities.

A video, now widely viewed on YouTube and other sites, has sparked considerable outrage on campus. "How, in the twenty-first century, can we allow this sort of thing to happen at a place like Devon? Student safety must come first," said Jaylen Biggs of the Afro-American Cultural Center. Others echoed similar sentiments. One student, however, who claims to be in the same class, remarked that the claims were "simply ridiculous," and that Russell was an "excellent teacher."

A panel led by Martika Malik-Adams, Dean of the Office of Diversity and Inclusion, will conduct the hearing.

D'Arcy and Eph approached the limestone façade of the beaux arts building that housed the Devon administration. It was a work of architectural elegance, adorned with Corinthian pilasters and classical balustrades. The ever-expanding administration had outgrown the twelve-thousand-square-foot confines of Stockbridge decades ago, but many of the top deans maintained offices there, as did President Strauss. Dean Malik-Adams had recently been installed down the hall from Strauss on the second floor. In a large room on the third floor the Devon Board of Governors met four times a year. D'Arcy occupied a desk in the president's antechamber.

They entered through the enormous double doors. "I wonder where I go," Eph said. D'Arcy pointed at a calendar of events on the wall. It had those little white letters someone would have to arrange and stick into the black felt every day.

### Bias Response Team—Third Floor

On the second floor, D'Arcy pulled Eph toward her and gave him a kiss. "This is where I get off. Go get 'em."

"Okay. If you can get away let's meet over at the Dix when it's done. I'll text you."

Eph continued up the marble stairs, steps echoing as he went. *Racist approaching!* His heart was working harder than a short climb would normally require. By the third floor, he had broken out in a mild sweat. Which room was it? He poked his head in the first door he came to and found himself in the antechamber for some administrator's office. It was enormous, bigger than any professor's. A woman behind a desk, perhaps an administrative assistant like D'Arcy, looked up and said, "Oh, you're looking for the Board of Governors Room. It's down at the end of the hall." *She knew him!* Just like that. Somehow he doubted this random administrative assistant could have identified him a couple of weeks ago. Was that a reproachful look? He felt a trickle of sweat find its way down the center of his back. Thank God he'd worn a blazer.

Walking down the hall, he heard voices. That must be it. He walked through the entrance into the biggest conference room he'd ever seen. An immense oval table dominated the space. Its wood was polished so finely it gave the impression of a calm, reflective lake. The ceiling was twenty feet overhead and decorated with elaborate white wood carvings set on a robin's-egg-blue background. It occurred to Eph that in a room like this, no one ever raised a hand and said, *Excuse me, but . . .* That was likely the intended effect.

"Professor Russell, welcome. I'm Dean Malik-Adams."

Eph's suspicion that Dean Malik-Adams had been the disruptive presence at Blue Nation Coffee that day was immediately confirmed. She and two others were already seated on the far side of the table's expanse. They made no move to get up. The fourth person present, to the side, was a stenographer, which made everything seem even more serious.

"Yes, hello. I see I've found the right place."

"Please, sit down."

Eph picked one of the twenty or so empty seats on his side of the table. Before he'd even pulled his seat in, the dean continued. "Seated next to me are the other members of the Bias Response Team. To my left is Professor Marcia Simmons of the African-American Studies Department, and to my right is Professor Jaime de la Cruz of the Sociology Department."

"Hello. I confess I'm confused. I see we have a stenographer?" *I'm* came out as *ahm*. The more nervous Eph got, the more South came from his mouth. "This isn't a court, after all . . ."

"No, Professor, it is not. We use a stenographer so we have an accurate record of the proceedings. This is simply a hearing where we wish to ascertain the facts of the case, both from you and others."

"Others?"

"Yes, Professor. We have already spoken to a number of stakeholders."

"I don't understand. What's a stakeholder?"

Marcia Simmons cut in, a strident tone in her voice. "Professor Russell, there are issues here that are of vital interest to the *community*, and we must take all views into account."

"If I may, have there been specific complaints?"

"Yes," Malik-Adams replied.

"May I know from whom, and how many?"

"That is confidential."

"The number of complaints is confidential?"

"It is. We realize you might find this upsetting, but confidentiality is vital. If we don't protect it, then it's easy to imagine there are those not brave enough to come forward in situations such as these."

"From what I saw in the paper and outside my class the last two weeks, they don't seem too concerned about confidentiality."

"I think we can begin now," said Malik-Adams, ignoring Eph. "That is, if that's all right with you, Professor."

Eph sensed he should demur. "Of course. Just trying to under—"

"Professor Russell, this hearing is to ascertain the facts about occurrences in English 240, Nineteenth-Century American Literature, a class that you currently teach, correct?" The stenographer began clicking away.

"I do, yes."

"On October fifteenth of last month there was something of a disturbance in your classroom, is that also correct?"

"Well, I suppose you could call it that, yes."

"Would you please describe it to us?"

"We were discussing Twain, specifically *Huckleberry Finn*, and one of the students, I actually don't think he's in my class at all, got up and just started reading."

"Reading what, Professor?"

*"Huck Finn."*

"Could you please be more specific?"

"The sections he chose had some language that some apparently found upsetting. But as I said, I don't think any of these kids were actually in my class. I'm not really sure—"

"And what language was that, Professor?"

"He was reading otherwise unremarkable passages, but they had, ah, the N-word, if you will."

"If I will *what*, Professor?" asked Malik-Adams.

"Uh, if you will accept my, uh, euphemism."

Marcia Simmons: "Do you mean the word *nigger*, Professor Russell?"

"Well, yes. That's the one."

"Isn't it true that you yourself also used this word in class, Professor?" continued Simmons.

"No, I did not."

"One of the students says you did," Simmons said.

"I most certainly did not."

"So you say," said Simmons.

"Yes, ma'am, I do."

"You may call me *professor*. I believe I've earned that right," said Simmons.

"Of course, my apologies, Professor."

"You said that some apparently found the passage upsetting. I take it that means *you* did not?"

"Well, I didn't say that exactly. But if I may . . . Professor, the word we're discussing is part of the book, and this is Twain we're talking about."

"The identity of the author is hardly germane to this discussion," Malik-Adams said.

"I believe it is. Twain is one of the giants of American literature."

"Are you aware that *Huckleberry Finn* has been banned from the curricula of a number of schools?"

"It has a long history of being banned, in fact. The library in Concord, Massachusetts, home to Emerson, Hawthorne, and Thoreau, banned it because its characters didn't use the Queen's English. But it was also controversial because *Huckleberry Finn* was the most powerful antislavery message of its day."

He shoots, *he scores!*

"Of its day," said Malik-Adams.

*Wait, what?*

"What concerns those of us on the Bias Response Team is not what effect the book had on the prosperous people who could afford books in the nineteenth century, but what effect it has on our community *today*."

Malik-Adams let the words hang there, and Eph could feel things slipping in the wrong direction. Time to shift gears. "If I may, Dean, Professors, I believe this entire incident was arranged by some students who weren't enrolled in my class. That boy, whom I'd never seen before, just got up and started reading, and others reacted in a very scripted way."

"*Boy?*" said Simmons.

"Student. They all seem so young these days." Eph laughed nervously. Hadn't the student been white, though? Still, that was an unforced error. "Forgive me, Professor."

"There is also a complaint that your course deliberately ignores authors of color. We have examined your syllabus and it would appear this complaint has some merit. Wouldn't you agree, Professor?"

"Well, that's true on the face of it, but as I told my students, African-American literacy rates were very low in that period, and I'd very much like to emphasize how tragic this is, but there just aren't many options from which to choose."

"What about"—Professor Simmons glanced down at the notepad in front of her—"Elizabeth Keckley?"

Eph wracked his brain. Elizabeth Keckley . . . Keckley . . . She wrote a single book, didn't she? . . . What was it again? *Crap, crap, crap.*

"Elizabeth Keckley," Professor Simmons continued, "who wrote a stirring memoir of her ordeals as a slave. Does Elizabeth Keckley not measure up to your course's standards?"

*Damn, now he remembered.* "Of course. Wonderful book. It's only that my class is meant to contrast the Romantics and the Realists, and—"

"Is slavery not real enough for you, Professor Russell?"

"Oh, certainly, very real, and a shameful mark on our nation's history . . . perhaps not including Keckley was an oversight on my part. I will be sure to add her to the syllabus." Eph wiped his sweaty brow with his blazer sleeve, finding no way to do it discreetly. He wondered if Professor Simmons had ever actually read Elizabeth Keckley.

"Professor, if I may . . ." Jaime de la Cruz weighed in for the first time. "Where are you from? I mean, originally. I notice a bit of an accent."

"Florida, mostly."

*Mostly. Sort of. Grad school, anyway.*

"I see," said de la Cruz. "I have family in Miami. Whereabouts is your family from?"

"Uh, we moved around a bit." *Sure, those vacations to the Gulf.* The redneck Riviera, Floribama. Opioid country. *Trump* country. The silence hung there as Eph willed the conversation to take a different direction. The stenographer was somehow still clicking away. He wondered if she was writing something like *awkward pause here.*

"I did my doctoral work at Florida State," Eph said, feeling the need to break the silence. It couldn't hurt to remind the panel they were speaking to someone with a Ph.D., even if it was from a state school.

"Thank you, Professor," said Malik-Adams. "Let's move on. I'd like to ask my fellow panelists if they have any last comments or questions."

"No, but I need to say, Professor Russell, that I'm not entirely satisfied with what I'm hearing here," said Simmons, arms folded.

"Professor de la Cruz?"

"Well, speaking as a *Latino*, I am troubled by all this. Deeply troubled."

*Speaking as.* The ultimate rhetorical battlement. The phrase was popping up with increasing frequency. *My status as a member of an oppressed group trumps anything you might want to say.* Eph had no truck with the plight of oppressed peoples, but shouldn't any argument be open to critical analysis?

"I believe we've heard enough," Malik-Adams said. "Professor Russell, you should be advised that the possible consequences in these situations range from nothing to a reprimand to outright dismissal. This panel will advise your department head of our findings when we arrive at them. The meeting is adjourned."

Eph texted D'Arcy and walked over to the Dix to meet her. She ducked out of Milton's office, saying she was running out for coffee. They met in a quiet pod.

"Well?" She looked anxious.

"Let me ask you something. Have you ever heard of Elizabeth Keckley?"

"Who?"

# DECEMBER

# The Faculty Club

**TITUS COOLEY ASKED** to meet Eph at the Faculty Club. Under normal circumstances, Eph loved spending time there. The conversations were always stimulating, and it was rare not to see at least one or two Nobel winners, hanging out, just like that.

Today, though, he found it difficult to suppress his anxiety, getting there fifteen minutes early. He took a seat near the corner with his back turned to the other professors. The waitstaff offered tea and he happily accepted a cup. He was normally a coffee drinker, but found tea calmed the nerves.

The shortening days reflected his mood. It had been almost a month since the hearing and still he'd heard nothing. *What is taking so long?* D'Arcy had been supportive, as she always was, but everyone else was keeping a polite distance. Sleep came in fits and starts, if at all. Devon, normally a protective cocoon, now felt distant, as if he were on the outside looking in.

Class attendance had never recovered since the "incident." He received official notice that a number of students were electing to drop the course. The protesters still got five or six people out in front of the building most days. Concentrating was a challenge. Way back when—a few weeks ago—his students looked at him with respect, even adoration, and he could feed off it, like tapping into a wondrous energy source. It focused the mind. But when every pair of eyes appeared filled with reproach, it was quite the opposite. The negative energy was like an oppressive weight. Sure, he knew many in the class understood exactly what had happened, and they probably sympathized with him, but he was in the press now. The trolls and digital vigilantes were unrelenting. His Rate My Professor score was now an unheard of 1.7. Even a kind interpretation of his circumstances had him woefully out of step with the campus zeitgeist.

His star had fallen.

Staring at a print of nineteenth-century Devon, he tried to think about anything else. The tweedy chuffing of nearby faculty conversations drifted his way. . . .

"So I had this student who wrote a paper—a paean, really—to Hayek. Can you imagine? Does he think this is Chicago? Who does this kid think he is?"

Eph's eyelids grew heavy. Someone else droned on.

"I understand it's a hunger strike, but the man seems to be enjoying the whole thing. Selflessness can't be an enjoyable act or it ceases to be selfless. From a strictly Kantian perspective it can't be called a moral act at all!"

Gradually, the faculty prattle became white noise, and Eph, stress and sleeplessness catching up with him, dozed off in his forest-green leather club chair . . .

"Well, glad to see you're a man who can still relax!"

Eph bolted upright, discreetly wiping drool from his chin. It was Titus. "Forgive me. I haven't gotten a lot of sleep lately. I must have nodded off."

"Out like a light, I'd say. Well, what of it? Half the fossils around here do the same thing every time they pretend to read *The New Yorker*." Titus laughed heartily at his own joke while Eph was trying his best to process being awake.

Sitting down in the next chair, Titus lowered his voice. "Listen, my boy. It was touch and go there, but you're in the clear."

"What?" That wasn't what Eph expected to hear.

"I've just come from Dean Malik-Adams's office, so I've got it right from the source. I got the distinct impression she wasn't entirely happy about it, though."

"About what?"

"About the lack of consequences."

"But I did nothing wrong, and this trigger policy, or whatever it is, isn't even in place yet."

"I know, I know, and that's fortunate for you, because then they might have had a way to construe this as a violation. You introduced Twain into the class without a content warning."

"Oh, come on!"

"You're preaching to the choir, my boy, preaching to the choir. But as it is, you can't be held responsible for violating a policy that doesn't yet exist, although, that being said, the good dean wasn't entirely deterred. She was still pushing to have you placed in some sort of workshop or other on privilege and racism."

"I'm not a racist, Titus."

"Of course you're not, but what's that got to do with it? Was it Beria who said, 'Show me the man and I'll show you the crime'?"

Eph recalled that Beria was Stalin's secret-police chief.

Titus paused, weighing how much more to say. "There's more you should know . . . *entre nous,* of course."

"Of course."

"Other factors that weighed in your favor." Titus leaned in closer. "President Strauss got involved."

"Jesus!"

The room suddenly quieted, and the Nobels turned and looked their way. The two men stayed silent until the others went on with their conversations. This wasn't how Eph imagined coming to the attention of Milton Strauss.

"Now, now, let me finish. While Milton is certainly sympathetic to issues of race—we all are, naturally—he also thought any further publicity around this would not be in the best interests of the school. It seems he came to this conclusion when an unedited version of the incident came to light, an audio recording. You turned out to be absolutely right—someone doctored the video."

Eph leaned back in his chair. "Thank God. Where did the audio come from?"

"I don't know, exactly. Whoever it was captured the whole thing and came forward. Strauss and Malik-Adams listened to it in its entirety, and it was pretty clear what happened. Not that it deterred the good dean, mind you. She said she didn't like your whole attitude. But Milton realized that making this an issue might not play well with the alumni, at least the ones who write checks. God knows, Breitbart or something would write a piece and it would get emailed around God's green acre and Milton would have had to answer phone calls all day."

"So that's it?"

"Where you are directly concerned, yes."

Eph leaned back, breathing a sigh of relief, but it was half a sigh at best. "I don't understand. Is there something else I should know?"

"Well, yes. You'll find out soon enough. As a result of all this, a group of students, many of them in our department, are making demands about the curriculum. They have circulated a petition over the last few days. The incident in your class was the spark, not that any of this falls on you."

"What sort of demands?"

"They insist that we *decolonize* the English curriculum. Yes, that was the word they used. *Decolonize.*"

"I'm sorry, but what does that mean?"

"It means less Chaucer and less Shakespeare and more, shall we say, exotic authors?"

Fred Hallowell would not be pleased, thought Eph. "Sir, if I may ask, will all this affect my position, I mean, with regards to my . . . prospects?"

Titus reflexively raised his hand toward his mouth, as if to draw on his pipe, before realizing he wasn't holding one. He reached for his teacup instead and took a sip. "I'll be frank, because you deserve it. My own view is that this incident was nothing but abject silliness. You're still my choice, but understand that I'm not the only voice. Our department's tenure committee must vote, and I don't know if you know, but the third spot on the committee, the spot opened by David Atkins's retirement, has been filled by Professor Blue Feather."

"Blue Feather?" That was the second thing Eph wasn't expecting today.

"Yes. With everything going on, there's been pressure on us to present a different face, you see."

Eph knew exactly what this meant: not white, not male, and in this case not exactly female either.

"Professor Blue Feather is an interesting one. She—er, *they*—have been trumpeting the works of Kishwar Naheed, a feminist Urdu poet from Pakistan. Can't say I ever heard of the woman, but they want to bring her in as a poet-in-residence."

"Excuse me . . . *they?*"

"Oh, you didn't know? There was an email from HR the other day—I thought everyone got it? They were very adamant on the point of personal pronouns where Professor Blue Feather is concerned. Hold on, let me read it to you." Titus took out his phone, holding it at arm's length like some foreign object. Eph remembered he might have gotten an email about Blue Feather, but the HR Department had taken to sending out so many emails he tended to ignore them. "Here it is." Titus began reading:

> Professor Sophia Blue Feather, having self-identified as pangender, will correctly be identified by the pronouns "they," "them," or "ze" in all matters. Self-identity is a right universal to all, and as such we will respect Professor Blue Feather's right as well. Furthermore, Professor Blue Feather will be heading up a newly formed committee to be called the Gender Violence Prevention and Support Group, which will focus on matters of gender communication within the Devon community.

"One wonders when this woman has time to teach!" said Titus, slipping his phone back into his pocket. "I'm not sure I totally understand any of this. Why would we use the plural? That's incorrect English!"

"I could hazard a guess." Eph had just done the research, after all. "Pangenderists believe they embody all genders within themselves, so I guess you could say there are a bunch of people in there."

"In where?"

"Inside their heads?"

"Isn't that what they call multiple personality disorder?"

"I'm afraid you're asking the wrong person, but I see Professor Potts over there from the Psychology Department, if we want to ask."

"And give him an opening to talk about Maslow's Hierarchy of Needs? I think not!" Titus sipped his tea. "You didn't hear me say that."

Eph smiled, but Titus suddenly looked tired. "You know, it's getting harder for old farts like me to keep up. I suppose that must be increasingly obvious. Anyway, Ephraim, back to you. We usually look for a unanimous vote from the committee. Right now, you have mine, and I think Hallowell likes you, but I don't know that you fit the, uh, profile that Professor Blue Feather has in mind. Honestly, I don't know that Smallwood does either, although he might be a little closer to the mark."

"Do votes have to be unanimous?"

"Technically, no. But once our committee makes a recommendation, it gets passed to the University Committee on Tenure. Generally, they're a rubber stamp, but they may wonder if our house is in order if we pass along a non-unanimous candidate. I don't think it's ever been done before. If I may, do you have a good relationship with Professor Blue Feather?"

"I can't say we know each other that well, but I think we get along." Eph cringed, thinking about how they first met.

*Yes, I'm pangender.*

"Well, you might try some old-fashioned sucking up, lad. And consider joining some committees. I think they're a pox, but the administration likes them. Gives us all the illusion of action."

Titus paused, as if pondering whether he should say what he was about to say. He leaned ever so slightly toward Eph. "Are you still seeing Milton's secretary?"

Eph knew what Titus meant, and he shifted in his chair uncomfortably. He couldn't claim to be innocent in this regard. One of his keenest fantasies was to take D'Arcy back to Ashley. He imagined parading her around town on his arm. It wasn't the Jim Crow South anymore, but cages would still be rattled.

"I'll keep that in mind, Professor" was all he could manage to say.

# Friday at the PSA

**THE DEVON CAMPUS** had a different hum on Fridays, one with a higher pitch. Students had a gleam in their eyes and greeted one another with gusto as they walked the campus corridors and courtyards. It didn't matter what clique you ran with, what gender or race you identified with, or what team you played on; Friday was about the promise of the next two days and nights . . . the parties, the protests, the games . . . the hookups. The Devon weekend lay before its people like a vast open field of possibilities. Any and all wonderful things could happen.

It was mid-afternoon at the Progressive Student Alliance. Red and the others were already comfortably high on a particularly pleasant strain of cannabis called Trainwreck. Someone said it was Snoop Dogg's favorite. Rufus was playing tunes.

They deserved a little relaxation after a busy few weeks camped out in front of Grafton. Passing students had given them raised fists of solidarity or finger snaps of approval, and the PSA even grew its ranks by four members. Rufus, who handled the PSA's social media accounts, pumped out constant links to the Russell video on Facebook, Twitter, Tumblr, and Snapchat, and the group's social metrics grew considerably. #DevonShame even trended regionally for a while. Red was particularly pleased that they'd managed to trash Russell's rating on Rate My Professor. *That redneck piece of shit totally deserved it*, Red thought.

He smiled as he thought of how they'd deliberately placed themselves in a randomly distributed pattern around Russell's class to make it appear they didn't know one another and that the whole thing had been spontaneous. That move was straight out of Red's dog-eared copy of *Rules for Radicals*.

"Good couple of weeks, man," opined Robbie Ochoa.

"True dat," Red replied.

"The PSA snaps its fingers and shuts that motherfucker down," said Robbie, giggling.

*Snaps its fingers* . . . it had almost been too easy. Not that Russell's class had been canceled entirely, but the dude looked like he was going down. Gaia came up with the idea for the petition to fire Russell, which she circulated using the website change.org. They had already collected 372 signatures. That was gonna get some media play, for sure.

With all the social tools they had at their disposal, it had become a simple thing to tap into a wellspring of progressive anger that extended well beyond the borders of campus. A retweet from the right person or a video that went viral and a whisper became a thunderous roar, truth to power, impossible to ignore. . . . They had the world's biggest megaphone at their disposal. How much more could they accomplish?

"Roof, how many more followers this week?"

Rufus examined his phone. "We are up to twelve hundred, double a week ago." Everyone snapped their fingers. *Amen, brother.* "You know, with a little effort, we could really get these numbers up there."

"You wanna take lead on that, bro?"

"Oh, no, man. No time." Rufus leaned back after another hit. "Gotta make time to get my DJ on."

"How's that going?" Gaia asked. She slung an arm around Red, who stiffened noticeably.

"Awesome. Got another gig tonight. Gonna make some coin."

*It's always about money*, Red thought. *Money, money, money.* That he had millions locked in a trust occasionally left him feeling conflicted. He told himself he would *so* give it to the Struggle, if only he were allowed to, but he had no access to the trust's principal. Instead he was forced to live on the several hundred thousand that the trust threw off every year in interest and dividends, and with that he was expected to cover his tuition, at least when he was enrolled. Those little Eichmanns who controlled his trust just didn't understand . . .

"Where's the party?" Robbie asked.

"Beta house," Rufus replied. "Bunch of assholes, but should be a smoke show."

"That is so sexist," Gaia fumed.

"Whatever."

Red's thoughts then shifted gratefully away from grubby pecuniary matters. He'd been having sex with Gaia on and off for the last year, but that was getting old. She was down with the Struggle, sure, but a guy like him couldn't carry extra weight. Gaia was turning out to be a bummer. It was time for some fresh. He wished she hadn't put her arm around him.

Henry Schott, a sophomore member, burst through the main door, out of breath. "Guys, Russell's off the hook."

"What the fuck are you talking about?" Red said.

"I just ran into Chris Huffman from the *Daily*. He told me."

"I can't believe that fuck didn't call me. We *gave* him the story!"

"He said he only just found out."

"Okay, so what else?"

"He didn't really know anything else."

"Fuck." Red got out his phone and dialed Jaylen Biggs. They needed to plan. "You hear about Russell?"

"Yeah, word's out."

"We need to escalate."

"I don't know, man. I'm not sure this Russell dude is the best play."

"He's white. Isn't he? And from the South somewhere. Asshole has privilege written all over him."

"Man, shut the fuck up."

"What?" said Red, taken aback.

"Seriously, just shut your hippie white ass up. You notta nigga, get it? You a rich cracker, so don't motherfuckin' talk to me about privilege."

Red was momentarily speechless, a rare event. "Hey, asshole. I set the whole thing up."

"And for that, we black people thank you. But this is our issue. Stay out." The connection dropped. Red was glad the others couldn't hear any of that.

"So what now?" Rufus asked.

"Send out some pissed-off tweets," said Red.

"Got it. That it?"

"I don't know, man, just let me think." Trainwreck was starting to make the task problematic, though, so Red leaned back, allowing himself to be swallowed by the enormous couch. He gave himself over to the steady beat of Rufus's EDM tracks. The words kept repeating . . . *love you, love you.* The effect put him in a mild trance. Then, another thought . . . not wholly crystallized, more like swirling brain dust trying to organize itself, but then forming, coalescing . . . another deep toke . . . ahhhh . . . wait, what? . . . oh, right, the thought . . . an idea . . . music, a bit of timing . . . the right social channels . . . yes, *it just might work.*

"Ah, hey, Roof," said Red. "Can you get me on the list for that party?"

"I dunno, dude. Those fraternity guys can be dicks."

"Just get me on that list." Red smiled, keeping his own counsel for the moment.

# Friday, Eph's Office

**EPH RETREATED TO** his office. He put some Tom Petty on his phone and connected to a Bluetooth speaker. That Tom Petty was the apogee of American music was the one thing on which he and Big Mike always saw eye to eye. Petty was from Gainesville, a stone's throw from southern Alabama. One time, Big Mike piled everyone into their old Jeep Wagoneer and drove them the two hours to Pensacola to see the Heartbreakers. It was one of Eph's best childhood memories.

Eph knew rock music wasn't in sync with the rest of campus. Students favored hip-hop, while the faculty leaned toward jazz and classical. But this particular part of his upbringing he refused to surrender. Popular music standards, in Eph's view, had been declining since roughly 1982, before he was even born. Where was the amped-up adrenaline of Led Zeppelin, the glorious menace of the Stones, or the soaring harmonies of the Beach Boys? There was some good country, which he liked, but today's pop dribbled like treacly syrup from the radio, written by soulless algorithms never programmed to understand interesting chord progressions or complex harmonies. And where did the guitar go? He would never tire of Petty's jangling, Byrds-like Rickenbacker. Rap music—ubiquitous in every dorm—struck him as a forced marriage between a rhyming dictionary and a drum machine. He thought it all sounded alike, a view he kept to himself in case anyone thought it racist.

Glancing at his watch, he saw it was almost five. He reached into his lower drawer and retrieved a bottle of Jack Daniel's. He wasn't a big drinker, but somehow listening to Petty always gave him the urge, another vestige from his younger days. He poured a couple of fingers into a glass he kept in the same drawer and took a sip. The warmth slipped down his throat, all the way to his gut. It was easy to understand why people made this a habit.

He wasn't sure how to feel right now, and he was hoping the Jack would help sort it out. Getting by the Bias Response Team had been a great relief, but he knew the cloud that followed him would not blow away so easily. His colleagues were treating him differently. It was subtle, but there. They were unduly solicitous, as though he had an illness or something. And if he was being honest with himself, Blue Feather was going to be an issue. He had to win her favor, but didn't have the slightest notion how, or if he even wanted to try.

There was a knock on the slightly open door. "Hi, Professor." It was the Harris girl. What was she doing here? These weren't office hours.

"Miss Harris. I wasn't expecting you."

"I sent you an email."

"Sorry, I must have missed it." Lulu Harris had taken to sending quite a number of emails to Eph, mostly about class, but sometimes they veered off-piste. A recent one included side-by-side pictures of Lulu in two different out-fits and asked him which one was more "literary." She was going to New York for a book party or something. Eph thought the email was odd but harmless. He answered, "Number two, but I confess I am out of my depth."

"I thought I'd catch you to hand in my paper," said Lulu.

"It's perfectly all right to email your paper in, you know."

"I know, but I wanted to hand it in personally." She nudged the paper across the desk. *Louisa May Alcott and the Birth of the Modern Woman.*

*Hmm, interesting title.* At least he wouldn't have to print it out. *Crap*—he realized the bottle of Jack was sitting right there. No way to hide it without being obvious.

"Looks interesting. I look forward to reading it."

"Thanks." Lulu stood there.

"I appreciate your bringing it by."

"Of course." She was still standing there. Eph eyed his bottle, desperately wanting another glass, but not until Harris left. "My dad likes this music."

"So does mine, and I seemed to have inherited his musical tastes, if noth-ing else."

"Cool." Lulu saw a picture of D'Arcy on Eph's desk and picked it up. "Who's this?"

"She's someone I care for."

"Girlfriend?"

Eph thought it odd to be getting personal questions from a first-year, but he had left the picture on his desk, so he supposed it was fair game. "Yes."

"She's gorgeous." Lulu closely examined the picture before putting it down. "You know, that whole thing in your class, it was a total setup. I mean, it was so obvious. Any idiot could see it. They even sat in different places to make it look spontaneous, but I've seen those guys hanging around."

"Thank you. It's been an unwelcome episode."

"I can imagine."

Lulu eyed the bottle of Jack. This was getting uncomfortable. Eph made a mental note to pour his drink directly out of his desk drawer next time.

"Sooo, can I have some?"

"What?" Eph hoped Lulu meant something other than what he thought she meant, but then she nodded toward the bottle, smiling.

"Oh, uh, I don't think that would be appropriate."

"I've been drinking since I was fourteen. I think I can handle it."

"Well, I'm pretty sure we'd be violating about twenty-five different clauses in my employment contract." *Why is she smiling like that?*

"Oh, you're no fun."

"It's true. Please don't tell my girlfriend. She doesn't know."

"Hmm, she's lucky."

"I think it's clear that I'm the lucky one."

Lulu twirled her hair and then looked back at the bottle. "Are we celebrating something?"

"What do you mean?"

"Rumor has it you're in the clear."

"How could you possibly know that?"

"You mean, other than because I was the one who got you off? Other than that, I'd say it's because there was something about it a half hour ago in the online *Devon Daily.*"

Eph was at a loss for words. Someone must have given the paper the scoop. He swiveled his laptop around and called up the *Daily.* There it was.

# Devon Daily

## Breaking—Russell Cleared of Wrongdoing

Ephraim Russell, an Assistant Professor of English, was cleared of any wrongdoing today by a panel chaired by Diversity and Inclusion Dean Martika Malik-Adams. There had been accusations from some students regarding the use of violent and offensive language in Professor Russell's classroom, including some that was considered racist. In a prepared statement, Dean Malik-Adams said, "While some of the language used in Professor Russell's class was regrettable, it appears that there has been no specific violation of any university codes, therefore no action will be taken by the university at this time. We look forward to more specific guidelines forthcoming from the Committee on Safe and Open Classrooms."

Dean Malik-Adams could not be reached for further comment.

"*You* made the recording," Eph said.

"I usually record my classes on my phone, in case I miss something. I get distracted easily."

"I guess I should thank you."

"I guess you should."

"Well, thank you. I mean it."

Lulu leaned forward. "Do you, Professor?"

"Of course."

Lulu grabbed the bottle of Jack and smiled. "Then I think we should *both* celebrate."

"Hey, you'd better put that away. Seriously." Eph glanced at his office door, which was still slightly ajar.

Lulu just smiled. "Sure thing, Professor." Instead of putting the bottle down, she tilted her head back and took several large swallows without the slightest grimace. "Frankly, Professor, I think I deserve more than just a thank-you."

"If this is about grades . . ."

"It's not about grades. . . ." She took another swig.

"Give me that!" Eph snatched the bottle out of her hands.

"You know, all the girls think you're hot." She leaned forward and teased with the top button of her blouse.

*Oh, shit.* Harris's intentions were now abundantly clear, even to Eph, who'd always been the last person to know when a woman liked him. "Well, yes, naturally . . . I mean, no . . . which is to say you're . . ." Eph was aware he was starting to sound like an idiot in front of this eighteen-year-old girl. Lulu stood up and walked around the desk. "Listen, I'm flattered, really, but . . ."

Lulu, apparently not interested in whatever Eph was saying, suddenly lifted a leg and straddled his lap. She then planted her mouth firmly on his, which was hanging conveniently open. It was on there like a suckerfish, tongue thrusting down his throat. All Eph could do was make a panicked, muffled sound. *Mmmffft!* Then Lulu leaned back and flashed innocent eyes, while simultaneously gyrating her hips. Eph tried desperately to not be aroused, a battle he was quickly losing.

"Something wrong, Professor?" Voices echoed outside in the hallway, sending sudden waves of panic through Eph. The door was still open. In another era, teacher-student dalliances were common, but the conventions regarding such things as student pelvises grinding on teacher laps had undergone a radical transformation.

Eph lurched, sending Lulu sprawling to the floor.

"Ow, fuck!"

*Damn, did anyone hear that?* Eph looked fearfully toward the door. "Shit! Sorry. Look, I can't . . . my job, and besides, you seem very nice, but I have a girlfriend." He helped Lulu back to her feet. "I'm flattered, really, and thanks for bringing your paper . . ." *Thanks for bringing your paper?* "I think it would be best if you left." He sat back down.

"So, what, I'm not *pretty* enough for you?"

"More like not old enough. Sorry, really. You're very . . . attractive, but I could get in trouble."

"*Attractive?* What am I, thirty? Well, fuck you, Professor." She made her way to the door, but suddenly turned and came around the back of Eph's chair. In one quick motion, she lowered her head next to Eph's and swung her iPhone around with her right arm. She pursed her lips like a duck and tapped the phone with a practiced thumb.

"Hey! Uh . . ." protested Eph, confused.

"Thanks, Professor!" And just like that, she was gone.

A few minutes later Eph's laptop beeped, indicating he had a new email. It was from Lulu. The photo of the two of them.

Eph reached for the bottle.

# The Brothers of Beta House

**DESPITE DETERMINED EFFORTS** over many decades by Devon administrators, fraternities remained a part of the school ecosystem. There was a time, back in the 1970s, when the administrators had almost succeeded in purging them, but then the drinking age was raised to twenty-one and off-campus fraternities sprouted like invasive weeds.

Tonight was party night at Beta Psi. Various pledges—*goats*, they were called—scurried around, making preparations and taking the edge off the general state of disarray. Beta's interior, with its uneven couches and secondhand furniture, was in a long-term war against entropy, with entropy consistently enjoying the upper hand.

The older brothers were mostly relaxing, enjoying that wonderful lull before the evening's coming pleasures. It was almost Winter Break, what used to be called Christmas Break, and with most of their exams in the rearview mirror, the Betas were in a partying mood. Tonight was sure to be a rager. They had that EDM guy, RoofRaza, plus the goats doing all the work.

*Swipe, swipe . . . swipe.* Digger was working Tinder hard. He, Tug Fowler, and the Mound, all seniors, were prone on the common-room couches.

"How's hunting?" asked Tug, president of the Beta house.

Digger Brooks didn't look up from his phone, still swiping. Digger was the *FOGO* on the lacrosse team, which stood for "face off, get off." It was his job to win face-offs and then run to the sidelines to be immediately replaced by another player. A lacrosse face-off resembled two people with sticks wrestling each other, and Digger's particular style lent him his nickname back in high school. His skills had earned him a 40 percent break on Devon's tuition, despite his being from a wealthy family in Greenwich, Connecticut.

"Hey, *dill weed*. Asked you a question."

Digger, without looking up: "It's a digital kennel out there, my friend. When we pre-gaming, anyway?"

Pre-gaming had first emerged in the mid-1980s, long before any of the current Betas were born. Congress, acting as institutional scold, passed the National Minimum Drinking Age Act, which withheld highway funds from states that didn't raise their drinking age to twenty-one. Most states caved immediately. Louisiana held out for a little while, but Northeastern states folded faster than you could say, "Jäger shot."

The effect on college campuses was complicated, and not at all what any Washington politicians might have imagined, assuming they'd given it any thought. Colleges were forced to implement compliance regimes to keep an army of avaricious tort lawyers at bay. Complicating matters, most seniors could still legally partake, while underclassmen could not, creating a great schism of haves and have-nots and a compliance nightmare.

No one really thought underclassmen were going to abstain; this was college, and no Devon freshman walked through Phipps Gate without having seen *Animal House*, howling at the sight of John Belushi smiting beer bottles on his head. The federal *fucking* government was not going to get in the way of a good party, no sir. But big, campus-wide parties? Those were now a thing of the past. Students slithered into the nooks and crannies, mainly dorm rooms and fraternities, consuming what they wanted behind closed doors where they wouldn't be caught by RAs and other mandated busybodies. Beer, the college beverage of choice since the first student was forced to read Proust, faded away. Too bulky. No way to sneak a keg into your dorm. Vodka was the new poison, its primary virtue lying in its efficiency—a mere ounce was equivalent to a whole beer, so it was easy to sneak around, and it mixed with about anything. Gatorade, say. No RA would be the wiser if you were sipping from a Gatorade bottle.

There were other, subtler consequences. Unintended ones. Social life became cliquey, balkanized. With the open-to-all, campus-wide parties gone, students now huddled in groups of six or ten or twelve. These groups had an irritating habit, from a progressive college administrator's point of view, of self-selecting almost completely along demographic lines. No one saw *that* coming, and no one much wanted to talk about it. The higher drinking age became accepted wisdom along with the parallel conceit that some sort of transcendent diversity had been achieved with new admissions policies.

A few college presidents squawked, mostly because they didn't like the liability. Some even signed a letter, but Mothers Against Drunk Driving was a powerful lobby, and no politician was about to commit career hari-kari by pushing for eighteen again. Twenty-one was here to stay.

Not that anyone in the Beta Psi house knew much of this. A few may have heard stories from their parents about the wide and varied social life that existed in their day. Devon in particular was once known for some legendary blowouts such as house-on-house chugging contests and a "saloon" night that featured a shot bar.

It might as well have been another planet.

Most of today's Devonites only knew the world they inherited, and they made the best of it. So, the idea behind pre-gaming was to get drunk in small groups before the party, just in case the party was dry.

Technically, the Betas didn't need to pre-game at all since they owned their own property and so could do whatever they damn well pleased. Tonight, though, they would get drunk before getting drunker.

A goat walked through the common room, carrying a case of Popov vodka, Beta's most revered of spirits. Tug and Digger nodded approvingly. Popov was described in a well-regarded spirits periodical as a "yeasty, vanilla putrescence," but it possessed the highest single virtue in the eyes of the brotherhood: it was cheap. Years back, one of the more analytical Betas, pondering how to reduce a spirit's usefulness to a single number, came up with the "Beta ratio," derived by dividing a liquor's proof by its price for a fifth. For instance, a fine single malt like Macallan had a Beta of 1.6. This was inefficient, even gauche. On the other hand, Popov's Beta was 7.3, a number worthy of approbation. When the house Alcohol Requisition Officer came back with anything new, the first question was always "What's the Beta?" If it wasn't 7 or higher, there were repercussions.

The only time anyone had ever seen a higher Beta than Popov's was when someone purloined several gallons of pure grain alcohol and made jungle juice, a grenadine-laced concoction mixed to look harmless by its friendly red color. House mythology put the Beta north of 10. It was said that Havenport General had to use stomach pumps on several of the female guests. The subsequent banning of Beta from all university activities for two years was enough to cut grain alcohol from the weekly shopping list, even as it cemented Beta's reputation as the best party house.

Finn Belcher, a slovenly but tech-savvy brother from the Midwest, came in, waving his phone. "I've been working on an app," he announced.

Everyone, it seemed, was working on an app. Jimbo Peters had one that required you blow into a Breathalyzer—attached to your phone—before calling or texting anyone you had previously tagged as an ex. The default blood-alcohol threshold was .08, same as drunk driving, but you could set it wherever you wanted. Someone else had an app where you could calculate your carbon offset based on how much you farted. You had to take the phone out and notify the app with every fart. The brothers, all recruited as beta testers, turned this into something of a contest. In the end, the Mound, a football player of prodigious girth, had no real competition. He was readily appointed House Flatulist.

Unlike most of the brothers, though, Finn was a Comp Sci major and actually had some coding chops. This had the others listening in semi-interest. "You point your phone at someone," Finn said, "push this red button, and the app randomly pairs a word with *douche*."

"A demonstration, if you will," suggested Tug.

Finn pointed his phone at Tug and pressed down. The phone suddenly spoke in an irritating, nasally voice. "Douche bucket!"

He pressed again.

"Douche nozzle!"

"Again!" said Tug, who sat up with growing interest.

"Douche licker!"

"Or if you want, you can stick with the classic . . ." Finn pushed a second button repeatedly.

"Douche! Douche! Douche!"

"You can also change the voice." Finn clicked again, this time producing a "Douche!" in basso profundo.

"That is fuckin' *awesome!*" squealed Digger. He and Tug high-fived. "I so need that."

"Of course, it's not completely random, since you can only pair with nouns, and not every noun is funny when you pair it with *douche*. Something like *douche motherboard* would, you know, suck."

"Would suck balls, sure," Tug said.

"But a surprising number of words actually work."

"How many you up to?" inquired Digger.

"Seven hundred and forty-two."

"Do you have douche *rocket?*" asked Digger intently.

"Nice one! Consider it added."

"Does this app have a name?" asked Tug.

"I was thinking of Douche Buddy."

"Belch, we are humbled," said Tug. "You are a credit to the fraternal order."

Another brother wandered in, Bryce Little from New York. "Hey, guys, I know this freshman chick from the city. Smoke show. Mind putting her on the list?"

"Our man Mound is manning the door. Hey, Mound, wake up!"

The Mound was buried in a nearby couch, sleeping.

He reluctantly rolled over. "The *fuck*." He meant, *Why did you bother me just now and what do you want?* Mound was gifted with an economy of speech.

"Bryce's got some chick he wants on the list."

"Name."

"Lulu Harris."

"Done." Mound rolled back over.

"Hey, Mound, any good hit-and-runs today?" asked Digger. Mound's thing was to tour Devon's newly designated transgender bathrooms where he'd lay down tremendous bowel movements. It was about as political as Mound got. The brothers tracked his progress with great interest.

From deep in the couch: "Fuckin' A." *Why, yes, I had some success in that matter.*

"Good man, Mound," Tug said.

The Mound was also an anchor on the Devon football team. Last year, he led the team with forty-eight tackles. He was not, however, destined to be remembered for gridiron heroics, but rather for an academic misadventure of sorts. During last year's football season, Mound had taken Art History 101 because he heard it was a blow-off. Students were assigned to pick any artist that was well represented in the Devon Gallery of Art and write a paper about that artist's stylistic evolution. Venturing to the gallery for the first time,

Mound examined the small labels next to each painting with care and picked an artist who seemed prolific, who painted in many different styles, and whose career was extraordinarily long.

That artist's name was "Circa."

Mound's teaching assistant handed the resulting paper back with *Are you a moron?* written in big red ink letters. That was it. Are you a moron. No grade. Apparently the F was understood.

Confused and seeking elucidation, the Mound made the mistake of showing the paper to his roommate, Jimbo, who was also in the class. Elucidation was not forthcoming. Jimbo promptly ran into the dining hall, laughing hysterically and wielding the paper for all to behold. One student wag pointed out, between fits of laughter, that if Mound had turned the same paper in as an ironic statement, he'd surely have scored an A.

The Mound was less amused.

Tug now barked some orders to some passing goats. Yes, this was a swell place, and it was going to be an epic evening.

# The Beta Party

**IT WAS TEN** o'clock and guests would start trickling in any minute. The Mound lumbered to the door with his final list. Digger was upstairs making sure his hair was disheveled just so. Tug, being president, was making the rounds to see that everything was ready-set-go. In the bar area, one of the goats, a kid named Mark Snyder, was stirring a large vat of Beta Punch with a sawed-off lacrosse stick. A huge block of dry ice was floating in the middle, giving off smoke. Tug walked by and dipped in a red Solo cup, testing the batch. "Hmm." He reached under the table and grabbed a handle of Popov, twisted open the cap, and emptied the contents into the vat. Testing the punch again, he pronounced it acceptable. (The recipe for Beta Punch was a closely held Beta secret, but for those in the know, it consisted of Natural Lite beer, frozen pink lemonade, and, of course, Popov. The brothers privately referred to it as "pink panty remover," although Tug had to caution them never to call it that while using the university email system.) For those who preferred beer there were also kegs of Bud. They would be needed for the informal beer pong tournament.

Tug wandered into the den to survey the pong tables. Once, beer pong had involved real Ping-Pong tables and paddles, or so his father told him. Now they used double-length card tables and the object was simply to throw a Ping-Pong ball into one of your opponents' cups before they could do the same to you. You drank when your opponents scored. The goats had set up two tables, complete with cups, filled pitchers, and extra balls. Billy Curtis, another senior, was supervising.

Billy was a legend for having pulled one of the great pranks in Beta history. When he was a sophomore, one of the goats named Joey Spears got really drunk and passed out on a downstairs couch, an opportunity no self-respecting Beta could let pass. Spears had this pathetic-looking mustache that had always gotten on Billy's nerves, so, taking an electronic beard trimmer, Billy carefully trimmed the sides until Spears had a perfect toothbrush mustache. Billy then found some shoe polish and made the remaining whiskers jet-black. Joey now looked exactly like Adolf Hitler. This greatly amused the brothers, who gave the passed-out pledge a number of *Sieg Heils* before heading off for bed. The next morning, Joey overslept. Realizing he was late for class, he bolted out the door, skipping his normal shit, shower, and shave.

The resulting campus furor focused unwanted attention on Beta for more than a week. Milton Strauss, whose family had distant relatives in the camps, ordered the chapter to be suspended until discovering that Beta was still on suspension from the year before. He slapped on another two years. It was symbolic, since the fraternity operated outside the school's legal authority. But Billy Curtis's place in fraternity lore was cemented, as was Joey Spears's, whose nickname from then on was, naturally, Der Führer.

Trusting the beer pong to be in good hands, Tug continued his rounds, making his way to the living room to check on the music. RoofRaza looked busy arranging his equipment and testing the sound. "Hey, RoofRaza!" Rufus pulled his Beats off one ear. "Ready for liftoff?"

"You know it, bra."

Rufus put his Beats back on, his thoughts tonight more focused on personal ambition than the progressive struggle. Those thoughts might have smacked of capitalist predation had they not been so, well, cool. He'd been doing some research and the top EDM stars, guys like Diplo and Zedd, were making 500K a gig. Half a mil. Once upon a time the Beatles made a mere sixty grand at Shea Stadium. He looked it up. The goddamn *Beatles*. Now guys were making that in about fifteen minutes. And these dudes (they were exclusively male, something that might have given Rufus pause, but *RoofRaza* didn't give it a second thought) hardly had any mouths to feed. They traveled light. Touring dinosaurs like U2 and Springsteen had crews of fifty, even a hundred, but the top EDM jocks would only have a couple of guys, max.

This summer, Rufus had mixed an EDM track that he called "I Want to Love You," which sampled Michael Jackson's "P.Y.T. (Pretty Young Thing)." He posted it on Spotify and it went viral with over half a million streams. It had him dreaming big. Playing to frat boy assholes for a few hundred bucks was a start.

He surveyed his equipment, which he'd spent the whole summer before last saving up for from his job at an Amazon Fulfillment Center near his home. (Red didn't like that, arguing that Amazon drove local merchants out of business. Rufus didn't disagree, but where else was he going to make the scratch? And besides, that was before he came to Devon and got, you know, woke.)

On the table was a Pioneer DDJ-SX2 Performance Controller, today's digital equivalent of two side-by-side turntables. That was where the magic happened. It was fed by his laptop, on which he had over seven thousand MP3s. To either side of the table were Mackie Thump15 thousand-watt loudspeakers that would blow the room away. Above him was a GigBAR, a horizontal bar on a tripod from which hung various lighting effects, including strobes and lasers. EDM shows were about all the senses, not just sound. Below the table was a Hurricane 700 fog machine, which Rufus could control with a foot pedal. Lastly, there was his mic, through which he would exhort the crowd to greater and greater heights. All this was connected with a tangle of black cables.

He tested the sound to his satisfaction, being particularly pleased with the giant, driving base. His plan was to play a mix of popular tracks as well as his own creations.

Partygoers had started arriving in earnest, with the Mound checking his guest list diligently. The list was primarily friends, although Mound was instructed to magically find the names of any hot girls. Someone laughed and shouted, "Hey, Mound, where's your toga?" Mound had once mistakenly worn a fitted contour sheet to a toga party, which lent the impression of a beluga whale.

An hour or so in, he could no longer live with the others getting drunk without him, so he handed the job off to a hapless goat. Even more than football, even more than befouling transgender bathrooms, drinking was Mound's core competency. It was said he could drink an entire case of beer in one sitting, and one of his favorite tricks was betting he could chug a whole pitcher before someone could name all ten Devon houses. That one was a consistent moneymaker.

Over at Fellinghams, the evening was off to a slow start. Lulu, India, Shelley, and five of the boys were pre-gaming, only at Fellinghams it was "cocktail-ing." With the changing of the seasons, Pimm's had gradually fallen out of favor. Most of the women were watching calories, so Tito's and soda with a splash of cranberry was the standard. The men favored Stella or Scotch. Win tried to stock the bar with Laphroaig, since Prince Charles, in a rare royal endorsement, had once proclaimed it the "finest whiskey." Regrettably, it was too expensive to drink in the manner of most college students, and truth be told, few of them had the palate for it. "Tastes like liquid dirt," said one member when Win was out of the room. They settled on Dewar's, an acceptable alternative despite its pedestrian use of several malts.

Lulu was drinking heavily, licking her wounds. She hadn't told anyone about the incident in Professor Russell's office, nor would she. There was nothing to gain from it. Sure, she'd been aggressive, but no one had ever turned her down like that, let alone heaved her unceremoniously onto the floor. Not even the ones with girlfriends.

He must have known where she was going—she couldn't have been more obvious, and she could *feel* him responding to her. How dare he humiliate her, especially after what she'd done for him! He'd be nailed to a cross right now if it weren't for her. Fortunately, the semester was ending in a few days, and her final paper was in, so she wouldn't have to see him again in class. For now, best just to self-medicate, which tonight took the form of several Tito's and sodas.

"Enough of this trifling badinage," Win said with a dismissive wave of his hand. It was almost eleven o'clock, and the crew was growing restless. "Surely there is amusement to be had. This sybarite wishes to be entertained."

Lulu remembered an email about something, or was it a Facebook message? She took out her phone, scrolling through emails . . . who was that from again? Not finding it, she searched her emails for the word *party*, which produced 472 results. The most recent was from a Bryce Little. She remembered vaguely they'd met once or twice in the city. She hadn't even realized he was at Devon. The email read:

Hey, Lulu. Pumped ur here @ DU! We're having a thing (party!) next Friday at Beta. Come by. Should be chill.

-Bryce
P.S. I put u on the list.

The most compelling of invitations it was not, and Bryce had the patois of a ninth grader, but still, options were limited. "I have something. There's a party at some fraternity."

"All those silly frat boys?" Win sniffed. "Their lips move when they read."

Lulu wondered absently if Win was gay.

"You have a better plan, scepter boy?" Shelley asked. "It's only eleven, and I don't want to go to Gino's."

"Very well, then," Win replied. "We shall officially slum it. I enjoin you all to breathe from your mouths for the remainder of the evening."

India bowed out, claiming no interest, which left Lulu, Shelley, and the five boys. They walked the few minutes over to Beta, which was one of a row of midcentury shingled homes behind the sprawling Patterson Gym complex.

Lulu, fueled with Tito's, kept circling back to her humiliation, sprawled on the floor of Ephraim Russell's office. She needed something else to think about. Sidling up to Shelley, she said, "So, I've been dying to tell someone."

"Do tell, then."

"I mean, it's not a big deal or anything, but next month, or maybe the month after"—Lulu paused for effect—"I'm getting the cover of *OTA*." Lulu had hinted as much through all her social channels, but maybe Shelley had missed it. Surely she would have said something.

"Holy shit, really?" Shelley well understood the importance of an *OTA* cover.

"Yuuuup."

"Fabulous news! You've already done the shoot?"

"Oh, yes, it was such a *hoot*. They put us in some killer outfits. In fact, shum of them may have made their way back with me." Lulu was starting to slur her words.

"You took them?"

"No, of corsh not! Well, maybe a little. Mostly it was swag, but maybe a bit extra. Maybe a little Dolce and Gabbana."

"So you stole something. You scamp!"

"It's not schtealing, that's such an ugly word. They *want* you to have stuff because you don't get paid, you know, and it's not like they don't get it all for free . . ." *Why were they talking about this and not, you know, the cover?*

"I happen to know Wendy Faircloth. She and my mother have lunch the first Thursday of every month at Le Bilboquet. Just so you know, she's pretty particular about things . . ."

"Oh, don't be silly."

"Look, honey, I don't care either way. I'm happy for you."

At that, they had arrived at Beta, discovering a knot of people outside the door, all clamoring to gain entry.

With Mound off somewhere else, likely on his twelfth beer, a freshman from the squash team now manned the door, clutching his list. His diminutive presence did not have the same effect as Mound's massive girth. Lulu wedged to the front of the crowd.

"Name?" asked the goat.

"Lulu Harrish."

The goat examined his list. "Uh, yeah, you're good." Lulu motioned to the others, who'd hung back inconspicuously. They tried to follow her in.

"Uh, wait a minute. Wait a minute. Are you all on the list?" asked the goat, not at all sure of himself.

"I'm sure we are," Win said.

"Names?"

"We're from the Society of Fellingham." It came out *fellium*.

"The what?"

"The Fellium Society!"

"I'm sorry, but I don't see anything about—"

"Look, what's your name?" asked Lulu of the doorman.

"Uh, Goat Number Nine." He had strict instructions to refer to himself that way until pledging was over.

"Well, listen, Mr. Nine—thasha strange name, by the way—there's reshiprocity, understand me?"

"There certainly isn't!" objected Win, horrified.

"Well, I don't see—"

"Who's your commanding offisher, Nine?"

"My what?"

"Who's in bloody charge?" interjected Shelley.

"If you mean the brother in charge of the list, that would be brother Mound. He's inside."

Win decided to jump in. "My good man, please entreat this Mound person—"

Lulu raised her hand. "Shut up, Win." She brought them here, she would get them in. "Look, Nine. He was shapossed to put us all on the list, not just me. Bryce Little said so," she said, making it up as she went. "So if you'll excuse us, we'll go shtraighten it out with him ourselves. You're cute, by the way." With that, Lulu and the others marched past.

Torn whether to abandon his post and go after them, Goat Number Nine decided the girl was hot, so he'd let it go. Plus, if he abandoned his post, the twenty or so other people who were there would all rush in. He hoped he was doing the right thing or else he'd soon be doing push-ups in a pool of spilled beer.

For Lulu, getting into parties where her invitation status was ambiguous was a practiced skill, but one she wouldn't need much longer. With the *OTA* cover she'd be on every list from New York to L.A. Just another month or so . . .

*"How's everybody doin' tonight?!"* cried Rufus into his mic. The crowd roared its approval. The party was hitting its peak. "I am the RoofRaza, yo, and you can stream my tunes on Spotify and follow me on Instagram!" More roars. He spun up his signature track, "I Want to Love You," and the crowd responded again. Did they know the song? He bounced up and down, feeding off the crowd's energy. A quick decibel-level check on an app on his phone: 107 dB. Perfect.

The crowd, fueled by Popov and hormones, took on a life of its own, swelling and receding with the music like a single organism. Strobes and lasers alternated from the GigBAR, firing shots of colored light into the fog-shrouded room. The crowd shouted his song's words, which repeated over and over.

*"Love you! Love you!"*

Lulu and Shelley soon found themselves in a spirited game of beer pong. Lulu hated beer, but every time she threw a ball into one of the little cups, people went crazy, so what the hell. Time seemed to skip forward and she found herself midconversation with some frat boy. She couldn't recall the conversation actually beginning.

"So Digger is wasted and hooks up with the chick, right? Spends the night, does his thing, and then tries to make like Casper the next morning. The chick wakes up and says, 'Where are you going?' 'Gotta squash game,' he says. Squash! Digger's never seen a squash court. Then, outta nowhere, this chick says, 'You don't remember my name, do you?' 'Of course I know your name,' he says. 'So what is it?' she says. Then Digger gets all defensive-like. 'I can't believe you don't think I know your name.' 'Then say it,' she says. 'Say my name.' This goes back and forth for a while and finally his hand is forced. 'Carmen,' he says, and then she says, 'It's Miranda, you asshole! He was just coherent enough the night before to know he'd better come up with a mnemonic, which he remembers, but then he realizes it only gave him a fifty-fifty shot! She starts throwing shit at him and he runs out of there. How classic is that?"

Another skip forward. The boy is gone, and she's followed the music into the crowded living room, which had been converted into a rave with strobe lights and fog. The bass pounded through the floorboards and up her spine. Closing her eyes, she raised her arms and started dancing in place, giving herself to the sound and light and alcohol. People were colliding and spinning, losing themselves to their more basic drives.

She became vaguely aware that someone was dancing with her. Win. He had been following her around way too much lately. Then his hands were on her hips, and before she could object, his mouth was on hers. It tasted like stale booze and years of dental neglect. She gave him a forceful shove and he banged into some other partygoers.

"What the hell was that?" he screamed over the music. He actually looked offended.

"Me, saying no interest!"

"Well, to hell with you!"

"Eggsactly."

Win scurried off.

After that things grew bleary, blending together, as if she were floating along outside herself. The sensation was not altogether unwelcome.

After a few more up-tempo tracks, Rufus knew he couldn't maintain the intensity much longer. Good DJs worked their crowds up and down the adrenaline ladder. He cued up a slow number next. Time for people to start pairing off. He liked to think he was a matchmaker, too, or at least a facilitator.

Just then, Red Wheeler sidled up beside him and said, "It's time. Next song."

Rufus, completely caught up in the music, had almost forgotten that he'd put Red and Gaia and some of the others on the list. He hadn't noticed them come in. Red's little scheme had slipped Rufus's mind, but he saw no harm in it. It was pretty damn clever, when you got down to it. He quickly shelved the slow number and cued up a rap song called "Solo," by Heavy Shoes. The song had over 150 million downloads, so the crowd would know it well, exactly what Red was counting on.

The opening staccato piano notes sounded and the crowd reacted with approval. Just before the vocals started, Red nudged Rufus, who then shouted into his mic, "You know the words, sing along!"

*Two a.m., Seven-Eleven*
*Got my burrito, oh thank heaven*
*Phone's blowin' up, back in the heezie*
*Yesterday's squeezie, gotta let'r down easy*

A bit later in the song, Red raised his iPhone, opened the camera, and hit the video record button. "Now," he said, and Rufus hit the system mute button. The song went silent, but the room did not. After a few moments, Rufus unmuted the song and looked at Red, who was grinning like a well-fed shark.

# The Morning After

**LULU RAISED HER** head slightly and tried, as best she could, to ascertain the facts. This wasn't an easy task: her head throbbed painfully with every heartbeat. But she was able to establish four things:

- She was entwined on a couch with some boy—man?—who was naked and hairy and passed out.
- Her clothes, including her underwear, were lying on the floor next to the couch. What appeared to be a dirty army jacket was the only thing covering her and the man-boy.
- She was in a living room of some sort and there were cups, empty pizza boxes, and other garbage strewn about the floor.
- The man-boy, whose face was inches from hers, had breath straight from the sulfuric depths of hell.

These were not altogether welcome facts. She forced herself to remember more. *Oh, right, the fraternity. Beta something.* The evening's events came back to her in fragments, but only up to a certain point in the evening. After that, it was blank, a void. She tried to remember more, but the effort required was way too taxing. She wasn't sure she wanted to, anyway.

The immediate priority was to extricate herself from the couch and the man-boy. This proved to be relatively easy, given his complete unconsciousness. She pulled his arm from around her waist and placed it carefully at his side. Since she was on the inside of the couch, she was forced to climb over the back to get off.

On her feet, Lulu was afforded a better look at her paramour. She recoiled in disgust, realizing she recognized him. This was *not* the direction her social life was supposed to be going. *Ugh, can't drink so much.* Flashing back to the previous day, she remembered the events in Professor Russell's office. *He made me do this,* she thought. She would never have drunk so much if he hadn't humiliated her like that.

*What a shitfest.* Thank God she was leaving for break today. Maybe by the time she got back from break this would all just be a bad memory.

Lulu noticed that others were passed out on nearby couches and realized she'd best leave before one of these slope-headed frat boys spotted her. She scooped up her clothes as quickly as she could and threw them on. Moving quickly toward the exit, she caught a heel on a sound cable that had been run across the floor and went careening. As she fell, her cheek struck the corner of a low coffee table with considerable force.

*"Fuck!"* she cried, as a pulsating pain spread through her head. The noise stirred some previously inanimate shape sleeping nearby under the beer pong table. He lifted his head slightly and peered at Lulu.

"I'm fine," said Lulu, trying to keep her voice low so as not to wake anyone else, especially the man-boy. "Go back to sleep." The boy lowered his head and resumed sleeping, no doubt thankful that his attention was not required.

The frigid December air outside made the stinging pain in her cheek even worse. She tried touching it and flinched. It was swelling quickly, and one of her eyes was beginning to shut. She shuffled back to Duffy, hoping not to run into anyone along the way. Fortunately, it was an early Saturday after a big party night, so the few Devonites walking the streets weren't ones she was likely to know.

In the lobby at Duffy, her luck ran out. There, putting up more goddamn posters, was the last person she wanted to see, her RA, Yolanda Perez.

Yolanda took one look at Lulu and gasped. "What happened to you?"

"It's nothing."

"The hell it is. You look like you stepped in front of a freight train."

"Yes. Turns out it was a bad idea."

Yolanda's eyes narrowed. "Did someone do this to you?"

"No, no one did anything."

"*Something* happened."

"Really, Yolanda, I just want to get a couple hours' sleep and then get out of here . . ."

"I smell alcohol, and your clothes are disheveled. What happened to you? Did you have sex with someone last night after drinking?" Yolanda's eyes were now two slits.

"Is there any other way it happens?" Lulu giggled, despite herself, which only made the pain worse. Why wouldn't this woman go away?

"You don't understand. By university policy, a woman cannot give consent while under the influence. Sex under the influence is automatically assault." Yolanda looked almost excited. As an RA, she'd had over thirty hours of mandatory training on sexual assault protocols, and she was sniffing the first opportunity to put her training to use.

"But not for the guy?"

"What do you mean?"

"I mean if the guy has drunk sex, does *he* have to give consent?"

"No. It doesn't work that way."

"Well, that hardly seems sporting."

"Didn't you learn anything at orientation?"

"Yeah . . . I'm a little fuzzy on that."

Yolanda grew frustrated. "You're not hearing me. In all likelihood, you've been *raped,* and on top of that someone obviously struck you. I'm a mandatory reporter, and—

"A what?"

"Mandatory reporter, which means I'm obligated by the Devon Committee on Title IX Enforcement to report this."

"Would you please relax? No one's been raped." Before Lulu could react, Yolanda whipped out her phone and snapped a picture. "Jesus, delete that!" Lulu shouted. She imagined how she must look, and God forbid anything found its way to social media. "It was a long night and I just fell, okay?"

"There was a party last night at that piggish frat, Beta, wasn't there? Is that where you were?"

"No, and it's none of your business." *Damn, this woman is annoying.*

"I don't believe you, Harris."

Lulu turned and started walking quickly toward her room. Yolanda, undeterred, followed in her footsteps. Lulu got to her door and fumbled her keys, dropping them on the floor.

"Harris, you need help! What was his name?"

What Lulu really needed was for Yolanda Perez to disappear. Then Lulu needed to get the hell out of Devon for a couple of weeks. Sheldon was taking her to St. Barts, where she would lie in the sun and forget about everything that had happened. She picked up the keys and finally got the door open, entering quickly and shutting the door behind her.

Yolanda knocked repeatedly, and her voice grew loud and angry. *"What was the prick's name, Harris?"*

Lulu turned.

"What the fuck happened to you?" asked Song.

# Winter Break

**NORMALLY, HE LOVED** the buzz of campus life, but now Eph cherished the quiet. A heavy, muffling snow blanketed Havenport, accentuating the silence. Things had gotten weird, and maybe winter break would give everyone some needed pause. D'Arcy had gone home for a week to New Jersey to spend Christmas with her family, leaving Eph to his own devices. He took advantage of her absence to go out for pizza, which D'Arcy hated. Havenport was famous for pizza. Big yet thin, irregularly shaped, and cooked in coal-fired ovens, the pizzas were a culinary transcendence. Eph loved the layer of tasty black soot on the underside, rumored to be charred cornmeal. His favorite order was white clam, which left his mouth in garlic-infused ecstasy.

Most of his time, though, was spent grading term papers. Forty students times twenty pages each meant eight hundred pages of reading, plus critiques. He was glad to have some time on his hands for this daunting task. As always, Tom Petty helped. Next year Eph might have to get a teaching assistant from the grad school.

Eph considered the pile in front of him. He still liked to mark up physical paper, unlike many of his colleagues who had gone completely digital. The first paper he pulled was titled "Gender and Sexuality in 19th Century Literature." He groaned, grieving for the next half hour of his life. Without reading a word, he knew that the paper would judge the nineteenth century through the lens of contemporary social standards. The author would be outraged, just outraged. He also knew that moral indignation would outweigh any deficiencies in grammar, syntax, or even logic, at least in the author's view. Eph noticed more students like this had been slipping through the net of the admissions department of late. Or did they get trained to think this way after they got here?

A few hours in, he came to Lulu Harris's paper on Alcott and Thoreau: "Louisa May Alcott and the Birth of the Modern Woman." It wasn't half-bad. Lulu theorized that Alcott's unrequited love for Thoreau, her much-older schoolteacher, may have influenced her political sensibilities, which then informed her later work. Alcott never married and became an outspoken feminist and often championed female protagonists, unusual for the era. Lulu made a reasonable if occasionally tenuous case. Overall, not bad for a freshman.

What happened that day in his office was still perplexing. If Eph was being honest, he was flattered, and he found the girl more than a little attractive. Was this why he hadn't told D'Arcy about the encounter? And even though he knew he shouldn't, he felt a lingering guilt over the unceremonious way he had dumped Lulu on the floor. But what else could he have done? After the incident in his class, even the suggestion of an inappropriate relationship with a student would have severe repercussions.

He gave the paper a B+, then took a break to eat some Chinese takeout, another culinary transgression only committed in D'Arcy's absence. He'd suffered more than one lecture on the evils of monosodium glutamate and high-fructose corn syrup.

D'Arcy.

With the distractions of the last few weeks, he felt that he hadn't paid much attention to her, and he'd been short at times. He missed her.

Christmas Day wasn't much different from the rest. Eph was raised a Baptist and still associated religion with the Bible-thumping, revival-tent world in which he was raised. He now fully embraced the secular version of Christmas, which in his case meant listening to a Christmas channel on Spotify and giving his sister, Ellie, a call. He didn't call her as much as he should, he knew, and he hadn't seen her in over five years. This was the source of some guilt, which he dealt with mostly by not thinking about it. He loved his big sis, but she was still in Ashley, and talking to her was kind of depressing. He got the call over with and Ellie sounded fine, her kids were fine, et cetera. Ellie's husband had left some years ago and wasn't in the picture and Eph hadn't seen his two nephews since they were little. They were playing football now, of course. Big Mike had been under the weather. They said their good-byes.

That out of the way, Eph was free to exchange presents with D'Arcy, which they did via Skype. D'Arcy's face filled his laptop screen. Eph gave her a yellow cashmere sweater, which she opened on camera and appeared to love. The yellow contrasted beautifully against D'Arcy's ebony skin. "It's gorgeous," she said.

Her present to Eph came in an envelope delivered the day before, which he opened. It contained two tickets to a contemporary art exhibit at the Whitney in Manhattan, *Moral Excavations: Deconstructing the New Urban.*

"Great!" Eph tried his best to appear enthused.

"It's in a couple of days. We can meet and go back to Havenport together."

"It's perfect." Eph forced a smile. Just then there was a knock. "Hold on a second, there's someone at the door."

"On Christmas? How odd."

Eph walked to the door—all of four steps in his small apartment—and opened it. Standing there was a man he recognized as a neighbor from down the hall. For some strange reason, especially since it was snowing outside, he had a bicycle. Then Eph noticed a big red bow on the handlebars.

"Hi, I'm Mike from 3C? I actually work at Devon, too. I'm a director in community engagement? Anyway, D'Arcy just texted me and asked me to make this delivery. I've had the bike for a couple of weeks."

Focusing on it now, Eph saw it was a Specialized Allez Sprint, an ultra-high-end road bike. "Holy shit."

"Anyways, Merry Christmas." D'Arcy's little Christmas elf handed the bike to Eph and wandered off.

Eph got on the bike and rolled it in view of his MacBook. "I can't believe you did this."

"Now you can get rid of that junker hanging on your wall." Eph eyed the ten-year-old Schwinn that was rack-mounted on the exposed-brick wall. *You served me well.*

"But how—"

"Mike? I've known him for a while. He comes by Stockbridge now and then. I only found out recently he lived in your building, and that's when I hatched my little plan. Couldn't very well gift wrap the darn thing, could I?"

"You might have tried . . ."

"Oh, shut up."

Eph lovingly examined the bike's shift pedals and carbon handlebars. "You are such a little schemer."

"By the way, you were a very good sport to pretend to like the tickets."

"But I do!"

"Liar! But I still think it would be fun to meet there on my way back from Montclair."

"Done. Love you."

"Love you, too, baby. See you soon, and Merry Christmas." The little *b-bloop* noise told Eph that Skype had been disconnected. He sat there, thrilled with his new toy and immediately missing D'Arcy. He also felt a little embarrassed—a sweater didn't quite match a Specialized Allez. He'd been outgifted. That D'Arcy was from a well-to-do family in the New Jersey suburbs—her father was a senior insurance executive—assuaged his guilt slightly.

Despite the snow, Eph decided to take his bike out for a short spin, at least around the block. Leaving the bow on the handlebars, he threw on some warm clothes, went downstairs, and rode off down the silent street.

The art show at the new branch of the Whitney met Eph's exceedingly low expectations. One artist made small Lucite cubes filled with garbage purloined right from New York City trash bins. There were cigarette butts and fast-food wrappers and even blobs of moldy food. Eph could hear one nearby aesthete gush about the artist's "urban truthfulness." Another artist featured a painting of a rose done entirely in menstrual blood. The flaw, Eph thought, was that blood dried brown, not red, but nobody seemed to be pointing that out. He also wondered what it had to do with the "New Urban."

"There are no words," said Eph, sotto voce in case the artist was lurking among the people nearby.

"Art is meant to provoke," said D'Arcy. "If you have a reaction, even a negative one, then the artist has succeeded."

"Then this art is really, really good." That comment earned an elbow jab from D'Arcy.

They wandered among the art world hangers-on until Eph thought he'd been a sufficiently good boyfriend. "Can we leave?"

"Fine, be a closet redneck."

"There are sometimes limits even to my considerable sophistication."

That made D'Arcy honk.

The Whitney was at the southern end of the High Line, so they climbed the stairs and headed north. The elevated park, a hit with both the public and critics since its opening in 2009, was crowded with tourists despite the cool weather. After a mile or so, they descended back to the street and found hot chocolate at a Starbucks. D'Arcy, checking her phone, said, "Oh, look. There's a Camille Thornton retrospective playing at the Film Forum."

"That is truly fascinating information." Eph knew where this was going. D'Arcy *loved* Camille Thornton. She had been the queen of romantic comedies for years but was now aging out of those roles. No doubt Thornton would be mortified to be the subject of a retrospective, but nostalgia cycles had been shortening up in recent years. (Eph thought it had something to do with culture itself speeding up, but he wasn't a sociologist.)

"*The Lost Diary* is playing. I love that one! She went to Devon, you know. The drama school."

Eph didn't know. "If you love it, I love it." D'Arcy had probably seen *The Lost Diary* five or six times, so he lied like any good boyfriend. It beat menstrual art, anyway. Camille Thornton it was.

"We can just make the five o'clock if we call an Uber."

# Milton's Winter Walk

**MILTON BUNDLED UP** against the Havenport winter, which was cold and humid as usual. It was January and the first day of the new semester. They called it "spring" semester, but most of the students would be gone by the second week of May. This was more properly called the "dead of winter," but Milton still enjoyed his morning walk across the campus from Church House, the stately Georgian brick residence where all Devon presidents lived.

He passed the site for the two new houses, at the moment a pitted landscape of pile drivers and construction vehicles. In addition to Foster's gift, they needed to raise $300 million more over the next two years, more than entire endowments at most smaller colleges. It was a seemingly daunting task, but this was Devon. Its alumni base was rife with billionaires and centimillionaires.

Milton had long become inured to the enormity of numbers like $100 million. You tried to fathom them for a while, then just accepted that you couldn't. They were an abstraction, like trying to understand an infinite universe. But these were the units by which many of Devon's alums kept score. Still others—sixty-two, according to the Development Office—used a different unit. Billions.

The fund-raising would take some of Milton's time, but it wouldn't be too onerous. The media department had produced a slick animation that was remarkably realistic. It offered viewers a virtual tour through the Gothic spires, shady walkways, and ecclesiastical libraries of the two adjacent houses. They'd put it out on YouTube, and wallets were already opening up like spring flowers.

Helping the process along were so-called naming opportunities. A million dollars got your name carved over the door of a seminar room. Five million scored a common room or a house library. Everything was up for grabs except the house names themselves. That honor could not be bought at Devon, it had to be earned.

By tradition, houses were named for Devon graduates who had contributed in some significant way to the school or society at large. The sifting through of potential honorees fell to a committee of administrators and professors. Ostensibly, they would take dozens of factors into account, but it was a given that at least one house would be named for someone of color, or perhaps someone from the LGBT community.

One ironclad rule, though, was that the person also had to be deceased, which presented somewhat of a problem. Devon didn't have minority students in great numbers until the seventies, meaning finding a deceased alumnus of color who had also made a profound mark in some way was proving to be a challenge. "A damn short list," confided the head of the naming committee to Milton privately (after deciding it was best not to convey the message in an email). As for gays, the task was even tougher. Today Devon was at least 20 percent openly gay, something in which Milton took great pride. But looking back, the vast majority of its gay community was closeted until sometime around the eighties or nineties. The committee chair suggested they might have their best luck by sifting through graduates of the Drama School. Some of Hollywood's finest actors were Devon grads. Camille Thornton herself was a Devonite. If only she were dead, thought Milton, who then immediately regretted the notion. (Milton, a film buff, loved Camille Thornton. *The Lost Diary* was his all-time favorite.)

Surely some famous and gay Drama School grad had slipped the surly bonds? With all the sexual assault allegations coming out of Hollywood, though, Devon would have to tread carefully. It wouldn't do to pick someone only to find out later insiders knew "all along" the honoree had a serial affection for minors. Milton shuddered at the potential damage to the brand.

Milton considered managing Devon's brand to be one of his primary responsibilities, and the last few years had been good. The endowment set a new record every year, helmed by the incomparable Wick Wilder, who had pioneered a groundbreaking approach to portfolio management. The acceptance rate had never been lower. The physical plant was in the finest condition in all of Devon's 315 years, with significant renovations having just recently been completed. The sports teams were faring well, with the hockey team winning a recent national championship. Not that he cared much for sports, but they kept the alums happy and therefore their checkbooks open.

One of the professors had recently written an op-ed in *The New York Times* objecting to Milton's use of the word *brand* when discussing Devon. "Our university is not a dish soap," the professor sniffed from his tenured perch in the Anthropology Department. This had privately annoyed Milton, but he started using the word *reputation* instead of *brand,* and that had quieted the good professor.

Keeping all of Devon's myriad constituencies happy was another major responsibility, and Milton always imagined he was good at it. He was popular, and personal popularity was a currency. He didn't get to be president of Devon by being disagreeable. Before taking on administrative duties, he'd been a professor of sociology. His course, Foundations of Modern Social Theory, was always the most popular offering on campus. It was light on requirements—a mere three five-page papers—and Milton was an easy grader. (If they were all smart enough to be at Devon, they were all smart enough to get A's, he reasoned.) Throw in that he was an entertaining lecturer, and word spread. Soon he was attracting nearly eight hundred students and his class had to be moved to Fairchild Hall, which was normally only for large concerts or significant guest lectures. That Milton played in a faculty jazz band and showed up for lots of Devon sporting events only solidified his standing as a man of the people. His rise through the political thickets of both the Sociology Department and the administration had been rapid.

Later today he was set to meet Foster Jennison, the school's biggest single benefactor. Milton was confident Foster would be pleased with the progress Devon was making under his leadership.

Head down against the cold, he crossed the bleak expanse of Bingham Plaza. A large red sculpture by Alexander Calder stood out starkly against the whites and grays of winter.

Looking up as he approached Stockbridge, Milton recoiled in horror. Beyond the Calder, in giant, dripping black letters, someone had spray-painted a message across the limestone base of the building:

*WELCOME TO RACIST U*

# Racist U

**MILTON BOUNDED UP** the stairs of Stockbridge two at a time. "D'Arcy!" he screamed down the hallway before even reaching his office suite. D'Arcy appeared in the hall in an instant.

"I know, sir. I've called maintenance. They're on their way."

"And get someone to throw some tarps over it in the meantime, before someone starts taking pictures!"

"Of course, sir, but I think we might have bigger problems."

"What are you talking about?"

"This, sir." D'Arcy held out her phone and handed it to Milton.

A video was cued up on the tiny screen. He hit play and tried to make out what he was seeing. It was dark, and there were flashing lights. People, lots of them, were jumping and dancing, pumping their fists in the air. "I don't understand. What is this?"

"Those are Devon students at a Beta Psi party. Here, let me turn up the sound." D'Arcy reached over and pressed the volume-up button a few times. Loud, tuneless music played through the phone's tiny speaker. People were singing along:

*Two a.m., Seven-Eleven*
*Got my burrito, oh thank heaven*
*Phone's blowin' up, back in the heezie*
*Yesterday's squeezie, gotta let'r down easy*

"D'Arcy, why am I listening to this?" Music today was all very angry sounding, thought Milton.

"Just wait." The song continued, but when the music suddenly stopped before the end, the partygoers, familiar with the lyrics, kept singing even louder:

*So keep it on the lo-lo,*
*This nigga runs solo,*
*Nigga runs solo!*

Milton sighed. "That word will be the death of us."

The video cut to a figure in a dark hood and a Guy Fawkes mask. "Welcome to Devon University, aka Racist U!" The voice was deep and digitally masked. "Listen as the rich white sons of privilege in their exclusive fraternities spout their hate! Tell President Strauss that hate and oppression have no place at Devon!"

"Where did you find this?"

"It's posted anonymously on YouTube. Also, the hashtag DevonShame is trending regionally on Twitter, so there are links to the video just about everywhere." Milton walked to his window and looked down. Several students had stopped and were photographing the graffiti.

"Goddamn it! Where the hell is maintenance? Will you call them again? And get someone down there right now to cover it up until they get here!"

"Right away, sir." D'Arcy, unsure which command to deal with first, decided to run out to look for blankets first.

Foster Jennison sat patiently. Much of his investment success owed to this legendary patience. Born in Massachusetts to the proprietor of a small sporting goods store, Jennison held part-time jobs to pay his way through Devon. He supplemented his income by deftly relieving money from the rich kids in dormitory poker games. His edge was his uncanny ability to read others, particularly when they were drunk and he was not. After working briefly for the legendary banking house Lazard Frères, Jennison set out for Los Angeles to found his own money-management concern, calling it Beaver Dam Capital (he liked the animal's famed industriousness). The move was unusual for the time. The money-management business was dominated by buttoned-up concerns located almost exclusively in New York and Boston. The West Coast lacked the requisite probity. But, whether by foresight or fortune, his timing was excellent. The sixties saw a surge in West Coast wealth, mostly from real estate and entertainment, and the newly moneyed class wanted not just probity but proximity. Jennison fit the bill on both counts. His favorite saying was "I like to help people. When they're desperate to sell, I help them by buying. When they're desperate to buy, I help them by selling."

For years he built his firm on consistent if unflashy returns. In times of severe market dislocation such as '68 and '74, Beaver Dam would pick up market share against its more aggressive rivals. But when he married and had his first child, Jennison began to view the social fabric of L.A. as too flaky for raising a family. He moved his company headquarters back East, to New York. This had the added benefit of being close to dear old Devon, and he was frequently seen at football games. In recent years, he was a regular guest in Milton's box on the fifty-yard line.

It was not football that brought Jennison to Devon today. Today was about making sure Devon and Milton Strauss continued to be careful stewards of Jennison's money. He'd come up by train this morning from the city and taken a Yellow cab from the Havenport train station. Limousines and drivers were an unnecessary expense and not to his taste.

"Foster! What are you doing sitting out here?" asked Milton, finding Jennison sitting in the hallway. He'd come into Stockbridge unannounced, and no one had taken notice of the quiet man on the bench.

"I didn't want to be a bother."

"Foster, you are never a bother." Milton shook Jennison's hand vigorously. Jennison had a mane of white hair and was wearing a sensible dark gray suit purchased in a two-for-one sale at Joseph A. Bank. "Come, I want to show you something."

Milton led him to his office, where the previous day the staff from Soren O. Pedersen Associates had installed a scale model of the new houses, complete with tiny trees and little people. The spires, turrets, and towers were all rendered in loving, painstaking detail. Miniature students could even be seen in the dining halls through miniature arched Gothic windows.

"It's beautiful, just beautiful." Jennison reached out and ever-so-gently touched one of the towers.

"I'm glad you like it. I've arranged for the people over at Pedersen to have another one made just for you. Might look good in your office, no?"

"Oh my gosh, this must have been very expensive. I think one is enough."

"Are you sure, my friend?"

"Quite sure. Put the money into the project."

"If those are your wishes. Come, let's sit."

They took seats by the fireplace.

"Foster, I wanted to talk to you about something sensitive. It's never come up in our previous conversations, and I think we need to address it. As you know, we have a long-standing policy about naming, which is to say we don't name houses or other major buildings after donors. But I think I have some ideas you might—"

Foster raised a hand. "Not necessary, Milton. I don't want my name on anything."

"You don't?"

"Absolutely not. It's unseemly, as far as I'm concerned."

Milton was surprised, although he knew he shouldn't have been, knowing Foster. Most donors got excited about having their names on a brick. "Foster, I can't say how honored we are by what you're doing for Devon."

"Nonsense. It is I who am indebted to you, or rather to this great institution. I made lifelong friends in these halls. My time here made me who I am. If giving some money lets a few more kids have that experience, then it is my privilege to make that possible."

*Oh, if only there were more such as this!* thought Milton.

"But . . ."

*But?*

"I have some concerns. . . ."

"About the project?"

"Most definitely not. The houses are magnificent."

"Then what?"

"Call it the culture."

"Please, tell me," said Milton in his most solicitous voice.

"I saw that Senator Potter was not permitted to speak here recently." Potter was a Republican and best known for his strident views on immigration.

"Oh, but he *did* speak."

"In an *off*-campus facility. He was scheduled to speak in Fairchild Hall. You moved him."

"Well, yes. But he still spoke and it was well attended."

"Milton, what kind of message are you sending—that conservative speakers aren't welcome on campus?"

"No, of course not. We welcome everyone. It's just that there were a number of threats and we didn't feel we could guarantee security. Safety must come first."

"So, free speech takes a backseat to the heckler's veto?"

The fine hairs on Milton's neck stood at attention. *Heckler's veto*—he associated that term with the odious alt-right movement. He threw up his hands. "A university like Devon has many constituencies that have to be pleased, Foster."

"Do they?"

"Do they what?"

"Have to be pleased?"

"Well, certainly, I mean, don't you think?"

"You know, you're the president of this august institution. Last I heard, that was a position of great influence. Try using it, Milton. Try being a leader. You might find it useful."

Milton turned a shade of ruby. Foster Jennison was famous for being direct, but the president of Devon University was not used to being spoken to this way.

"Allow me to be more specific," continued Foster. "Leadership means occasionally saying no and living with the fact someone may be angry as a result."

"I say no all the time! Why just the other day the faculty asked for their own gym and I told them there was no room in this year's budget."

Foster just stared. "Let me ask you something," he said finally.

"Please."

"What percentage of your faculty do you think gave money to Donald Trump?"

"I don't know offhand."

"Zero. The data is online."

"Foster, the man's a buffoon. We have a very sophisticated faculty."

"Do we? What percentage gave to Mitt Romney, then?"

"I don't know."

"Zero."

"I see."

"Do you wish to know the last Republican candidate who received financial support from even a single member of our faculty? George Bush. Not George W. Bush, George *H. W.* Bush. One of our computer science faculty gave two hundred dollars. That was in 1992, in case you're a little foggy on the dates."

"Well, this is New England, Foster. It's a pretty liberal place."

"Don't misunderstand me. I don't expect Devon to be some Southern Christian college, but balance is needed or people will forget how to think. Heck, Milton, the place was liberal when I was here, too, but all views were respected. There were no—what are they called?—safe spaces."

"We don't have safe spaces here, Foster. That whole thing is being exaggerated by certain elements of the media." *Fox News.* Milton discreetly looked at his watch. He was going to be late for dinner.

"I would suggest that the entire campus has become a safe space. What was that nonsense with Mark Twain?"

"The professor in question was completely cleared."

"Cleared of teaching Twain?"

"Yes—er, no. Not exactly. It was a misunderstanding. Some students exaggerated what really happened."

"And those students were disciplined accordingly, I take it?" Milton looked like he was struggling for the right way to respond. "Don't bother, I know the answer." Foster went over and looked out Milton's window. "Tell me, what do you suppose would happen if I set up a Right to Life volunteer table down there in that plaza?"

Milton looked Jennison right in the eyes. "Foster, free speech is an unassailable right on this campus. It is the linchpin of our core mission to pursue the truth."

"Fine words, Milton. I hope they are more than that."

# Jack Russell

**EPH AND D'ARCY** were trying out Havenport's newest restaurant, Saigon Taste. The arbiters on Yelp said, "Finally, Havenport gets Vietnamese."

D'Arcy watched as Eph struggled with his pho, trying his best not to slurp. "Is there any way to eat this gracefully?"

D'Arcy grimaced as a piece of beef slipped off Eph's spoon and splashed into his bowl. "It's a good thing this isn't our first date," she said.

They'd been dating for well over a year now, but D'Arcy still felt some invisible barrier that Eph wouldn't let her past. She knew he was self-conscious about his roots, but she didn't care about any of that. No, that wasn't quite right. She *did* care, because it was part of who he was. She loved that person, the whole person. It hurt her to think he was holding back, even with her, particularly when it came to his family.

She decided to take advantage of a lull in the conversation. "You know, you never talk about your brother."

"I know."

When Eph didn't follow up, she quickly retreated. "I didn't mean to pry. I'm sorry."

"Don't be. It's just that there're some things I try to leave in the past."

They ate in silence for a bit. D'Arcy feared she'd spoiled the mood. Eph looked as if he was struggling with something. He looked up. "You really want to know about Jack?"

Jack was always Big Mike's favorite. Eph learned this at a young age. He didn't like it—what child would?—but he accepted it. Jack was handsome and charming and confident in all the ways Eph wasn't. Jack also inherited Big Mike's physical presence, which he put to use in the way all physically gifted Alabamians do, on the gridiron. As a linebacker, he set an Ashley High School record for tackles in a single season. And, yes, his full name was Jack Russell, like the dog. Not John or Jackson, just Jack. Big Mike thought it was funny and just liked the sound of it, so he kind of forced the issue with Millie at the time.

It couldn't have been a surprise when people started barking at Jack when he got older. It wasn't meant to tease, it was more like respect—we know who the big dog is. Whenever he made a tackle, everyone in the stands barked. Two thousand people, barking. Eph was sure if that song had been around— "Who Let the Dogs Out"—the fans would have chanted it every time the defense came on the field.

Thankfully for all concerned, that song came later.

Even though he was eight years younger, Eph floated around in Jack's wake. All things considered, it was a good place to be. Sometimes, Jack would take him squirrel shooting. Eph didn't much care for it, but he was happy to be included. Jack also let Eph tag along when he went to the Dairy Queen.

Being undersized, Eph might have suffered the usual preteen cruelties had he been forced to navigate public school hallways on his own. Wedgies and swirlies were the stock-in-trade of Ashley's bullies. But being Jack Russell's brother conferred maybe not respect, exactly, but at least an occasional reprieve from the worst predations of his classmates. It helped that all of Ashley's grades were housed in a single building, so Jack was always somewhere near.

One time, Jack came into the boys' room only to find three of Ashley's more notable delinquents cornering Eph, who looked terrified. The boys went white at the sight of Ashley's football star standing there, demanding to know what in all hell was going on.

"Nothing," answered Bobby Fincher, the pimple-faced scourge of Ashley Middle School.

"Is that a fact? I notice my brother's pockets are inside out. Now why would that be, Bobby?"

"Dunno."

"Eph, where is your pocket money?" Eph just shrugged and pointed to his inside-out pockets. "I see. Gentlemen, we have a problem, so I'm afraid an example needs to be set. But first, fork it over."

Bobby sheepishly dug into his pockets and pulled out a small wad of one-dollar bills. He handed it back to Eph.

"That all of it?" Jack asked.

Eph could only manage a nod.

Jack turned to Bobby and hoisted him in the air. Sensing an opportunity for escape, the other two moved toward the door. "Uh-uh, you two are going to watch," Jack said. Such was his reputation that the other two froze despite Jack's hands being clearly occupied.

Jack nudged a stall door open with his knees. Lifting a squealing Bobby even higher with his left hand while reaching around with his right, Jack hung Bobby by his Fruit Of The Looms right there from the coat hook. He dropped about a foot and there was a great tearing sound, but the underwear held. Bobby hung there, howling.

"I think there's serious doubt about you having children one day, Bobby." Jack looked at the other two, who were wide-eyed, desperately hoping to avoid the same fate. "You pick on Eph and you answer to me. You hear?"

They nodded vigorously.

"Okay, then. Ya'll have a nice day. C'mon, Eph, let's leave our new friends here."

Some boys might have been resentful at having to be rescued by an older brother. Not Eph. He worshipped his brother, who might have been the only person who made life in Ashley tolerable. But when Jack reached senior year, Eph knew his time under his brother's protective halo would soon come to an end.

# 𝔇𝔢𝔳𝔬𝔫 𝔇𝔞𝔦𝔩𝔶

## Club Item Goes Missing

The Society of Fellingham, an off-campus club that bills itself as a haven for foreign and socially elite students, has reported the theft of a valuable bejeweled scepter. According to the club's president, Winslow Gubbins, the scepter was a centerpiece of the club and originally belonged to a Lord Herebert Fellingham, an ancestor of the club's founder, Sir Alexander Hargrove.

"This is a great loss for us, and we are quite bereft," said Gubbins. Club members have been known to march with the scepter through campus and nearby streets after nights of partying. Other sources tell the *Devon Daily* that they doubt the scepter is in any way a historical artifact, and that the jewels are likely reproductions.

The Society of Fellingham was founded nine years ago by Hargrove, then a Devon first-year. Interviewed by the *Daily* at the time, Hargrove was quoted as saying the society was a "refuge from those who eat ice cream in the street." He declined to elaborate further, and no mention was made of the scepter.

It is not known at this time if the Havenport police have been contacted. Anyone with information about the scepter is urged to call campus police.

# Jaylen Doesn't Heart Red

**JAYLEN BIGGS WAS** pissed. He'd just watched the YouTube video of the Beta party. *Bunch of frat boys singing "nigga" like pretend gangstas?* Whatever. What made him mad was that he never approved the play. How *dare* those two-bit raggedy-ass revolutionaries do this without his say-so!

Jaylen pushed through the doors of the PSA. *Why they get such a dope building, anyway?* There they were, sitting around, getting high, as usual. Middle of the damn afternoon. "Man, that all you motherfuckers do is smoke weed?"

Red smiled. "Jaylen! Welcome, my brother!"

"Don't brother *me*, asshole."

"I thought you would be in a better mood today, Jaylen. What brings you by?"

"Fuck you. *That's* why I'm here. Who said you could up and do another race play?"

"I don't know what you're talking about, my friend."

"Bullshit. I *know* you posted that video, the one with them dumbass frat boys."

"Oh, you mean the one where they use that abhorrent language? Yes, we saw it, but damned if I know who made the thing. Good thing, though, right? Fucking racist fraternities."

"Whatchoo think I'm stupid? Your boy Roof here was spinnin'." Jaylen glared at Rufus.

"Hey, that's all I was doing," Rufus said. "Whatever else was going on was none of my business."

"So, I'm confused," Red said. "When I saw it, my first thought was 'Boy, my man Jaylen's gonna kill with this.'"

"Not the point. When you brought me and the Cultural Center into your little play with that teacher, that was one thing. It was little shit. This here is bigger, especially with that graffiti. You went rogue."

"Graffiti?" Red asked.

"Oh, shut up, motherfucker. There's probably still paint on your hands."

*"Moi?"*

Some of the others snickered.

"Okay, listen up. Y'all can bitch all you want about LGBTIA-whatever-the-fuck-letter-comes-next, or unionizing the grad students, or fucking fracking, or *whatever*, but as president of the Cultural Center, this kind of thing is our turf. Don't get me wrong—we gonna run with it, cuz it presents an opportunity, know what I'm sayin'?"

The last words came out *nome sane*. Despite Jaylen's having grown up in affluent Rye, New York, gone to private school, and being the son of a prominent neurologist, he could don a ghetto affect when it served his purposes.

"But understand this," he continued. "Race is *our* thing, not yours. I already told you once, and I ain't gonna tell you again. From now on, keep the fuck out. You hear me? Stick with yo' hippie shit and *keep the fuck out.*" He turned and left.

"A thank-you might have been nice," Red said.

# Double Date

**EPH STARED ACROSS** the table at Sophie Blue Feather and her—*their*—date, whose name was Darrin. Eph warily pondered Darrin's genetic provenance, an exercise he well knew should be a silent one. The longer Eph spent in the Northeast, the more aware he became of the cultural minefields. In his thought bubbles Darrin was "she."

Outwardly, Darrin was a beautiful woman, although for Eph her completely shaved head complicated the picture. She was considerably younger than Blue Feather and had delicate pale features. A silver ring pierced her nose, while a series of smaller rings climbed the outer edge of her right ear. A tattoo on her neck read DO NOT RESUSCITATE. Eph wondered where Darrin placed herself among Facebook's fifty-eight genders but decided he lacked the required perspicacity to sort it out.

Getting to this dinner had involved no shortage of awkwardness. Eph popped his head into Blue Feather's office one day and, screwing up his courage, just blurted it out: "We haven't had a chance to get to know each other, and I was, ah, wondering if you and a . . . friend? . . . would like to join my girlfriend and me for dinner some night?"

Blue Feather stared back, expressionless. "What would we eat?"

"I hadn't thought that through yet, but we could go wherever you like."

"I have a number of dietary restrictions. Also, I am still new here and am not yet acquainted with the culinary landscape."

"Oh, well, this town's not half-bad for food. Bit of a renaissance in the last few years. I'm sure there's something you would like."

"Very well."

Eph decided to push his luck. "Will you be bringing someone?" He didn't want to say "a date," even if he wasn't sure why. He was treading carefully.

"Yes," said Blue Feather, elaborating no further.

They settled on Calendar, a new restaurant that varied its menu based on the time of year and what could be locally sourced. The amateur critics on Yelp liked it, one reviewer saying it was a "fresh newcomer on the burgeoning Havenport food scene, offering a mélange of seasonally correct cuisine." It was mid-January, so Eph hoped the menu had something other than root vegetables.

The four of them arrived at the same time and Eph held the door. D'Arcy and Blue Feather entered, but Darrin stopped and glared. Eph smiled and motioned with his free hand for her to walk on through.

"Patriarchy," said Darrin, not moving.

"Sorry?"

"Your behavior. It's patriarchal."

"Just trying to be polite . . ."

"That's what you've been trained to think, but it's a lie."

"Well, my mother trained me, and I'm pretty sure she'd be upset, wherever she is, if I walked through that door first."

"Then she'll have to be upset."

There was a brief standoff, but other people now wanted to enter, and a small part of Eph could see her point. "Okay, forgive me, Mom." He looked up at the sky as he said it, then walked through first. Standoff resolved.

Darrin ordered an apple martini, while Blue Feather surprised Eph by ordering Maker's Mark, neat. Eph went with an IPA and D'Arcy a cabernet.

The menus were made from some kind of particleboard. At the bottom was printed *Made from 100% American hemp*. Eph was relieved to see a varied selection of meats, game, and vegetables.

"So, how long have you two been together?" Eph asked, hoping he might steer the conversation back to how long he and D'Arcy had been together. He shoved feelings of shamelessness into a deep pit where they could not be re-trieved. Tenure was tenure.

"About six months," Blue Feather said.

"How did you meet?"

"At a poetry slam in Brooklyn. Darrin is a poet."

"That is so awesome," D'Arcy said, looking for a way into the conversa-tion. "I love poetry. Are you published anywhere?"

Darrin fiddled with one of her many earrings, which appeared to be bother-ing her. "I don't write any of it down. I don't believe in it."

"Where does it go?" D'Arcy asked.

"I only speak it aloud, and only once. Sometimes in front of others, and sometimes all by myself. I spoke my last work to a small copse of trees."

"How intriguing. Why don't you like to write it down? I'm sure people would enjoy it."

Darrin lowered her apple martini, which was disappearing quickly. Her face betrayed the slightest hint of contempt. "True poetry should be as fleet-ing as a momentary gust of wind, relevant only to the moment, the right now, and then as disposable as our culture. I compose for only the present, not for yesterday or next week."

"I see," D'Arcy said, not sure at all that she did. "That is *so* interesting."

"Is it?" Darrin looked absently into space.

Lacking anything else to say, all went for their drinks. Eph was throwing back his second beer as fast as he could without being obvious. Darrin seemed content to glower.

Thankfully, Blue Feather broke the silence. "So, D'Arcy. How long have *you* guys been together?"

"About a year."

"D'Arcy works in President Strauss's office," Eph said.

Blue Feather shot him a look that said, *I think the woman can speak for herself.* "Impressive." If Blue Feather was in any way surprised that Eph's girlfriend was "of color," she wasn't letting on.

"It sounds more impressive than it is. I'm basically a secretary, although we don't call it that anymore. But it keeps me busy, and some pretty interest-ing people come through. I've met three U.S. presidents!"

"Sounds like the heart of the patriarchy," Darrin said in a monotone.

"I don't know if I'd quite put it *that* way," D'Arcy said. "Milton is awfully nice."

After ordering dinner and their third round of drinks, Eph said the only thing that came to mind. "I didn't take you for a bourbon gal, Sophie." He immediately kicked himself for *gal.*

Blue Feather fixed an unblinking stare on Eph. "What are people like me supposed to drink, Russell? Just curious."

"No, ah, I didn't . . . what I meant to say is . . . ," Eph stammered, shifting in his seat. *This dinner is a huge mistake.*

"Relax, Russell." Blue Feather smiled. "I'm just busting your chops. I grew up in Kentucky. We're weaned on the stuff there."

"Well, *I* think it's vile," offered Darrin.

"So, you're from the heartland," Eph said. *An opening.* "How did you end up here? At Devon."

Blue Feather leaned back. "Let me ask you something, Russell. I grew up in the middle of Kentucky nowhere, a town called Junction City, population twenty-two hundred. How do you suppose blue-haired, gender-fluid teenagers from ethnic backgrounds got along in a place like that? You think I was on the pep squad?"

*From* ethnic *backgrounds? Damn, the woman is obtuse,* Eph thought. "I suppose you got along about as well as an undersized bookworm in the football-mad town of Ashley, Alabama."

D'Arcy gave Eph a surprised look. She'd never heard him mention Ashley with anyone else.

"You can't be talking about yourself," said Blue Feather. "Alabama?"

"Yes, ma'am. Roll Tide." He said the words with a heavy Southern lilt. "Looks like we're both outsiders, Ms. Blue Feather."

"I'll be damned. I took you for Northeastern establishment all the way."

"We become what makes us most comfortable, I guess. Besides, if I played up my roots, it might set off some kind of alarm around here."

Blue Feather laughed. "I hear ya."

"If I may," Eph said, "I don't think you are in much danger of being outed as a denizen of Junction City, Kentucky."

"Probably not. I haven't been back there since the day I got out of high school. Went to NYU and haven't looked back."

"Do you have family back there?" asked Eph.

"Some, but they've never known what to make of me, and I think I just embarrass them. Easier for all involved to go our separate ways. You?"

"Same story. More or less."

"Do you miss them?"

"Sometimes." Eph preferred not to elaborate.

Blue Feather raised her glass. "Well, here's to us closet rednecks."

The four of them clinked glasses.

"Isn't it interesting how much you two have in common," D'Arcy said. "Although, Eph, I'm going to have to insist you remain gender nonfluid, at least for the time being."

D'Arcy honked at her own joke, but Eph froze, hoping she hadn't crossed a line. But then Blue Feather broke into a smile and laughed. Even Darrin offered what Eph could only assume was her version of a smile.

"I may have misread you, Russell. You struck me as someone who was—how to put this?—not in tune with the times. Do you plan to remain stuck in the nineteenth century, academically speaking?"

"What do you mean?"

"I can't imagine you want to go the rest of your life teaching Mark Twain." Blue Feather's elocution dripped with contempt at *Mark Twain*. "I mean, with the proposed steps toward decolonizing the curriculum, you need to adapt."

Eph could feel D'Arcy's hand give his knee a hard squeeze under the table. "Adapt . . . uh, naturally one should always try to stay . . . relevant," Eph sputtered.

"I'm glad you feel that way. What was that book you wrote?"

"It was called *Ralph Waldo Emerson: Muse of the Private Man*."

"I understand it did quite well."

"Six thousand copies. I don't think Stephen King feels threatened, but I was pleased."

"So that's your yardstick? Book sales?"

"Is there a different one?" Eph shifted in his seat.

"Books are meant to be written, not read," offered Darrin.

"What's important," added Blue Feather, "is what you have to say, not how many consumers you can snooker into clicking BUY NOW on Amazon."

"I guess all things being equal," Eph said, "I'd like someone to read my books. They do take some time."

Their main courses arrived. Eph looked down at his lamb and brussels sprouts. His serving appeared as a small island in the middle of an expansive plate. D'Arcy had pumpkin ravioli, while Blue Feather and Darrin were both eating some sort of vegan stew.

"So, Russell," said Blue Feather, digging into her stew. "There's a march for trans rights next Saturday, right here in Havenport. I think it would be amazing if you two joined us. Darrin's dressing as a pussy. I'm still trying to decide what works."

*That must be complicated*, thought Eph, willing his face into a bland neutrality. He glanced sideways at D'Arcy, looking for help, but she just smiled pleasantly while giving his ankle a swift kick under the table. *Overall collegiality* was one of the criteria for tenure. That was the nebulous factor that had tripped up more than a few candidates in the past. Collegiality was strictly in the eyes of the beholder.

"Amazing, yes. Can't think of anything better."

"It's settled then. I'll email you the details. You know, we might even have some extra costumes."

Eph raised his hand to catch the attention of their waiter. "Excuse me. More drinks please?"

# Milton Gets Occupied

**IT TOOK TWO** days to remove the graffiti on the base of Stockbridge. The paint had seeped deep into the pores of the building's limestone, and several applications of borax had been required, followed by blasts of heated water at high pressure.

Milton Strauss longed for a return to normalcy. It didn't seem an extravagant request. He hoped things had blown over and he wouldn't have to open the next Board of Governors meeting discussing the video and the graffiti.

Sorting through some paperwork on his desk, he heard some distant chanting from outside somewhere. It grew louder as he listened. He looked out his office window to see several dozen students, all African-American, in an angry knot making their way up Mathers Walk. Some pumped their fists as they poured into Bingham and steered right toward Stockbridge, a peloton of inchoate rage. Milton knew his longing for quiet was shot to hell.

What were they chanting? He strained to make it out, but couldn't. Despite the cold, he opened his window to hear better.

*"We are through with Racist U!"*

He watched them file in downstairs. Sitting down, he had a pretty good idea of what was coming next. The chants echoed inside the marble halls, coming closer.

Moments later, D'Arcy rushed in. "Sir, I tried to stop them!"

"I know. It's all right. Let them in."

They streamed around D'Arcy into his office, still chanting. Milton tried to speak but was drowned out. He knew he was just going to have to wait them out.

"Should I call security?" D'Arcy was doing her best to be heard.

"No, I'd like to hear what they have to say." More streamed in, perhaps thirty in all. After a few more chants, they stopped, as if on cue.

"President Strauss. My name is Jaylen Biggs, and I am president of the Afro-American Cultural Center. We are here to occupy your office until our demands are met."

Milton spread his arms wide. "Oh, welcome, welcome! It's great to see everybody. Really great. And please, call me Milton."

"We are through being Devon's second-class citizens!" declared Jaylen. The protesters, who now occupied every square inch of Milton's office, many sitting on the Persian rug, snapped their fingers repeatedly. It sounded like the clucking of many tongues.

"I understand, I really do," Milton said in his most solicitous tone. "Would anyone like some coffee? It must be very cold outside. D'Arcy, would you be kind enough to round up some coffee for everyone?"

"Oh, sure, let the woman of color play servant!" said one of the female students.

"Oh, well, we can all get our own coffee, if that would be better. Or tea. Please remember to use coasters."

"We are here to be heard, sir!" More snapping. "As a white person of privilege, you will never know what it's like to walk by a building named after a slave owner, or into a dining hall surrounded by portraits of dead white people, no people of color at all. You don't know, and you can't know."

"You're so right. How can I know? Why don't you help me? I'm here to listen. D'Arcy, you'd better cancel my appointments." Milton adopted an expression of intense interest, one that said, *I'm here for you. Share with me.*

One of the female students took up the reins. "This place, this place you call Devon, is white, white, white. It's violent, in your face, everywhere you go. You, the university president, *you're* white. It's oppression. But know this: we owe you *nothing.* It's Devon that owes us everything. *We* built this. This is ours. This place was built on the backs of our people, and yet we are second-class citizens on this campus!" The girl was so worked up tears were now steaming down her face.

Milton nodded, as if in profound agreement, deciding not to point out that slavery was largely nonexistent in eighteenth-century New England when Devon was founded and was completely abolished by the time most of the current campus was constructed. But surely the girl was speaking metaphorically, and her pain was plainly real. "Please, tell me how I can help."

Jaylen Biggs produced a sheath of papers. "We have a list of forty-seven demands. First, the fraternities . . ."

# Lulu Finds Out About Survivors

**ALL OF HAVENPORT** rendered in gray scale. It wasn't as if Devon was that far from her New York home, but somehow winter was worse here, the way the January wind blew off the water right through your bones. Lulu noticed a general sense of depression among her classmates as campus life settled into a somewhat dreary routine. For Lulu, this meant classes, assuming she woke up in time, and working out at the university gym. At least she'd managed to avoid the dreaded "freshman fifteen," something she made easier by assiduously avoiding student dining halls. Most meals, to the extent she ate them at all, she took just off campus at a chopped-salad place that wasn't horrible. Socialites were whippet-thin; gaining weight was out of the question.

Years ago—Sheldon thought it was in the seventies—some Devonites decided that the month of February was wanting and, well, something had to be done. Opting for overkill, their solution was to have a party every night of the month. They dubbed it the 28 Club for the number of days in February. Every night, a different group volunteered to host, and it was open to all, assuming one was wired enough to know the schedule. Lulu had been to a couple out of boredom, although she skipped the one at Beta. No need to be seen there again.

When Lulu first got into Devon, she didn't react the way most did. She didn't film herself screaming with excitement reading her electronic acceptance letter. She didn't humble-brag on Facebook, *Guess I'll be spending the next four years in Havenport. I hear the winters are terrible!* Truth was, she was surprised to get in.

She figured she'd go to NYU, a school much more geographically desirable for her purposes. But there was Sheldon to consider, plus she found that being accepted at Devon while simultaneously making it clear she didn't give a shit infuriated people. That part was fun. Anyway, Lulu figured she'd stay long enough to please Sheldon, then get on with things, with the *brand*. But now she wasn't so sure. There were some people here—not many, to be sure—that she didn't find completely horrible and might even miss a little if she left. This was an unexpected development. In particular, the Fellinghams lot, they were friends she imagined she might keep. She *did* have to ward off Win's advances that one night, which proved painfully awkward. Win was too light in his loafers for her tastes. But on the whole, other than that and a roommate she wanted to pack off on the next cargo ship to Rangoon, things were tolerable. Almost pleasant.

Campus was blanketed with snow from an all-day blizzard, and the paths were only partially plowed. It was the kind of wet snow that caked tree branches, giving everything a winter wonderland look. Deciding her Stuart Weitzmans were not up to the task, Lulu pulled on some Bean boots and made her way to the campus post office. The walk was not made easier by her hangover, courtesy of Fellinghams the previous evening. She could swear a small man with a ball-peen hammer had taken up residence somewhere just behind her eyes. She would open her third Diet Coke of the day as soon as she got back to her room.

The PO was practically deserted. Once, maybe back in Sheldon's day, the PO had been a hub of activity, but no longer. The internet had seen to that. Today, though, it was a place that held infinite promise; Lulu was there to pick up this month's *On the Avenue*. Surely, this would be the one.

*OTA* had an online presence, of course, but its glossy articles and oversize pages were meant to be a tactile experience. The magazine encouraged this by delaying online content until the print version had been out for a couple of days.

Peering into the window of her little box, Lulu could see it was stuffed with mail. After checking her phone's Notes app for her box combination, she spun the little dial and opened it up. Mail spilled out, almost all junk. Lots of credit card offers. She picked up the pile and rifled through it, throwing almost everything in a nearby trash can. She found a card from the PO that said, *You have additional mail at the desk.* She handed the note to the postal worker behind the counter, who, seemingly in slow motion, retrieved another bundle. "You should get your mail more often."

"Why?"

Lulu dumped the mail on a nearby table, and the big, glossy copy of *OTA* was hard to miss. Right away, she could see she wasn't on the cover. A shot of some society-matron types was under the heading "The New Astors." *Old people, who cares.* She flipped rapidly through the pages . . . boring article . . . boring article . . . nothing. *Where the hell is it?* It should have run by now. She was briefly tempted to call Wendy Faircloth, but thought better of it. Too eager.

She walked back to her room, which was blissfully devoid of Song. Plopping down on her bed, she leafed through *OTA* at a more leisurely pace, flipping to the party pictures first. It was the usual benefits and openings. Cassie Little, one of Lulu's erstwhile modeling partners, was shot at an opening for a contemporary art show at the Odeon Gallery in Chelsea. The show featured the work of up-and-coming artist Lucien Smith. Lulu thought his paintings looked like a bunch of black dots on a white background, but a *New York Times* art critic had dubbed Smith the "new Dada," so she took it on faith that his work was important. It annoyed her to think of Cassie sashaying around the Odeon Gallery, pretending to understand everything, especially when photographers were nearby. *Bitch.*

Now bored, Lulu tossed *OTA* aside and thumbed through *Newsweek,* a free copy of which had also been stuffed in her box. She guessed they were looking for younger subscribers, although she didn't know a single person her age who subscribed to a newsmagazine. The very idea seemed ridiculous.

About halfway through, past the hard news, an article caught her attention. Called "Campus Nightmares," it was about the wave of sexual assaults on American campuses. The victims—known as survivors—were bravely coming to the fore, exposing their pain for the common good. There was a lot about Emma Sulkowicz, the famous "Mattress Girl" at Columbia, who had carried a mattress around campus for an entire year to protest an alleged assault by a fellow student. Lulu thought there must be less exhausting ways to get attention, but she couldn't argue with the results. Sulkowicz had become a campus celebrity and a feminist hero. She even got invited to one of Barack Obama's States of the Union. Lulu googled *Mattress Girl,* and there were 2.7 million hits.

Another girl had accused a teacher of assault and her whole campus had rallied around her cause. She was hailed with words like *brave* and *pathbreaking* and was said to be taking on the "power imbalance" between teacher and student.

Something new was happening here. *Victims as celebrities.* Yolanda Perez had kept on her about that black eye last month, the one that forced Lulu to hide her first week in St. Barts. Perez had even shown up at her door with some woman from a campus feminist group. They pressed Lulu hard for a name, promising to "title nine his ass." As much fun as it might be to get the hairy man-boy in trouble, Lulu didn't have time for a bunch of dykes. As a likely English major, she was, however, intrigued that *title nine* was now being used as a verb.

The article also reminded her uncomfortably of her encounter in Professor Russell's office. The anger she had felt afterward had devolved into something that most people would understand as shame, although in Lulu the feeling was banished to a dormant level of consciousness before it was allowed to be recognized as such. Alcohol helped with that. And then, to get that B+ on her final paper! She was still smarting over that. Not that she gave a shit about grades, and not because she gave a rat's ass about Louisa May Alcott, either.

Craving a distraction, she made an exaggerated frown into her phone's camera and posted the shot to Instagram with the hashtag #SoBored. She was up to two thousand followers. The near-instantaneous likes and comments that caused her phone to vibrate put her in a better mood.

That the picture captured more than she intended she would only come to realize later.

# Devon Daily

## Students of Color Continue Occupation

The occupation of Stockbridge Hall by minority students entered its fifth day yesterday. Echoing iconic demonstrations of prior generations such as the Columbia protests of the 1960s, minority students, led by the Afro-American Cultural Center, have occupied Stockbridge Hall since Tuesday. They have vowed to stay until their list of demands is met. The office of Devon's president, Milton Strauss, was the initial focal point, but as the protest has grown, other offices have been occupied as well, bringing many university services to a halt.

The Cultural Center has cited recent incidents on campus, including a recent party at the Beta Psi fraternity and the alleged racism last semester in the English Department as evidence of a hostile and unsafe atmosphere for minority students. The campus is so on edge that police were called on Thursday to the site of the new residential houses, where a noose was reported hanging from a construction girder. It was later determined that the rope was there to keep electrical wires safely away from construction workers.

There has been increased scrutiny of Devon by the press and on social media, with some questioning Devon's commitment to social progress. Many believe this to be a seminal test of President Strauss's tenure.

The Cultural Center posted its list of forty-seven demands online as well as on the door of Stockbridge. Among them, they instruct the university to:

- *Ban membership in Beta Psi and other fraternities and convert the houses into living space for all members of the African diaspora*
- *Eliminate tests and grades in certain non-STEM majors*
- *Change the names of various buildings and permanently remove plaques honoring Devon's graduates who died fighting for the Confederacy*
- *Eliminate cultural appropriation in all forms, including ethnic food nights in the dining halls*
- *Create a new student-run committee to monitor all forms of oppressive behaviors on campus, including those that are racist, sexist, transphobic, cissexist, misogynist, ableist, homophobic, Islamophobic, and climate denying*

Reached by phone from President Strauss's office, Cultural Center president Jaylen Biggs issued the following statement:

"Our demands are fair and reasonable. It is the university's responsibility to provide a safe environment for its students and it has failed to do so. We will occupy this office and others until they are met."

It is reported that President Strauss, in a show of unity with the protesting students, has vowed to stay with them inside his own office until an agreement can be reached. The *Daily* has also exclusively learned that an emergency session of the Steering Committee of the Board of Governors has been called for tomorrow.

Reading the *Daily* with growing anger, Red Wheeler took special note of Jaylen's demands, which now bled into matters of LGBT, feminist, Latino, and Islamic rights. Shit, Jaylen even threw *ableist* in there. And climate! That *fucker*. After his big speech about the PSA staying out of race issues, he'd gone and laid claim to every goddamn thing. Ableism, for Christ sake! What the fuck did Jaylen care about ableism? And this, after Red had handed him this whole damn play on a silver platter. The fucking nerve!

Over at the Beta house, Tug Fowler had just finished reading the sports section of the *Daily*. The Devon hockey team was making quite a run this year. Seven members of the team were in Beta. Having a few more minutes before he had to leave for his next class, he decided to glance at the front page.

"Fuck, have you guys seen this?"

# Eph Gets a Visitor

**IT ALWAYS FELT** colder in Havenport than it actually was. It was the humidity, people said. Eph wondered if he'd always be a biological Alabaman, shivering in the Northern climes when others went about unfussed. The snow this year had come in December and stayed, with each storm piling more inches on the last until the paths on campus became narrow channels from building to building.

"Is the whole winter like this?" asked Ellie.

"Most of them." His sister, Ellie, had shown up somewhat unexpectedly. A personal matter had taken her to New York, so she called and said she'd like to come up for a day to visit. It was her first time at Devon, and the first time Eph had seen her in over five years. He'd always had a soft spot for Ellie. Ellie the peacemaker. He was touched she'd made the effort.

Not sure what else to do, Eph was giving her "the tour," a crisscross through the snowy pathways and quadrangles. He showed her the classroom where he was teaching his second-semester courses, and they walked by the occupied Stockbridge. Eph explained what was going on.

"What is it they want?" asked Ellie.

"It's quite a long list, actually. Some of it is kind of out there."

He decided not to tell her of his own misadventures. She would be supportive but wouldn't understand.

Farther on they ducked into a stone archway, which led to the courtyard of Hewitt House. Hewitt was one of the larger residential houses and thought by many to be the most beautiful. The courtyard was almost a football field in length and had several weeping willows, which somehow hadn't yielded their foliage to the assault of winter. Surrounding the yard were gracefully arched entryways that led to smaller courts, as well as peaks and turrets of varying height. At one end was a dining hall with a façade of stone and lead glass so airy and light it looked as if the two could dance. At the far corner rose Hewitt Tower, one of the largest freestanding stone structures in the world. Within its higher reaches was housed an immense carillon, which a handful of music students learned to play every year. Built in the most detailed Anglican style, the tower looked like an elaborate, vertical wedding cake.

"Students get to live here?" asked a wide-eyed Ellie, taking in the sweep of the place.

"Yes. This house, and others."

"It's so beautiful. I had no idea."

Just then, the carillon began to play. The sound of the bells was peaceful and serene. Whatever was happening elsewhere in the world, this place, Devon, existed calmly outside time. The bells, this courtyard, it was all thus a century ago and would be thus a century from now.

They listened for a minute until the cold caught up with them, so they retreated into the dining hall to warm up. Medieval-looking pennants hung from the wood rafters of the twenty-five-foot ceilings. Around the walls hung formal portraits of housemasters past, only they didn't call them masters anymore. They were *heads of house* now, lest anyone grow faint at the word *master*.

It was the afternoon lull between meals, but the dining hall stayed open for drinks and light food. Eph grabbed a coffee, Ellie a hot chocolate, and they sat in the almost-empty hall.

"I can't believe this place," Ellie said. "All of it. It's like living in *Harry Potter* or King Arthur's court."

Eph smiled. It wasn't the first time he'd heard the campus compared to the *Potter* books. "Sadly, it turns out my skills as a wizard are wanting, so they've got me teaching English."

"I read your book, you know."

"Oh, you're the one."

They laughed, then sat in silence for a bit, getting warm. Ellie looked tired. They had avoided the elephant in the room all day.

"So how is he?" asked Eph.

The Russell farm had been in the family for three generations. Everyone was expected to help, including the children. Technically, the government says you can't work the family farm until age twelve, but Big Mike didn't take much stock in what the government had to say about much of anything. It was hard work, particularly during harvest season. Migrant workers helped, but the family couldn't afford many of them.

Like most boys, Eph grew up in awe of his father, but it was Eph's older brother, Jack, who was undeniably the chip off the old block. Jack and Big Mike had a bond that made Eph's heart hurt in every way that it could. Eph tried things that he thought might win his father's approval, but it never quite worked out. There had been Eph's disastrous turn on Pop Warner football, of course, and then later he wrote a school paper on famous authors from Alabama, which he thought Big Mike might like given the family's long history there. Big Mike looked at the paper and sort of grunted. "Never read any of them," he said, handing the paper back. Eventually, Eph just stopped trying.

Ellie met Eph's gaze. "He's been better. To tell you the truth, I worry about him. Ever since we sold the farm, he hasn't had a purpose. Men need a purpose."

"I suppose they do."

"He moved in with us, as you know, and mostly he watches TV or sits on the porch. On good days, he might go out shooting squirrels, but there've been fewer of those."

"Is it hard on you?"

"We get by." She paused. "I have a small confession to make. I didn't really have to be in New York. Mostly, I wanted to see you."

"Sis, you didn't need an excuse. It's always great to see you."

"It looks like you have a nice life here."

"Some of the people are a bit different, but this is a special place. It's home now."

"And your girl?"

"D'Arcy. She's my angel. Can you stay for dinner? Let's all three of us go somewhere. I'd love for you to meet her."

"I can't, I'm sorry. I have to get back for a flight this evening. Maybe some other time."

The conversation flagged the way it can between two people who love each other but have drifted apart with life's natural currents.

"You know, he won't say it, but I think he might like to see you sometime."

Eph suspected that was coming. "I don't know, Ellie . . ."

"He's not getting any younger, and you two just need to get on with it, if you ask me."

"Hey, Sis, I know you mean well, but I'm crazy busy here—did I tell you I'm up for tenure?"

Things were, in fact, looking up for his tenure prospects. He knew Fred Hallowell and Titus Cooley stood in support, and Eph seemed to be making progress with Sophie Blue Feather. He did his best not to reflect on the costume he'd donned for the trans rights march.

"I am so proud of you, I can't even say. He is, too, in his way."

"It doesn't sound like he's exactly asking for me. It might be a long trip for a short conversation."

"Will you think about it?"

"Sure." Eph looked at his feet.

"Well, I should get going. There's a bus I should catch." Eph didn't even know buses came to Havenport. "You have a wonderful life here. And I promise to make time to meet your gal next time. D'Arcy."

Eph walked her out to the street to find a cab.

Ellie gave him a big hug. "Don't be a stranger."

"I won't."

"Promise?"

"Promise."

# Stillman Weathers

**STILLMAN WEATHERS POKED** at his tuna tartare and looked out the cabin window. With a cruising altitude of forty-two thousand feet, his company's brand-new Gulfstream G650 didn't offer much to see. Even the clouds looked far below. He rubbed the soft Spanish leather on his armrest. It smelled as if it had been tanned yesterday. The G650 seated eight, had a crew of four, and a top speed just shy of Mach 1.

He liked saying that. *Mach 1*. The speed of sound. The G650 waiting list was long, but Stillman's company had always been a good Gulfstream customer, so they got the fourth one off the line. He noticed it was the only one parked at Davos last month.

With its final configuration, the tab to his company came to $72 million. This had given Stillman some pause, but he worked hard, and it wouldn't do to waste half his days in commercial airports, not with what his time was worth. It wouldn't do at all. And besides, his company, Broadreach Industries, made $3.2 billion last quarter. The shareholders wouldn't squawk, that's for sure. Not with numbers like those.

"Will that be all, Mr. Weathers?" asked Jenny, the plane's flight attendant.

"Yes, thank you, Jenny. You can knock off for a bit."

Today, Stillman was the only passenger. As the chairman of Devon's Board of Governors, he was heading to Havenport for an emergency meeting of the Steering Committee, which was basically the small subset of the board that actually got things done. The board had forty-five members, a size that maximized financial gifts but rendered productive meetings impossible. When you got right down to it, the broader board didn't do much, not that anyone on the outside had to know.

The unscheduled trip was an inconvenience, but Stillman was quietly pleased to think he was riding to the rescue. Being chair of Devon's board pleased Stillman almost as much as being CEO of Broadreach. No, that wasn't right—it pleased him *more*. For better or worse, the corporate world was tainted. They were moneymen, strivers, never completely respected in the corridors of media and political power. He'd given over $100 million of his shareholders' money away last year to various charities to wash himself of the stain, and naturally he signaled his disdain for the current administration in Washington at every opportunity, but still . . . the stain remained. He felt it.

Academia, on the other hand, was still the province of an intellectual nobility, people who toiled in the pursuit of pure truth, not mammon. While Stillman projected an image of serene authority, he was secretly as thrilled as a little boy about his ascendency to the Devon chair. It conferred, in the circles he cared about, a legitimacy that could not be bought. And heck, he still loved the place, having spent his undergraduate years as a history major and heavyweight rower. In many ways, those were the best four years of his life.

The situation with the black students would have to be handled with tact. When he was a student back in the early seventies, there were minority students on campus, but nothing like today, what with outreach being such a priority. At his last reunion, a classmate of his—whose son had recently been rejected—quipped that back in their day, if you saw a black student, you'd whisper the person was likely a football or basketball player. Now, the joke went, if you saw a preppie blond kid, you might mutter, "Probably a lacrosse player." Like most successful jokes, it had the air of truth. Times had changed, and part of Stillman's job was to help the school navigate that change. He couldn't allow anything to undermine Devon's reputation and, not unimportantly, his own. In Stillman's world, a well-maintained order was the most virtuous state of affairs.

But he wondered about Milton. What kind of show was he running? Events were spinning beyond his control. Stillman would bottom-line this thing and put it in the rearview mirror. That's what he did. If some knuckles had to be rapped, so be it.

Since this was his first trip to Devon in his new iron, his people had had to call to make sure Havenport Airport's lone runway had the necessary length. It did, if just barely.

*Iron.* It's what CEOs called their planes when they were in one another's company. He loved that word.

The G650 started its descent.

# Busted

**THE KNOCK ON** Lulu's door came at an unpleasantly early hour, not even ten o'clock. There had been a rally last night in support of the occupation and all the chanting from that rabble had kept her up. Song was long gone, of course, probably in a lab somewhere. Lulu rolled out of her twin bed and threw on a robe. The knock was irritatingly persistent.

"Just a goddamn minute!" She flung open the door, ready to vent her irritation, and saw it was two campus rent-a-cops. One was quite obese. Didn't they have fitness tests for these sorts of jobs? The presence of campus gendarmes did not alter her general state of agitation, but she decided not be obvious about it.

"*What!*" She wasn't successful.

"Miss Harris?"

"Yes."

"We're with campus security," said the fat one. "We'd like to come in and look around, if you don't mind."

"Can you come back later? I was asleep. And why on earth would you need to come in my room anyway?"

"We just want to look around."

"Well, this isn't a good time. I'm not even dressed. And don't you need a warrant or something?" Sheldon repped a few actors on *Law & Order*, so she knew a thing or two.

"This isn't your property, miss, so no."

"Why don't you just tell me what you want? And shouldn't you be over at Bingham making sure those people don't start a riot?" Lulu couldn't imagine what this was about. She didn't have any drugs. Drugs weren't really her thing ever since she went to the ER after that Lower East Side rave a year ago. She had ingested more than the doctor-recommended amount of ecstasy.

"We'll just be a minute." They walked right around her into the room. The sight of fatty rummaging around her things made her nauseous. When he leaned over, his uniform shirt rode up, exposing a roll of corpulence. *Yuck.* Lulu had no patience for fat people. If they didn't respect themselves, why should she have to? Mostly, though, she just found them unattractive. Maybe she should call Sheldon. . . .

"Got it," said the not-fat one, who had been digging in her minuscule closet. He turned, holding the Fellingham scepter.

"*That's* what you're looking for?"

"Yes, miss. It was reported stolen."

"It's from my club. Of which I am a member. It can't be stolen if I'm a member, now can it?" *Officer Blart,* she wanted to add.

"Well, all we know is that it was reported stolen by the club, which filed a report, and then we got a tip it might be here. So here we are, and now we need to take this thing with us."

"And then what?"

"Miss?"

"I mean, you're just going to return it and that's that?"

"Miss, our only job was to come find this here . . . scepter. Anything else, you'll need to take up with the university. We will need to file a report, and that's the end of it as far as we're concerned."

They left. The fat one had to turn slightly to fit through the door, Lulu noted with horror.

The scepter. She'd taken it one night out of boredom. No other reason. She frequently took things out of boredom. She would have given it back, but after everyone at the society started bitching about the goddamn thing—Win and Frazier were being *dreadful* bores—and then there was that story in the *Daily,* she just hadn't found a moment to return it discreetly. She'd never heard people go on so much about something so silly. They should be happy she had it and not some common thief, who would have thrown the damn thing in the trash as soon as he found out the jewels were fake.

But how did someone know she had it?

She found out that bit of information the next day. Returning from her American Studies class—a new offering, American Precarity in the 21st Century—she came upon an oversize envelope at her door with her initials on the outside. No other markings. Curious, she opened it up and out fell a small gold plaque. *Her* plaque.

She grabbed her phone and immediately texted Shelley: "What the hell is going on?"

There was no immediate answer and Lulu grew anxious, texting again: "?????????????"

A few minutes later the reply came: "Meet me at the Dix in 30."

The Dix. Not Fellinghams. Shelley almost never set foot in the Dix other than to grab coffee at the Starbucks kiosk. Lulu threw on her black Moncler coat, the one with all the puffy rows of down, her Stuart Weitzman boots, and trudged over.

Anxious, she found herself there early. She sat down in a pod, but then decided she felt ridiculous, so she went and waited in line at Starbucks even though she didn't want anything. At the head of the line, she ordered a short latte (skinny, vanilla), paid with her phone, then considered where to wait. She imagined everyone was looking at her, but that was silly. Settling on the end seat of an empty nearby table, she got out her phone again and tried to look busy by scanning her Snapchat. One of her New York friends had sent her a snap from an East Village party, which didn't make her feel any better.

"Hi." Shelley dropped her class books on the table and took a seat. Lulu hadn't seen her walk up.

Lulu reached into her bag and pulled out the plaque. Might as well get right to the point. "So what's with this?"

"That's their way of telling you," Shelley said matter-of-factly.

"Telling me what?"

"That you're out, of course. Off the Wall of Belonging and all that."

Lulu had feared as much, but *what the hell.* "Out of the society? Over the fucking scepter?"

"You *knew* how they loved the damn thing. You knew it!"

"Oh, come on. It was just a prank. I was going to return it."

"Well, frankly, it didn't seem that way. It was in the paper weeks ago and you've heard the boys going on about it, and when they specifically asked if anyone knew where it was, you didn't say a thing."

"I just wanted some time to return it, you know, quietly. I didn't know it would be a thing."

"That was a month ago. You need to get real about this. That scepter is the society's symbol. I think that was pretty clear."

"It's not even real. The jewels are glass! Someone probably bought it on goddamn eBay."

"I'm not sure anyone thinks that matters. The society may be a bit of a lark, we all know that, but some things they—*we*—take seriously. People feel betrayed. Plus you took that other stuff, you know, from *OTA*. Seems like a bit of a pattern."

"The stuff *OTA* gets for free?"

"You don't know that, and I'm fairly certain Wendy Faircloth wouldn't see it like that."

"So, what, I'm out? Just like that?"

"Yes. I'm afraid so."

"This is so fucking unfair. I actually like the place, you know."

"That's awfully big of you."

"Oh, stop. You know what I mean."

There was a pause.

"Well, if that's all . . ." Shelley started to get up.

"You can't do this."

"It's done."

"Won't you help me?"

"Lulu, I *agree* with it. No one trusts you anymore. And they think you're a bit of a climber."

Lulu recoiled. "A *climber?*" Shelley had hit the mark. "That is so absurd."

"Is it?"

"How did they know I had the damn thing, anyway?"

Shelley picked up her books. "You might want to check your Instagram posts. Oh, and It Girl? Good luck with *OTA*." With that, she walked out, leaving Lulu alone in the Dix.

She wanted to hole up in her room, but Song was there, so Lulu settled on a remote section of the Goodwin Library, an immense cathedral-like structure with countless reading rooms and labyrinthine stacks. The Devon campus was filled with architectural nooks and crannies where one could get lost, and this was one of Lulu's favorites, a tiny book-lined recess with two leather reading chairs, a refuge within a refuge.

She curled up in one and started scrolling through her Instagram posts. There were forty-two in the last month. She realized she was pursing her lips, making "duck face," in most of them. Perhaps she was getting too old for that. Nothing stuck out, otherwise. The typical picture had a couple hundred likes. Nothing wrong with that. *Who do they think they are at Fellinghams, anyway?*

She decided to look through the comments. Not much there. Lots of "GORGEOUS!!!" mostly. Then, under one post where she'd used the hashtag #SoBored, she saw a comment posted yesterday from someone named lionheart32:

"So you had it, bitch."

She scrolled back up to the photo. Just an off-angle selfie from her room. Then she saw it.

Her face took up most of the frame, but to one side you could see into her open closet. There, poking up from behind her Stuart Weitzmans, you could see fake rubies reflecting the camera flash. It was the scepter. The goddamned scepter.

Even though the idea mortified her, she considered sending an apology email to Win. Maybe that would patch things up. What the hell was she going to do around here without Fellinghams? Hang out with those priapic frat boys? Not a chance. Go to hockey games? The student production of *The Vagina Monologues?* Please. Study all the time? What for?

Switching to email (which she almost never used socially), she tapped out a note.

Win,
So sorry about the confusion over the scepter. I'm sure you know
it was just a lark, and to tell you the truth, I'd almost forgotten I

had it. OF COURSE I was going to return it. Anyway, it should be back over the mantel by now, and I hope there are no hard feelings.

Sincerely,

Lulu

She hit send and her phone made that swooshing noise. Almost immediately came a reply: "Bugger off. Do NOT email or text again!"

A deep feeling of unease came over her. This was worse than she had realized. They couldn't do this! Desperate to dispatch the unaccustomed knot in her stomach, she remembered the new *OTA* might be arriving today. That would show them. She exited the library and made her way to the PO, which was in its usual state of inactivity. She hadn't returned since last month, so her box was stuffed with junk. Once again, she took the small notice and handed it to the slow-motion worker drone behind the counter, who returned with a small pile.

"You know, you really should pick up your mail more often," the woman said.

"Excellent advice, thank you." Lulu took her pile to a nearby table and immediately found the latest *OTA*.

There it was, on the cover: "The New Philanthropists."

*Yes!*

Also on the cover, in full glossy splendor, were Cassie Little, Chrissie Fellows, Aubrey St. John, and . . . that was it. They had cropped Lulu out of the shot entirely. Panicking, she whipped through the oversize pages until she found the article, with several more shots. She wasn't in a single one. Perhaps she was mentioned in the article? Ugh, that was useless, worse than a comment deep in a text thread with no hashtag. But she needed something. She quickly scanned the text. Nothing. Her panic swelled as she tried again, forcing herself to read through every paragraph. Had she missed it?

Nothing.

The chasm in her gut threatened to swallow her whole.

*What happened?* Did Shelley say something to her mother? It must be. *Shelley told her mother, who told Wendy Faircloth.* Tears welled in Lulu's eyes as the realization of just how far she'd fallen in one day washed over her. *Who do these people think they are?* She turned toward the wall to hide her face just in case someone happened by. For no particular reason, she looked up and saw a poster that said:

*Are You a Survivor?*

Then, under the glaring lights of an empty post office, Lulu Harris quietly had a nervous breakdown.

# The Steering Committee

**D'ARCY POKED HER** head into Milton's office, where students still littered the floor. Many more spilled out into the hallways and other offices. The university had brought in sleeping bags and set up a portable food and beverage service in the hallway. Professors had quietly been instructed to allow any missed work or tests to be made up later.

True to his word, Milton had not left the premises since the start. D'Arcy had run back to Church House twice to retrieve basic toiletries and fresh clothes. A small shower was just off his office, but he couldn't very well use it without allowing everyone else to, and there were just too many. The office of Devon's seventeenth president had by now acquired a pungency rivaling that of the locker room over at the hockey rink.

The protesters had grown largely quiet, having made their case with stridency. Jaylen Biggs went out on Milton's small balcony several times to lead outside supporters in some chants, especially after they saw the local media trucks with their big slogans drive up. CHUCK CHAPMAN IS ON YOUR SIDE! But now it was a waiting game. The protesters passed the time on their phones promoting the sit-in through social channels. #DevonShame was once again a trending hashtag, but this time it was national, not just statewide. #OccupyDevon was another popular one.

D'Arcy had been too busy to allow herself to get caught up emotionally. Between manning the phones, juggling Milton's schedule, and coordinating with food services and the like, she'd been on call twenty-four seven. As an

African-American, she sympathized with some of what the protesters were saying, but thought a few of the demands were just silly, even damaging. A dorm set aside exclusively for minority students? That one stuck in her craw. Hadn't they waged an entire civil rights movement precisely to get away from segregation? And how did such notions square with the goals of diversity? Weren't students from different backgrounds supposed to learn from one another? How would that happen if they built walls?

"Sir, may I have a word?" she asked Milton. They slipped out and ducked into a small office clear of students. "Stillman Weathers is here. I put him in the boardroom with the others. Also, you should know we're getting a number of calls from the media, and some are quite persistent. They're parking their trucks illegally. I called the city and police are issuing tickets, but they don't seem to care."

"Thank you, D'Arcy. Put the media on hold for a little longer. I'm going to the boardroom."

"Oh, and, sir? Dean Malik-Adams is insisting on meeting with you as well."

"Tell her to come straight to the boardroom."

"Yes, sir."

Milton entered the boardroom and found the Steering Committee gathered, talking in a corner. Stillman was holding court with the others. There was Patrick Colley and Ben Clifford, along with Allen Devereux, Devon's senior counsel. "Gentleman, so good to see you all!" Milton gave everyone his signature vigorous handshake.

"I had to step over people to get up here!" Ben exclaimed.

"Yes, we have a few students enjoying our hospitality, as you know," Milton said.

"But there are so many. And goodness, the smell!" They turned to see Martika Malik-Adams standing at the door. She looked angry, glaring at Ben.

"Ah, Dean Malik-Adams," Milton said. "Please join us. Let's all sit down and discuss this, shall we? I'd like to think we have an opportunity on our hands."

An hour later, Milton emerged and asked D'Arcy to summon the Cultural Center leadership to the boardroom, where they and the Steering Committee met collectively. D'Arcy, who had no idea what was going on, sat just outside in case she was needed. Ten minutes later, all came out as a group.

"D'Arcy, please tell the media people to gather outside in thirty minutes," said Milton. "We have an important announcement to make." The group, which numbered almost ten, then walked down to Milton's office to speak with as many of the camping protesters as could fit.

Outside, Bingham Plaza had grown dark in the late February afternoon. It had been a quiet day, but now students began to materialize, summoned by those on the inside through their social media channels. The "real" media began to show, too, those with TV cameras. The local affiliates for at least two national networks began setting up shop in front of Stockbridge. As the crowd reached a critical mass, they began to chant.

"No justice, no peace!

"No justice, no peace!"

Minutes later, the enormous double doors swung open and a beaming Milton Strauss walked out, followed by Stillman Weathers and the Steering Committee as well as dozens of students. Their appearance prodded the growing crowd to chant louder still. Milton stood on the top step, illuminated by the bright lights of television cameras. He waited a few moments to let the moment build. There was no microphone, but someone handed him a bullhorn. He felt like a young revolutionary again.

Motioning with his arms for the crowd to quiet, he raised the bullhorn to his mouth. "It's so great to see everyone here today. I just want to let you know how much I appreciate everything you do to promote justice and social equity."

More cheering.

"Dean Malik-Adams and I just met with Stillman Weathers, the chair of Devon's Board of Governors, as well as the board's Steering Committee, and students representing the Afro-American Cultural Center. We are pleased to make the following announcement. Devon University will immediately earmark $50 million to further the goals of racial diversity and inclusion."

A *whoo-hoo* of surprise and delight coursed through the crowd. By this time, Malik-Adams had shouldered her way up so she was next to Milton. She grabbed his hand and waved their intertwined hands in the air, lending the impression of running mates. Camera flashes popped everywhere.

Milton beamed and once again motioned for quiet. "But that's not all."

# Drop the Mic

# Devon Daily

February 14

## President Strauss Announces New Minority Initiatives

President Strauss announced yesterday that the university will undertake broad new initiatives for minority diversity and inclusion. Speaking to protesters from the steps of Stockbridge Hall, Strauss said that Devon will allocate $50 million toward various goals including boosting faculty representation for marginalized voices, ongoing sensitivity training for faculty members, and the hiring of at least a dozen new counselors and staff psychologists of color.

Responding to accusations from minority students that the curriculum is "hegemonic," Strauss is implementing a new course requirement for all incoming first-years called Identity and Privilege. The course, to be constructed by student leaders and professional diversity consultants, will focus on "micro-aggression self-awareness" and "understanding voices of oppressed peoples."

In the wake of an incident of racist language at Beta Psi fraternity, Strauss said he will also be asking the board to consider ways to phase out the fraternity system. A new panel, called the Committee on Fraternal Life at Devon, will be convened immediately to consider the matter.

Lastly, a $1 million grant will also be made to the endowment of the Afro-American Cultural Center.

These announcements came after the extended occupation of Stockbridge Hall by protesting students and an emergency meeting of the Board of Governor's Steering Committee. The developments appear to have brought the occupation to an end as students were seen dispersing from Stockbridge. However, Afro-American Cultural Society president Jaylen Biggs sounded a tempered note, saying, "Fifty million dollars does not buy off centuries of oppression. It's a start."

Stillman Weathers was once again at forty-two thousand feet, enjoying a medium-rare chateaubriand with a glass of 2005 Volnay En Carelle. He settled back in his cabin chair. Things had gone well. The black students should be pleased, and order had been restored. He was slightly bothered by the rather large amount they would be spending in the search for black professors. Not that they couldn't afford it, and not that he had anything against more minority faculty, per se, but he just wasn't sure how many black physics professors there were to go around. (Was he racist to wonder that?) To get the numbers of new hires to which they had publicly committed, they would have to hire minority professors where they could find them, and that likely meant further building out the "studies" departments like African-American Studies. This, in turn, meant finding more students to fill those classes, which meant further boosting minority enrollment. Not that he had a problem with *that*, of course, but those departments did tend to radicalize their students. The Steering Committee had come to a consensus quickly; there hadn't been any real discussion or analysis . . . he wondered whether they had just poured fuel on a longer-term fire.

Ah well, he would probably be off the board before all that happened, if it even did. He pushed the button in his armrest to summon Jenny, who materialized from behind a small curtain.

"Yes, sir. Can I get you something?"

"Thank you, Jenny. I believe I will get some shut-eye. Would you mind dimming the cabin lights?"

"Of course, sir." Jenny dimmed the lights as the Gulfstream G650, master of the skies, slipped through the reaches of the stratosphere.

# Lulu Meets the Dean

**LULU WAITED IMPATIENTLY** outside Dean Choudhary's office, dressed in her spin clothes. Right now, she didn't give a shit how she looked for some dean. Her crossed leg bounced up and down. She was pretty sure she was experiencing some sort of clinical depression. Even Song had asked if something was wrong.

In the days since that little scene in the post office, she had holed up in her room. No one at Fellinghams was responding to her emails or texts. She simmered with frustration and hurt when she thought of them. And then *OTA!* What had gone wrong? Had Shelley said something to her mother about the clothes or that ridiculous scepter? Lulu had thought about reaching out to Wendy Faircloth but realized it smacked of desperation. Her inability to do anything was more frustrating than anything else.

What the hell was she doing at the dean's office, anyway? Shitty grades were why most students got hauled in here, and she had no issues there. Her grades were tolerable, mostly B's, although about to head south on account of her not going to class in almost two weeks. The dean of students was someone she might have been just as glad to never meet.

The email had only said:

Ms. Harris,
Please come meet me in my office tomorrow at 11 am. There is a matter I'd like to discuss with you.

Dean Choudhary

Who the hell does that? Just summons you without giving the slightest hint why? What was this "matter"? He could have said he wanted to "catch up and chat," say, and that could have been anything. *Have you thought about going out for a play, Ms. Harris?* Or: *We were hoping you might volunteer for some community outreach.* Instead, it was a "matter." Was it about the scepter? Seriously? She didn't care what some goddamn dean had to say. She was probably just going to drop out anyway. Sheldon would get over it.

The door swung open. It was the dean. "Ms. Harris, would you please come in." She walked in and saw that her nosy RA, Yolanda Perez, was there. What the hell was *she* doing here? Didn't she have posters to pin somewhere?

"Have a seat, please," said the dean.

Lulu settled into one of those wooden "college" chairs, the ones with the spindles and a college crest on the top of the frame.

"Ms. Harris . . ." began Dean Choudhary.

"If this is about the scepter, I can assure you that it's all a silly misunderstanding."

"Yes, about that: I'd like to personally apologize if you were upset by how campus security handled the matter. We're going to make counseling available to you should you want it."

Hmm, that wasn't what she expected. Yolanda still hadn't said a word.

"*However,* I feel obliged to point out that stealing is an expulsion-level offense. Are you aware of this, Ms. Harris?"

Lulu said nothing, but she was thinking she wanted to drop out before the bastards could kick her out. The last thing she needed on top of everything else was people in New York talking about how she got the boot. Oddly, though, the dean didn't sound angry at all. He sounded . . . conciliatory?

"Ms. Harris?"

"I didn't know that, specifically, but really, I didn't steal it."

"There are those who believe otherwise."

"I know, but I am a member of Fellinghams. How could I steal it?"

"*Were* a member, is my understanding."

*Christ, did everyone know about that, too?*

"Ms. Harris, be that as it may, it's come to my attention there may have been an . . . incident."

*Now what?* "Sorry, I'm not sure I know what you're talking about."

"Your RA, Ms. Perez here, has made us aware of something. Something troubling. Yolanda, would you please explain?"

Lulu could see the bulges of Yolanda's flesh pressing through the spindles of her chair. *No one should have to see that,* she thought. Yolanda produced her phone and showed Lulu the photo Yolanda had taken the morning after the Beta party. At least a quarter of Lulu's face was a purplish blue, causing her to instinctively recoil.

"Not pretty, is it?" Yolanda let it sink in. "Harris, I think you were a victim of sexual assault. Actually, I *know* you were. You spent that night somewhere other than your room, you were disheveled and had clearly been drinking, and I don't think you hit *yourself* in the face. We've spoken to members of your former club, and they confirmed you were at the Beta house the night before. One of those animals did this to you, and you need to help us by telling us who it was."

"What Ms. Perez is trying to say is that we'd certainly appreciate your assistance with this," said the dean. "The fraternities have been a troublesome aspect of our culture here at Devon for some time."

"Isn't this my business?" asked Lulu.

"If there's a sexual predator—or predators—on this campus, it's everyone's business," said the dean. "We'd like to identify who it is so appropriate measures can be taken."

"This is all just a big misunderstanding. Really, it is." Lulu looked out the window, wishing she were anywhere else. She should just get up and walk out right now.

"Like the scepter?" asked Yolanda. "You seem to be at the center of a lot of misunderstandings."

Dean Choudhary jumped back in. "Ms. Harris—*Lulu*—we're really just here to help. We—the university, that is—are willing to overlook the whole incident with the scepter if you could assist us in this matter. We need to identify the individual or individuals who did this to you. Under Title IX rules, you will not have to personally confront anyone. I think you will find the process . . . unobtrusive. Indeed, you might find it personally restorative to unburden yourself. It must be a terrible thing to carry around."

Lulu thought about waking up next that hairy thing on the Beta couch. *Ugh.* She was pretty sure she had been a willing participant, but really, who was to say? She couldn't remember a damn thing. Maybe the hairy man-boy roofied her. *He probably did, the creep.* But did she really need to go through any of this shit? It might be fun to get the man-boy in trouble, but if she fessed up, everyone would know she'd had sex with that ape, forced or not. *Yuck!*

She looked at Yolanda and the dean, who both leaned toward her. What was that look on their faces? It was . . . eagerness.

Yolanda jumped in. "We have a whole support network for you here, Lulu. There's no shame in it. You are a survivor." Yolanda was practically glowing as she said the word.

*Survivor.*

Through the hazy fog of her depression, Lulu remembered the article in *Newsweek* about Mattress Girl and how she became world-famous, fêted globally by the media and women's organizations, even attending the State of the Union. She had 2 million followers on Twitter, even more than Cricket Hayes. Lulu's mental gears, addled as they were, ground away as she weighed her options. *Maybe there's a way forward.* Sitting there, with the eager faces of Yolanda Perez and Dean Choudhary boring in on her, it came together.

"All right, it's true."

"Could you be more specific, please?" asked Choudhary.

"There was drinking, then I was assaulted. There was no consent. That bastard did it."

A look of triumph swept over Yolanda's face.

# Rusty's Bar

**THE INVITATION WAS** unexpected. Eph received an email from Fred Hallowell with the subject line *Drink?*

Fred was very senior in the department, and they'd never had much inter-action outside the occasional departmental cocktail party at Titus Cooley's house. Hallowell was on the tenure committee, so this was an invitation Eph could scantly afford to pass up. Besides, he couldn't help but be curious about why Fred was reaching out. Perhaps he would share some insight on how tenure conversations were going.

Hallowell suggested meeting at Rusty's, a bar Eph had only been to once or twice back when he first arrived at Devon. It was about a ten-minute walk, and it was a pleasant evening for early March, so Eph decided to hoof it.

Things turned a bit gritty off the north side of campus, the neighborhood where Rusty's had planted its flag back in the 1950s. Other than Devon and its orbit, Havenport had always been a working-class town, although much of its industry had long departed for other countries or cheaper states down South. In recent years, the university began incentivizing its employees to buy homes locally, so there had been some improvement. You could see the odd restored Victorian here and there right next to another that was falling apart. Crime, while down, was still a fact of life. One walked with awareness, at least at night.

Eph reached Rusty's, which was marked by a blinking neon sign of a yellow-and-white beer mug. It was early, so things were quiet. A few middle-aged men were sitting at the bar, with no students in evidence. That would change later in the evening. The air was pungent with the unmistakable smell of stale beer and grease. The lighting was low, punctuated by neon beer signs and multicolored lights from a classic-era pinball machine. There was also a juke-box, one that still played 45s.

Eph ordered an IPA at the bar and claimed an empty booth. He had the notion that a little privacy was in order, even if he wasn't sure why. He'd thought about bringing D'Arcy, but the setting implied this was to be men only. Women didn't care much for Rusty's. It was a place to drink, and drink hard; a blue-collar bar dressed up in the paraphernalia of *collegium historiae*. Long-forgotten lettermen posed in fading photographs above wooden booths carved with gen-erations of initials.

Each evening, Havenport's workingmen quietly drank Schlitz drafts and blackberry brandy shots at shift's end, then gradually yielded to fist-bumping undergrads with fake IDs, who wouldn't have noticed the postal workers and stevedores at any rate. If asked, most students would have expressed solidar-ity with the Workingman, and indeed, many had taken the time to "like" the cafeteria workers' Facebook page during the recent dining-hall strike. But they were young—Devonites!—and the world lay bare at their feet. There were worlds to conquer and beers to drink. Their sweeping sense of propriety made them blind to certain things.

Fred Hallowell arrived, and Eph's first impression was that he looked im-mensely tired. There were bags under his eyes and his hair looked noticeably grayer around the ears than Eph remembered, which was odd since Eph saw him all the time. Eph didn't know how old Fred was, but guessed midfifties. Fred smiled in Eph's direction and motioned that he would stop at the bar first. (There was no such thing as waitress service at Rusty's.) He returned to the booth with a draft beer and two shots of whiskey. He pushed one toward Eph.

"Uh, it might be a little early for me," Eph said.

"Fair enough." Fred threw back both shots.

*Hello.*

"Are we celebrating something?"

Fred didn't answer right away. He chased the shots with a deep slug of beer, about a third of it disappearing down his throat. He then wiped his mouth with the back of his hand. "You know, I've always had a soft spot for this place. Used to come here when I was an undergrad. My initials are still in one of the booths, I think."

"I didn't realize you went here."

"Class of '84. Other than my Ph.D. stint at Chicago, been here ever since."

"I imagine things were different back then."

"You could say that." Fred smiled slightly. "Somehow the place got by on a couple billion dollars."

"Tough times," Eph said with the appropriate smirk.

"Devon still looks more or less the same, but everything else about it is different."

"What do you mean? Are you saying things have gone downhill?"

"Not entirely. All the money has its uses. Devon has opened up to a much-broader set of students, and that can only be a good thing."

"But . . ."

Fred stared at his beer a bit. "The kids, for starters. *They've* changed. Sometimes I just want to wring them by the neck."

"Why?"

"I first started noticing it about fifteen years ago, the sense of entitlement. And you know who feels the *most* entitled? The ones who come for free, the ones with no skin in the game. Go figure. No one will say it, but it's true."

"I think there's plenty of entitlement to go around," Eph said.

"You know, when I was a kid, we grew up without a lot of supervision. We were left to solve our own problems. If someone called you a pussy, you called them a pussy back. If they took a swing, you took a swing back. But then parents began to hover, became micromanagers, always there to intermediate, to make sure no one ever got hurt. The kids got it in their heads that someone else would always be there to solve their problems. At the same time, they were constantly told how special they were, even if they hadn't done a goddamn thing to deserve it. So what do you know? Those kids started showing up at Devon a few years later. Buncha vapid infants who were—*are*—completely confident they possess the entirety of the world's received wisdom. Why do we even need to teach them?"

Eph wondered why Fred was unburdening himself to him. They had rarely spoken beyond collegial pleasantries.

"And how, my friend," Fred went on, "does our great university respond to this? By catering to their every whim, by continuing to award shiny trophies for showing up."

"I've heard the word *snowflakes* thrown around. About the kids."

"And don't get me started on the Diversity Industrial Complex," said Fred, apparently moving on to a new thread. "What do those people do all day? Seriously, when they get to their desks in the morning, and they sit down, what do they do?"

"I guess I know more about that than I'd like."

"And no one seems to notice that the more diverse we become, the more fractured things get. Have you looked around a dining hall lately? Segregation is back, only now it's self-imposed. If I hear the word *diversity* one more time, I might lose my shit because they're all in little tribes now. And speech they don't like is being shut down because diversity can't thrive if students hear something that challenges their infantile view of the world. It's a shame, really. And did you hear the black students want their own dorm? Their own goddamn dorm. Martin Luther King is rolling over in his grave."

"I heard something about that. I agree with you on that one, it seems like a step back." Eph took a sip of his beer. "Why does everyone seem so mad all the time?"

"Because outrage is now its own virtue, or hadn't you noticed? They move like a pack from one grievance to the next, never stopping, even for a moment, to appreciate where they are or how far we've come."

A Stones song came on the jukebox. This place was old-school before anyone used the term.

"I'm going to get another," said Fred. "What will you have?"

Eph sensed he didn't have a choice. "Another of these, thanks." He pointed to his IPA. Fred rose and went to the bar, leaving Eph in the booth, still wondering why he was here. Not that he didn't enjoy the chance to get to know one of his senior colleagues better, but he couldn't help but think that something was yet to be said. Was he here to talk about tenure? Whatever the case, Fred was clearly in an impolitic mood, which made Eph uneasy.

Not knowing what else to do, Eph examined the carvings at his table, all preserved under multiple coats of shellac. It was mostly initials with graduation years, like *EJM '82.* Another just said *Mound,* whatever that meant. It looked fresher than most. Someone, decades ago from the looks of it, had carved *Suck my dick* in deeply gouged, two-inch letters. Eph wondered how many hours it took to carve. The effort showed a real commitment to the message. But *Suck my dick?* That was what the table carver, so many years ago, needed to say?

Fred returned with the beers and set them down. A look of sadness crossed his face like a shadow. "I'm tired, Eph. Tired of all of it. I keep getting told what the 'community' wants, or what the 'community' thinks. How many times did we hear that word in the last staff meeting? Blue Feather and Smallwood can barely manage a sentence without saying it. Well, rest assured that every time you hear that word they are not talking about you or me."

"I think the teachers here mean well, at least for the most part. Don't you?"

"A knot of pit vipers, if you ask me, the biggest gossips I've ever met. And I swear, they are as self-entitled as the students. Maybe more."

"I guess." Eph feared the conversation was navigating toward dangerous waters.

"It just wears you down. Do you know I kept track of my time last year? There's an app. Forty-seven percent of my time was spent responding to emails, attending departmental meetings, or dealing with HR."

"Don't you think that's the case everywhere?"

Fred ignored him. "Most of us are just dialing it in, you know. One of the best-kept secrets in the world is how easy this job is, not to mention how overpaid we are to do it. I remember the first time I taught a class; it was a lot of work. You had to construct the course from scratch: figure out the syllabus, the assignments, the tests . . . I'm not telling you anything you don't know. But then the next year rolls around and there you are, teaching the same course. All the heavy lifting is done. Just repeat everything from the year before. Copy and paste. Sure, you tweak here and there, but after a couple of years you can do it in your sleep. That's what it's become, sleepwalking. Is it any wonder most of us drink way too much? Self included." As if to underscore the point, Fred downed another slug of beer.

"I have to say, Fred, I really like teaching. I'm sorry you've grown bored with it, but for me it's a calling. There's nothing I'd rather do."

Fred smiled. "It was like that for all of us at one time or another."

"And also, I like it here. Devon is home to me." Eph hoped he wasn't being too confrontational, but the conversation was starting to annoy him.

"Hey, I get it. The bubble can be seductive. We float around this beautiful campus all day, maybe go see a famous guest lecturer or meet brilliant visiting fellows, do a little research. But it's not real, none of it. Getting less so. Do you know what they charge for tuition these days?"

"Around seventy K, isn't it?"

"Seventy-five. To live here and take eight or so classes over two semesters. Every year it goes up to pay for all the new deans who push paper around. But the bubble is so comfortable that no one wants to talk about how it's going to pop. Eph, I tell you, there's a tidal wave coming for higher ed, and it's going to take out a lot of schools. Excuse the mixed metaphor."

"But you don't think that could happen here, do you?"

"Oh, Devon will survive. It has the brand. And the money. Devon will be here when the sun cools. But it will slowly lose relevance."

"Okay, I get it now. You invited me here to give me a career pep talk. I have to tell you, Fred, you're not very good at it."

Fred leaned back. "I'm sorry. You're nice to let me vent a little, or a lot, but it's wrong of me. You're idealistic and I admire that. Please accept my apologies."

"Sure, it's no problem. Really."

Hallowell took a deep breath. "Listen, I'm aware of the elephant in the room. You should know I think you're a good guy, a good teacher, and the best candidate."

"I appreciate that." Eph allowed himself to swell with optimism, but then he noticed Fred wasn't exactly sharing in the moment of colleague-to-colleague bonhomie. Something was off, something Fred wasn't saying.

"I'm afraid to ask . . . was there a *but* in there?"

Fred now looked, what, nervous? "There's something you should know, Eph. Something I was informed of earlier today. It's why I asked you here." Fred took one more sip of beer.

"A student named Louise Harris has accused you of sexual assault."

# The Tarzan of Anderson House

**HOLED UP IN** her altogether pathetic room, it was not lost on Lulu what a shitstorm her accusation was about to unleash.

She was counting on it.

If she felt badly for what she was about to put Ephraim Russell through, those thoughts were fleeting. Mostly, there was the despair at *her* new circumstances—her dénouement at the society and callous treatment at the hands of *OTA*. The weight of these things, the public embarrassment, required dispatching. Throwing in with the feminists didn't exactly thrill her—they were *so* unattractive—but it was a necessary course correction.

But . . . she needed some time to think. This had to be played just right.

She needed a plan. Simply being another run-of-the-mill "survivor" would not suffice. That market was getting crowded. Some of the early girls got a lot of play, sure, but only Mattress Girl had transcended her own campus. The mattress angle was clever, but it had been done. Lulu needed a bigger play, something original.

She wasn't sure why, but a story that Sheldon had once told her about his freshman year popped into her head. She did some googling to refresh herself on the details.

Late one night, all those years ago, someone had lowered a window on the fifth floor of Anderson House, a freshman dorm in East Quad right across from Duffy. Yelling into the darkness, he executed a perfect Tarzan call, right out of the back-lot jungles of Metro-Goldwyn-Mayer. It went largely unnoticed, but then he did it again the next night. And the next, and the next after that, all at precisely the same time: 11:09.

After a week or so, a small crowd began to gather, eager for the nightly Tarzan call. That no one knew the would-be Tarzan's identity added to the crowd's general sense of ironic self-amusement. (No one liked arch, ironic humor more than Devonites.) It was always dark and Tarzan never stuck his head out far enough to be identified. No one in Anderson was talking, either. When the *Daily* wrote a piece about it, the crowds got larger, numbering in the hundreds each night, their excitement often fueled by alcohol. Tarzan developed a sense of drama, now delaying his nightly calls by a few minutes to build the anticipation. Other pseudo-Tarzans would call out from Pope and Kimball, but these pretenders were always roundly booed. Only the Anderson House Tarzan was worthy of the crowd's adoration. They chanted, "Tarzan, Tar-zan," building in volume until, at last, he would come.

As the fame of the Anderson House Tarzan grew, someone at the *Daily* wrote, "I was reminded of those old film reels from Mussolini rallies in the thirties, where the crowd would scream 'Il Duce' over and over until he appeared on the balcony." Tarzan-themed parties sprang up around campus, serving "jungle juice" (naturally), and campus conversations were of little else. Things in East Quad eventually got so unruly that the administration felt the need to intervene. They narrowed the possible Tarzans down to five and let it be known through the Anderson RAs that Tarzan could have one final call, and then no more.

That night, over a thousand people gathered in East Quad, many dressed as Tarzan or Jane. There were one or two ape suits as well. The Devon Marching Band showed up, playing "The Lion Sleeps Tonight" over and over, it being the only jungle-themed song they knew. A reporter from the *CBS Evening News* even came, planning on doing one of those human-interest pieces that come at the end of the broadcast, the ones that always start with "And finally tonight . . ." All this had the effect of whipping the crowd into a barely contained frenzy. One observer later described them as a "mob, coiled as a spring." Finally, the window opened, and a single hand emerged to silence the faithful. As a midnight calm fell, there came the most beautiful, perfectly executed Tarzan call that anyone had ever heard. When it stopped, there were a few moments of reverent silence, the crowd moved by the beauty of what they had just heard.

And that's when everyone pretty much lost their minds.

They became a mob in seconds, throwing rocks at Anderson, smashing most of the windows. Were they angry that they could no longer have their Tarzan? Perhaps. Or were they just whipped up into a frenzy of self-amusement? Those asked later didn't have an answer. It just seemed like the thing to do.

Having dispensed with Anderson, the mob moved out onto Dudley Street, trampling cars, tearing off their shirts, making apelike jungle noises and beating their chests. By the time the Havenport police arrived, over a dozen vehicles had been damaged. Two dozen students spent the night as guests of the city. The *CBS Evening News* got its story, but it was no longer of the human-interest variety. The lead-in was "Violence Erupts on Devon Campus."

No one ever did figure out who Tarzan was. Sheldon said that at his twenty-fifth reunion at least seven classmates claimed the Tarzan mantle for themselves, though he knew the real Tarzan would never be one to take personal credit.

Reading the story, and further considering the tale of Mattress Girl, Lulu hatched a plan. She'd have to put herself out there, really out there, but that's what it would take to separate her from the pack. It might just work. In Silicon Valley, they called this a pivot.

Lulu 2.0.

She flipped open her MacBook Air and jumped on eBay, entering a search term. They had everything on eBay. Sure enough, they had over a dozen of what she was looking for, although she required only one. She opted for "Buy It Now" and arranged for overnight delivery. The only thing left was deciding what to wear.

That always took some thought.

# The Passion of Lulu

**LULU STOOD IN** the vestibule of Grafton Hall, home of the English Department and Ephraim Russell's classroom. The dilemma regarding what to wear for her social experiment had been resolved neatly. Most—well, *all*—of her clothes were designer, and she hated the idea of ruining them. Also, rich and privileged wasn't what she was going for here. She had considered blue jeans, but they would rip, and nothing said chic like distressed jeans, so jeans were out, too. Then she'd had an idea, one she thought terribly clever. She ran out to the—*ugh*—Gap that morning and bought three pairs of khakis and a couple of blue button-down shirts. Back at Duffy, she tried them on and examined herself in the mirror. God knows, she wouldn't be caught dead wearing something like this under normal circumstances, but the outfit hit the mark. Khakis and blue button-downs were exactly what Ephraim Russell wore every day. That the outfit was vaguely butch was an added bonus; it would play with the militant fems. She'd also made it a point to go without makeup and not wash her hair.

She picked up a gym bag she'd brought and removed the lone item inside: an old cast-iron ball and chain. There had been plenty to choose from on eBay, including fake plastic ones, but plastic wouldn't do. It cheapened the message. The real ones ranged in weight from seven to fifteen pounds; she'd gone with the seven-pounder. No need to make this any harder than it was already going to be.

Tossing the gym bag aside, Lulu clasped the bracket around her right ankle and slipped a pin through the small hole to secure it. She wore heavy socks, hoping to avoid too much chafing.

She walked out the door, ball in her arms, and glanced at her watch. It was a cheap Casio purchased that morning. (Her Cartier?—not on earth.) It was precisely nine p.m. She'd deliberately chosen a quiet hour so there would be no confusing her "mission" with anything else that might be going on. *This is going to be a serious pain in the ass, but fuck it. Fuck all of them.*

Taking a deep breath, she dropped the iron ball onto the stone path. It made an enormous *clank.* A couple of nearby students turned and looked, but only briefly. Strange things were always happening on campus. Lulu then dropped to all fours and began.

To crawl.

She painted her face with a look of tragedy, one she'd practiced in the mirror earlier. And she crawled. It was slow going, but she crawled.

Her route was carefully thought out. Beginning at Grafton, it crossed Bingham Plaza, traveled down Mathers Walk, across Dudley Street, and through the East Quad gate. Fortunately, Duffy was the first house on the Quad. Crossing Dudley might be tricky, but traffic should be light this time of the evening. All told, the journey was about 250 yards, and it was going to completely suck.

As she crept across the largely empty Bingham Plaza, the iron ball made a metallic, scraping sound as it dragged behind her. Bingham was a broad granite space bordered by Grafton, Stockbridge, and the Dix. Piles of snow were still around but the path was clear. Just a puddle here and there.

The iron ball didn't seem to be an issue yet, but her knees concerned her. It wasn't like she'd ever crawled hundreds of yards on stone before, plus it was fucking *cold.* She only had the button-down, plus a T-shirt underneath. The granite felt even colder than the air, and the feeling of it seeped up through her hands and arms. Gloves would have been nice, but they might also have lessened the visual, the *authenticity.*

She almost laughed at that thought. This was perhaps the least authentic thing she'd ever done, but if she'd noticed anything in her half year at Devon, it was that people here were gullible as hell, particularly if the message was something they wanted to hear.

A few students noticed her, but only laughed. Was it sorority pledge season? Perhaps an art project? She made her way down Mathers, with its rows of antique streetlights poking through the snowbanks. Some other students came from the other direction but gave her a wide berth. *God, I feel stupid*, Lulu thought.

Arriving at Dudley Street, she considered her situation. Mathers dead-ended into the normally busy street, and she needed to get across. There was a crosswalk, and a traffic light that was activated by a large metal button. She crossed here several times a day and knew that pushing the button activated a green light with a fifteen-second countdown timer. That wasn't much time (city planners hadn't taken potential crawlers into account), but standing and walking was out of the question. Reaching up, she pushed the button. A few seconds later the light changed to green and several cars came to a stop. She crawled out into the street, one hand after another, right through the glare of headlights. Both her hands and knees were in considerable discomfort. Half-way across, the orange numbers on the countdown timer said five seconds. She was shuffling as fast as she could, considering she was dragging a large iron ball, but it wasn't fast enough. Still, she refused to stand. When the timer ran out, she had at least twelve feet to go. Several cars started honking. One man leaned out his window and yelled, "Crazy bitch!" Another just drove right around her, horn blaring. Lunging the last few feet, she finally reached the other side. She waited a few moments, catching her breath and allowing her pulse rate to subside. *Shit, that was no fun.* Thankfully, the gates to East Quad were right in front of her. It only remained to go through them, take a brief left, and she was at the entrance to Duffy.

Three stone steps led up to Duffy's door. When she reached there, some-one came out, a classmate. "Hey, are you okay?"

Lulu said nothing. She didn't—*wouldn't*—respond. The boy walked on, perplexed.

She made her way up the three steps, each bowed by generations of under-graduate feet. Standing at last, she turned to face East Quad. The large yard had crisscrossing paths and six separate freshman dorms. It was mostly empty at this hour, with most of her classmates either in their rooms or at a library. She could see maybe a dozen people out near the center of the quad walking this way or that.

Then, to an audience of none, Lulu drew a deep breath of cold air and threw her arms back, as if offering herself. And she let out the longest, loud-est scream of her life.

# The Story Breaks

## Devon Daily

March 18

## Professor Accused of Assault

Assistant Professor of English Ephraim Russell has been accused of sexual assault by one of his students, the *Daily* has learned. According to a source inside the administration, the assault took place in Grafton Hall in December. Dean Arjun Choudhary has confirmed Professor Russell has been suspended pending an investigation. Graduate students in the English Department have been asked to take over his two classes.

This is not the first time Professor Russell has been at the center of troubling events. In October, he was accused by students of allowing racially insensitive language to be used inside his classroom, a charge that was ultimately dismissed.

In a possibly related story, a student, identified as first-year Louise Harris, has been waging an unusual protest for the last several days. At the same time each evening, Harris has been seen crawling with an iron ball and chain from Grafton to her dorm on East Quad. There, she stands each night and screams. A handful of students have started to accompany her on her nightly journey and have joined in the scream. Drew Stokes, a sophomore, is one of those who has been following Harris on her nightly crawl. "Clearly, this is a cry against gender violence," he told the *Daily*. Others seemed to agree.

Harris herself has not responded to repeated requests for comment, and she remains steadfastly silent during her nightly procession. It can be confirmed, however, that she was a student in Russell's English 240 class this fall. Furthermore, Russell's classes are given at Grafton, where Harris begins her crawl each night. One person even noted that Harris's clothes are similar to those typically worn by Russell. While these facts are suggestive of a connection between Harris and the accusations against Russell, it cannot be confirmed at this time.

Eph stared blankly at the brick walls of his apartment. All he'd been told was that he was suspended pending an investigation. Teaching assistants would take over his classes. He could have learned all that in the *Daily*.

After he got word, he'd headed to Grafton to collect some things from his office. They only allowed him in after conducting a "search." For what, Eph had no idea. He noticed that a couple of the departmental offices near him had SAFE SPACE stickers on their doors. Were those there before?

He'd hardly been able to function since his night at Casey's with Fred Hallowell. D'Arcy had been sympathetic, but Eph could swear he heard doubt in her voice. They'd met earlier in an empty classroom to talk.

"Why do you suppose that girl would make something like this up?" she asked.

Eph had played that day in the office over and over in his head. "How the hell should I know?" He allowed his frustration to show. "I think she was annoyed I wasn't interested in her. Or, maybe she's just crazy. In fact, based on my experience with her, I'm quite confident that's the case."

"I recognize her from around campus. She doesn't strike me as the militant type. She's always wearing expensive clothes, for one. And why would she bail you out on *Huck Finn* just to do this to you now? It doesn't make sense."

"Not to me, either. But she apparently now thinks it's good sport to ruin my life." Eph also told D'Arcy something else Fred Hallowell had told him that night: that the university had a photo of Eph and Harris, in his office, dated the same day as the alleged assault. He recalled that Harris had sent him that photo. Did the university look through his emails? The thought made him nauseous.

"I don't get it. Why did you take a picture with her?"

"She just ran around my chair and took it. It was a selfie. I don't know why."

"But why would she just *do* that?"

Eph was getting angry, although more at circumstances than D'Arcy. "Again, I don't know. Maybe she planned all this. Or maybe, as I said, she's batshit crazy. Just look at what she's doing, crawling around and screaming every night like some animal."

"Hey, I'm on your side. I'm just trying to understand, okay? Maybe you should tell me everything."

"She came to my office to drop off a paper. She hands in her paper and then tells me *she* was the one who cleared me on *Huck Finn.* Then she starts talking all flirty, and just when I'm trying to process the shift in the conversation, she jumps on my damn lap and plants her face on mine. I shove her off, she gets up, takes the picture, and leaves. Door was open the whole time. End of story."

"And that's it?"

"She came by my office one previous time to talk about her paper topic. Also, she emailed a lot, but it seemed like harmless stuff. Other than that, she was a face in the crowd."

"Why didn't you tell me any of this at the time?"

"I don't know. I should have, but it was right around that other stuff, and I guess I didn't want you to think I was some kind of magnet for trouble."

D'Arcy thought about this. "Listen, I believe you. Of course I do. This will work out, just like the last time. I think this girl may be troubled. Let me keep my ear to the ground and see what I can find out."

"Don't do anything that'll get you in hot water. Please."

"I'll be careful."

Sitting alone in his apartment, Eph knew what had been left unsaid, that the stakes were higher this time, much higher. Devon had erected a wall of silence. Not even Titus was returning his calls. Tenure? That was a fantasy Eph could put to bed. This was about survival now.

His apartment seemed even smaller than usual.

# The Crawl: Day Ten

**"THE CRAWL" HAD** turned into a growing nightly procession. Yolanda Perez mustered some troops from the Devon Womyn's Collective. The collective's president, Pythia Kamal, started coming by the fifth day. Kamal was a Fourth Wave feminist, believing in the use of modern technology and social tools to advance the cause. The Crawl was tailor-made for Fourth Wave feminism. Others who came didn't go to Devon at all but heard about Lulu through the collective's outreach. There were better than a hundred now, many carrying candles in silence.

Lulu never spoke, not a single word. Nor did she make eye contact or engage with anyone in any way. It lent the impression of a fugue state, a damaged soul. She just crawled and crawled, the iron ball scraping along behind her. The others let her lead, following slowly in her wake, a slow-motion parade. By the eighth day, Pythia realized that complete silence didn't translate well on social channels so she started a chant. She would yell, "Crawl!" And the others would answer with "Peace!"

*"Crawl!"*

*"Peace!"*

Even though Lulu wasn't talking, it was widely understood she was the victim in the Russell case. The clothes, the route, the timing . . . the message was there for anyone to decipher, and she was gaining considerable stature from her choice to protest symbolically. There was a power to it.

Part of the way down Mathers, a familiar voice cut through the chanting. "Lulu, what the fuck are you doing?"

It was Shelley. Lulu kept crawling, eyes focused on nothing.

"I had to see for myself. You know damn well this is bullshit. Do you hear me?"

Pythia Kamal quickly interceded. "How *dare* you. Lulu's a *survivor*. We honor survivors on this campus!"

"Kiss my ass. *No one is buying this,* Lulu. And, not that I really care, but when your bullshit is exposed, you're only going to make it harder for *real* victims to come forward. What about them?"

Several people stepped up and surrounded Shelley. "You need to leave. *Now.* This is a peaceful march," said one male student, striding toward Shelley, chest thrust out.

"So these are your new friends, Lulu? Attractive lot you've hooked up with." A few marchers hissed at that, which struck Shelley as pathetic.

Lulu still gave no indication she knew Shelley was there, which was hard, because she wanted to belt Shelley in the nose. But how could she? She was in a fugue state.

"All of you can piss off," Shelley barked. With that, she turned and left.


Lulu's followers had solved the problem of crossing Dudley each night. Once the light turned green, they made two lines across, forming a human channel. The light would always change when Lulu was about halfway, but traffic had effectively been blocked. Horns would blare, but not a single person would break rank until she was safely across. The honking also served notice to the nearby dorms in East Quad that the Crawl was close. Dozens would run downstairs to join the primal scream. Most were supporters, some just enjoyed a good scream.

Turning the corner into the quad, the crowd waiting in East Quad appeared twice as big as yesterday. Not sure what the appropriate reception was, some snapped, while others clapped, and they came to walk next to Lulu for the final few feet. Making it to the top of the steps, Lulu stood. She breathed heavily, her chest heaving with the effort. On her face was a thousand-mile stare, fixed on nothing and no one. The crowd quieted at this moment, as they had learned to do. Then Lulu threw back her arms, looked to the sky, and screamed. This deep and tortured scream went for as long as she could hold a single breath. The crowd stood, transfixed by this perfect distillation of distaff rage. When her voice finally trailed off, Lulu simply turned and entered Duffy. There was a pause, then the crowd answered with their own scream, throaty and maniacal, a single contrapuntal note.

*We understand your pain.*


When Lulu got up to her room, she was thankful Song wasn't there. Song rarely got back from the library before eleven. Lulu removed the ball and chain from her ankle and stripped off her crawling clothes, donning a terry-cloth robe. *Someone needs to teach those women how to dress,* Lulu thought, flopping on her bed. All denim and flannel and unfortunate looking T-shirts with phrases like SMASHING THE PATRIARCHY IS MY CARDIO.

Lulu's khakis were thoroughly frayed. This wasn't an issue, of course. A ragamuffin appearance only reinforced her victim status. Her knees were in pretty sorry shape as well, even though she'd started taping them every day. Fortunately, she'd found a halfway decent day spa, and she slipped in there quietly every morning to get a massage and soak in one of their Jacuzzis. It was a few blocks from campus and pretty much off the beaten track. Her daily visits required missing several classes, but whatever.

Lulu giggled to herself thinking about what she'd overheard one marcher say, that she admired Lulu's "purity of purpose." What an idiot. But what was that phrase? *Useful* idiot?

The whole "suffering in silence" routine was playing out better than she could have imagined. Offered no specifics on which to grasp, her supporters were coming up with all sorts of progressive click bait on their own. One chick in the *Daily* said that Lulu's silence was a "pregnant commentary on gender power imbalances." Another marched with duct tape over her mouth in sympathy with Lulu's silence. (It was a good visual on Snapchat but a dilemma for those who preferred to chant.)

In the beginning, Lulu had kept silent so she wouldn't have to engage with these clowns. Now it was something more. Her silence was infused with meaning.

Perhaps the hardest thing, other than the toll this was taking on her body, was maintaining a tragic mien. *Crawl. Peace. Crawl. Peace.* Lulu did her best not to laugh when they started up with that. She was the one who thought that up. It was enormously frustrating that she couldn't share what she was pulling off. *God,* she so wanted to tell someone.

It had been around day four she'd come up with the phrase *Crawlpeace,* using it as a Twitter hashtag. It was getting real traction. Lulu had never bothered with Twitter before, dismissing it as the realm of political nerds, but now she found it quite useful. Her Twitter bio simply read, "Student. Friend. Crawling for peace." She diligently avoided specifics, instead throwing bumper-sticker memes into the ether and letting people think what they wanted. What she may or may not have meant by *peace* or anything else was left to the observer. Her last couple of tweets had been *Unity = Disruption. #Crawlpeace* and *Change is the new normal. #Crawlpeace.*

She boned up on progressive nomenclature, too, peppering her tweets with words like *intersectionality, agency,* and *transmisogyny,* all while really saying nothing at all. She let others create the narrative. This meant she was bulletproof, no matter how this played out. There was no story, nothing to defend. Let people project their own stupid issues. The nut jobs here have enough of them. Undergraduate culture was a petri dish of psychoses.

That she was, behind the scenes, falsely accusing someone had given her pause at the start. The feeling passed. Collateral damage was acceptable in every war, even if this was a war about which she didn't particularly care.

She *could* have, though. Cared. If she were one of those strident fems, the butchy ones who were always angry about something, well, then collateral damage was easily justified for the greater cause. That she wasn't a butchy fem and was merely playing the part seemed a minor detail.

This morning, when she'd checked her social media accounts at the spa, she had nine thousand followers on Instagram, up over a thousand from just the day before, and about five thousand on her new Twitter account. She'd decided to delete all the old frivolous social posts on Instagram, especially the duck faces. That was Lulu 1.0—Lulu 2.0 was a more serious affair.

Pulling out her phone now, she checked on the Reddit page someone had created about Crawlpeace. There were over seven hundred comments. Then she checked again on her usual socials—Instagram, Snapchat, Twitter . . . *Holy shit.* Sarah Silverman had retweeted her! Silverman had added, "So brave. Keep crawling, sister!" She even used the #Crawlpeace hashtag. Sarah Silverman had

12 million followers. *Twelve freaking million.* Silverman's retweet had already been retweeted itself sixteen thousand times and had twenty-five thousand likes. *Ho-ly shit!*

Lulu fell back on her bed and squealed, kicking her legs at the air.

*Fuck you, Shelley Kisner. You, too, Aubrey St. John.*

*Fuck all of you.*

# Milton's in a Bind

**MILTON TOOK HIS** usual route. In the last few days, the stone pathways had been transformed from their natural slate gray to an explosion of bright colors. On many campuses, "chalking," as it was known, had become a vibrant means of political expression. Pathways at schools like Oberlin and Wesleyan had become veritable chalk tributaries. Officially, Devon had a policy against it, although Milton knew this stemmed from aesthetic concerns more than anything else. He wasn't about to kick the hornet's nest over some pink and orange chalk. Besides, important speech issues were involved. As he would remind anyone who listened, freedom of speech was one of Devon's core principles. Chalking was just how the students were exercising theirs.

Sometimes, of course, Milton had to make a judgment call. People like Foster Jennison needed to understand the full picture. For instance, just recently the Devon Republican Club had invited that conservative provocateur to speak on campus, the one who believed transgenderism was a mental disorder. After multiple threats of violence Milton canceled the event. Safety of the students had to come first. And really, the man was crazy. Devon was not obligated to confer its prestige on crazy people.

The messages covering Mathers all concerned this girl, Harris. Milton walked over ones saying such things as

Devon stands with survivors

and

Lulu for President!

Also *#Crawlpeace* was chalked everywhere. Catchy, he thought.

Milton had a growing admiration for Lulu Harris. Last night, he'd worked late and watched the procession cross Bingham from his office window. There was a religiosity about it he found moving. He could feel the poor girl's agony as she crawled along in tattered clothes. Clearly, she had suffered a great trauma and was striking a chord with the community. The crowd must have been three hundred strong, and they followed solemnly behind her, chanting sometimes. Minutes after he could no longer see them, he heard the tortured scream all the way from East Quad. It was haunting.

Milton knew all eyes would be on him to see how he dealt with this. What a crazy year it had been. Just when one problem died, another sprang up. How could something like this assault have happened at Devon? This was an enlightened institution! This professor, Russell, it was the second time this year he was in the thick of it. Well, all that would be taken care of soon enough. Lulu Harris clearly wasn't making this up. No, that was impossible.

Inside Stockbridge, D'Arcy intercepted him before he could even enter his office. "Sir, Stillman Weathers is on the phone for you."

Milton sighed. He fantasized how much easier life would be if he didn't have to deal with a board. Or alums. "I'll take it inside," he said. Shutting the door, he traversed the vast space of his office and picked up the receiver. "Stillman! How are you?"

"Not happy, Milton. Not happy at all. I'm in the middle of closing a deal and I have to field an angry call from Foster Jennison. It seems he was watching one of the morning news shows today, and his beloved university is getting national exposure for what? A new scientific breakthrough? Nobel Prize winners? No, for some goddamn girl crawling around in ripped-up clothes because we apparently have a faculty full of rapists! Christ, Milton, we just finished putting out a fire and now this. What the *hell* kind of show are you running up there?"

Milton blanched. People from the outside had a directness he found regrettable. "I understand your concerns, Stillman, I do. But this girl is free to express herself." Milton picked up a pile of his messages and started flipping through them.

"But this is the same goddamn professor as before, right? Just get rid of the sonuvabitch. Then the problem of the girl goes away."

"He's been suspended. There is a process we have to follow." One of his messages jumped out. George Carrillo from the DA's office. *Please call re Ephraim Russell.* "And it looks like the DA is now interested. I just got a message."

"The DA? Shit. More publicity."

"Well, that cat's out of the bag, I'm afraid."

"Yes, but the legal process is slow, and the publicity will drag on. Just fire his ass and then he's not our problem anymore. Need I remind you that most of Foster's gift for the new houses is still only a pledge? A pledge, as in, *the money is not in the bank.* And I can tell you the man is not happy."

"I assure you, Stillman, this situation is my top priority."

"I can only assume it is." Stillman hung up, leaving Milton staring at the phone.

There was a quiet knock at the door.

"Yes, come."

It was D'Arcy. "Sir, Dean Malik-Adams would like"—Martika marched in around D'Arcy before she could finish her sentence—"a word."

"There's something you and I need to talk about," Martika said.

"Go a—"

"It's the Russell situation. We need to immediately convene the Title IX Tribunal to deal with this." Devon's Title IX Department reported to Martika, as it happened.

"Yes, Stillman Weathers just called, the DA's office, too." Milton waved the message in the air. "You don't think we should let the justice system take care of this? There *is* an alleged crime, after all."

"Absolutely not."

"I beg your pardon?"

"We don't want them involved. This is a university matter."

"But a crime may have been committed, Martika. He's not tenured. We could just fire him and let the legal system deal with it. In fact, that's what Stillman wants to do."

"We can let the justice system have Russell later."

"Why?"

"Failure to act expeditiously in a case like this—one that's receiving national attention—could easily land us on the OCR watch list, and I think you know what happens then. . . ."

"The OCR . . . ?"

"The Office of Civil Rights within the federal Department of Education."

"Oh, right." He'd forgotten the acronym. The OCR. The people who could turn off the federal spigot. How many research projects would he have to kill? *All those angry professors . . .*

"You remember what happened with Beta Psi a few years ago . . ."

He did indeed. "But isn't firing him acting expeditiously? What's more expeditious than that? Plus, he's out of our hair."

Martika sat down on the couch. "I can assure you that the OCR won't see it that way. They will want a faster result than the criminal justice system can provide, and they are watching schools like ours to make sure we have the procedures in place to deliver those results."

Milton looked confused, so Martika continued. "Let me put it this way. Title IX allows us more . . . *latitude* in how to conduct things. Title IX procedures, as laid out by the government itself, do not constrict us in the same ways as the criminal justice system."

"So what you're saying is that justice might be served more . . ."

"Expeditiously. We can find guilt with a preponderance of evidence—fifty point one percent—which is far more straightforward than the 'beyond a reasonable doubt' standard in courts. We can't send this bastard to jail— hopefully that comes later—but we can deal with him here in our own way, quickly. If the DA gets involved, the whole thing gets bogged down in discovery motions and evidentiary procedures and whatnot, and then we might not be seen as justified in firing Russell until there's a guilty verdict. If we keep things in-house, we can do things our way. *Fairly*, of course."

"But this won't impinge upon Professor Russell's rights in any way, am I correct? I mean there's due process, right?"

"There's a process."

"What does that mean?"

"Let me put it this way. Professor Russell will have the same rights as everyone else who gets accused of a Title IX violation."

Milton considered his conversation with Stillman. A quick resolution was certainly desirable, and Milton *did* just get Martika's assurance that Professor Russell would be treated fairly. "Of course, the Harris girl may file a complaint with the DA. Then I suppose it's out of our hands . . ."

"*Woman.*"

"What?"

"Harris *woman.*"

"Yes, of course. The Harris woman."

"She hasn't filed a thing."

"How do you know that?"

"I have a friend in the DA's office, so I took the liberty of checking. She hasn't filed. Right now, all that's happening is that the DA sees all the publicity and is trying to horn in. This is a potentially high-profile case and it happens this is an election year. They are welcome to have Russell when we're done here."

Milton weighed the pros and cons. His first instinct in any situation was to be cooperative. In his experience, that was almost always the best course. On the other hand, he worried deeply about tangling with the OCR.

As for the Crawl, despite his personal feelings, he was starting to have misgivings there, too. What Lulu Harris was doing was admirable, but not everyone saw it as the creative exercise of free expression that it was. Foster Jennison certainly didn't, and Milton hated to think how much work would be involved making up for Foster's gift should things go south. It could be done—this was Devon—but it might have a knock-on effect to the capital campaign. The development office would scream bloody murder. No one, including Milton, liked asking for money, and ground had already broken on the new houses.

He decided to table the Crawl issue for now. Russell was the more exigent matter. "Very well. Convene the tribunal as soon as you can make it happen."

That will be easy, thought Martika, since she was the tribunal's sole member.

"I will talk to counsel and have them tell the DA that we view this as strictly a university matter for now," Milton continued. "Maybe that will hold them off for a bit. Of course, if the Harris . . . *woman* goes to the DA directly, it's out of our hands."

"Of course. Wise decision."

Martika walked out and went to her own office, the one just down the hall.

# The Summit

**RED WAS BROODING,** angry, but more than that he was panicked. This thing, the Crawl, was taking off without him, and he needed to find a way in. On top of that, his mojo, his status as *the* progressive leader on campus, had been totally hijacked by Jaylen Biggs, who was now having private weekly meetings with Milton Strauss. Jaylen thought his shit didn't stink because the Af-Am boys scored that $50 million check. Red set that up! Now, he was watching the same thing happen with the Harris chick. The PSA was standing like idiots on the sidelines with their dicks in their hands.

Red had only met Lulu Harris once. She was doing the whole Manhattan rich-girl thing at that frat party, at least until she was fellating him on the couch like a pro. The girl was definitely a player. Now suddenly she's Joan of Arc? *Give me a fucking break.*

He knew his skepticism hardly mattered. The true test of an idea was not its provable truth, but its utility. That's Progressive Strategy 101, and the Crawl had big-time utility for sure. It had evolved very quickly into a national phenomenon. Red joined the procession every night, but mostly because he needed to be in the game. #Crawlpeace was trending everywhere, bigger than any hashtag the PSA had ever floated. Fucking *New York* magazine did a feature, even calling Harris "The New Face of Feminism." It showed her crawling, from the front, with that thousand-mile stare, exuding hopelessness, a small army of her people walking behind her. (Red briefly wondered if feminists wanted their new face to be one of such abject victimhood—what ever happened to Rosie the Riveter?—but that ship had clearly sailed.)

The exact nature of Red's problem was becoming apparent, and it had been brewing for some time. The Progressive Student Alliance was born in the sixties. Originally a chapter of Tom Hayden's Students for a Democratic Society, it was the first serious activist group on campus. There had been the Devon Democratic Club, of course, but they were about earnest editorials and genteel debates and all that polite crap. The times had called for direct action, not *Robert's Rules of Order*. Growing quickly, the PSA was the only game on campus for committed progressives. They were a big tent for causes of the day . . . the ERA, acid rain, unionization drives . . . Vietnam, of course.

But over time, specialized constituencies broke out and formed their own groups. The greens, LGBTIAQ, the blacks and Hispanics—each now had a major campus organization. Going forward, things threatened to get even more granular. (For instance, there was grumbling in the trans community that LGBTIAQ had too broad an agenda and that issues specific to trans were getting short shrift.) All this left the PSA with a somewhat ambiguous mandate, and despite the overall rise in student activism, the PSA had been losing members steadily. When an issue became hot, students joined the organization that served that particular cause. PSA press exposure had declined as well. When they needed a quote, reporters seldom called the generalist. Red was forced to admit the PSA had become a half-assed group that mostly liked to get high.

On top of all this, Gaia had totally ghosted him. Red heard she'd gone over to the Womyn's Collective. He swore sometimes women should come equipped with user manuals.

Red needed to do something bold to reassert his primacy over Devon's progressive hierarchy. Jaylen had outmaneuvered him on racial issues, and now here he was again, but this time it was the fems grabbing the reins. How odd it was that Professor Russell was once again in the crosshairs. Russell was *his* find, but the fems had moved in, smelling their own big payday courtesy of Uncle Milt.

*Fucking Lulu Harris.* What was she up to? Red, too, had grown up in Manhattan's moneyed quarters, so he knew her type. Upper East Side rich chick, bored by everything. Hooking up with her had been amusing, but he could have been anyone. He was a convenience, a plaything. Not that he had any problem with that, mind you. He also had to admit she'd had the decency to split before he'd woken up.

Red asked the leaders of the various progressive groups on campus to come to the PSA house for a meeting—a "summit," he called it. He promised free beer. All agreed and arrived at the PSA with two or three representatives. No one was entirely clear on the specifics of why they were there, other than a discussion about the Crawl. When everyone was settled, Red stubbed out his clove cigarette on the stone fireplace and hopped up on the raised platform at the end of the room. He saw Gaia was there with the Womyn's Collective. Jaylen also came, which Red hadn't been sure about. They hadn't spoken for some time.

At Red's side was someone the others didn't know. He looked older. Next to both of them was an easel on which rested a blank poster board.

"Thank you for coming and welcome to the PSA," Red said. "Brews are in the tub back there, plus munchies are on the table. I've asked you here tonight because the eyes of the world are on this campus, and I believe we are seeing a moment of cultural impact, a rare opportunity when the needle actually *moves*. I think we should discuss how to best work together. I speak of course about the Crawl, which I know many of us have been joining every night."

"Go, Lulu!" shouted someone in the back. The group, which numbered about thirty, all snapped fingers.

"To this end, I have invited a guest, one with extensive experience in group action, to talk about where to go from here. *Together*. Let's give it up for Julian Knudsen."

Knudsen looked to be early thirties. He had bushy black hair and was dressed in Timberland boots, frayed khakis, and a T-shirt that said YUCK FOU in big white-on-black letters. In the sixties, campus cops would have called him an outside agitator. Red had met him the previous year at Burning Man and was immediately drawn in. Julian took his Marx straight up, no chaser.

"Brothers and sisters, I am honored to be here among you, among the *committed*. Seriously, give yourselves a hand." Julian started snapping to the audience and they responded in kind. "I'm with a group called OSP—Organizing for Social Progress. We are a national organization focusing on collective action at the grassroots level, and let me just say what's going on here is fucking amazing. Just fucking amazing."

More snaps.

"Let me ask you all something. Why are we here? Those of us in this room. What is our greater purpose?" Julian began pacing back and forth like a caged cat.

"Well, *we're* fighting climate crimes," said Mark Levine of the Climate Action Group.

"And we're fighting for LGBT rights," said Kenny Merrill of the LGBT Coalition.

"No, no, *no*," said Julian. "We each have our specific goals, sure, but why are we *all* here? What is our collective purpose?"

"To support Lulu."

"Okay, yes, but I'm thinking more broadly."

"To advance progressive causes," someone said.

"Yes! But how?"

"By defeating our enemies!" someone else shouted.

"Wrong. Precisely wrong. You don't want to defeat them. We want to lose—strategically."

"That makes no sense," came a reply.

"Let me put it differently. The price of any successful attack is a constructive alternative. Alinsky said that. *Alinsky.* Think about it. What happens if you make demands and the other side says yes? That's the moment you have been bought and paid for. They *own* your ass. That's why any demands should always be unreasonably high—*impossible* to comply with. *Never* give the enemy something they can say yes to. My brother Red here told me how Jaylen played it, making dozens of crazy demands. What happened? Devon cut a fifty-million-dollar check, and Jaylen and his crew stay outraged because they didn't get everything on the list. The struggle continues. Why do you think the Palestinians don't have a state? Everyone since Jimmy Carter has offered them one, but they just move the goalposts. Why? Because the moment the struggle succeeds is the moment it ceases to exist, and that is when you lose all power. *True* power lies in the permanent revolution. Arafat knew that. Castro knew that. If you're fighting the establishment, you can't *become* the establishment.

"This is why demands must always be unreasonable. Just as importantly, your outrage must be diffuse, impossible to pin down with specifics. This is also why, my friends, Lulu Harris is a fucking genius. She's taking it to another level. Everyone's making assumptions, but has anyone heard her actually say anything? No. She hasn't said a goddamn thing to anyone, other than some vague shit on social media. And look, she's a national news story."

Julian stopped pacing. The room had grown quiet. Was this guy making some sort of crazy sense? A hand went up, Kirk Browning from the Devon Sustainability Initiative (they had split from the Climate Action Group several years earlier). "This is really confusing. You're saying we want power, but we *don't* want it?"

"We want power—we will *have* power—but we don't want our names on the door. We want to *control* whoever's name is on the door. As progressives, we play the long game. It's the accrual of power through a process of constant agitation. Chip away at the power structure until that same power answers to you. Never provide constructive alternatives because it's a trap—everything becomes your responsibility, and responsibility slows us fucking *down*."

"So what are you suggesting we do?"

"Any mobilization strategy requires a face around which we mobilize anger. Alinsky said pick a target, freeze it, personalize it, and polarize it. The issue of the moment is gender violence, right? So who do you think will be the object of our anger?"

"Men!" offered someone from the Womyn's Collective.

"Hey!" cried Kenny Merrill.

"Come on, people. Think more strategically than that. *Way* too broad. We are but ghosts in the wind about specifics except for this one thing, the *target*."

"Ephraim Russell!"

"Better, but Russell's already roadkill."

"Devon?"

"And who is the face of Devon?"

"Milton Strauss?" someone offered hesitantly.

"Yes!" Julian walked to the easel and flipped over the poster board. There was a large picture of a smiling Milton Strauss. "This is the target. *This* is the man whose name is on the door. Freeze him, and then make demands."

"But he's a progressive, and if I'm being honest, I kinda like him," said Kirk Browning.

"It doesn't fucking matter. You understand me? He is the establishment. He runs a school that houses sexual predators on its staff. We connect the dots between Strauss and Russell. It was all Milton Strauss."

"But if he gets fired, the next guy could be worse. At least Milton shares most of our beliefs."

"The Milton Strausses of the world are obsessed with power and influence, or at least the appearance of it. They will do almost anything to keep it. Look, one of two things is gonna happen. A: he hangs on, but you control him because he's terrified of you. I mean, look how fast he cut that fifty-million-dollar check, am I right? Or B: he goes down, in which case the next guy will be even more terrified of you cuz you took the previous guy out." Julian's eyes glowed with the fullness of a man who was doing precisely what he believed he was on this earth to do. He smiled, seeing understanding dawn on the young ones' faces.

Red stepped in. "I propose we call a student strike. We bring this school to a standstill, blame Milton, and wreck their precious 'brand.' We mobilize around the Crawl, and then we issue a shitload of demands."

"Excuse me." It was Mark Levine, the greenie. "But where is Lulu Harris? Shouldn't she have a say in this?"

"We reached out, several times, but never heard back," Red said. "She seems determined to go solo. But this is bigger than Lulu Harris. Who says she gets to own the underlying issues? No one."

"I don't know," Mark said. "I mean, she started this. I don't see how we do anything without her involvement."

"Did she ask any of us to crawl with her? No, but we do it anyway and I don't hear her complaining. Besides, I'm sure they have been speaking to her at the Womyn's Collective, right?" Red looked over to Pythia Kamal for help.

"Of course," Pythia replied, sounding defensive.

"Well, what does she say?"

"I'm not sure that's any of your business."

In reality, Pythia had absolutely no idea what was on Lulu's mind. Lulu wasn't speaking to them, either, or even to her RA, Yolanda Perez, who was a collective member. The collective had no involvement at all, other than showing up for the Crawl every night. This had been a matter of growing frustration and debate within their ranks, and there were bitter arguments over what to do about it. They had settled mostly on promoting Lulu as an über-survivor. But as far as Pythia was concerned, Red Wheeler didn't need to know any of this.

"You know, Red," Pythia said, "I don't know why we're even here."

"We're here to organize!" said Red.

"No, why *we* are here." Pythia motioned to her fellow reps from the collective. "This is clearly a gender issue, and we're already heavily involved. We don't need your help."

Jaylen Biggs jumped in. "Shit, Red, you just trying to hijack this thing for yo'self—make your little group of hippies relevant again. I know your shit." Pimp-rollin', trash-talkin' Jaylen was here tonight. Rye, New York, Andover-educated Jaylen was nowhere to be seen. "And while we at it, where does this bitch get off using a ball and chain? That's slave shit. She's *appropriatin'*!"

"I beg your pardon?" Pythia stood up, facing Jaylen.

"Cut the shit, Jaylen, we're all on the same side," Red said.

"*Fuck* we are. I know what's up here. We got our fifty mil and you been pissed ever since. You just want some of our action."

Pythia sat back down as the confrontation swiveled back in Red's direction.

"Jaylen, please. You know I think you guys deserved every penny."

"Actually, *we* would like to know something," interrupted Kirk Browning. "How come *them*?" He was looking toward Jaylen and the Af-Am members.

"What?" Red said.

"How come *they* get fifty million dollars? I mean, no one here doubts the struggles for people of color, but seriously? Sit around Milton's office for a few days and you get fifty million dollars? What about the rest of us? We all have valid causes." There was much murmuring at this. Brown was saying what many were thinking but reluctant to say themselves.

"I agree." It was Atepa Smith from the Devon Native American Society. "No one has been more oppressed than we Native Americans. We are the victims of genocide, and we don't understand why African-American causes have been the sole beneficiary of the school's largesse."

Jaylen sneered, "You think you're more oppressed than black people? We were fucking slaves, yo. And how many Indians are at Devon, anyway? Like three? Fuck off."

"But *we* are thirty percent of Devon, and no one gave us fifty million dollars either." It was an Asian kid Red didn't recognize. Who invited *him*?

"You ain't oppressed, so you can fuck off, too," offered Jaylen.

"On the contrary, we built the railroads as slave labor, we were rounded up into internment camps in World War Two, and now our reward is we have to get perfect SAT scores to have any hope of getting into Devon, whereas they roll out the welcome mat when one of you guys nails a twelve hundred. Twelve hundred sucks!"

"Fuck you, man! Go back to the fuckin' library."

"Excuse me," interjected Aaron Gershman from the Devon Hillel Society. "But we came here tonight on behalf of Jewish students to object to the use of the term *survivor.*"

The room erupted in shouting and finger-pointing.

"This is bullshit," Jaylen said. He and half a dozen others from the Cultural Center turned and left, Jaylen waving his middle finger on the way out.

The feminists looked like they were getting ready to leave, too, and Red knew he'd better step in before the meeting completely fell apart. "Comrades, comrades! We are all part of the larger struggle, are we not? Now let's put our heads together and work this out."

"Sorry, Red," Pythia said. "I think the collective can handle this one all on its own." She motioned to her people, and they promptly walked toward the door, including Gaia.

"Pythia, come on!" cried Red, trying his best not to sound desperate.

"Bye, Red." They were gone.

He took stock. Maybe two dozen people were left, but not the right two dozen. Left were the Asians—*useless*—the greens, the Native Americans, the Latinos, the gays, and the Jews, all of whom were now shouting about which group laid claim to the top spot on the hierarchy of oppression. The people Red really needed were gone.

"I thought you said you owned this place," Julian said.

# Devon Daily

## Tribunal Convened as #Crawlpeace Enters Fifteenth Day

The Devon Title IX Tribunal concerning the accusations of sexual assault against Professor Ephraim Russell will convene in the coming days, the *Daily* has learned. The hearing will be conducted by Dean Martika Malik-Adams. The case is widely believed to concern an alleged assault on Louise Harris, a first-year in Duffy Hall. Although Harris has never made an accusation publicly, it is believed her nightly crawl across campus is a symbolic protest over the alleged assault.

Further details about the tribunal are unknown at this time.

Meanwhile, #Crawlpeace has become a phenomenon extending far beyond the confines of the Devon campus. Many livestream the event on Facebook or YouTube. Adding to the spectacle, members of the Devon Womyn's Collective are now pulling a pink cardboard construction on wheels meant to represent the female vagina.

The primal-like scream that concludes each night's Crawl has been adopted on other campuses across the country, occurring each night at exactly the same time as in East Quad. The largest such gathering was two days ago at UC Berkeley, where over one thousand gathered in Sproul Plaza to scream in sympathy.

Earlier this week, the Crawl persisted despite four inches of late-season snow. Concerns about Harris's mental and physical health have been expressed within the community. Ms. Harris has steadfastly refused to comment to this paper or any other media, and it is not known how long she intends to continue her protest.

# Title IX

**MARTIKA MALIK-ADAMS EXAMINED** the photo before her and her blood boiled. While this was not an uncommon emotional state for her, the feeling was particularly acute today. The photo showed the badly beaten face of Lulu Harris. Yolanda Perez had provided it during her testimony.

*Ephraim Russell will pay for this.*

For too long, Martika knew, campuses had been playgrounds for sexual predators. The consensus fact was that 25 percent of all female students were sexually assaulted. A study said so. Title IX was changing all that by finally bringing justice for survivors.

Those who suggested that a woman—*any* woman—would fabricate an allegation of abuse further angered Martika. A growing chorus on the right, from odious places such as Fox News, was trying to create a counternarrative by exploiting one or two instances with confused women, such as the one at UVA on the cover of *Rolling Stone.* If Martika's first mission in life was to help survivors, her second was to see people like that suffer in hell.

Of course, in Lulu's case there could be no question. The evidence was all too clear.

A few short years ago, she knew, justice for Lulu would have been difficult at best. Allegations were swept under the rug, as was most anything that posed a threat to the collegiate "brand." Title IX came like a cleansing storm, washing away decades of filth. Most people didn't understand it, thinking it was about gender equity in athletics, and it did start that way, back in 1972. The initial effects saw an increase in the number of women's varsity sports programs at most colleges.

That was fine as far as it went, but for Martika and other activists, it was nowhere near enough. They lobbied for more. In 2009, the Department of Education sent out a communication now famously known as the "Dear Colleague" letter. It stated that the intent of Title IX was not simply equal access to athletics, but rather equal access to *education,* and any college that didn't provide this access was in noncompliance. Noncompliance meant an investigation by the OCR. These investigations were extremely time-consuming and expensive, costing hundreds of thousands in legal and compliance. But far worse was the implicit threat of turning off the funding spigot. This hung like the sword of Damocles over the Milton Strausses of the world. Last year, Devon pulled in a whopping $720 million from the federal government, mostly in research grants. Even with all of Devon's riches, it could not afford to make an enemy of Uncle Sam. While it was legally murky whether some DOE bureaucrat could pull the plug over Title IX noncompliance, the bureaucrats were happy to leave the impression they could. Poking the bear was simply not worth it.

But how, some wondered, were colleges not providing equal access? Weren't colleges already over 50 percent female? The "Dear Colleague" letter cleared up any confusion; there simply *was* a campus rape culture—again, that study said so—and by definition such a culture created a hostile and unsafe environment. Such an environment might well discourage women from applying in the first place, and *that* constituted unequal access.

Colleges were on notice. They had to get their acts together—or else.

In the years following, Devon and others built out expensive infrastructures to ensure compliance. Martika's Title IX group, a subdivision of her Office of Diversity and Inclusion, had twenty-seven employees, plus outside counsel.

Devon had endured a single OCR investigation, something Martika was determined to never have happen again. It happened about six years ago. Members of the Beta Psi house sent their pledges down to the Womyn's Collective, where they stood outside and chanted, "No means yes, yes means anal!" Someone filmed it, and it got lots of play on CNN. A team of officials from OCR was practically on the next plane. The ensuing investigation lasted seven months and cost Devon upward of a million dollars. (The Betas said they didn't mean it literally, they were just trolling the feminists. They considered it good sport.)

Lots had changed in six years, and if a fraternity pulled a stunt like that today, Martika had no doubt the OCR death penalty would result, regardless of how the university handled it. Chop-chop. No more federal funds. How misogynist and exclusionary organizations like fraternities still had a presence at Devon was beyond Martika, but she was making progress on that front.

For any college to keep the OCR happy, it had to show results. Filing quarterly reports with no cases of assault wasn't an option. While it might suggest the Devon campus was a halcyon island of sexual accord, the OCR would be suspicious. With assault rates at 25 percent, *someone* was doing something. Given this, the colleges had to encourage women to come forward. Victims had to be educated as to what constituted assault because often they didn't fully appreciate their own circumstances. Lulu Harris, for instance, could not have given consent because, according to Yolanda Perez, she had been drinking.

At the outset, Lulu, like many others, had not been sufficiently knowledgeable to understand her own abuse. Recent campus "awareness" initiatives were helping. For instance, just because a woman was in a sexual relationship didn't mean consent was given each time sex occurred. And even if an encounter starts as consensual, women have every right to withdraw consent during the act. Importantly, consent withdrawal can include nonverbal cues such as silence or passivity. Male students were being taught, under her office's guidance, how to read such nonverbal cues. All first-years were now required to attend a two-day workshop on proper sexual procedures. The result of these initiatives was a 500 percent increase in reported incidents, an improvement Malik-Adams had used to great effect in her last compensation review.

The illegitimate billionaires now running the U.S. government were trying to say "Never mind" about the "Dear Colleague" letter, but most schools, including Devon, were having none of it. The machine was built, and it was doing what it was supposed to do: expose and remove sexual predators.

But Devon had never reeled in a professor. There had always been rumors, and Martika chased each whisper down every rabbit hole, but bagging a prize had proved elusive. In the world of Title IX, a professor was considered a big-game trophy. The Title IX head at Whitby College got the keynote nod at last year's Equity and Inclusion Conference in Las Vegas after she toppled a fully tenured professor, one of some fame in physics circles. He had taken a grad student to an academic conference, and they ended up in a single hotel room where sex occurred. Both the professor and the student maintained it was consensual, but the power imbalance in their relationship made this impossible. The professor lost not only his job but also his pension. The publicity rendered him unemployable, and the last anyone knew he had retreated to Mexico for the lower cost of living.

Visions of keynotes played in Martika's head as she looked up from her notes at Lulu Harris.

# Yeah, No

**LULU SAT ON** a comfortable couch in Martika's spacious office, along with two other people, introduced as Rhonda Stern, a Devon staff psychologist, and a stenographer. Lulu wondered how long this was going to take. She had an appointment with the ladies at the day spa.

"I know how difficult this must be," said Martika. "I want you to know how courageous you are in coming forward. And what you're doing—your protest—I can't even tell you how inspiring it is for all of us."

"Thank you, Dean," said Lulu between chews. She was working over a piece of appetite-suppressant gum.

"Please, call me Martika."

"Okay, Martika."

"I want you to know that Rhonda here has a lot of experience with our survivors. She's here to help you through this."

"It's nice to meet you, Lulu. I hope we can be friends," said Stern.

"Nice to meet you, too."

"I see you don't wear your crawling clothes *all* the time," said Stern, attempting to break the ice. She and Martika did their best to chuckle. Lulu was wearing a simple shawl from the Donna Karan winter collection.

"They get pretty torn up."

"You know, I don't want to get overly serious, but a lot of us are concerned for you," continued Stern. "How are you feeling?"

"Fine."

"It's okay to say something if you aren't. You should know that everything discussed here is completely confidential, and at no time will you be made to talk to anyone else or to the person who did this to you. This is a safe space. Both Martika and I and the whole university are bound by the same rules."

"So nothing I say leaves this room?" Lulu continued to work over her piece of gum. She wanted to get through lunch on only a small salad.

"We will use what you say to establish what happened and make a case against your assailant, if warranted," said Martika. "But the only person you need to convince is me. As Devon's chief Title IX officer, I both investigate and adjudicate the case. This is completely normal, and it's to protect your privacy. No one else will know what is said here. Do you understand?"

"I do. You've been very clear."

"So . . . how are you feeling?" asked Stern. "This must all be so difficult."

"Well, Rhonda, my knees are pretty shot and I've got hands like one of my dad's landscapers, but other than that, not too bad."

"But how do you *feel*? Emotionally speaking."

"Oh, you know."

"Perhaps you could tell us."

"I feel peachy, Rhonda. I'm worried I'm a bit behind on my work, though."

"You don't concern yourself with that. We will contact all your professors and provide you with notetakers," Martika said.

"With what?"

"We will have grad students sit in and take notes for you. It's often done in cases like this. We mean you don't have to go to class."

"Seriously?"

"Seriously. No one should have to go through what you're going through, and we know that meeting your class schedule under these circumstances is difficult."

"Well, that would be nice."

"Is there anything else we can do to ease this process for you?"

Lulu sniffed an opportunity, and her eyebrows rose almost imperceptibly. "I'm sort of embarrassed to say . . . my room. . . . I'm stuck there a lot of the time now, and I have a roommate who is not very sympathetic, and it feels so . . . claustrophobic, like the walls are closing in. It's suffocating."

"Would you feel better in a single?" Martika asked.

"I think that would help." Lulu allowed her lips to quiver ever so slightly. *Song can suck it!*

"Done. I'll make one available for you." Martika made a note on her legal pad. "Now, Lulu . . . honey, I know this is difficult, but if you would, in your own words, tell us what happened that day. We'd like a contextual understanding."

"Which day is that, Martika?"

"The day of the assault."

"What assault?"

Stern and Malik-Adams looked at each other quizzically. "The day Professor Russell assaulted you. Can you tell us what happened? In your own words."

"Nothing."

"What do you mean?"

"I mean nothing happened."

"But you indicated to both Dean Choudhary and Yolanda Perez, your RA, that Professor Russell assaulted you."

Lulu took out her spent piece of gum and cast about for a place to put it. Martika produced a napkin. "Yeah, no," Lulu said, retrieving another stick of gum from her bag.

"I'm afraid I don't understand," said Martika.

"What's that?"

"Are you now saying he *didn't* assault you?"

"That's what I'm saying."

"But you were quite clear with Yolanda and Dean Choudhary that he did."

"You know, Martika, I feel like they were putting a lot of pressure on me."

"What kind of pressure?"

"To name someone. I mean really, they just wouldn't let up. Yolanda— jeez, she wouldn't shut up about it. Plus they practically threatened to throw me out for that stupid scepter thing if I didn't hand them someone. I feel like they put me in an emotionally stressful situation."

"But, Lulu, what about this?" Malik-Adams pushed across the table the picture of Lulu that Perez had taken.

Lulu recoiled at the sight of it. "Ugh, that awful picture. I wish you people would lose it."

"But you've clearly been assaulted."

"Nope. Fell. Hit my head."

"You fell."

"Yup, fell."

"Where did this happen?"

"At the Beta house. I was really shit-faced." Lulu laughed at the memory. "Whew, yeah. Quite the bender."

"So you're saying you just . . . fell down."

"Yup. Hurt like a sonuvabitch, Martika."

Something was clearly wrong. Rhonda Stern decided she needed to intervene. "Lulu, we know how upsetting these things can be, but burying your emotions can only cause greater trauma down the road. Please believe me when I say you need to address this head-on to start on a healing path."

"Nope. I'm good. Do you guys have any coffee?"

"Of course," Martika said.

As she walked to the door, Lulu could scarcely contain her horror over the vast swath of gold spandex stretched like Saran wrap over Martika's ass. It looked like two squirrels fighting over a Ritz cracker under there. Martika came back with coffee, and Lulu tried hard to think about something else.

"Lulu," said Martika, striking a more serious note all of a sudden. "We've conducted a search of Professor Russell's emails, and we know you met with him that day. We also have evidence that you were drinking with him. There is a picture of the two of you and alcohol is clearly visible."

"Yup. May have had a pop. I mean, hey, Fridays, am I right?"

"So you acknowledge that Professor Russell gave you alcohol."

"Well, not exactly. I just grabbed the bottle and had a belt."

"You grabbed it."

"That's right, Martika."

"And drank right out of the bottle."

"Yup."

"But the bottle was sitting out, correct?"

"Correctamundo."

"What was a bottle doing out during a scheduled meeting between a student and professor?"

"Not sure he knew I was coming, to tell you the truth."

"Was it after alcohol was consumed that he made an overture toward you?"

"I suppose so, but I kissed *him*, not the other way around. He's pretty hot, don't you think? I mean, ladies, have you seen that ass? That's what *I'm* talkin' about. He wasn't interested, though." Lulu shrugged.

"Forgive me, but after the accusations you made, this is all a bit hard to grasp." Martika looked like she was starting to hyperventilate.

"Like I said, everyone was all up in my grill, so I felt pressure to name someone. Probably shouldn't have done that, so sorry. Yeah."

Martika's and Stern's faces betrayed states of extreme flabbergast. "But *the Crawl*," said Stern. "Help us understand."

"Oh, yeah, that. I think gender violence is a terrible thing. Don't you, Martika? Just terrible. I thought I should make a statement, do my part and all. Don't you think that's a worthwhile statement to make?"

"Certainly," Martika said, "but your clothes, when you crawl . . . they're just like Russell's."

"Are they? I hadn't noticed. Frankly, I just needed something sensible. You couldn't very well expect me to ruin my Dolce and Gabbana, could you?"

The two administrators looked at each other. The interview had left the tracks. "Uh, Lulu, perhaps we could continue this another time."

"Okay, Martika. Do you think I could get another coffee to go?"


Lulu's walk back to Duffy traced much of her nightly route. Every face she passed gleamed with recognition, even admiration. Some said, "Peace, Lulu!" Others snapped admiration with their fingers. One person yelled, "Crawl on, sister!"

She glided over one chalk tribute after another. Part of her hated the chalk; it got into the cuts on her hands and knees and took forever to clean off. It also wafted up and coated the inside of her lungs, which gave her coughing fits. Still, it made for good reading. One chalking, done in Lenten purple, said SAINT LULU and had a little halo above it.

Totally worth it.

Today had been great fun. The hardest part was not laughing out loud, particularly at "contextual understanding" and "healing path." She found digging a sharp fingernail into her thigh an effective way to keep a straight face.

A few days earlier, Sheldon had made a surprise visit. He arrived in his 750i, chauffeured by his usual driver, Pauly. Sheldon's midnight-blue Savile

Row suit, complete with folded handkerchief, stood out against the sartorial frumpiness of campus. His salt-and-pepper hair was combed straight back. He was the image of Manhattan success.

Word of the Crawl had reached him, of course, and he imagined his only child had . . . what? Been attacked by some professor and become a crazed feminist? He didn't know what to think, but his alarm was real.

Lulu came clean with him, at least about Russell's innocence. Sheldon didn't need to hear about the hairy man-boy. He also didn't need to hear about the Great Scepter Affair, either, although Lulu was now certain her growing fame had put that issue to bed.

"But you've accused him, this professor!" Sheldon was confused, which Lulu granted was understandable.

"Only to my RA and a dean. They kept bugging me for a name because they thought I'd been raped or something. I hit my head one night and had a big bruise on my face. Remember, from St. Barts? It was no big deal."

"You told me you fell."

"Exactly."

"But everyone thinks you're some tragic victim!"

"People think what they want."

"And you're telling me the truth."

"No one raped me, no one assaulted me, and I told my RA as much at the time. She got angry. I think she was actually disappointed."

"So . . . this crawl business?"

She couched the Crawl as kind of a performance art project, omitting that she wasn't enrolled in any art classes. (Sheldon wouldn't have noticed either way.) "I started doing it, you know, almost as a lark, and it just turned into this thing. It was all rather spontaneous. Can't say I thought it through, exactly." *Okay, that wasn't exactly true.*

"Jesus Christ, Lulu, that may be the understatement of the year. Do you understand Russell could sue you—sue *us*? You've made this look like it's about *him*."

"Well, like I said, I never actually said anything about Russell publicly. People assume whatever they like. I can't be responsible for what people assume, can I, Daddy?" Lulu knew full well how to play to Sheldon's affections. She did everything but bat her eyelashes.

"But I still don't understand—the Crawl, any of this. Help me out here."

"It's *something*. People are responding. Do you know I hit a hundred thousand followers on Twitter yesterday? I barely started the account!"

That got Sheldon's attention. Lulu knew that ninety-nine in a hundred fathers would have responded with bewilderment or even scorn, but not Sheldon. Sheldon knew the value of branding. "So . . . what now? You're a feminist superhero or something?"

"Or something." Lulu gave her best girl-next-door smile, the kind few fathers could resist. She could see Sheldon's wheels turning. He was weighing the angles. It's what he was good at.

"All right, then. I had a talk before I came over here with a Dean Chu . . . Chow . . ."

"Choudhary."

"Right smarmy son of a bitch. He informed me that this is now a Title IX matter and wouldn't tell me anything else. Said it was to protect your privacy. Hah, can you believe that? I'm your goddamned father. Who does he think pays your tuition? Anyway, I called the office, and one of my partners knows a top Title IX guy. Apparently it's a red-hot field. Who knew? You and I are going to speak with him as soon as possible."


And they did, to one Leo Silver. This was when Lulu learned she was bulletproof, at least where the school was concerned. She could say pretty much anything to the Title IX people and there would be no consequences. "They can't touch you," Silver said.

Ephraim Russell was another matter. While *his* rights under Title IX were virtually nonexistent, it was entirely possible he could bring a civil suit. Silver argued strongly that if Lulu hadn't actually been attacked, she should immediately recant her accusations. Otherwise, any civil suit would be adjudicated outside Devon's aegis, and there was no telling what might happen there. "Russell would have rights," Silver said.

She'd been smart, he added, not to go public. No need to recant public statements she'd never made in the first place. She just had to straighten things out with the administration.

Lulu knew that where the public was concerned, the truth no longer mattered. She had observed her followers carefully these three weeks, and she'd realized the narrative was everything. The Crawl was now bigger than a single incident, one that may or may not have occurred. It was about something larger. Media requests were piling up. She no longer needed the likes of Yolanda Perez or Martika Malik-Adams.

"This is worse than I thought," said Stern. "The poor girl clearly has PTSD. She's repressing. The only way she's found to express what she's *really* feeling is by crawling and screaming. I've seen a lot of trauma but I've never seen a case like this. The girl needs serious therapy. It's heartbreaking."

"I smell a rat," replied Martika, flexing her fists repeatedly.

"What do you mean?"

"I think that bastard Russell got to her. I think she's being threatened."

Stern thought about this. "We can't discount the possibility. And it may not even have been an overt threat. The power imbalance of their relationship is such that she may feel implicitly threatened, and he may have exploited that. Predators don't always resort to a single playbook."

"The fact is, she didn't report this for months. I think she was frightened to death."

"You may be right."

"I *know* I'm right." That several professors had called as character references for Russell, including Sophie Blue Feather and that dinosaur Fred Hallowell, did not alter Martika's thinking. She knew predators could often be charming. She got up to signal it was time for Stern to leave her office. "I meet with Russell on Thursday, and I will get to the bottom of this. I can assure you that."

Martika briefly wondered whether she'd been premature in leaking Russell's name to the *Daily*, but decided it didn't matter.

# Fucking Fucks

**EVERY TUESDAY,** the Betas gathered for a meeting to deal with fraternity matters, such things as setting annual dues or deciding whether vomiting off the second-floor balcony was an acceptable activity. The brothers hated these meetings because it was the only time all week when no alcohol was permitted. This had the salutary effect of keeping meetings remarkably short.

Tug herded the brothers into the common room. Most had been in the pong room, where they were playing Splat, a traditional Beta pastime in which brothers scored points by hocking loogies to the ceiling and then catching them in their mouths when they eventually succumbed to gravity.

Tug called the meeting to order. He waved the latest *Devon Daily* in the air. "My brothers. We have a serious problem. We are under assault." He began reading.

# Devon Daily

## Panel Proposes to Crack Down on Fraternities

A committee of professors and administrators convened by President Milton Strauss has recommended sweeping reforms that call into question the future of the fraternity system at Devon. While most fraternities are off campus and not themselves within legal reach of the university, the Committee on Fraternal Life at Devon is recommending a series of moves it feels will diminish the appeal that fraternities hold for some undergraduates. Among the recommendations up for consideration is to prohibit fraternity members from holding leadership positions on campus such as sports captaincies, club chairs, or editorships. Further, the panel suggests that Devon decline to provide fraternity members with recommendations for prestigious scholarships such as the Rhodes or Marshall.

These potential steps come after a well-publicized racial incident earlier this year at the Beta Psi house. Further, Devon officials cited various studies that suggest sexual violence is endemic in the Greek system. "Recent events on campus have focused the nation's attention on rape culture, and it is simply not an option to sit on the sidelines and do nothing," said Professor Martha Geddes, a member of the panel.

A spokesman for Milton Strauss said that the administration would review the committee's recommendations in the coming weeks.

Tug lowered the paper as the brothers booed and howled. "Well, that blows," said Mound.

"As usual, brother Mound is a font of insight and brevity," Tug said. "Strauss appears to be serious about this."

"Guy's a total nob," Finn Belcher said, an observation that met with much agreement.

"Complete asshat," offered a junior named Pudge.

"All true, but our clarity around this does not solve the problem."

"This is all because of that stupid bitch crawling around campus every night," Billy Curtis said.

"But seriously, what the fuck did *we* do?" asked Pudge. "It was that English prof, what's-his-name."

"Russell, I think. They are using the whole thing to take us down. They've been looking for a way for years," Tug said. "Russell, Lulu Harris—it's all just an excuse. Bryce, don't you know this chick?"

"Yeah, kinda. She's a social type that I used to see around the city when I was at Collegiate, and the next thing I know she's Lena fucking Dunham. She came to our party in December, but she blew me off as soon as she got here. She was pretty hammered. Think she might have hooked up."

"Oh, I *know* she hooked up," said Finn. "Right on that couch."

Mound was on the couch. He looked down at it and made a snorting noise that most interpreted as a chuckle.

"She was with that asshole from the PSA," continued Finn. "The one with the dreadlocks. I happened to come down the stairs really late and saw them on the couch. Almost forgot cuz I was so wasted."

"That commie douche got laid here? Only we're supposed to get laid here," said Digger.

"Fuckin' A," said Mound. *I am in agreement.*

"Well, I say this bitch is full of shit and is messing with the wrong fraternity," said Digger.

The brothers growled at that and pounded their hands on tables.

"Well, technically," Tug said, "she hasn't said a word about us, but she's definitely the catalyst here."

"Same difference," said Digger.

All in the room knew that President Strauss's proposals would effectively end Beta Psi and every other fraternity at Devon. A particularly sore point was the ban on captaincies. Beta had no fewer than three current sports captains. Those positions were résumé burnishers, frequently leading to positions on Wall Street and elsewhere through a well-established network. Tug himself had a job lined up as a financial analyst at Morgan Stanley. The Mound, well, he was working on it.

"Does anyone have any ideas?" Tug asked.

The room fell silent. The meeting had been longer than usual, and a keg waited in the next room as soon as they were done. Solving for their very existence *tomorrow* had to be weighed against drinking *today*, and it was a close call.

"Jimbo," said Tug. "You're the sergeant at arms. That's kind of like being a lawyer. Any suggestions?"

Jimbo looked startled, like the kid who just got called on who hadn't done his homework. The sergeant at arms was mostly responsible for handing down drinking penalties, so what did he know? "Uh . . ."

Joey Spears, he of Hitler fame, raised his hand, bailing Jimbo out.

"Der Führer wishes to speak," Tug said.

*"Sieg Heil!"* yelled everyone, as was the custom.

"What if we did something for, you know, the community. Some charity bullshit. Then, you know, told people about it."

"Excellent thinking. The older alums who come here and get hammered after football games tell me Betas did that kind of stuff once. What could we do? Ideas?"

More silence and blank stares. Mound gazed with longing toward the keg in the next room. It was silver and shiny.

At last one of the sophomores spoke up. "We could go to a hospital and, like, hang out with sick kids . . ."

The brothers thought about this before Mound, breaking his mind meld with the keg, said, "I hate fucking hospitals. That idea sucks."

Everyone quickly agreed with this assessment, relieved they didn't have to pretend otherwise.

"How 'bout we do the big brother thing?" someone else suggested.

"That's a good thought," Tug said, "but I'm afraid we need to make a quick impression. We couldn't gear that up fast enough."

"What about we clean up all that goddamn chalk!" offered Digger.

Everyone laughed, knowing full well what a Category 5 shitstorm that would create.

Mound had had enough. He silenced the room with a single pound of his fist to the table. Raising his impressive girth up off the couch and stabbing the air with a beefy finger, he said, *"How 'bout we tell all those fucking fucks to go fuck themselves!"*

Everyone rose as one to their feet and cheered, *"Mound! Mound!"*

Tug, after briefly marveling at Mound's ability to use *fuck* as an adjective, noun, and verb in the same sentence, tried his best to yell over the crowd. "Guys, I don't think we can blow this off!"

Someone changed the chant. *"Fucking fucks! Fucking fucks!"*

Seeing it was hopeless, Tug cried, "We have a motion to tell those fucking fucks to go fuck themselves. All those in favor!"

*"Aye!"*

"The motion is carried!"

*"Fucking fucks! Fucking fucks!"*

Tug threw in the towel on the meeting. The brothers were a crazed mob now, a single organism descending on the glistening keg in the next room.

# The Tribunal

**EPH SUPPOSED THIS** was what purgatory was like, assuming he believed in such things. He'd been told to stay off campus grounds while his case was being "processed." This left him hanging out in his small apartment most of the time. He tried reading some Melville—*Billy Budd*—but found himself reading the same lines over and over, his thoughts constantly drifting to his current plight. When the walls closed in, he'd go for a ride on his new bike. He and D'Arcy went to the movies once or twice when she had time. Sometimes she spent the night.

One afternoon he looked himself up on Rate My Professor. He knew he probably shouldn't, but morbid curiosity got the best of him. His rating was now an almost-unheard-of 1.6. Over four thousand people had rated his classes. Doing a quick calculation in his head, he guessed he'd had no more than eight hundred students in all his classes since starting at Devon.

At a local newsstand he saw last week's *New York* magazine had Lulu Harris on the cover. "The New Face of Feminism," it said. Against his better judgment, he forked over five bucks and took the magazine home. The article featured extensive quotes from a Woman's Studies professor from Reed College named Tonya Washington.

*"One sees the self-abnegation, the pathos, in this brave young woman's eyes as she gives up her body in the name of a movement that she herself started. We feel her agony as every inch of this mostly silent drama plays out in front of us. The silence is broken*

*by a lonely, cathartic scream, only to have the cycle play out again. Lulu Harris is a cry for all those whose voices have gone unheard for so long."*

As he read on, Eph's heart sank when he saw his name.

*While Ms. Harris has never explicitly stated the reasons for her protest, or even the cause it represents, many on the Devon campus believe they are tied to a professor named Ephraim Russell, who is currently facing Title IX charges thought to involve allegations from Harris.*

The press had been calling his apartment and sending him emails almost constantly. He knew better than to engage. His sister, Ellie, even called, but Eph wouldn't answer. He was mortified that word of all this might have spread to Ashley.

Eventually, Eph gave in to a combination of curiosity and sheer boredom. Throwing on a hoodie, he went to see the Crawl for himself. There was some risk, he knew, but it was dark and he drew the hood well over his face. He was confident no one would recognize him.

The cherry blossoms had bloomed and the scent of lilac was in the air. Devon had emerged from its winter hibernation. He decided to approach Mathers discreetly from a perpendicular walk. Rounding the corner, he was astonished by the scene unfolding before him. Along the colorfully chalked path, hundreds of people walked in procession behind Lulu Harris like medieval flagellants. Many of the women wore duct tape over their mouths, and a few wore hijabs, which he didn't quite understand. Others had signs that said highly unpleasant things about him and Milton Strauss. A typical one said:

*Russell + Strauss = Devon Rape Culture!*

Dozens more lined either side of the walk, with more than a few filming the procession on their phones. Those videos would be on YouTube within hours, he knew. Some were probably livestreaming already. The media were there as well.

One of the reporters, followed by a cameraman, approached Lulu and thrust a microphone into her face. "Ms. Harris, can you tell us why you're out here every night? What happened to you?"

Lulu, as usual, appeared to be in a trance and gave no response. Another student intervened. Eph recognized him as one of those who had sabotaged Eph's class, the one with the red dreadlocks. "No questions, my man—back off!" he yelled. Several female students wearing T-shirts from the Womyn's Collective went over and shoved him out of the way, seemingly more upset with their fellow crawler than the reporter. That was curious, Eph thought. If Lulu noticed any of this internecine drama, it wasn't clear.

When the marchers came to Dudley Street, they formed a human alley, blocking traffic until Lulu could safely cross. Traffic backed up for several blocks. There was a considerable police presence, too, as well as campus security. They were assisting with traffic control.

Eph followed along cautiously, head down. At Duffy, Lulu stood and screamed. As usual, it was the only sound she made the entire time, save for the scraping of her iron ball. The long and tortured scream was done on a single breath, leaving little doubt among observers that it welled up from a deeply personal place. It was loud enough to echo off the other buildings in East Quad. When the last sound of it died away, the assembled crowd responded in kind, making for an enormous roar. Then Lulu disappeared inside.

Eph felt like he'd just witnessed some sort of atavistic ritual. How had he gotten mixed up in all this?

As the crowd disbursed, one couple walked in his direction. A flash of recognition came over the girl's face. *"Hey . . ."*

Eph realized he'd been standing there a bit too long. He turned and walked briskly toward the nearest gate.

"That's *him*."

Eph broke into a jog.

"That's him . . . the *rapist!*"

As others turned to look, Eph broke into a run and disappeared out onto the street.


Two days later, Eph was back on campus, staring across Bingham Plaza. It was finally time to meet the Title IX people. He wore a blazer and tie and a baseball cap lowered over much of his face in case anyone noticed him. For insurance, he had a lightweight Columbia jacket with the collar pulled up. The hearing was in Stockbridge, but a phalanx of demonstrators were camped out-side the entrance. Someone must have tipped them off. Giving the demon-strators a wide berth, he walked around behind Stockbridge looking for another way in. He found a door in the back but it was locked. Taking out his phone, he dialed D'Arcy. Luckily, she answered right away and came down to let him in.

"I'm so sorry you have to go through this," she said.

"Hey, another day, another hearing. I might get good at this."

"I'm going to talk to Milton."

"Don't. It won't make a difference, and you'll just get yourself in trouble. But did I mention I love you for offering?"

"Well, come on, then. I'll show you where it is." D'Arcy led him to a small, windowless conference room in the basement. They seemed to be sending a different message this time. There, he found that once again Dean Malik-Adams held his fate in her hands. She and two other women sat across the table.

"We meet again, Professor," said Martika.

"Dean." Eph took a seat. He had been specifically told he had to come alone—no counsel. He had reluctantly called a lawyer at D'Arcy's urging, someone who had been involved with several Title IX cases. The lawyer told him that counsel wouldn't be allowed into the process but he was happy to give (paid) advice from a distance, and even happier to be Eph's plaintiff lawyer when he sued Devon later, the idea of which Eph found horrifying. He de-murred.

"You'll come around," the lawyer had said.

"This is a convening of the Devon University Title IX Tribunal," said the dean, wasting no time. "To my right is Stephanie Coughlin, who will act as counsel to the university in this matter. To my left is Linda Gomez, who will act as stenographer." Linda Gomez was Eph's old friend from last time. He could swear she was giving him the stink eye.

"Excuse me. A question, if I may. Where is the rest of the tribunal? If Ms. Coughlin is counsel, and Ms. Gomez is the stenographer, that just leaves . . . you."

"That's correct."

"So where is everyone else?"

"I *am* the tribunal, Professor Russell."

"Just you?" That lawyer warned him it might be the case, but Eph had found it difficult to believe that the university would put his professional future in the hands of a single person.

"The majority of Title IX cases are adjudicated by a single person; it's well within the federal guidelines. It's a question of efficiency."

"Will there be an investigation? How does this process establish facts?"

"I also perform that role, and it has already begun."

Eph tried to process this. It occurred to him he should have done more research into the whole Title IX thing. "So, and again, I apologize, but this is all new to me—you act as sole investigator, plus judge and jury, while I am apparently allowed no counsel?"

"I don't make the rules, Professor. If you have a problem, I suggest you take it up with the Office for Civil Rights at the Department of Education in Washington. Now let's proceed." Martika poked her reading glasses up her nose and began flipping through papers. "Professor Russell, you teach a fall-semester class called English 240—Nineteenth-Century American Literature. Is this correct?"

"It is."

"And you had a student in that class named Louise Harris, correct?"

"Yes, I did, but I think you already know that."

"We are just establishing the background facts for the record. How would you describe your relationship with Ms. Harris?"

"She was my student. Beyond that, there was no relationship."

Martika looked down at some papers. "An examination of your university email account shows that she sent you fifty-seven emails last semester, considerably more than any other student. Would you say that's normal, Professor?"

"I suppose it's more than normal. I was under the impression she liked the course."

"In one email, she asks for your opinion on which dress to wear. Wouldn't you say that's an odd question for a student to ask a professor?"

"I suppose it is, yes, but I didn't think much of it at the time."

"And why is that?"

"Sometimes students try to ingratiate themselves in different ways. They hope that by establishing a rapport they might get a better grade."

"And did any other students ask you for clothing advice?"

"Not that I recall, no. But I just thought she was an engaged student."

"And you know this because of the emails."

"Yes, but she also contributed in class now and then."

"You made quite an impression on Ms. Harris."

"I am a teacher. I believe that's in my job description."

"Still, she was emailing almost daily."

"Was she? I honestly didn't give it much thought."

Removing her reading glasses for effect, the dean then asked, "Professor Russell, how long had you been having a sexual relationship with Ms. Harris?"

"I have never had a sexual relationship with Ms. Harris. Never. Not one time."

"Are you sure that's the story you want to stick with, Professor?"

"If I may, what are the exact charges being brought against me?"

"You may not," interjected Stephanie Coughlin, the lawyer.

"I'm sorry, what?"

"Under Title IX regulations, we are not obliged to offer specifics, including information about the charges. Our role is merely to gather testimony and evidence and then come to a just conclusion."

"Well, I object!"

"Noted, Professor," Coughlin said.

"I'd at least like to get Ms. Harris in here to talk to her directly."

"That will not happen, Professor."

"Excuse me? I wish to confront my accuser. That is a universal right. Everyone knows that."

"I'm afraid you are very much mistaken," Coughlin said. Eph could swear Malik-Adams was trying to suppress a smile. "Title IX proceedings operate under a different set of guidelines than the criminal justice system. The process is designed to encourage survivors to come forward. Studies show that forcing them to directly face their attackers has a chilling effect on reporting."

"How about the goddamn chilling effect on my rights?"

"We've been through this already, haven't we, Professor?" said the dean. "We will move on. Isn't it true, Professor, that you and Ms. Harris kissed in your office?"

"It's partially true."

"How can this be partially true? You either kissed, or you didn't. Could you be more specific?"

"She tried to kiss me."

"So you admit you and she kissed."

"I admit she kissed me."

"And why would she do that?"

"Why don't you just ask *her*, for Pete's sake. It sure as hell took *me* by surprise."

"And you just sat there, I suppose?"

"No, I pushed her away."

Martika reached into her pile of papers and pushed a photograph across the table. It was the one that Lulu had taken in his office of the two of them, with Lulu making duck face. It must have been found in a search through Eph's emails. "Can you please explain this?"

"Yes. It's a photo she took in my office."

"We know what it is, Professor. Can you *explain* it?"

"You mean why would this girl try to kiss me and then take a selfie of the two of us while making that ridiculous face? No, I can't. I can't explain any of it. I can't explain a *goddamn* thing. Why is the sky blue? I don't know. Why is this girl out of her mind? I don't know that either. Maybe she's on drugs. Have you asked her that?"

"Or perhaps alcohol?" asked Martika, eyebrows arched so high Eph thought she might pull a muscle. "Would you please examine the photo more closely?"

Eph looked at it carefully. *Shit.* In the background, you could see part of a bottle. The word *Jack* was clearly legible.

"Were you and Ms. Harris drinking?"

"I keep a bottle in my desk. A lot of us do. It was Friday evening and I was having a glass when she walked in."

"Do you often drink alcohol before meeting with students?"

"No, of course not, but it was after office hours and I wasn't expecting anyone."

"And yet there is an email to you from her saying she was coming."

"Well, I didn't see it until later."

"Did you offer her a drink?"

"No. She grabbed the bottle and took a sip. I suppose I should have put it away when she walked in, but I didn't think it was that big a deal."

"Professor, would you please read the time stamp on that photo?" Martika asked.

"December nineteenth, five-oh-eight p.m."

"Now, would you please examine *this* photo." Martika pushed another photo across the table.

"Jesus!" exclaimed Eph. The picture showed Lulu with violent bruising across one side of her face. It looked as if someone had taken a two-by-four to her face.

"Now, Professor, would you please read the time stamp on the second photo?" Martika's eyebrows were arching again in a way that suggested her prey was wounded and she was circling in for the kill. It was starting to get on Eph's nerves.

"December twentieth, seven forty-two a.m."

"So, the next morning."

"It would seem."

"So the established facts are that Harris was with you, you were drinking and kissing, and that sometime between the time on that photo and the next morning she was attacked. Perhaps it would save time for all involved if you just told us what really happened."

Eph wondered what the dean otherwise did with her time that made it so precious. "I did nothing to harm Lulu Harris. I have no knowledge of how she was hurt. Whatever happened must have occurred later in the evening."

"Professor, have you ever threatened Ms. Harris?"

"What? No!"

"How many times have you spoken to her since the date of the incident?"

"Zero."

"I see. Tell us, can you *prove* you didn't do any of this?"

"I'm sorry, but isn't it the other way around? Isn't the burden of proof on your side?"

"I don't have a side, Professor."

"I'm glad to hear that."

"We are here to see if there's a preponderance of evidence. Nothing more, nothing less. In that spirit we are asking if you have any exculpatory evidence to offer."

"I'd like to ask *you* something. Did Lulu Harris actually *say* I did any of this?"

"Ms. Harris's testimony is protected by confidentiality."

"Seriously? This is a joke."

"I can assure you, Professor Russell, this is a *very* serious matter, and you would be advised to take it as such."

"Perhaps this would be a good point to end this session, Dean," said Coughlin, looking to defuse things.

Martika looked like she was just getting started, but relented. "Very well. We'll meet for a final session Thursday. What time works for you?"

# The Internet Says So

**"SO, WHAT ARE** we going to do? I mean, this is terrible!" said Milton, who paced back and forth on his Oriental rug.

Martika looked unconcerned. "Isn't it obvious? He's clearly guilty." She sat, watching Milton wear a path in the carpet.

"But you said that their stories match up. They both say nothing happened."

"It doesn't matter. I have a lot of experience with cases like these, and so does our counseling staff. We are in agreement that Lulu Harris is clinically traumatized and Russell's lying through his teeth to save his skin. There's a clear preponderance of evidence."

"This makes me uncomfortable, Martika."

"Russell is a bad seed. First, he shows no cultural awareness over racist course materials, that business in his class, and now this. You know, I've been looking at his file, and I'm not sure how he ever got hired. He's a fish out of water. You should have seen him in the hearing—utterly disrespectful of the process. The bottom line is that he attacked one of our students. I'd stake my career on it."

Martika gauged Milton's expression and didn't note the appropriate alarm. Possessed of an astute understanding of Milton's priorities, she tried a different tack. "Think of it this way—do we need this one man blowing up our school's reputation? They're saying we protect predators."

Milton looked up. *"Who's* saying that?"

"Everyone. The internet."

"There's a process, and we're respecting it. No one can fault us for that."

"Process? You think people are paying attention to those kinds of details? Please. They want to see results. I get that we have a process, but it must be expeditious or our reputation will suffer."

Milton shifted gears. "Martika, what are your thoughts on the Crawl?"

"She's a brave girl. It's her means of expression, the only way she's found her voice."

"If she's clinically traumatized, as you say, should she be out there doing this?"

"It's her way of healing."

"You say Russell makes us look bad—what about this? The Crawl's becoming a circus."

"I think it shows we are a united campus that embraces free expression and will not tolerate violence."

"Not everyone sees it that way, you know."

"Who?"

"Some alums, for one."

Martika's expression grew dark. "And are you going to allow a bunch of out-of-touch old white men to dictate how this school is run?"

"Am *I* not an old white man?"

Martika shifted in her seat. "Milton, *you* are in touch with the feelings of the students and have earned their respect. Look at how you handled the students of color this winter. They came to you with serious issues and you treated them with the respect they deserved."

"Some of the 'crawlers' seem to have a different view of me. They have signs."

What Milton wasn't sharing was the panicky call he had recently received from Pete Whitson in the development office. According to Whitson, Devon was becoming nationally synonymous with the Crawl, and it was all the alums were talking about. Younger, more progressive alums were upset because the Crawl drew attention to Devon as a playground of sexual predators. The older, more conservative alums thought social justice warriors were now controlling the school. Whitson was getting it from both sides, the practical consequence of which was that small and middling donations were drying up.

Whitson had added, sotto voce, that losing progressives wasn't of great concern since they never gave much anyway. (Devon had reams of data on demographic giving habits, although it was kept tightly under wraps for fear of causing offense.) But losing the conservative alums, the ones who wrote 10K checks every year, was more concerning. Sure, Milton knew, many were out-of-touch cranks who refused to keep up with the times. But their love for "Old Devon" was normally unshakable, and most of the time they were easily managed. A winning football team and boozy reunions—held safely after potentially offending students had left for the summer—did the trick. But this time felt different. Whitson pleaded with Milton to put an end to the Crawl.

"Those 'out-of-touch white men' pay our salaries, Martika."

"Are you gonna tell me that with twenty-eight billion dollars in the bank we have to worry about what Chip Worthington the Fourth from the all-white, all-male class of '59 thinks?"

"How do you think we got the twenty-eight billion dollars in the first place? These people need care and feeding. Part of that is allowing them to think that their Devon, the Devon they knew, is still today's Devon. You follow me?"

"Maybe. I'm just glad that care and feeding is not part of my job description."

"But it *is* part of mine." Milton realized he should have anticipated everything that was happening, but support for Lulu Harris was so pervasive on campus that sometimes it was hard to remember that a broader spectrum of opinion existed.

Out there.

Simply shutting the Crawl down, though, would be tricky. Campus activists were not a bunch of shrinking violets. Violence was not out of the question. Just as concerning were the free speech implications. Shut down the Crawl and the ACLU, an organization Milton otherwise fervently supported, would probably show up at his office the next day.

Then there were the signs. About *him.* There were more every day. One particularly upsetting one said GIRLS: DON'T SIT ON UNCLE MILTIE'S LAP! Even the normally supportive @FakeUncleMiltie Twitter account had turned against him, suggesting this was all somehow his fault.

How could they say such things? About him! He had been supportive of the Crawl from the beginning, even making sure campus security maintained safety. He was a champion of progressive causes!

Perhaps the solution was the usual one: money. He could provide a generous package for campus feminists. The playbook was clear from his experience earlier in the year: more tenured positions in Women's Studies, a bigger budget for women's health services, some direct cash into the Womyn's Collective and other organizations . . . He would also approve that fraternity committee's recommendations and make it part of the package. This had also been on the African-American students' list of demands, so he'd score some points there as well.

This couldn't appear to be a quid pro quo for ending the Crawl, but he was confident it could be handled. As for Professor Russell, perhaps all parties would be best served if he left Devon. Yes, this seemed the best course.

"Martika, I agree the Russell matter needs to come to an end. Respect the process, but make it fast." He knew exactly how the process would conclude. "And Lulu Harris needs to be reined in. She's made her statement and we respect her for it. But let her know it ends this week. This campus needs to return to normal."

"Speaking of which, I need to talk to you about the fraternities."

"You are reading my mind. I believe I will accept the committee's recommendations."

Martika smiled. This had turned into a most productive year. "It's the right decision. You will be praised for it."

"They are a vestige of another era, as you say, and do nothing to add to our cultural fabric. But we need to ensure it goes down smoothly."

# The Enemy of
My Enemy

**EYES PEERED THROUGH** the slotted door of the Fellinghams clubhouse.
They could make out little but a mess of red tangles. "Who calls?" the voice
said through the slot.

"My name is Red Wheeler."

"State your business, Mr. Wheeler."

"A mutual friend of ours. Lulu Harris."

After a pause, the voice said, "We have no affiliation with anyone of that
name."

"C'mon, I know she used to be a member of your thing here. I just want a
minute of your time."

"Miss Harris is a nonperson to us. We returned her plaque."

*Her what?* Red decided he didn't care. "Well, I think she's a dick, too." The
little slot closed and the door remained shut. "Look, man, would you just open
the door for a minute. I think we may have a common interest here."

The door remained shut. "I have information," Red said finally.

Red heard a lock turn and the door opened. The guy stood there, wearing an ascot and red velvet smoking jacket. This took a moment for Red to
take in. What a complete douche.

"Enter. We may speak here in the vestibule. Nonmembers are allowed no
further."

"Ah, yeah." Red stared farther in to the living room with its tired furniture. "I can live with that."

"Very well, Mr. Wheeler. My name is Winslow Gubbins. Tell me why we have the pleasure of your company today."

"You can call me Red. Everyone does."

"We've only just met."

"Okay, then."

Another time, Red might have taken great pleasure in focusing his progressive attentions on Winslow Gubbins and the Society of Fellingham, but now was not that time. *Perhaps next year*, he thought.

"I believe you and I have common cause. She fucked you guys over, am I right? Stole your scepter? I saw it in the *Daily*."

"What of it?"

"Well, this crawl of hers. I'm not a buyer."

"Meaning what?"

"I think it's bullshit. Chick is a player. I know firsthand, if you know what I mean."

"I do not know what you mean."

Red sighed. *What is with this guy?* "Do I have to spell it out? Chick rode me like she was roping calves. And it's not like I'm the only one."

Win was gobsmacked. Lulu Harris had made carnal congress with this walking pestilence? That Harris had been lavish of virtue, he knew. She was a bloody sexual philanthropist, but he himself had been rebuffed, left to his own ministrations. That the harlot went and shagged this common hippie compounded the shame.

The rejection had made the decision to expel Lulu from Fellinghams that much easier. (In the wake of her departure, the society decided going forward to refer to expulsion as "getting plaqued." That bit of cheeky taxonomy pleased Win, so at least something positive had come out of *l'affaire Lulu*.)

"So, look," Red said. "I don't know what happened with her and the English teacher, but whatever it was, I don't see her as the victim type, do you?"

"We are in agreement."

"Did you know she's doing her final Crawl on Friday?"

"Slither."

"What?"

"We prefer to call it the Slither."

Red chuckled. "Hey, that's good. Anyway, word is the administration's had enough, and they told her to wrap it up."

"Everyone knows that. It was in the *Daily*. Although Friday . . . isn't that the Fling?"

The Spring Fling, or Fling as it was always called, was a big blowout the day after classes ended, which was also the beginning of reading period. Exams followed a week later. The event centered on Bingham Plaza and always featured a name act. Last year it had been the cowpunk revival band Drunk Bob and the Confessions. This year it was a famous West Coast rapper, Killa C Note. Killa was legit ghetto, from Compton, so students were excited.

"It is," said Red.

"Although I suppose the Fling is during the day, and she slithers at night."

Red grinned broadly. "So, dude, here's the thing. That's exactly what the administration thinks, but there's something they don't know. She's changing her last crawl to three in the afternoon, right in the middle of the Fling. It could be a circus."

"How do you know this?"

"I know everything that goes down on this campus, man." In reality, he had been informed by Chris Huffman at the *Daily*, who had been tipped by the Womyn's Collective, which had, in turn, been told by Lulu. For some reason she had let them in, if only just this once.

"Okay, so what of it? We don't care what that woman does anymore."

"Well, maybe you don't care. Maybe you don't mind at all that she's a thief who fucked you over after you so nicely made her a member of this fine establishment and then went out and got famous on a lie. Maybe I was wrong and you don't care about any of that at all."

Win looked toward the scepter over the mantel in the other room. If it was worth a hundred dollars, he'd be surprised. Truth be told, he hadn't given the scepter much thought lately. What still burned was that night at the Beta house. He'd been dancing with Lulu and thought he'd read the signals right, but the wench had shoved him away like he was some smelly homeless person asking for money. Was that the night she'd ended up with this *orangutan*?

"If I may," Win said, "I recognize you. Aren't you a campus provocateur? I would think you quite approve of Miss Harris's activities. Why are you bringing this information to us?"

"Let's just say I think she's a fraud and leave it at that. I don't like frauds."

"I see." Skepticism was written on Win's face. He imagined Red Wheeler was well acquainted with any number of frauds in the campus activism racket, though Win didn't particularly care one way or the other. The Fellinghams crowd was happy to keep its distance from all that. "So you are proposing . . . what?"

"Nothing. I just thought you should know, in case you thought you wanted to . . . do something."

"Do something."

"Right. And by the way, did you see this?" Red pulled a magazine out of his backpack and handed it to Win. It was the latest copy of *People* magazine. On the cover, a flag on the right corner said, "Feminism's Rising Star," and there was a tiny head shot of Lulu. Win looked aghast as he flipped through the magazine, trying to find the article. *Hideous treacle,* he thought, skipping over pages of journalistic puffery. Then, there she was, posing with her ball and chain, mustering her most plaintive look. The title read, "Lulu Harris—a Crawl for All."

Win quickly scanned the piece. Notably it said, "While Ms. Harris declined to be interviewed for this article . . ." Yet there she was, clearly posing for the money shot. Her complicity was clear.

"That conniving *whore.*"

"Thought you might find that interesting."

"Thank you, Mr. Wheeler, for bringing this matter to our attention."

"Anytime. You can keep the magazine."


Red Wheeler could not have cared less whether Lulu was a fraud. Maybe Ephraim Russell—that sap who taught *Huck Finn*—hit on her, maybe he didn't. Red suspected not, given the girl's inclinations. It didn't matter, though, because she had captured the moment, the zeitgeist. He had to hand it to her. It was rare that he saw his own talents as a campus incendiary outmatched, and by a first-year no less.

But it created an unacceptable situation. His normal dominion over the campus left was in grave jeopardy. He felt his power sliding away like Jell-O off a spoon. The *fucking* Womyn's Collective was milking this thing for all it was worth, and the other groups were going their own way. It was all about specialization now.

The *ingrates.*

Had they already forgotten about the oil company divestiture? *That was all Red Wheeler!* The summit he called was a disaster, and his attempts to call a campus-wide strike had fallen on deaf ears. They were all too busy elbowing one another for Milton's table scraps. And now the Womyn's Collective was "expelling" him from the Crawl. *Bitches!*

The seeds of chaos must be sown.

Red walked purposefully toward Patterson Gymnasium, a building he had never visited in his seven years at Devon. Today would not be his first. His destination was behind the gym: fraternity row.

# Betas Are Boned

**THE BETAS WERE** not known for their sense of industry, or, for that matter, anything else that required real effort outside of athletics. Occasionally, though, something fired their collective imagination. There was that time they'd taken the empties from an entire semester—the ones usually thrown into a pit in the basement until one of the goats could return them for deposit money—and constructed a near-perfect fifteen-foot replica of the Great Sphinx of Giza. For almost a day they danced around it, wrists bent, hands pointing like funky Tuts. It was meant to be the centerpiece for an Egyptian-themed party where guests were invited to come dressed as their favorite plague. But, perhaps inevitably, someone slammed into it, right into the missing nose. He was followed by others, who destroyed the structure in mere moments, leaving a pile of over two thousand cans. The party was nonetheless a great success, the empty cans being repurposed into something like a children's ball pit.

Today's events, Teddy knew, required a similar level of motivation and creative thinking. Milton Strauss had approved recommendations from the Committee on Fraternal Life at Devon, and it was a death sentence. For all their outward indolence, the Betas were motivated on levels most took care not to show. They had all made it to Devon, after all. Something got them there. Secretly, many had excellent GPAs, and most were elite Division I athletes. Some harbored ambitions for Wall Street or law school. Others wanted to teach. Being shut out of leadership positions and recommendation letters was a nonstarter. Something had to be done.

Technically, they were having a meeting, but mostly they were lying around the living room hungover. The smell of stale beer permeated the woodwork.

"We are so boned," said the Mound.

The others moaned their agreement.

Billy Curtis asked to be recognized. "We and the other fraternities are all off campus, and none of us publish membership rolls. How the hell are they gonna know who to fuck over?"

That very question was the subject of great speculation. Rumors were going around that Devon would employ snitches who might employ devious means to ferret out offenders. One rumor had them loitering across the street, monitoring the comings and goings of members—block watchers, like in old East Germany. Someone else heard that anyone up for leadership roles would have to sign an affidavit swearing he didn't belong to any all-male organizations.

That rumor had credibility.

"Well, there *is* one way out," said Tug. He knew that the committee had cited the single-sex nature of fraternities as the core problem. The statement said, in so many words, that men spending time with men created a ferment of sexual predation. "Toxic masculinity" was the phrase everyone was throwing around. The statement further suggested there was a way forward for any fraternity agreeing to expand its membership to women, who would presumably exert a civilizing influence. "We could admit women."

Tug was met with a blizzard of red Solo cups heaved in his direction, drops of yesterday's beer hitting his face.

"Mound's right," said Der Führer. "We're boned."

"There is another solution," Finn Belcher said, looking up from his phone.

"Brother Belch, by all means," said Tug. "You have the floor." Belch had the highest GPA in Beta, so the brothers generally listened to what he had to say.

"So, you know how the university recently decided to allow anyone to self-identify?"

"Huh?" Der Führer asked.

"Self-identify. You are what you feel you are. When you apply to Devon, you can now check any box for gender. It's the new thing."

"They said that?" asked the Mound.

"Yes, it was everywhere. Didn't you read . . . never mind."

"Yeah, so what of it?" asked Der Führer.

"Okay, so hear me out on this. One of us changes our official Devon iden-tity to female. By their own rules, they're not allowed to question it. Seriously, it could work." Finn smiled, pleased with his cleverness.

"But who would it be?" said Billy Curtis. "I ain't becoming no chick."

"Fuck no," said Mound. *Nor will I.*

"But, Mound, you already have experience with transgender bathrooms," said Digger. "You're halfway there!"

Everyone laughed.

"You wouldn't have to become or even act female, numbnuts. Just *say* you were," said Finn.

"So who would it be?" Tug asked.

"I don't know. Maybe we could draw straws."

"Not fuckin' doin' it," said Mound. *I respectfully decline.*

That pretty much did the idea in. The brothers all shouted it down. Some made lip farts of disapproval.

Tug threw up his hands. "So we're finished. Is that what you're all tell-ing me?"

Belch looked up, a thought percolating. "Wait, we still have till the end of the year, right?"

"Yeah, as far as we know," Tug answered.

"And you said that commie dude told you there's a Crawl during the Fling?"

"That's right."

"What's left in the treasury?"

"Six hundred and forty-seven bucks. Why? What are you thinking?"

"Anyone know how to make papier-mâché?"

No one did, but the answer was found quickly on the internet. Finn out-lined his idea and there was vigorous approval all around. "And one other thing. I almost forgot about this." He held out his phone for all to see. "Like I said, I was pretty hammered at the time."

There was a whoop of excitement as it dawned on the brothers what they were seeing. "Holy shit," Tug said.

It was agreed. If they were going down, they were going down like Betas.

# Captain Jack

**"EPH, HE'S NOT WELL.** They think it's Parkinson's. I know he'd like to see you."

"Since his first choice isn't available?"

"That's not fair," Ellie said

Eph knew it wasn't, but he figured he'd earned the right to some self-pity.

"Listen, I read about what's going on up there, this Crawl. It was on the news, so I googled it and your name came up. I tried calling but you didn't answer. I was concerned about my baby brother."

"I know, I'm sorry. I guess I didn't want to know people back home were talking about it."

"Are you okay?"

"Yeah, Sis, I won't lie, it's been a rough patch. Hopefully it works out. I didn't do any of the things they're saying."

"I know you didn't. You don't even have to say it."

Unlike Eph, Jack Russell never went to college. He was one of twenty-three in his graduating class of Ashley High School to enlist in the army. For some, it was just something to do when few other avenues were available. Others, though, felt the call, like a lot of boys across the South. Jack sported a buzz cut his whole senior year and decorated his bedroom with military posters. He'd felt the call for years.

Off they all went, all twenty-three, on a bus one morning to Fort Jackson in South Carolina. The Russell family saw them off, and a tearful Millie handed Jack a bag of her famous pecan tarts for the long drive.

Like a lot of boys from Alabama, Jack was a crack shot, and the army soon trained him as a sniper. After several months at Fort Jackson, he was transferred to Fort Irwin, in the Mojave Desert, where soldiers could acclimate to conditions similar to those in Afghanistan. He called home every Sunday and sounded eager for deployment. For someone who had never been outside Alabama and the Florida Panhandle, it was all a great adventure.

Eventually Jack got his wish and became the first Russell to leave the country. He quickly built a reputation as an effective sniper. He was often called on to protect patrols from a distance, acting as lookout and, if necessary, protection, courtesy of his Winchester Magnum. In one engagement, while positioned on top of a water tank almost a mile away, Jack held off a group of insurgents who ambushed his company while on IED patrol. He had six confirmed kills and bought enough time for his company to evacuate. For his actions he received the Bronze Star. They wrote a big article about it in the *Ashley Standard.* Millie cut that one out for her scrapbook.

Jack's absence made things tougher for Eph. His heart wasn't in farming and he no longer had Jack's coattails at school. Big Mike was a good man, but didn't know how to relate to a son who liked to read all the time. Tension grew as the months passed and Ellie frequently had to act as a buffer, the way daughters sometimes do.

The knock on the door came on Jack's second tour. Millie saw the chaplain and the notification officer, solemn faced, walking up and refused to open it, knowing what waited on the other side. She wanted just a few more moments of a world where her boy was still alive. Big Mike summoned all the stoicism a man could muster and let them in.

Jack Russell had died a hero, which was only natural. Nine men in his company had come under heavy attack by an al-Qaeda militia. Heavily outnumbered, they sought refuge in an abandoned farmhouse. As the militia closed in, Jack, aided by his spotter, picked them off one at a time from their nest in a stand of trees some five hundred yards away. Unfortunately, his steady fire allowed militia members to make the nest and they fired mortars. As shells exploded around him, Jack kept picking the enemy off, knowing if he abandoned his position the farmhouse would be overrun. It was later confirmed

that Jack had had an astonishing fifteen kills before the remaining militia retreated. Angry over their losses, though, the jihadists had fired a few more
mortars from behind a building. One got lucky and hit the tree over Jack's
nest and instantly killed his spotter. Jack himself took shrapnel but was still
alive when those whose lives he'd saved got to his position. He died in the
transport on the way back to base.

The Russell family's first trip to the nation's capital was to bury Jack at
Arlington. Millie was presented with the burial flag and Jack's posthumous
Medal of Honor. It was the only time Eph saw Big Mike cry.

Millie would never get over the loss of her eldest boy. She succumbed to
an aggressive cancer a year later. She didn't fight it very hard.

Eph was pretty sure that every time Big Mike looked at him he was reminded of the better son. Ellie tried to keep up spirits, but over time the house
grew silent. Eph grew resentful that a normal childhood had been stolen from
him and resolved to find his way out. After a year at a nearby community college he won a scholarship to Samford and never looked back.

He wasn't sure Big Mike even noticed.

# Gherkins Are Small Pickles

**EPH ONCE AGAIN** made his way across Bingham Plaza to Stockbridge. Students were scurrying everywhere with final preparations for tomorrow's Fling and were too preoccupied to notice a disgraced professor in their midst.

An enormous stage had been erected in front of the Dix and sound checks were being performed. Adjacent to the stage was a twenty-foot video screen. Eph had never heard of Killa C Note but he wasn't surprised. He didn't know much about the rap world.

Electronic music blared from the speakers . . .

*Love you! Love you!*

The Fling was probably the high point of the year for most students. Classes were over and they had a week off until exams. The administration understood the constant pressure most students felt and that periodically steam needed blowing off. Best that it be done in a largely enclosed space like Bingham where campus security could keep an eye on things.

Eph wished he could share in the collective mood. Titus had called earlier and told him the tenure committee was going with Toes. Toes was going to be the Edward S. Phelps Professor of English.

"I suppose this doesn't come as a surprise, after everything," Titus said in a sympathetic voice.

It didn't, but it still stung. Minutes later D'Arcy showed up and said, "I'm afraid I have bad news."

"You should take a ticket and get in line."

"Why?"

"Toes got the tenure spot."

"Oh, God, baby. I'm sorry." She gave him a supportive hug, but with the news she was about to share, it was hardly a shock.

"Okay, go ahead. Throw another log on the bonfire of my discontent."

"So, I can hear what happens in Milton's office, right? I usually tune it out, but I heard Milton say your name. He was talking to Martika. The second hearing is just for show. They've already made up their minds."

"I should have known as much. I'm such an idiot."

"I am going to hurt that woman." D'Arcy explained that the meeting was to paper things over in case Eph sued later. "After Milton left, I went onto his university email account, which I have access to. I did a search for your name. Dozens of emails came up, mostly from Martika and counsel. From what I could gather, universities are sued on Title IX decisions all the time and frequently settle, but those settlements are peanuts—'small beer' was how Milton put it—compared to how much they receive in federal funding every year, so all in all they view it as a reasonable trade-off. But they still try to minimize the damage."

"D'Arcy, I love you, but you have to stop."

"The point is, they think you'd win a case against them."

"Sweetheart, you're going to get fired."

"I'm not sure I care."

"I do."

Was this his last time on campus? He wasn't sure why he was even going to the hearing. Did he need to play along with their star chamber? He also didn't know why Lulu Harris still had it in for him, but he was strictly forbidden from contacting her. Title IX, he was told, again. He sighed, knowing it was in his DNA to follow the rules, even when rules were rigged. On some level, too, he still felt love for this place. He couldn't just turn it off with a switch.

Those feelings did not apply to Martika Malik-Adams.

A secretary led Eph back to the same conference room as before and told him to wait. He could still hear the thumping beat in the plaza outside with someone occasionally saying, "Check, check."

A full half an hour later Martika, Stephanie Coughlin, and the stenographer came through the door and took their seats. "This is the second session of Professor Ephraim Russell's Title IX hearing, called to order," Martika began, wasting no time. "Hello, Professor, how are you today?" She flashed some feral teeth. Eph assumed it was an attempt to smile.

"Under the circumstances, I don't know how to answer that question."

"I feel like we got off on the wrong foot last time, and I apologize for that. We're not on anyone's side, we're only trying to establish the facts."

"That strikes me as a difficult task when it's one person's word against another's," said Eph.

"We all do the best we can, don't we? I should say we are very appreciative of your help in understanding what happened." Martika waited for a response from Eph, but it wasn't forthcoming. "Anyway, I'd like to put aside the day in question for the moment. If you would, tell us a little bit about yourself."

"I don't understand."

"We'd like to know you better. Indulge us. We want to understand Ephraim Russell, the person, so we can make this process as fair as possible."

Martika was taking a different tack today, and despite everything D'Arcy had told him, a small part of him wanted to believe. This was Devon, a place where the highest ideals were supposed to be upheld. A place of beauty and truth. But, no. His naïveté could only be pushed so far. She, and by extension the university, was lying to his face. This was a game he didn't need to play.

"Well, Martika, I like riding my bike and eating pizza, especially with clam sauce. I'm not really a morning person and I'm partial to long walks in the rain."

Malik-Adams stared blankly. "I see. And do you walk in the rain often?"

"Oh, yes. I monitor the forecasts for bad weather."

Martika took some notes. *Is she really writing that down?* His stenographer friend was clicking away.

Martika forced another smile. "Oh, you're making a joke." She tried her best to chuckle. "But seriously, tell us what makes Ephraim Russell, the man. I believe you have roots in the South somewhere?"

"I thought we covered that at the last rodeo."

"We'd hate to overlook anything, especially something that might help. Wouldn't you say that's a good thing?"

"Okey-dokey. But I don't see what it has to do with whether I laid a hand on Lulu Harris. Which I didn't, by the way. Did I mention that?"

"Professor Russell, it is within our purview to ask any questions we like."

"Then I take the Fifth."

"About where you're from?"

Stephanie Coughlin leaned in. "I'm afraid that the Fifth Amendment is a legal construct that doesn't apply here, Professor."

"Okay, I plead the Fourth."

"Professor, there's no such thing, and again, you are confusing this with a legal procedure. This is not a court of law. Please answer the question, if you would."

"Fine. I'm Southern."

"Whereabouts?" Martika continued,

"Here and there. Does it matter?"

"I'm having trouble understanding your defensiveness, Professor. I believe you told the Bias Response Team that you were from Florida, is that not right?"

"That's where I spent a number of years, yes."

"But not where you were actually raised . . ." Martika shuffled through some papers until she found the one she wanted. "If I were to look at a copy of your background file from HR, is that what it would say? That you're from Florida?"

"Excuse me, but once again, what does this have to do with Lulu Harris?"

"It gets to character and veracity, Professor. How about your spare time? Are there organizations you get involved with?"

"Scrabble."

"I'm sorry?"

"I am a member in good standing of the National Scrabble Association. Great game, Scrabble. Did you know I once scored one hundred and eight points on a single word? *Gherkin.* It's a small pickle."

"I see." Martika wasn't sure if her chain was being yanked, which it most definitely was. "What about political inclinations? Could you share your thoughts there?"

"Absolutely. I am stridently opposed to inclinations."

"*Professor—*"

Stephanie Coughlin leaned over and whispered something in Martika's ear.

"I withdraw the question." Continuing, Martika said, "You wanted to talk about Ms. Harris. Let's do that. Would you say she seems like a troubled girl?"

"Well, you've seen her crawling around campus just like I have. I'd say she's flat-out nuts."

"But what about before?"

"Before what?"

"Before this recent behavior."

"I have no idea. But the girl hit on a professor and then lied about it, so yeah, maybe." *Lied* came out *laah'd*.

"Would you say she's attractive?"

"What?"

"She's a very pretty girl, wouldn't you say?"

"I don't know."

"I think anyone would agree she is. She's also quite young, isn't she?"

"Relative to what?"

Martika ignored the question. "So here we have this young, pretty girl, one that is also troubled, all alone with you when you'd been drinking. The situation must have seemed all too easy."

"Easy for *what*?"

"Easy to take advantage of. Tell me, Professor, do you like young girls? Do they turn you on?"

Eph had been clenching and unclenching his fists so hard that his nails had drawn flecks of blood. His head throbbed. *How did I get here?* He looked across at Martika, sitting there like a ravenous vulture. What gave her the right? *What?*

A feeling of pure clarity came over Eph for the first time since this all began. It came as if a voice, and that voice said, *Screw it.* He sat up bolt straight and said, "Lady, I am from Ashley *fucking* Alabama. I like country music, I hate kombucha, and I think dressing up as a vagina is idiotic. Furthermore, as we say in Ashley, Lulu Harris is some serious sugar, but I never laid a hand on her. I think both you and this hearing are a complete joke, and just to be clear, for about five minutes I considered voting for Donald Trump." Eph leaned back and put his feet up on the conference table. "Now what else would you like to fucking know?"

The two women stared in shocked silence. Martika turned the shade of a ripe eggplant and her mouth twitched. "Professor Russell! You were warned for the last time to take this proceeding seriously. I will be forced to report you did not!"

Eph gave Martika the most serious, forehead-furrowed look he could muster.

Then he winked.

*"Mr. Russell!"* She was screaming now. *"You are—"*

"Dean, perhaps this is a good time for us to take a break," said Stephanie Coughlin.

*"No!"* Martika yelled. She turned the full focus of her fury back to Eph. "Look at me, Professor. Look very carefully. You want to treat this as a joke, be my guest. It makes my job easier. But you should take me very seriously. You *will* take me seriously!" Waves of heat radiated off her and bits of spittle flew from her mouth. Suffused with the rage of someone whose obvious importance was not properly recognized by those around her, she then rose out of her chair to say something else. It was at that very moment, Martika Malik-Adams, Devon dean of diversity and inclusion, farted. Not a small, sneak-it-out kind of fart, but an emphatic, clarion one, finding its full voice through a thin barrier of straining spandex.

Eph's eyes went wide, and for the first time in weeks, he laughed. As Martika stormed out of the room, he laughed and laughed until tears came to his eyes.

# America's Sweetheart

**D'ARCY POKED HER** head into Milton's office. "Sir, there's someone here to see you."

"Not now, D'Arcy." He was about to call the Steering Committee to share the latest developments. The ship had been righted, as it were. The Crawl was coming to an end, women's groups had been mollified (albeit with some generous funding), and the historical scourge of fraternities would soon be over. All in the last week. It felt good to lead.

"Sir, it's Camille Thornton," said D'Arcy in an exaggerated whisper.

"Camille Thornton? *Here?*" He'd always hoped they might meet, but she'd never come back to campus. Until now.

"Yes, sir. She'd like a moment of your time. I'm supposed to remind you she went to the drama school."

"Yes, of course. Send her in!"

"Right away."

"Oh, and, D'Arcy, please reschedule the call with the Steering Committee."

"Of course, sir." Milton tried to compose himself, but when Camille swept into Milton's office, his heart fluttered. *That smile!*

"Ms. Thornton. I am honored," he said, beaming.

"Thank you, President Strauss. The honor is mine." She flashed her trademark smile again. It was broad and elfin and had melted the hearts of a generation of moviegoers. If it had lost any of its luster, Milton wasn't noticing.

"Please, call me Milton."

"Milton. Thank you for seeing me without an appointment. And call me Camille. Please." She touched him lightly on the forearm.

"My pleasure, Camille. It's always good to welcome back one of our lost lambs."

"Lost no more!"

For a few moments, Milton just stared, grinning foolishly.

"Do you think I could sit?"

"Oh! Yes, of course." Milton led her to the sitting area. "What can I get you? Some coffee? A glass of wine, perhaps?"

"I'm fine, thank you."

"So tell me, how can Devon help one of her favorite daughters?"

"I've flown across the country to speak with you. It concerns Lulu Harris."

"Ah, our crawler. Very impressive girl. May I ask your interest?"

"You certainly may. I'm making a film, and it would be helpful if I could talk to her. For research."

"A new film. Wonderful! Are you allowed to tell me what it's about?"

"Of course. It's called *Gender Games*. I play a woman named Molly Fletcher, the mother of a college-age girl—"

Milton waved a hand dismissively. "College age? Impossible!"

Camille laughed. "Flattery will get you everywhere, good sir, particularly where I'm from. Is this how you raise all that money?"

"Merely stating the obvious." A goofy smile was still plastered to Milton's face.

"Anyway, the girl is off at college, and as it happens, she suffers an assault at the hands of several boys. When the girl publicly accuses them, they set about destroying her reputation. This leads tragically to her suicide. The mother, my character, comes to campus to seek revenge."

"Sort of a feminist *Death Wish*? You're the distaff Charles Bronson?"

"You know your film history! Yes, but perhaps a bit more topical and definitely edgier. My character exacts her revenge in fitting ways, if you know what I mean."

"Oh, dear." Milton crossed his legs reflexively. "It sounds like a hit!"

"That's so nice of you. Perhaps we could put you in a cameo. Much of the film is set on a college campus . . ."

Milton's face lit up. "You know, I used to be somewhat of a thespian myself! I played the Stage Manager in *Our Town* my freshman year." Milton held up a theatrical hand and looked into the distance. "'So this is the way we were in the provinces of New York . . . the way we were in our growing up and our marrying and our living . . . and in our dying.'"

"Bravo!" Camille clapped. "I'm sure we can arrange something."

Milton visibly blushed. "It's amazing how easily it comes back."

"Yes, I'm sure. Anyway, I always like to research my roles thoroughly, and I'm sure you can see the parallels here, so I was hoping I might meet Miss Harris."

"Have you tried reaching out to her?"

"Well, from everything I've read, she's quite private and hasn't been talking to the media or anyone else."

"That's true. She's been quite the cipher." Needless to say, he wasn't sharing Lulu's recanting of her story with anyone, not even Camille Thornton. Poor girl was confused. "You know, tomorrow is her last Crawl, which means there's one tonight as well. It might help your research. In fact, you could watch from here if you wanted . . ."

"That's very gracious of you. I think I'd like to talk to Lulu before I do anything."

"Certainly, if she's willing. I can't imagine she'd say no to Camille Thornton!" Milton walked to the door and stuck his head out. "D'Arcy, a moment?" D'Arcy entered with pen and notepad. "Ms. Thornton would like to meet Lulu Harris. Would you mind arranging it straightaway?"

"Certainly, sir, although she apparently never responds to calls or emails. I can walk Ms. Thornton over to Duffy . . ."

Milton turned back to Camille. "It's a beautiful day. Why don't I take you over to Duffy Hall myself and we'll see if we can find the enigmatic Ms. Harris together?"

"That would be lovely. Thank you so much."

Milton imagined people seeing him squiring Camille Thornton about. Just another day as president of an elite university. Perhaps @FakeUncleMiltie would have something to say . . .

———

Camille Thornton wondered how Milton might react if he knew the truth.

At one time she had been the top-grossing actress in Hollywood, starring in a string of massively successful romantic comedies, famous for her girl-next-door persona. As is the way of Hollywood, though, younger actresses asserted themselves and offers gradually dried up. In an effort to stay youthful, Camille embarked on a series of ill-advised plastic surgeries, the combined effect changing her trademark fresh-faced look into something faintly alien. Her lips were puffy from collagen and her skin unnaturally shiny from a face-lift and Botox injections; not the Camille Thornton her fans knew. It also didn't help that in real life she wasn't the bubbly sprite she was on-screen. She had a well-earned reputation in the industry for being "difficult" on set. Now forty-five, she hadn't had a real role in over three years.

Publicists, agents, studio execs . . . they all fed her the same crap. *We love you, Camille. The next great role is right around the corner, Camille.*

She was tired of getting smoke blown up her ass.

Walking down Mathers, Milton and Camille got plenty of shout-outs and wide-eyed stares. No one actually stopped her for an autograph, which disappointed Milton, but Devon students imagined themselves too sophisticated. So much cooler to just shout famous lines from her movies.

*"It's so cute!"*

That was Camille Thornton's signature line from *That One Weekend,* her equivalent of "I'll be back." It was her character's response to this creep who thought dropping his pants on a first date was the path to her affections. She heard it most places she went, and invariably people thought they were being clever. Bill Murray once told her that "It's in the hole!" was his own particular cross to bear.

It's so cute. A career, distilled to three words. There had to be more, a role that meant something, a role that changed people's lives. She believed with every fiber of her being that Molly Fletcher was that role. *Gender Games* was topical and it was dark. Total Oscar bait. Molly Fletcher was the role of a lifetime, the kind of strong woman audiences were demanding these days. Camille Thornton, girl next door, was about to be buried. Camille Thornton, avenging badass, would be born.

But she needed to take matters into her own hands or nothing would get done.

Just like Molly Fletcher would do.

"All this graffiti, it's for her?" she asked Milton.

"It is. We call it chalking. It's not uncommon on campuses these days, but I'm not sure any have matched this." Graffiti now covered every inch of Mathers Walk.

"Incredible."

They arrived at Duffy and walked the two floors up to Lulu's new room. "We moved her to a single so she could have more privacy," Milton said. He knocked on the door; there was no answer, so he tried knocking harder. "Hello?"

"Who the hell is it?" came a voice from behind the door.

"Lulu, it's Milton Strauss. May I have a moment?"

After some shuffling inside, the door swung open. Lulu had on a terry-cloth bathrobe and a face mask of avocado-colored cream.

"Hello, Milton!" She sounded hoarse. Primal screams had taken their toll. She appeared pleased, though, perhaps because the president of the university had come to *her*.

"Hello, Lulu, it's a great pleasure to finally—"

"Wait." She'd noted the presence of another, the great Camille Thornton, America's Sweetheart. "What the fuck is *she* doing here?"

Milton's face broadened with shock. "*Excuse me*, young lady, but—"

Camille cut him off with a dismissive wave, looking intently at Lulu. "Is that any way to talk to your mother?"

# It's Only a Motion Away

**"I DON'T SUPPOSE** you could take the mask off?" asked Camille. They were alone now, a flustered Milton Strauss having practically run off.

"What the fuck are you doing here?" Lulu left the avocado cream where it was.

Camille took in the space. "These rooms are small, aren't they?"

"I'll repeat the question. What the fuck are you doing here?"

Camille's tone softened. "Don't be like that. I come in peace."

"But why have you come at all?" Lulu asked, arms folded.

"Listen . . . Lulu, I know this is odd, my just showing up like this. I would have reached out, but I wasn't sure you'd respond, and I wanted to see you."

"You know what that's like, don't you? Not hearing back from someone."

"I deserve that, I know." Camille took a chance and sat down on the edge of Lulu's bed. "I hope you're open to hearing this because it's very difficult for me to say. I've had a lot of time to think, and I feel badly about, well, everything. I was very young . . . I just didn't know how to handle things . . ."

"Things."

"Marriage, motherhood . . . a child. All of it. I wasn't that much older than you, you know."

"So you just show up at my door one day unannounced and think you can snap your fingers and everything's peachy? You must be kidding."

"I wasn't sure you'd agree to see me . . ."

Flashes of red were starting to show around the avocado edges of Lulu's mask. "Pretty good fuckin' instincts there, Camille. Let me ask you something. All these years, you had a child you kept a secret. How do you suppose that made the child feel? Just curious."

It was true. No one knew that Camille Thornton had a child. The marriage to Sheldon had been a spontaneous, justice-of-the-peace sort of thing. They had known each other for nine weeks, and Camille—April Gilmartin, back then—was already pregnant. The pregnancy forced her to decline a small part in a Broadway play and she was almost immediately resentful, blaming both Sheldon and the unborn child for hindering her career. Almost as soon as she could leave the hospital, she left for L.A. and changed both her name and her look. Things were slow at first, but a year back east at Devon Drama School provided some key contacts, and before long she landed her first movie role—all of seven lines. But "Camille Thornton" was on her way.

For a fresh-faced Hollywood newcomer, though, an abandoned child and busted marriage were flies in the career ointment. Camille offered Sheldon full custody in exchange for signing a nondisclosure agreement. The whole affair, including the existence of a child, was officially buried. Sheldon was barred from telling Lulu about her mother's identity until her sixteenth birthday. That would give Camille's career some leeway. Sheldon's resentment toward Camille ran so deep that this suited him just fine, although he hadn't anticipated the guilt he felt every time Lulu asked him about her mother.

"I can't even imagine," Camille said. "I am so, so sorry. But please understand how different things were then. I was trying to make it in Hollywood, a place run entirely by men. There was a lot of pressure to . . . present a certain image."

"Way to take a fucking stand," said Lulu, still covered in cream. "Does Sheldon know you're here?"

"It's been a long time since your father and I have spoken."

"I tried to call you, you know. When Sheldon told me. Many times. You never called back. That was only two years ago. I suppose you were still trying to present a 'certain image'?"

"I know you did. I was scared, if you want to know the truth. I didn't know what to do or say. I felt this horrible guilt and tried to put it—*you*—out of my mind. It worked for a little while, but then I saw you in the papers and in *People*, of course, and I just felt so awful about everything."

"So now *I'm* famous you suddenly show up unannounced at my door? Do you think I'm some kind of idiot?"

"No! I just so admire what you're doing. Honestly, you're taking the kind of stand I never did."

The two were silent for a minute, each taking the other's measure.

"I'm sure you know," continued Camille, "that sexual assault has been a big issue in the film industry."

"I hadn't noticed."

"I myself have had the misfortune of seeing Harvey Weinstein discard his bathrobe, as if anyone wants to see that. Of course, I said, 'It's so cute,' before I ran out the door. What a fat, self-deluded asshole, I hope he rots in hell." Camille sighed. "I suppose that's as close to taking a stand as I've ever gotten. Tell me, were you really attacked?"

"Does it matter?"

"Of course it matters, but you don't have to tell me. Anyway, I thought . . . what you're doing . . . perhaps I could help your cause."

"My cause." Lulu chuckled slightly.

"I thought I could bring . . . attention, maybe more press."

"I seem to be doing pretty well with that on my own, *Camille*."

"Of course you are, but we all want more attention brought to this issue, and it's finally starting to happen. We women are in this together. Aren't we?"

"Not interested. Go home."

"Don't underestimate celebrity, Lulu."

"I prefer to think of it as not *over*estimating you."

Camille turned toward Lulu. "Look, I'm not claiming to be a good person, and I know you got the short end of the stick in all this. I was quite selfish in my younger years. But when I saw your picture, staring back at me at a newsstand, it affected me deeply. I had this *daughter* out there, doing great things, and it tugged at my heart. I was so proud and so ashamed all at once. And I'm doing this film, you see, and it's all about this! About what you're doing, in a way. It's called *Gender Games,* and one of the central characters could be you! When I read about you and the Crawl, I felt it had to be a sign, that I somehow had to make this right." Camille wiped away a tear.

"Make this right. By doing what?"

"I'd like to march with you. And . . . I'd like to tell the world you're my daughter."

Lulu considered this. The wheels turned. "Really?"

"Really. If you'll let me."

Lulu's expression softened for a moment. Camille took this for a sign and leaned in to hug her daughter at long last.

Lulu thrust a stiff arm straight out. "You are so full of shit."

"I'm sorry?"

"Get the hell out of my room."

# Screw Warhol

**CAMILLE DECIDED TO** show at that night's Crawl. It wasn't as if Lulu could stop her. Camille had Noah Stein, her agent, slip word to some paparazzi. Havenport wasn't exactly their beat, but the photo op was potentially good enough that a few made the drive up from New York. Camille had also slipped word of her plans on Twitter, so tonight's Crawl was the biggest yet.

She followed solemnly just behind Lulu, listening to the ball go *scrape, scrape*. A single candle was held in her hands; it would make for a good visual. She had hoped the story line was going to be more dramatic than simply another celebrity backing a cause. *An anguished mother comes to her long-lost daughter's side in her hour of need.* Now, *that* would have been solid gold. But she would take what she could get.

Cameras flashed and dozens of spectators were livestreaming. A few reporters yelled questions, but Camille thought she would let the imagery speak for itself, at least for now.

She cringed just a bit at the ten-foot vagina on wheels. That might have been a bit more abstract, she thought. Very cinematic, though. Noah might be able to pitch this.

When they reached Duffy, Lulu crawled up the three stone steps and stood. As the crowd came to complete silence, she screamed. Only, it wasn't her normal scream, the full-throated roar of a woman releasing her pain. She was losing her voice, and it sounded almost like a desperate whisper, like when you try to scream in a nightmare but nothing comes out. Her faithful could see she was trying harder and harder to project, but the harder she tried, the more her voice failed. As the whisper-scream faded to nothing, many were moved to tears. The imagery was one of an anguished, defeated woman.

Camille sensed an opportunity. Before anything else could happen, she hopped up next to Lulu and took her hand. The camera flashes were blinding. She drew in a deep breath and began to scream herself. As a trained actress, this was something she could do. There were those one or two regrettable horror films early in her career.

When her breath finally gave, there was a moment of awed silence. The crowd was profoundly moved. Then they responded, not with their usual responsive scream, but with unbridled, joyful cheering.

Camille raised Lulu's hand over their heads as if they were politicians who just won nomination. Camille then leaned over and whispered in Lulu's ear, "A good actress always knows how to improvise, my dear."


Camille followed Lulu inside, and Lulu knew she couldn't very well do anything about it. She'd been outfoxed. She let Camille into her room and slammed the door shut. "Very clever," Lulu said, unclasping the iron ball.

"Only trying to help." Camille lifted the iron ball, as if to test its weight. "Jesus, this thing is heavy."

"You are so transparent, you know that?" Lulu removed the clasp from around her ankle.

"I don't know what you mean. You sound horrible, by the way. Can I find you some tea somewhere?"

"It's your movie. It's having problems, isn't it?"

"What?"

"*Gender Games*. It's in . . . what do they call it out there? Development hell? Google makes for fascinating reading sometimes." Lulu had kept quiet track of Camille ever since she'd learned her true identity. She knew *Gender Games* was supposed to be Camille's big comeback, but it was in Hollywood purgatory. Lulu knew few movies ever made it out. People moved on.

"It's coming along. The script just needs one more rewrite."

"Sure it does. How many would that make, exactly?"

"If you've been doing all this research, then you know it's part of the process."

"So, correct me if I'm wrong on any of this." Lulu rubbed Nivea cream around her ankle. "You haven't had a role in years, this movie is your way back onto the red carpet, and you think announcing to the world I'm your daughter, a daughter who conveniently has become a feminist media hero while you're trying to make this girl-power movie, will kick-start your career. So you come in here and think if you cry a few phony tears we can get the show on the road. That about right, Camille?"

"Lulu! I never would—"

Lulu glared. *"Cut the shit."*

Camille sighed, sensing defeat. "You're a smart one. I guess that's why you're here. I'd like to think you got that from me, but those genes are probably Sheldon's. You're right, I could use the help. Women my age, Hollywood has little use for us. And yes, *Gender Games* is stuck in the mud. I confess I thought coming here . . . might ignite something. Maybe we can help each other. But I also wanted to get to know you. I truly did—*do*."

Suddenly, this was a relatable person, one Lulu understood. Camille was an operator, but who was Lulu to cast the first stone? It was almost something she could admire. Could she forgive Camille for nineteen years of absence? Probably not. But it was nice to be *needed*. This bitch needed her. Camille's fame was fading while Lulu's was on the rise. Still, the name Camille Thornton was known the world over. If Lulu let her get involved . . . the possibilities popped in her mind rapid-fire . . .

The Crawl was coming to an end, and Lulu needed a follow-up act. Fifteen minutes of fame was not an acceptable outcome. *Screw Warhol.*

Lulu started changing out of her crawling clothes. The khakis were shredded and the blue button-down frayed at the cuffs. "The answer to your question last night . . . it's no."

"I'm sorry, which question?"

"No, I wasn't attacked."

"Seriously?"

"Seriously."

"Then . . ."

"The Crawl? I wasn't having a great time here, if you want to know the truth. It started because I was pissed about some other stuff and I just had a feeling it would strike a chord, even if it's total bullshit."

Camille's jaw dropped. "Jesus."

Lulu smiled slightly. "Honestly, it was something to do. The people here are so pathetic and predictable, so I'm using it. I'm building a brand."

Camille was stunned. "You're doing all this . . . just for exposure?"

"Why not? College sucks anyway. And have you seen how many followers I have?"

"Oh, my God. That is so . . . brilliant."

"Cool, right? Honestly, I've been dying to talk to someone about it. But at this point I can't wait till it's over. I'm losing my voice and I have hands like a migrant worker."

"So . . . now what?"

Lulu looked up at Camille. Was that admiration in her eyes? Lulu then looked down at Camille's phone and smiled. "Go ahead."

"Are you sure?"

"Yes."

Camille picked up her phone and opened Twitter, where she had over three hundred thousand followers. She typed:

So proud and honored to tell the world Lulu Harris is my birth daughter. Reunited at last! C u at #Crawlpeace tomorrow!

She then sat next to Lulu and they hugged each other for a selfie, which she attached to the tweet. She handed her phone to Lulu for approval. "So, we're doing this?"

"We're doing this." Lulu held the phone up and hit send.

"Holy shit. People are going to go crazy." Almost immediately, Camille's phone buzzed with a call. "My publicist. His head is probably exploding." She declined the call. "I can talk to him later. Listen, would you get a bite to eat somewhere? I know it's late, but I'm starving."

Lulu smiled. "Why the hell not. Let me just call Sheldon before he hears this from someone else. I owe him that. But tell me something first."

"Anything."

"When Harvey Weinstein dropped that robe . . ."

"It was like being threatened by an angry kidney bean."

They both laughed like schoolgirls.

"Tell me more," said Lulu.

# The Fling

**IT WAS THE** largest event Rufus—*RoofRaza*—had ever played. He figured that at least three thousand people were stretched across Bingham. Several beach balls were getting knocked about. The crowd throbbed up and down in waves to the EDM beat as he warmed them up. The feeling was godlike.

A bow-tied a cappella group, the Swell Fellows, had been onstage as an opening act. (Devon was lousy with a cappella groups—you couldn't throw a stick on campus without hitting one.) The crowd politely tolerated a few numbers, but then "Surrey with the Fringe on Top" proved a musical bridge too far. The crowd booed and someone hurled a pillow shaped like a poop emoji, inexplicably. The Swell Fellows wisely cut their gig a couple of songs short. This teed up Roof to really start the party.

Sure, he was only an opening act, but still. Things were on track. Backstage he even got to meet Killa C Note. The man had two Grammys!

It was unnaturally hot for April and the skies to the west looked threatening. The forecast was favorable, but Rufus didn't like the looks of it. There was a lot of sick equipment up here, better and louder than anything he'd worked with before. He told members of the Fling Committee they should go find some tarps, just in case. There was apparently a lot of confusion about the exact location of spare tarps at Devon.

But it wasn't Rufus's equipment, so whatever.

"How you all doin' out there!" he yelled. "Who's ready to paaarrrr-tay?!"

The crowd threw fists in the air and roared. Oh, yes, they were. Officially, this was a dry event, but college is college. *Who they kidding?* Rufus thought. Drinking had begun in earnest hours ago. He saw one passed-out dude get carried out already before the music even started.

Rufus didn't have long before he had to give things up to Killa, so he made sure to play an extended cut of "I Want to Love You."

*Love you!*
*Love you!*

"Well, all right!!" he yelled, as the song faded. "Let's put our hands together and give it up for the one, the only, Grammy-Award-winning artist . . . Killa C Note!"

Rufus yielded his turntables to Killa's DJ, and Killa emerged, strutting, stripped to the waist, baggy jeans held perilously in place by unseen means. The video screen beamed a twenty-foot Killa to the far reaches of the crowd as he launched straight into one of his hits, "Pigs in Blue."

*Brothers cryin'*
*Souls say why in*
*Hell we gotta take*
*This life we tryna make*
*Jackboots, badge brutes*
*Hands up, don't shoot*

"Everyone!"

*Pigs in blue*
*I see you!*
*Pigs in blue*

Killa held the mic out to the crowd.

"I see you!" came the thunderous response.

A girl from the back was hoisted by the crowd and passed forward on a sea of arms. She made it all the way to the stage, as if an offering, and Killa swooped her up, then dipped her low, planting his face on hers.

"That's what I'm talkin' 'bout, yo!"

The crowd roared its approval as the girl was hustled off by security.

After finishing his set, someone came from backstage and whispered something to Killa, who then said, "Listen up, yo. I'd like to introduce Devon's very own boss man, the man who puts the action in yo' Jackson, Milton"—Killa leaned over as the assistant whispered in his ear—"Strauss. Lemme hear it!"

Milton emerged from the side of the stage, waving. Killa gave him the mic and disappeared backstage. The crowd chanted, *"Milt! Milt! Milt!"*

"Thank you, Devon! And thank you, Killa C Note." Milton pronounced it *killer*. "Isn't he great, everyone?" More cheers, but with less enthusiasm. Rufus, spying from the wings, knew they smelled a speech.

Ah, here they were. *His people.* Milton loved these opportunities. What a crowd this year! He was also pleased with the size of the media presence. At least seven or eight vans were parked just outside the plaza. Naturally, Devon's PR staff had tipped some reporters about whom he was going to introduce, knowing it would increase exposure for his important announcement.

"It's so great to see everyone together as one community. Because that's what we are, right? We're a community. *Una Crescimus.* Together, we grow! Am I right?"

There was scattered applause. Backstage, Rufus could feel the energy being sucked out of the plaza.

Milton hardly noticed. "But we're still a long way from perfect, aren't we? As you know, one of our community has been drawing much-needed attention to that fact in a very dramatic and selfless way. I'm talking, of course, about Lulu Harris. Can we have a hand for her?"

The plaza gave respectful applause.

"So, with Lulu as our inspiration, I'd like to make an important announcement. Devon University will pledge fifty million dollars toward making our community more gender inclusive. Thirty million dollars will be allocated toward the hiring of female faculty, including four new tenured positions in the Women's Studies Department, ten million dollars toward women's health initiatives, and ten million dollars toward the construction of a new women's cultural center!"

Applause was polite at best. Where was Killa?

"And, of course, Devon is leading the way toward inclusiveness by evolving beyond the need for single-gender organizations."

The crowd's tone changed slightly; boos mixed in here and there with a few cheers.

"With that, I'd like to introduce one of Devon's most illustrious graduates. Some of you may have seen her around campus the last couple of days, and she just shared some amazing news with us. . . . Here she is, the talented and wondrous . . . Camille Thornton!"

Camille made her way to the mic to polite applause. Rufus could tell patience was running thin with the liquored-up and adrenaline-fueled crowd, and this wasn't a rap star. More like some actress their parents liked. But she was a Devonite, and famous, so that was cool. Plus she was Lulu's mom! They would give her some rope.

Camille's master plan was back on track as she stood in front of an audience, the place any actor was meant to be. Maybe everything was turning around. She even liked Lulu, which was a nice bonus. It could easily have gone the other way.

The media were here in force, owing to her dramatic revelation that Lulu Harris was her long-lost daughter. Just why she was "lost" wasn't being asked, not yet. For now, the feel-good story was quickly sweeping through entertainment news and even into mainstream news. Someone from *People* was here. The magazine was sure to be sympathetic, especially since they'd just featured Lulu in their last issue. This was a home run for them. Camille's publicist and agent were both beside themselves with glee. The timing was "perfect," according to Noah. "I can't believe you managed to keep this a secret all these years. No one can do that these days. Not in this town."

"Just get the damn film out of development, would you?"

"Oh, I'll be making calls all day. This is gold. Love you, baby!"

Camille cried out now to the sea of faces, "Hello, Devon! It's so great to be back, and thank you for the kind reception you've given this old actress."

"We love you!" someone shouted.

Camille laughed. "I love you, too!" A beach ball was batted to the stage and she gave it a good kick, prompting cheers. "As you may have heard, it's here at my beloved Devon that I was just reunited with my daughter, Lulu, after so many years. She is *so*, so special. Aren't I just the luckiest person on the planet?"

More cheers echoed around the plaza.

"Lulu has been suffering for a cause, a cause we all care dearly about, and one I plan to make a film about. It's called *Gender Games*, and I hope you'll all come and see it."

"Where's Killa!" someone yelled.

As an actress, Camille was adept at reading crowds, and she knew she couldn't hold this one much longer. She'd gotten her plug in. It was time.

"I'd like to say one more thing, just one . . . *Crawl!*"

*"Peace!"* came the response.

*"Crawl!"*

*"Peace!"*

"Let's hear it for Lulu!" Camille motioned toward the archway in the corner of the plaza that led into the Dix. Out from the arch's shadow emerged the long-lost daughter . . . crawling.

*Oh, crap,* thought Milton. He quickly ducked backstage and dialed Martika. "Where are you?"

"Up in my office, watching."

"What the hell is going on? I thought the last Crawl was tonight when everyone was cleared out."

"That makes two of us."

"I don't like this, not at all. Half these kids are probably drunk."

"Well, I don't see what you can do about it," said Martika, leaving the distinct impression that whatever happened, it wasn't her problem. Milton noticed Martika's choice of pronoun—*you.* "Stop this thing and you could have a riot on your hands."

The Crawl was now fully emerging out into Bingham, where the throng was doing its best to make way. Behind Lulu, out of the archway, emerged row after row of supporters. The vagina on wheels was there, as was the entire Womyn's Collective. The newly tenured Professor Smallwood was also there, trying with some difficulty to ride his recumbent bike in slow motion.

Milton hung up the phone and immediately dialed Jimmy Trout, Devon's head of campus security. "Jimmy, don't intervene, but have your men close, just in case. I don't like the looks of this."

"Well, sir, there's gonna be a problem with that. As of five minutes ago, my men staged a walkout and the union is backing them."

"*What? Why?*"

"Let's just say they have an issue with the entertainment."

"What are you talking about? Tell them to get back on the job right now! We'll work out any issues later. You *know* I'm a big supporter of the union, but I've got three thousand drunk kids and a protest going on."

"Perhaps the university should have thought of that before it hired a cop-hating rap star. But I'll be sure to pass your message along." The connection was severed.


Moving up the time of the Crawl had been Lulu's idea. Camille was impressed with her instincts. So much more exposure. But Camille knew crowds were fickle things, and this one wanted Killa back. The Crawl was old news. Time to pump them up again.

"*Crawl!*" Camille cried into the mic.

"*Peace!*" replied the crowd.

"Louder this time. *Crawl!*"

"*Peace!*"

The crowd parted for Lulu like the Red Sea as she slowly made her way toward the center of Bingham.

Camille paused when she heard a sound, a musical sound, that didn't belong. What was that? She tried to spy where it was coming from, but Bingham Plaza was like an echo chamber. It could be anywhere.

Wait, was that . . . a *bagpipe?*


The full complement of Fellingham members emerged into Bingham from around the back of Grafton. They were led by none other than Sir Alexander Hargrove, their erstwhile leader. He wielded the sacred scepter, waving it back and forth as he marched. Accompanying him was a bagpipe and tenor drum. The others followed in neat rows, men dressed in traditional Scottish kilts and women in matching tartan skirts.

Earlier that week, Hargrove had received a call from Win Gubbins, who explained the situation. Win called Lulu an "affront to civility," sensibly omitting his own particular grievance.

Hargrove was confused at first. "Wasn't this woman removed from the Wall of Belonging?"

Win reminded Hargrove of the scepter heist and argued that no one who had treated Fellinghams in such a manner deserved to be fêted as a heroine. This was a matter of principle; a statement needed to be made, one that was *just so*. And besides, it might be a bit of a hoot. Perhaps Sir Alex could be persuaded to come back for a visit?

Hargrove checked his calendar, and upon remembering he had no gainful employment interfering with his ability to fly four thousand miles for a good wingding, he readily agreed. Besides, he hadn't been back to gay old Devon since graduation. He arrived on a plane from London the next day.

The crowd, sensing the kind of ironic amusement they loved so well, made way for the Fellinghams column, which vectored directly toward the Crawl. The two groups came to a head in the middle of the plaza. Win Gubbins motioned to the bagpipe and drum and they went silent.

Alexander Hargrove handed the scepter to Win and raised what appeared to be a scroll.

"Good people of Devon," Sir Alexander cried. "We, the good members of the Society of Fellingham, officially register our objections to this farcical display known to some as the Crawl. Miss Harris violated our trust just as she violates yours. We declare her to be a fraud and a strumpet."

The crowd was conflicted, and there rose an unsettled murmur as people considered how to react. They loved Lulu, of course, but on the other hand, whatever was going on here appeared to be amusing.

Representatives from the Womyn's Collective, though, weren't conflicted at all. Pythia Kamal, Yolanda Perez, and others looked like they wanted blood. "Get out of the fucking way, white boy!" yelled Yolanda at Hargrove.

Lulu, as usual, looked oblivious.


From a window on the third floor of Grafton, Red Wheeler quickly forgot his anger over the sudden enrichment of the campus feminists. Watching his handiwork unfold below, he laughed himself silly in an empty classroom. This was working out even better than he'd hoped. Bagpipes! Those guys were classic!

Sir Alexander was not finished. Still reading from the scroll like a town crier, he said, "We also declare the existing drinking age to be a barbarous New World edict and demand its immediate revocation."

That drew some laughs and more than a few cheers.

Hargrove, for his part, was clearly enjoying himself. "And furthermore—"

"Look!" someone yelled.

The crowd turned as one toward Mathers Walk. There was something large a couple hundred yards away, something that wasn't there a minute ago.

*Oh, dear,* thought Milton.

"Is that a . . . ?" asked Pythia Kamal to no one in particular.

It was, and it was coming their way.

The Betas had arrived.

# Along Came a Phallus

**THE BETAS HAD** spent the last several days in feverish activity constructing their last testament, their magnum opus, their final *fuck you*. Using a trailer bed for a base, they worked up from there with a wood lattice, which was then covered with cardboard and finally papier-mâché. Vibrant swirls of pink and purple paint were added for realism.

The structure was so tall they had to lay it on its side to transport it to Mathers. When raised, it would be stabilized with thin wire cables running to each corner of the trailer bed. Pulling it along were eight brothers, four each on a pair of ropes. Mound captained one rope and Digger the other. Tug supervised while the rest marched to the sides, all dressed identically in gym shorts and white T-shirts.

After rounding the corner onto Mathers, just where it dead-ended into Dudley, they stopped. They dropped the two lead ropes and grabbed two thin cables attached to one end of the structure. At this, Tug yelled, *"Ooh!"*

All the brothers responded with *"Ahh!"* and those manning the cables gave a mighty pull.

Tug, again: *"Ooh!"*

The brothers: *"Ahh!"* And with it another tug.

*"Ooh!"*

*"Ahh!"*

With each pull, the structure rose a bit higher until, pointed skyward, it stood twenty-five feet if an inch. The brothers secured the cables, took up the lead ropes, and were on the move again. Tug changed the chant.

The crowd in Bingham grew even more confused. Was this all part of the Fling? First the Crawl, then the odd people with the bagpipes . . . and now, what the hell was going on down Mathers? Coming toward them was, unmistakably, a big penis. It easily matched the vagina statue in its blushing anatomical precision. Clearly visible on the float's front and sides was the word *#Dickpeace.* Gradually, they heard the chant.

"*Dick! Peace!*"

"*Dick! Peace!*"

From his perch in Grafton, Red Wheeler jumped up and down with glee. Surely, this was his crowning achievement, an unmatched work of performance art. It wasn't exactly aiding the Struggle, but he was allowed a day off now and then, wasn't he? If only there were a canvas to sign or an audience to accept his bow. He was the maestro of chaos.

He pressed his face to the leaded glass, eager to see how the final movement would play out.

*Now, there's something you don't see every day,* thought Eph. A giant penis and a giant vagina on a collision course. Plus, people in kilts. What could go wrong?

Forgetting today was the Fling, Eph had come to campus to gather some last remaining items from his office. He hadn't officially heard from the administration regarding his fate, but he didn't need to. His life at Devon was over, and a dark depression had settled over him. When he came upon the Fling, he was grateful for the distraction, although distraction was perhaps an understatement.

Eph had on a baseball hat and glasses just in case, but there was little chance of his being noticed, not in the middle of this circus. He stopped at the spot where Mathers connected to Bingham, the enormous phallus moving slowly in his direction. The boys manning the rope lines reminded him of Egyptian slaves, pulling stones for the pharaoh. Equal parts curiosity and amusement glued him to the spot.

The Crawlers had used the distraction of a giant rolling penis to push their way around the Fellinghams people. Lulu's well-established route would exit the plaza and take her straight toward the Betas. Eph felt a few drops of rain beginning to fall. He glanced up; the skies looked ominous.

A minute or so later, the two groups ground to a halt in a standoff right in front of where Eph was standing. It occurred to him that most rational people accused of sexual assault would not choose to stand right next to a large protest where said person was the primary focus. He was done caring, though, and this was too entertaining to just walk away. He did, however, pull his baseball hat a bit farther down his face.

Clearly, no one was quite sure what to do, standing there, all staring one another down. Did the Betas look pleased? If it was their goal to stop the Crawl, they had accomplished that. For the moment.

Breaking the momentary silence, Yolanda Perez yelled, "You irrelevant, privileged pigs! Out of our way!"

The Betas took out their phones, tapped them once or twice, and held them in the air. The tinny electronic voice of several dozen phones spoke as one.

*"Douche Crawl!*

*"Douche Crawl!"*

Teddy nodded his approval to Finn Belcher, the creative genius behind Douche Buddy. Finn pushed another button and a large Bluetooth speaker mounted on the float came to life.

*"DOUCHE CRAWL!*

*"DOUCHE CRAWL!"*

A few of the Crawlers started yelling, "Fraternity pigs!" and hurled clumps of dirt and grass they tore up from just off the walk. At that, the Betas tapped their phones again.

*"BLOW ME!"* came the booming electronic voice, as if from the great phallus itself.

Mere weeks ago, Eph might have been upset with the events unfolding on his beloved campus. He might have still tried to care about Foucault and to understand the nuanced differences between fifty-eight genders. Mere weeks ago, he really did dress up as a vibrator at a trans-rights march. But that was then. Today a broad grin emerged through his depression, and he wondered how it had taken so long for the campus tribes to come to a head. He also wondered where the hell campus security was.

Then, not for the first time that afternoon, there was a sound that was out of place. It was loud, *really* loud, and coming from the stage speakers.

It was unmistakably the sound of two people having sex.

The Betas silenced their phones and the Crawlers stopped throwing dirt. All heads turned toward the stage. As rain started to fall in earnest, the grunting and moaning continued through the speakers, each moan testing the limits of the subwoofers. Suddenly, the big video screen came to life, and there, in high definition, were two people having sex on a couch.

Enthusiastically.

Also unmistakable was that one of the stars of the video was Lulu Harris. Many recognized Red Wheeler as the other participant.

Of little note to all but a few in attendance was the time stamp, clearly visible at the bottom of the screen. December 20, 3:57 a.m. The night Eph had allegedly attacked Lulu Harris. But Eph noticed. "Holy shit," he said to no one. Lulu's face showed no sign of bruising.

Elsewhere, reactions differed.

"Crap," said Martika from her office window. She, too, was aware of the significance of the time stamp.

"Oh, shit," said Red from one building over, before deciding it was time to slip away.

"Fuck me," said Milton Strauss, for perhaps the first time in his life.

The Mound, who was mere feet from Lulu, looked down at her and said, "You. Look." He pointed to the screen.

Breaking weeks of precedent, Lulu stood, and she saw. There she was, riding the hairy man-boy like a cowgirl at a rodeo. *Didn't see that coming,* she thought. She was inclined to be upset before remembering that sex tapes had launched any number of personal brands. Paris Hilton, Kim Kardashian, Pamela Anderson . . . This might play, although how would it sync with being a feminist hero? That would require some thought, which was difficult at the moment considering everyone around her was losing their mind.

Up on the stage, a furious Camille Thornton turned on Milton Strauss. "Do something!" she screamed. But Milton was frozen with indecision. This scenario wasn't in the college president's handbook. Taking matters into her own hands, Camille ran backstage to find that boy, the one who was playing music between sets. "You!" she cried, grabbing Rufus by the collar. "Where is that coming from?"

"What?" Rufus was confused. He was busy making himself a sandwich at Killa C's buffet spread and was oblivious of events outside. But wait, was that *sex* he was hearing?

"The video, you little shit. You tell me where it's coming from right now or I'll have Milton throw your ass out of school!"

"Uh, it's a USB stick, plugged into the console," he said, still confused. Some guy from Beta had slipped him five hundred bucks and a promise of more gigs next year to play it. Said it was just a gag on a rival fraternity. Rufus then remembered there wouldn't *be* any fraternities next year, but, hey, five hundred bucks was five hundred bucks.

Camille ran out to the console and found the USB stick. She yanked it out, but by then over three thousand people had seen Lulu Harris grinding away on Red Wheeler. The crowd booed when the screen went blank. They wanted more. The scene had not quite concluded, biblically speaking.


Down by the float, the Womyn's Collective seethed as one. Was that prick Red Wheeler behind this? They were momentarily unsure where to direct their fury. Not toward Lulu. Who cared if she had some recreational sex? It only demonstrated her agency. How *dare* they try to slut-shame her. On the other hand, this could be the handiwork of the Betas, and *those* pricks were right in front of them.

Exactly what to do about it was decided for them when Digger stepped up. "Hey, Lulu, we at Beta Psi just want you to know . . . that was totally hot."

As the rain turned into a torrent, Yolanda pointed a fleshy finger at the Betas and screamed, *"Bastards!"*

That was pretty much when all hell broke loose.

The Crawlers surged around Lulu, shaking the float and tearing at the #Dickpeace signs. The Betas tried shoving them away but were heavily outnumbered. To the side, a fistfight broke out between two onlookers, and others joined in. Still more bodies flowed out of Bingham toward the mêlée, including the Fellinghams contingent. Seizing the moment, the bagpiper resumed his duties while Alexander Hargrove swung his scepter from side to side, clearing a path. The media people buzzed around the periphery like flies, barely containing their spasms of joy, all scrambling to get the best shots.

The Crawlers succeeded in denuding the sides of the float and began climbing up onto it, hungry for more. The Betas knew it wasn't a great idea to exchange blows with women, so they settled for hurling insults and fat jokes. This further enraged Yolanda and Pythia, who were now wet and whirling blurs of female fury. They set their sights on bringing down the phallus. As they worked to untie the support cables, the rain caused streams of beige and violet to run down its sides, lending it a surreal artistry.

"Done!" shouted Yolanda from her corner, hopping off to safety. Pythia and the others untied their cables, too, and yet the phallus stood, undeterred, mocking. The Crawlers mounted the float again and began pushing it back and forth. Little held it in place other than papier-mâché and some thin wood slats. After a few shoves, audible cracks could be heard in the support structure.

The great phallus was toppling. Eph realized with a start that it was about to come crashing down right on top of Lulu Harris, who hadn't moved since she got up to watch herself in the porno. Without another thought, Eph dashed forward and shoved her out of harm's way, although not quite fast enough to avoid the crashing structure himself. It caught him squarely on the side of the head. Adrenaline fueled, he felt nothing.

Chaos surrounded them with rain falling in thick sheets. The diminished visibility provided an anonymity that emboldened some to even greater violence. A casual observer, dropped from the sky, would have had trouble saying who was fighting whom or why. With a bloodlust, the Crawlers destroyed every last remnant of the float. Then there came a *pop pop pop* as people hurled rocks through overlooking windows, perhaps just because they could. Inexplicably, the bagpiper played on. Sir Alexander was shouting something about the queen.

Eph put an arm protectively around Lulu. Looking for a way out, he saw none. They were in a narrow stretch of Mathers, about forty feet wide with residential houses on either side. Toward Bingham a wall of people came in their direction, eager to be closer to the action. In the other direction, Mathers was clogged with the float and flailing bodies still randomly destroying things. There were just too many people. They were trapped.

"Eph, over here!"

It was Toes. He'd abandoned his recumbent bike and stood in a nearby gated entryway that led into Draper House. Normally, house entries required key cards, but as luck would have it, Toes had one.

"C'mon!" shouted Eph. He grabbed Lulu's hand and they started to run, but Lulu was still attached to her ball and chain. Eph scooped it up and they scrambled awkwardly for the entryway.

Once through the gate, Toes slammed it shut. No need to give the hungry mob another place to pillage. They were in a short stone tunnel that led to the Draper courtyard. They caught their breath and wiped water out of their eyes.

"I'm a Draper Fellow," said Toes, by way of explanation, holding up his key card.

"Are you all right?" Eph asked Lulu.

"I'm fine, thank you." She stared blankly.

"That sure went *Lord of the Flies* in a hurry," said Toes.

"You know, maybe you could take that damn thing off at this point." Eph pointed to the ball and chain. Lulu examined her Good Samaritan for the first time. The falling phallus had relieved Eph of his hat and glasses.

"It's you!"

"If by *you*, you mean your former professor whom you falsely accused of sexual assault and whose life you are intent on ruining, then, yes, it's me."

"Hey, Eph, your head is bleeding," Toes said.

Eph was still focused on Lulu, who was removing the pin from the bracket around her ankle. "I need to ask . . . Why?"

"You should know I'm sorry. They were putting so much pressure on me to give someone up, and I was still mad at you, so your name, well, it just kind of popped out. They seemed excited and one thing just led to another."

"Do you understand what you have done to me?"

She looked at Eph quizzically. "Even after I set them straight?"

"Wait . . . what?"

"Eph, we really should let someone look at that," Toes said.

If Eph knew Toes was there, it wasn't clear. "What the hell do you mean you set them straight?"

"I told them you didn't do anything."

"When was this?"

"I don't know. A few weeks ago? At the hearing with that dreadful woman, Martika something something. Why?"

"A few weeks ago." Eph broke out in laughter, which both Toes and Lulu found confusing, especially since blood was now streaming down the side of his face.

"Eph, I'm not trying to be a pain," said Toes, *"but I really think we need to get you to an emergency room."*

Eph turned to look at him and did his best to smile. "You know"—Eph had to think for a moment what Toes's real name was—"Barrett, you're really not such a bad guy."

Then everything went black.

Up on the stage, Killa C Note surveyed the chaos as wet equipment sparked and popped around him. He stood next to Milton, who remained frozen, mouth agape. "This be one fucked-up place you got here, Milt."

# The Following September

# Devon Daily

## Spring Fling Fallout

Last year's Spring Fling, which ended in a violent debacle now referred to by many as the Devon Gender Riot, has resulted in a number of developments. Spring exams were canceled and the school year came to an abrupt end, so precise details were slow to emerge from the confusion. Ensuing investigations over summer break have lent considerable clarity.

Violence erupted during a break in a musical performance by rap artist Killa C Note. Members of two university groups, the Beta Psi fraternity and the Fellingham Club, sought to block an ongoing peaceful protest known as the Crawl. There were a number of injuries, and several dozen students were taken for treatment at Havenport General Hospital. There was also over $1 million in damage to Draper and Hunter Houses.

The Crawl, a daily personal protest against gender violence by a first-year student named Lulu Harris, had gained thousands of followers and significant national attention. Violence was triggered when a sexually explicit video appeared on the Fling's big screen depicting Harris and Aldrich Wheeler, a well-known campus activist, known to most as Red. Exacerbating the problem, members of Devon's security staff had staged a walkout moments before in a protest over a song by Killa C Note that they perceived to be anti-police. (Contacted in Los Angeles by this paper, a spokesperson for Killa C Note said he apologizes if anyone was upset with his performance, but he denies any responsibility for the ensuing violence. "Killa is a messenger of peace," said the spokesperson.)

The focus of the conflict was a parade-style float depicting a twenty-foot phallus, brought by Beta Psi members. Many students and other onlookers found the imagery highly offensive, particularly as it contrasted with the Crawl's message of female victimhood.

A student DJ unwittingly played the video of Harris and Wheeler, saying he was unaware of the content. The Committee on Student Violence and Gender Abuse, hastily formed in the days following the Fling, determined that a Beta Psi member named Finlay Belcher was the source of the video. Belcher has been expelled from Devon.

In a dramatic turn of events, Milton Strauss, Devon's president, resigned from his position in June. Devon's Board of Governors, led by Stillman Weathers, expressed dismay at Strauss's handling of events, particularly concerning the amount of alcohol consumed by Fling participants, most of whom were underage. Last week, Weathers appointed Dean Arjun Choudhary as interim president while a search committee looks for a permanent replacement.

In other developments:

—Fraternities will no longer be recognized by Devon. Any students found to be a member will not be eligible for leadership positions and will not receive university recommendations for postgraduate scholarships such as the Rhodes.

—Seven members of Beta Psi, including former chapter president Theodore "Tug" Fowler, have been suspended for one year. Reached at his home by the *Daily,* Fowler said, "Whatever."

—The university will have to make do without Foster Jennison's $250 million gift to fund construction of the new houses. Publicly upset with developments, he has withdrawn his support. The administration stated that while they are disappointed, the hole in the construction budget was filled by the endowment's finishing the June fiscal year up 8 percent instead of the expected 7 percent. The endowment was aided by a strong recent rally in hedge funds.

—Lulu Harris has withdrawn permanently from Devon. The Crawl came to its violent end after the dramatic revelation that Harris was the long-estranged daughter of film star Camille Thornton. Despite the prurient content of the video, Harris has been embraced in feminist circles, with supporters dismissing the graphic video as "slut shaming." She recently auctioned off the ball and chain used in her protest for $75,000 on eBay, donating the proceeds to Code Pink.

—In a bizarre twist, the video that triggered violence exonerated Professor Ephraim Russell of assault charges on Harris. Russell was thought to be at the heart of Harris's protest and was brought up by the university on Title IX charges. The *Daily* has learned the time stamp on the video proved the assault to be impossible. Devon's Title IX Committee subsequently cleared Russell of assault charges but found him guilty of promoting alcohol consumption by an underage student. He is on a one-year leave of absence. Who might have actually assaulted Harris, or whether she was assaulted at all, remains unclear.

—Dean of Diversity and Inclusion Martika Malik-Adams, who ran Professor Russell's Title IX investigation, also resigned after questions were raised regarding her handling of the case. She now runs diversity initiatives for the entire University of California system, reportedly for a salary of $850,000 a year.

—Aldrich Wheeler is not currently enrolled at Devon and his whereabouts are unknown.

# Moral Turpitude

**"YOU NEVER BOTHERED** to read the terms of the trust, did you?"

Red Wheeler sat there in his grandfather's office, glum faced and slumped in his chair, tangled dreadlocks obscuring much of his face. He didn't answer. It was his trip to the woodshed and he just wanted to get it over with.

"No, of course you didn't. That would have involved some sort of actual work. Allow me to bring you some clarity." His grandfather put on his reading glasses and flipped through the pages of the trust. "Part Two, Section Three: Payments from the trust to a beneficiary may be suspended temporarily or permanently for reasons of moral turpitude."

*Moral turpitude?* That didn't sound good.

His grandfather flipped a few more pages. "Section Four: Moral turpitude is defined as committing an act or acts in violation of generally accepted standards of moral conduct." He lowered his glasses and glared at Red. "The trustees are friends of mine and they have looked the other way on your behavior for many years. But guess what? They don't think that starring in a pornographic video that then sparked a riot is a *generally accepted standard of moral conduct.*"

"I never gave consent for that to be filmed!"

"You should just sit there and shut up. At market close yesterday, your trust was valued at thirty-eight-point-two million dollars. You and your brother are the sole beneficiaries and receive dividends and interest. These payments, at least to *you*, are being officially suspended and placed into abeyance for a period of three years."

Red slumped even further. "What the hell does that mean?"

"It means, as far as you're concerned, that the trust is frozen until you meet certain conditions. Once those conditions are met, you will once again be eligible as a beneficiary. I checked your personal accounts and I noticed you've been spending everything you've been getting so, son, it means you are flat broke."

"That's not fair!"

"Really. That's an interesting viewpoint. I'm curious what you did to earn any of that money." His grandfather sat there and waited for an answer.

*Damn him, using his money like a weapon,* thought Red. *Typical capitalist. I should just tell him what he can do with his money.*

"Nothing? Was that what you were going to say? Because I happened to work damn hard for it."

Red looked up resentfully at the family patriarch. The old man was framed by the Manhattan skyline behind him. *Surely this is a bluff.*

"You know, Red, you've spent much of your life in a childish Marxist fantasyland, railing against the very system that made everything around you possible. The trust, your education, the iPhone in your pocket, the very clothes you're wearing . . . where do you think it all comes from? Maybe you think there are magic iPhone trees? Or maybe it comes from a workers' paradise like Cuba? Where do you think the money came from to build your beloved Devon? From community organizers?

"I tried to give you every advantage, the best education, every resource at your disposal, and yet our family embarrasses you so much you still use your mother's name. This is my fault. It was a mistake to give you so much. I see that now."

"I do important work!" Red had to make a stand.

"You play at campus radical while living off money you didn't earn. You're free to continue doing so, but not with my money."

"I'm not leaving Devon. I still need a few more credits plus I'm over twenty-one! It's not your call."

"Is that so? How do you plan to meet the seventy-five-thousand-dollar tuition?"

Red was silent, looking out the window at all the nearby office towers, filled with their work slaves. He saw no hope there. "What are these conditions?"

"I'm glad you asked. I'm going to do you an enormous favor, although you will not see it that way. My company owns a significant stake in a company called Youngstown Steel in Ohio. I have arranged for you to start Monday on the factory floor."

"No fucking way."

"I haven't finished, and I will thank you not to use that language in my place of work. You will work there for no fewer than three years. Should you do this and get satisfactory reviews from the floor manager, you will once again be the trust's beneficiary. Should you not meet these conditions, the beneficiary shall be changed to the United Negro College Fund. Frankly, I like their odds."

It was no longer possible for Red to slump any further in his chair.

"So, as I said, it's your call. You can sit there as long as you like. I have a meeting."

Foster Jennison stood up and left the room.

# Where the Skies Are So Blue

**AFTER THE RIOT,** Eph spent two days at Havenport General with a severe concussion. As soon as he was released, he packed up his Kia Sportage and drove west, planning on seeing some of America. He hadn't yet officially heard from the Title IX Tribunal, but needed to get away regardless. His musical heroes always sang about the restorative nature of the American road. *A last-chance power drive*, like Bruce said.

Eph would find out.

Anyway, it sounded better than teaching another summer session at Devon, even if he'd been allowed. D'Arcy understood he needed some time.

At a diner in Snow Shoe, Pennsylvania, he read the email about his suspension. They'd got their man, one way or another. He was banished, if temporarily, from Valhalla. He wasn't sure how that made him feel. The blueberry pie in front of him seemed more important right now.

He deliberately took off roads through rolling farmlands and small towns. Here, in America's gaps, the radio played country. The open landscape was punctuated with grain silos and grazing cows. The towns had VFW posts, a church, and maybe a deli. Eph always thought, though, that every town had a story if you bothered to ask. Many of his literary heroes had done exactly that and then written it all down.

He stopped in Clyde, Ohio, inspiration for Sherwood Anderson's short-story collection about a sad town called Winesburg. Eph planned next to stop at some birthplaces: Oak Park, Illinois (Hemingway), and Hannibal, Missouri

(Twain, of course), but halfway across Indiana he took a left, heading south toward Kentucky and the Appalachian Plateau. Without allowing the thought to fully form, he had known all along this was going to be the way. On a whim, he pulled over in the tiny town of Winchester, Tennessee, for a couple of days just to read. At a motel on a pretty lake he made himself at home in an Adirondack chair.

Eph stood for a while on the porch of the small house Big Mike and Ellie had moved to when they sold the farm, It was closer to town and had a modest yard with a swing hanging from its only tree. That must have been left there by the previous owner, Eph thought. He reached out and rang the bell. When Ellie opened the door, she ran out and threw her arms around Eph and wouldn't let go.

"Why didn't you tell us you were coming?"

"I didn't know myself until a few hundred miles ago."

Releasing Eph from her bear hug, she looked past him at the Kia in the driveway. It was loaded with stuff, and Eph's bike was mounted on a rack. "Are you staying for a while? Tell me you are!"

"Maybe. I don't know exactly. Is there a spare bed?"

"You know there is, little brother."

Big Mike appeared at the door. There was an uncomfortable silence and Big Mike examined Eph without expression.

"Hi, Dad" was all Eph could manage.

"I see you finally got some meat on you," said Big Mike.

Over the summer, a summer that stretched out languidly like those of Eph's youth, father and son repaired their relationship. There wasn't much conversation, but then Big Mike had always been a laconic man. The shadow of loss still hung over him, but Eph grew to think he'd been a little harsh in his judgments as a teenager. Maybe even an idiot. One night over beers on the porch, they reminisced about Jack. Big Mike laughed when Eph told the story about Jack coming to his rescue that day in the school bathroom. Ellie said Bobby Fincher was doing three-to-five at Holman for robbing the Circle K.

Big Mike was officially diagnosed with mid-stage Parkinson's. He had trouble with his balance but could mostly get around without help. There was still time—years—and Eph was grateful for it, even if Big Mike occasionally called him a "Yankee pussy."

Eph got to know his nephews, Ellie's kids. Little Mike and Brian. They were good kids, both busy with the business of being boys. Little Mike was in high school already.

D'Arcy came down for the month of August. Eph was concerned about what kind of reception she'd get—or more to the point, what kind of reception *they'd* get—but those concerns soon passed. People were warm and welcoming. Maybe the South had grown up some while he was away. After Labor Day, she went back to Devon, and things between them were left up in the air. Eph wanted to be with her, but wasn't sure what to do about it. Did he want to stay in Alabama all year? It wouldn't be fair to ask her to quit her job—now with Acting President Choudhary—just to come South for a year, and he wasn't going to loiter around Devon with his tail between his legs.

One day Eph drove up to Samford, his alma mater. He didn't have any particular reason for going, he just thought he would. It was still summer vacation, so campus was quiet, but he ran into Emmet Weaver, one of his old teachers, who was now faculty dean. They went for coffee at Lucy's, a small diner next to campus. Eph told his story, warts and all, and Emmet offered him an adjunct position on the spot. They didn't get many Devon professors coming around this way, he said. Eph was surprised and happily agreed. It solved what to do for the year.

"You know, if you ever wanted more . . ." Emmet said it half laughing, knowing he was unlikely to lure a Devon prof—even a "tarnished" one—full-time.

Toward the end of September, Eph got a call from Titus Cooley, who struck a surprisingly upbeat tone over the phone.

"Ephraim, my boy, how've you been?"

"No complaints. Catching up with family."

"That's good, that's good. Family is important. Listen, I never got a chance to say how sorry I was about everything this past spring. You got a raw deal and the university should be ashamed of itself. I dare say Milton got what he deserved, though, in the end."

"Thank you, Titus."

"Tell me, what plans have you made?"

"Samford University, my alma mater, offered me an adjunct position for the year, so I've started teaching a class there."

"I see. Good, good. Anyway, to the point . . . I call with news. I'm going to retire after this year."

"I'm sorry to hear that." Eph truly was, but he wasn't sure why Titus would call to tell him.

"Oh, let's face it, I'm a dinosaur. The world belongs to the Blue Feathers now."

"I hope not, Titus."

"Well, I do, too, and that's actually why I'm calling. As you know, Professor Smallwood was granted the tenure position. However, my retirement will open up another slot. I've spoken to Acting President Choudhary, and we think that spot should go to you. We hope you will come back and teach next semester, and tenure would be made official as soon as I leave. Choudhary will even put it in writing."

Eph was flabbergasted, his mouth agape.

"Ephraim, are you still there?"

"Yeah—*yes*. Are you serious?"

"As a heart attack, my boy, as a heart attack. Between you and me, I think Choudhary is afraid you will sue the school back into the last century, but to hell with him. You're a damn fine teacher, all that nonsense is behind us, and this is something you deserve."

"I don't know what to say." Eph had to sit down because the room was suddenly spinning.

"Say yes, you foolish man! This is what you worked for. Tenure at Devon University! You've ascended the mount, my boy."

"Wow. I can't believe this."

"So what do you say?"

"I say yes."

"Good man! Call back tomorrow and we'll start the paperwork."


That night the whole Russell family had dinner: Eph, Big Mike, Ellie, the boys, and even a few cousins who lived nearby. Ellie made roast chicken with mashed potatoes and fried okra, served along with beer, plus lemonade for the boys. They set up a big table out on the porch and enjoyed the cool evening air. A light wind carried with it the smell of fertilizer, something no one minded at all. Little Mike said the Ashley football team looked strong this year. One of the cousins said a Walmart might be coming to Dillon, the next town over. There was talk of a record harvest season.

For dessert, Ellie brought out pecan tarts, made with their mother, Millie's, famous recipe. The boys ate theirs in about three big bites and asked to be excused to throw a football in the front yard. Little Mike looked to have a cannon for an arm.

"I have some news." Eph wiped some crumbs from his mouth. "I got a call today, from the head of my department at Devon. It seems some different people are running the show up there now and I've been offered tenure."

Everyone, save Big Mike, cheered and clapped.

"My brother, the genius!" proclaimed Ellie.

"I don't know about that. I guess they were desperate."

"That pay much?" asked Big Mike, from the head of the table.

"It would be a nice raise, yes."

Big Mike grunted in what could have been approval, but it was hard to tell. He'd been silent for most of the dinner. He looked at his untouched tart, almost solemnly. One hand was shaking, as it increasingly did of late. "I'd like to say something," he said. He paused for a few moments as if collecting his thoughts. The words came out slowly. "We are blessed here, those of us at this table. We are blessed by this food and by God and country and family. Ellie, thank you for this fine meal. You have honored your mother with it, and she would be proud to know the mother you yourself have become to those fine boys out there."

Ellie visibly teared up. "Thank you, Daddy."

"Eph?"

"Yes, Dad?"

Big Mike looked as if he was struggling for what to say. "It's nice you're here, Son."

It grew dark and the night sky lit up with a million stars. The outer band of the Milky Way was a brilliant white sash. Eph had forgotten what a deep-country sky could look like. The others left or went inside, but Eph and Big Mike remained there, sipping beer, quietly taking in God's universe.

———

The following day, Eph was back at Samford.

"Good morning, Professor!" called a passing student with a wide smile. Eph returned the greeting. He was running one or two minutes late, so his class was already full. He had maybe twenty students in all. They sat around a large Harkness table.

"So, let's begin with a question. Why do you suppose Hemingway said all American literature descends from *Huckleberry Finn*? What made it so great?"

Hands shot up and Eph chose a girl on the far side of the table.

"It was the first novel to portray common people as central characters."

"Yes, very good. Novels before this almost exclusively featured the rich and well educated. Twain wrote about a different America. Anything else?" A boy to his left raised his hand.

"It used language as people really spoke it."

"Correct. Twain's characters did not have access to the *Oxford English Dictionary*. They used the language of nineteenth-century rural America, some of it quite colorful, and some of it even offensive, at least to the modern ear. At the time, this was the equivalent of a literary earthquake, and we can follow the technique's lineage through the Realists right to Hemingway and all the way to modern writers like Tom Wolfe. It all started with Twain.

"You know, in real life, Twain didn't have much time for the smart set. He wrote them off as posturing 'city folk.'"

Eph stole a glimpse through the window. It wasn't leaded glass, and the campus wasn't one of Gothic elegance, but Samford had its charms. The students were earnest. Maybe not possessed of that knife-edge intellect he was used to at Devon, but likable. There was less entitlement, and no one was confused about what pronouns or which bathrooms to use. Either way, it felt good to be back on the professorial stage.

After class he went outside and sat on a bench and watched students walk by. He meant to start reviewing the next assignment, but it was a beautiful day, so he let his eyes close while he soaked up the sun. A calmness settled on him and he realized the personal and professional anxiety that had followed him around for much of the last year was gone.

Pulling his phone out of his pocket, he dialed Titus Cooley's number.

"Titus, it's Eph."

"Ephraim, good. I need to give you over to HR to get the paperwork going. There's so much of it these days!"

"Titus, that's the thing. I really appreciate everything you've done for me, but I think I'm all set."

"All set. All set with what?"

"All set here. I think I'm going to stay. In Alabama. I think maybe I like it here."

"I am hearing this correctly? You're turning down a tenured position at Devon University?"

"I guess I am."

Howls of laughter came through the phone, not the reaction Eph was expecting.

"Titus?"

"Bully for you, Ephraim, bully for you."

Eph didn't know anyone else who could get away with saying "bully for you" without sounding ridiculous. "I'm confused."

"Ephraim, I wish I had your balls. Do they have a full-time spot for you down there?"

"They have suggested it, yes."

"Well, good. I don't think I've ever met anyone in our little world who could turn something like this down. But the university mistreated you badly, and frankly, we don't deserve you. And if you want to know what I really think, I think this place is going to hell anyway. Devon is like a big pot of stew with lots of ingredients, only they'd never been mixed. Last spring an immense spoon came and mixed the stew and we discovered it was inedible all along."

"I'm not the spoon in this, am I?"

"You're not *the* spoon. You're certainly *a* spoon."

"And if it's a stew, wouldn't the ingredients be mixed to begin with?"

"Hmm. Perhaps salad would have made a better metaphor . . ."

"I never meant to be a spoon."

"The best spoons never do."

"I thought you'd say I was crazy turning this down. A big part of me thinks I am."

"Not crazy, not crazy at all. And let me just say again how lucky the good folks at Samford University are to have you."

They wished each other well, and Eph slipped his phone back in his pocket. He should go see Emmet about a more permanent arrangement, but right now he had a more immediate need: some peach crumble at Lucy's. He'd heard good things.

He wondered how D'Arcy would react. She'd be upset she wasn't consulted, or at least act the part. He'd barely consulted himself, but it felt right, as right as anything he'd ever done. Would D'Arcy move down here with him? She, too, had grown disenchanted with the madness at Devon. He decided he'd fly back North next weekend and get down on bended knee. If she still loved him, his odds were good.

Eph arrived at the entrance to Lucy's at almost the same moment as a young woman. He grasped the door handle first, pulled it back, and stood to one side. "After you."

"Why, thank you, sir."

He followed her inside.

# Epilogue

**"IS SHE HERE YET?"** asked the producer.

A nervous-looking production assistant, one hand holding a clipboard and the other the side of her head, strained to hear through her earpiece. "Her limo is three minutes out. There's a lot of Midtown traffic."

"Good. Get her past that rabble outside and straight to prep. We're running close."

Across town, the Mound, now more commonly known to his coworkers at Goldman Sachs by his real name, Dennis Flugelbaum, emerged from the shower. As was the dressing habit of any Wall Streeter, he turned on CNBC to watch *Morning Squawk*, but then his phone buzzed with a text. Dennis often received texts this early; it was probably an update from the Hong Kong trading desk.

Glancing down, he saw it was from his buddy Digger. It simply read, "Turn on GMA."

Dennis grabbed the remote and changed to ABC.

"Welcome back this hour to *Good Morning America*. I'm your cohost George Stephanopoulos. Our next guest is the daughter of Hollywood film star Camille Thornton, an emerging star in her own right, and rumored to be the new face of Revlon, all at the tender age of twenty-one. If you're one of the few that doesn't know her already, you will soon. I'm speaking of Lulu Harris." The camera lens drew back to reveal Lulu emerging from side stage to the audience's enthusiastic applause. She wore an Alexander McQueen leather jacket and a tight red-and-white tartan skirt. She sat on the high stool next to Stephanopoulos, allowing the producers to keep Lulu's long legs in the shot.

"Lulu, welcome to *Good Morning America.* So great to have you here."

"Thank you, George, although I don't know how you get up this early every day!"

Stephanopoulos and the audience dutifully laughed.

"So, I happen to have an advance copy of something here that you may not have seen yet." He reached down and produced a large glossy magazine, which he held up. The cover revealed a head shot of Lulu. "This is *On the Avenue* and it reads, 'Lulu Harris, a New Kind of It Girl.' Congratulations to you."

"Thank you." Lulu smiled. It was okay to smile once you were on the summit looking down, she'd decided. Besides, it was time for Lulu 3.0.

"What a remarkable story. After you left college, you joined your long-estranged mother, Camille Thornton, in Hollywood and took a small role in her movie *Gender Games.*"

"Yes, well, Camille was wonderful to me and I was just grateful for the opportunity."

"And what an opportunity it turned out to be. As everyone knows, *Gender Games* was nominated for Best Picture last year, and many thought it should have won."

"It was an honor for all of us just to be nominated."

"*The Jurist* edged you out, of course. What did you think of it?"

"A wonderful film and a deserving winner. So moving." In truth, Lulu thought it the most tedious two hours of her life. Some Supreme Court judge comes out of the closet? Who the hell cares?

"It certainly has put your mother back in the spotlight."

"Was she ever out of it?"

The audience laughed.

"Speaking of your mother, you two were estranged for many years. How is your relationship?"

"Just wonderful. We're the best of friends." *Sure, when it's convenient.*

"Well, your role in *Gender Games,* while small, got you noticed, and you now have a significant supporting role in a new film coming out this Friday called *The Indecent.* Tell us about that."

"Well, I play a suburban au pair who has a secret affair with my employer, who is married of course. But he's quite controlling, and my character is quite malleable, so my existence becomes subsumed to his."

"Now, I understand there's been some controversy about this."

"Has there?"

"I'm sure you saw there were some protesters outside."

"I saw one or two. I thought they were lost."

The audience laughed on cue.

Stephanopoulos's brow furrowed slightly. "Some see the subservient nature of your new role as not being, well, very modern. The man is in control."

"They are certainly entitled to their opinions." *No matter how stupid they are.*

"Lulu, you first came to national prominence with a protest against gender violence at Devon University, didn't you? You gained almost iconic status in certain circles, particularly feminist ones. Those supporters now seem to be turning on you, both because of this film and the rumor that you will be the new face of Revlon. They see the beauty industry as, and I'm quoting one blogger here, 'a multibillion-dollar industry that preys on and profits from women's deepest insecurities about their bodies.'"

*Another dumb cow,* Lulu thought. And wasn't this interview supposed to be softballs? It was *Good Morning America,* for Christ's sake. Wait till she got her agent on the phone.

"Well, George, I can't comment about Revlon, but don't you think that women should be able to decide for themselves how they want to present themselves? Aren't we supposed to be empowered to make our own choices? If you want to strive for beauty, that should be your personal choice, your truth. If you want to grow hair under your arms and shave your head, that's your choice, too. Just don't expect anyone to want to look at you, know what I'm saying?"

Stephanopoulos looked taken aback, but the audience laughed.


By the end of the segment, the protest had doubled in size as word spread quickly. Hell hath no fury like a movement scorned. ABC assigned two burly security personnel in black suits to get Lulu from the side door to her idling limousine.

Staffers had created a small channel through the phalanx of pink hair and body piercings.

Lulu and her guards reached the door and one said, "We're gonna hustle to the car, do you understand?"

Lulu nodded. As they emerged, the protesters screamed in anger. Lulu and her bodyguards walked quickly, but then Lulu stopped. "Wait."

"*Excuse me?*" said the first bodyguard.

Lulu didn't answer. She just stood her ground amid the growing chaos. *Not my first rodeo, bitches.* She held both her hands out in a universal gesture meant to ask for silence. Incredibly, the racket subsided. For the moment, curiosity trumped outrage.

"My friends . . ." Lulu tilted her head back and screamed, primally, the sound of it echoing in the canyon-like side streets of Manhattan. It was as loud, loud as any scream issued from the steps of Duffy Hall, but then she abruptly stopped. The protesters seemed at a loss. Was Lulu, *their* Lulu, returning to their embrace? Lulu stared, absorbing their confusion.

Then she laughed.

That it was a mocking laugh was immediately understood.

"In the car, *now!*" said the first bodyguard, who practically carried her to the limo and slammed the door shut. As soon as that happened, the crowd turned into a mob, screaming and banging their fists on the car. As it pulled away, Lulu turned to look out the back window.

She smiled.

# ABOUT *CAMPUSLAND*

*Campusland* is a work of fiction. Kind of. The American college has evolved into a strange place, and while *Campusland* is written as satire, it doesn't stretch the truth by much, and sometimes not at all. Title IX, as depicted, is true to life. If you want some good nonfiction on the subject, I suggest Laura Kipnis's excellent (and horrifying) book *Unwanted Advances*. (Note: As of this writing, the Department of Education has begun reviewing some of Title IX's more troublesome aspects.)

# ACKNOWLEDGMENTS

Many friends deserve to be thanked. Several took the time to read the first draft and give me their thoughts, including Kathryn Tohir (we miss her), Bob Potter, Mike Balay, Alison Belknap, Rob Schade, Judy Lewis, Eric Mogilnicki, and Stephan Skinner. Thanks also to the Manuels (Charlie, Amo, and Tristan), Scott McNealy, Mark Anderson, Andrew Ehrgood, Ralph Gill, Daniel Tenreiro, the Deplorables (Dave Tohir, Dan Mahony, and Bill Sawch), Melissa Fleming, Scott Edmonds (for legal advice), and Shelley Dempsey of Families Advocating for Campus Equality, who generously assisted with my understanding of Title IX practices. Special thanks to Elizabeth Beier of St. Martin's for taking a flier on a first-time novelist, and to my brother, Sim Johnston, a better writer than I.

Lastly, thanks to my family, Kelly, Tucker, Caroline, and Brady, for not thinking this was a crazy idea. (Okay, that's not exactly right. . . .) Particular thanks to Tucker for telling me when I was getting college argot totally wrong.